Anonymous

Memorial of Samuel Finley Breese Morse

Including appropriate ceremonies of respect at the National Capitol, and elsewhere

Anonymous

Memorial of Samuel Finley Breese Morse
Including appropriate ceremonies of respect at the National Capitol, and elsewhere

ISBN/EAN: 9783337307783

Printed in Europe, USA, Canada, Australia, Japan

Cover: Foto ©Raphael Reischuk / pixelio.de

More available books at **www.hansebooks.com**

MEMORIAL

OF

Samuel Finley Breese Morse,

INCLUDING

APPROPRIATE CEREMONIES OF RESPECT AT THE NATIONAL CAPITOL, AND ELSEWHERE.

PUBLISHED BY ORDER OF CONGRESS.

WASHINGTON:
GOVERNMENT PRINTING OFFICE.
1875.

TABLE OF CONTENTS.

CONTENTS.

HISTORICAL.

BIOGRAPHICAL SKETCH.

PROFESSOR S. F. B. MORSE.

Prof. Samuel Finley Breese Morse, the inventor of the electro-magnetic telegraph, was born in Charlestown, Mass., on the 27th of April, 1791. His father was the Rev. Jedidiah Morse, D. D., pastor of the First Congregational Church in Charlestown. He was the eldest of three brothers, Sidney E. and Richard C., the founders of the *New York Observer*, being respectively two and four years his juniors. Samuel Finley graduated at Yale College in 1810, and, having resolved to devote his life to art, he went the next year to England with Washington Allston, to study under his tuition and that of Benjamin West. He produced a model of a dying Hercules, which gained for him a gold medal from the Adelphi Society of Arts; but Providence had reserved him for other works than those of the pencil and the chisel, though he always retained his early fondness for such pursuits. He made a second voyage to Europe in 1829 to complete his studies in the chief cities of the continent, where he produced a number of paintings, which are held in high repute. He was one of the founders of the National Academy of Design in 1826; he was its first president; he was about the same time lecturer on the fine arts at the New York Athenæum; and during his second residence abroad he was elected to the professorship of the literature of the arts of design in the University of the City of New York. It was on the voyage home in 1832, to enter upon the duties of this position, that he conceived the great invention to which he owes his world-wide fame. The new discoveries in the science of electro-magnetism had a special attraction for him, and he had discussed them over and over again with his friend Prof. J. F. Dana. On board the Havre packet *Sally*, which brought him home in

October, 1832, the subject formed one day a topic of conversation among the passengers. Dr. Charles S. Jackson, of Boston, described an experiment recently made in Paris, by means of which electricity had instantaneously been transmitted through a great length of wire. "If that is so," said Morse, "I see no reason why messages may not be instantaneously transmitted by electricity." Before the packet reached New York the invention of the telegraph was virtually made, and even the essential features of the electro-magnetic transmitting and recording apparatus were sketched upon paper. Of course, in reaching this result, Professor Morse made use of the ideas and discoveries of many other minds. It is not sufficient that a brilliant project be proposed; that its modes of accomplishment are foreseen and properly devised; there are, in every part of the enterprise, other minds and other agencies to be consulted for information and counsel to perfect the whole plan.

Various forms of telegraphic intercourse had been devised before; electro-magnetism had been studied by *savants* for many years; Franklin, even, had experimented with the transmission of electricity through great lengths of wire. It was reserved for Morse to combine the results of many fragmentary and unsuccessful attempts, and put them, after years of trial, to a practical use; and though his claims to the invention have been many times attacked, in the press and in the courts, they have been triumphantly vindicated alike by the law and the verdict of the people, both at home and abroad. The Chief-Justice of the United States, in delivering the decision of the Supreme Court, said:

"It can make no difference whether he" (the inventor) "derives his information from books or from conversation with men skilled in the science; and the fact that Morse sought and obtained the necessary information and counsel from the best sources, and acted upon it, neither impairs his right as an inventor, nor detracts from his merits."

Part of the apparatus was actually constructed by Mr. Morse in New York, before the close of the year 1832, but it was not until 1835, that he succeeded in putting up an experimental line, consisting of half a mile of wire stretched around and around a room, and exhibiting a telegraph in actual operation. In 1837, he gave greater publicity to his scheme by an exhibition at the University. The invention attracted a great deal of interest, but very few persons could be persuaded of its financial value. At the close of the year Mr. Morse went to Washington, and asked Congress for an appropriation to build a telegraph-line from Washington to Baltimore. The House Committee on Commerce, at the head of which was the Hon. F. O. J. Smith, of Maine, gave him an attentive hearing and a favorable report, but the session passed without further action, and the disappointed inventor went to England and France. He met with no encouragement in Europe, and struggled on for four years longer, renewing his appeal at Washington year after year, and still hopeful in the midst of poverty and trouble. On the last night of the session in March, 1843, he left the Capitol entirely disheartened, after patiently waiting through the long day. But the next morning, to his amazement, he learned that in the hurry and confusion of the midnight hour the expiring Congress had voted $30,000 for his experimental essay.

Even after the appropriation had been made by Congress, the completion of the line of telegraph-wire from Baltimore to Washington was effected only through the effective aid of Ezra Cornell, who took a warm interest in the enterprise; and through the skill and experience of Amos Kendall, companies were organized by which the invention was brought into general use, and by which, contrary to almost universal experience, the inventor soon realized a fortune, which he lived to enjoy, together with the gratitude of his country and the world.

Then came a long series of vexatious lawsuits. Morse's patents

were violated; his honors disputed; even his integrity was assailed,
and rival companies devoured for a while all the profits of the business. But these troubles were finally overcome, and no inventor has
ever had prouder satisfaction in the acknowledgment of the benefits
which he had conferred upon his race. All the principal nations of
Europe gave him tokens of distinction. So early as 1848, the Sultan
presented him a decoration set in diamonds. Gold medals were
awarded him by Prussia, Austria, and Württemberg. France made
him a Chevalier of the Legion of Honor. Denmark gave him the
cross of Knight of the Dannebrog. Spain, the cross of Knight Commander of the Order of Isabella the Catholic. At the instance of
the Emperor of the French, representatives of the European States—
France, Russia, Sweden, Belgium, Holland, Austria, Sardinia, Tuscany, the Holy See, and Turkey—met at Paris to decide upon a col-
lective testimonial to him, and the result of their deliberations was a
vote of 400,000 francs. Scores of learned societies all over the world
admitted him to membership. In 1856, the telegraph companies of
Great Britain gave him a banquet in London. In 1858, the American Colony in France entertained him at a grand dinner in Paris.
On the 29th of December, 1868, the citizens of New York gave him
a dinner at Delmonico's. In June, 1871, a bronze statue of Professor
Morse, erected in the Central Park, New York, by the voluntary contributions of telegraph-employés throughout the country, was formally
unveiled, with an address by William Cullen Bryant; and in the evening a reception was held at the Academy of Music, where one of
the first instruments used on the original line between New York and
Washington was placed upon the stage and connected with the wires,
that Professor Morse might send, with his own hand, a word of greeting to all the cities of the United States and Canada.

The latter years of Professor Morse's life were spent quietly in the
City of New York, and at his summer residence in Poughkeepsie.
Although having passed the age of fourscore, his mental faculties

remained in full vigor, and he continued to take a lively interest in all that transpired in the world, and in the church.

The last public service which he performed was unveiling the statue of Benjamin Franklin, in Printing-House Square, New York, on the 17th day of January, 1872, in the presence of a vast concourse of citizens. He had cheerfully acceded to the request that he would perform this act, remarking that he would do so if it were to be his last. It was so eminently appropriate that Morse should thus inaugurate a statue of Franklin. The great philosopher of the Revolution discovered the identity of electricity and lightning; drew it from the clouds, and protected our homes and our public buildings from its terrible power; the philosopher of our own day subdued the subtle and mighty element, making it a docile minister, and a most useful agent for the business and comfort of man.

Professor Morse was a man of decided religious character, having been the superintendent of one of the first Sabbath-schools ever held in this country, in Charlestown, Mass., in his father's church; and in all the vicissitudes, and struggles, and successes of his remarkable career, he maintained under all circumstances, the most conscientious and devotional habit of life, such as becomes a humble and consistent Christian. While yet a young man, he wrote a series of able and forcible papers, afterward published in a volume, purporting to unmask the designs of the Jesuits upon the liberties of the United States. He brought to public attention the saying, attributed by some to Lafayette, "If American liberty falls, it will fall by the hands of Romish priests." He was a communicant in the Madison Square Presbyterian church, of New York City, (Rev. Dr. Adams',) and adorned his profession by a spotless life. His gifts to objects of benevolence were many and very large; various institutions, religious and literary, in New York, in the West and the South, and countless individuals, receiving his generous contributions.

Comparing the contributions made by any one inventor to the

wealth and comfort and usefulness of mankind, we may place the art of printing, and the use of steam-power, above that of electricity; yet they have been in use these very many years, while the inventor of the art of telegraphing, lived to see his invention revolutionize the means of intercommunication for the business of the world. It was a sublime result when the beating of the nation's heart at Washington was instantly felt at the farthest outposts of the broad republic; but that was small compared with the instantaneous transmission of thought across the ocean, and over continents beyond, so that the sun himself was outstripped by the speed of Morse's messengers; and in a moment, his lines were gone out into all the earth and his words to the ends of the world.

The genius and labor of such a man reflect glory upon his country, so that his name becomes part of the national heritage and treasure. The unanimity and magnanimity with which kingdoms and empires acknowledged their indebtedness to the great inventor, were not less creditable to them than to him, England remaining almost alone among the great powers of the earth in withholding from him the meed that was his due. Now that he has gone, attempts may be made to rob his memory of the honor that surrounds it; but so fresh in the minds of men are the facts, and so well are they established by the testimony of still living witnesses, and by unimpeachable documentary testimony, we may be as sure as we can be of anything in human experience, that Samuel Finley Breese Morse will, in all future time, be known and honored as the inventor of the Electro-Magnetic Telegraph.

LAST YEARS.

The last two or three years of Professor Morse's life were spent in quiet at his home on Twenty-second street, near Fifth avenue, New York, in winter; and at his country-seat, one mile south of Poughkeepsie, on the Hudson, in summer. The latter was the old homestead-farm, and the mansion he left as a sacred relic on the drive leading up to his palatial residence. He spent his time in reading, writing, and receiving his friends. He was specially devoted to his wife, who, strange to say, was a mute ; and he was married when he was about fifty-five years of age. In sentiment a Presbyterian, but catholic in his feelings, religion was his favorite theme during his last years. During the last two years of his life he became specially interested in the Rutgers Female College ; presided at a course of lectures given there in February and March, 1871, and made a donation to it of $2,500 for a lectureship. Through him Stone's vase, commemorative of the advancing spirit of American invention, illustrated by freedom, giving the torch successively to Franklin, Fulton, and Morse, designed for the National Morse Monument, was presented to the college. His last public appearance was at the Academy of Music, on the inauguration of his statue in Central Park. The death of his brother Sidney, some months after, seemed to be the final blow that shattered his yet remaining powers.

RECOLLECTIONS OF PROFESSOR MORSE.

(BY IRENÆUS.)

More than thirty years ago—it was in the year 1840—I first met Professor Morse. He was then bringing out, not his telegraph, but the daguerreotype. He had become intensely interested in the invention and the inventor, from whom it takes its name, and he introduced it into this country. I was among the first whose portraits were taken by that art on this side of the sea. He said that it would not hurt the business of the portrait-painter, for *it would not flatter*. His prophecy was and is fulfilled, and the reason he gave for it is quite likely to be true. Nature tells the truth, and the photograph makes the defects as well as the beauties radiant and indelible. The painter can make a good likeness, yet make it look better than the original in the eyes of every one but those of the original.

He was now patiently at work upon the machinery to make the telegraph a practical success. After it was an accomplished fact, and a line was in working order between Washington and New York, he gave me the first things he ever made toward the great work. He said that having cut a mould, he melted lead in an iron spoon, and made castings of a model of what he would hope to perfect as an operating apparatus. Those lead forms I presented to the New York Historical Society, and they were deposited in its archives, together with the strip of paper bearing the dots and dashes of the first message that ever reached New York over the wires. I presume these memorials are still preserved.

He told me then that the invention had cost him a thousand sleepless nights and more anxious days, and he added, "It is not done yet." And now, after the lapse of thirty years, it is probably in its infancy. Like the art of printing, it has, indeed, leaped into being complete, but, like that art also, it is not perfect. Every generation will add to the facilities and economies of its use, while the invention itself is *the* thing that will never be improved upon.

I very rarely met Professor Morse in my own study or his, or on the street, when there was an opportunity for conversation, that he did not introduce the subject of personal religion, making it the easiest and pleasantest theme of quiet, genial discourse. He was the most simple, pure, unaffected, humble man whom I ever knew. When I say the *most* so, I mean just that, because I never knew any man who had attained so much honor among men, and was not puffed up at all. I was with him in Paris during the great exhibition of 1867, and often saw him under circumstances that would easily develop the vanity of inferior men. Royal personages would send to know at what time it would be convenient for him to receive them, when they would call at his modest lodgings to pay him the tribute of their respect. But he a, peared no more elated than by the expectation of a call from a friend. He did not affect to undervalue such attentions, nor to despise the honors that come from men. Esteeming them at their proper value, he had a just sense of the glory which his invention has necessarily purchased for him and his country, and he always gloried, as was becoming, in the usefulness and happiness which his invention had added to the common stock enjoyed by the human race.

One day as he was going to a certain office in the city of Paris to transact business in connection with international telegraphic communication, he asked me if it would be proper for him to wear any of the badges of distinction which had been conferred upon him by various governments in recognition of the value of his invention. As those whom he would meet would display whatever tokens they might have of position and power, it might be for the advantage of the object he sought to accomplish to appear with the prestige which such decorations might confer. Yet he shrunk from what might appear ostentatious, and preferred to rely only on the merits of his case.

His interest in the American chapel in Paris was great and earnest. His children were teachers and scholars in its Sabbath-school. And when an effort was made to pay off a debt then embarrassing it, he started the subscription with a thousand dollars in gold.

The most impressive recollections of this illustrious man's life which remain with me relate to the attempts that were made at various periods of his life to rob him of his well-earned fame as the inventor of the telegraph. When his patents were granted he could maintain his rights by law; but to meet the detractions and injustice of envy or avarice required constant vigilance, and often protracted labor. He felt keenly the wrong done him, especially by the British claimants, who, with pertinacity that would have been commendable in the interests of truth, have down to this day denied to Morse and America the meed that all the rest of the world most cheerfully award. In Paris there was a revival of this claim during the Exhibition, and I was with him in repeated conferences as to the expediency of meeting the adverse claims with a defensive pamphlet. The serenity of his spirit in those exciting times was wonderful and beautiful. It was difficult for him to summon temper enough to make a fight for himself. He had the case in his own hands, and could easily demolish his enemies; but he had done it so often, that he could not rouse himself to do it again. And he let it go. He contented himself with putting in order the irrefragable testimony on which his rights rested, and these will in due time be given to the world.

The verdict of the world is generally right. Merit gets its own in the long run. Columbus did not give his name to the hemisphere he found, but who ever speaks of Americus as its discoverer? I do not know a meaner business in which men are ever engaged than robbing the dead of the glory that gilds their graves.

Morse in his coffin is a recollection never to fade. He lay like an ancient prophet or sage, such as the old masters painted for Abraham or Isaiah. His finely-chiseled features, classic in their mould and majestic in repose; his white hair and heavy flowing beard; the death-calm upon the brow that for eighty years had concealed a teeming brain, and that placid beauty that lingers upon the face of the right-eous dead, as if the freed spirit had left a smile upon its forsaken home—these are the memories that remain of the most illustrious and honored private citizen that the New World has yet given to man-kind.

HISTORIC FACTS CONCERNING MORSE'S ELECTRO-MAGNETIC TELEGRAPH.

(BY DR. L. D. GALE, OF WASHINGTON, D. C.)

In the winter of 1836–'37, Samuel F. B. Morse, who, as well as myself, was a professor in the New York University, city of New York, came to my lecture-room, and said he had a machine in his lecture-room, or studio, which he wished to show me. I accompanied him to his room, and there saw resting on a table a single-pair galvanic battery, an electro-magnet, an arrangement of pencil, a paper-covered roller, pinion-wheels, levers, &c., for making letters and figures to be used for sending and receiving words and sentences through long distances. This machine consisted of three elements. The first was a wooden clock-movement, to be wound up for the operation, containing the vertical pencil with its point resting on the paper-covered roller, connected with and moved by the keeper of the electro-magnet, used to make the marks or letters on the paper-covered-roller. The second part of this machine was the port-rule, (of which there were several,) consisting of a long wooden horizontal rod, with a deep slot on the upper surface, in which slot are received the type, letters, or words of the message, arranged in sentences. The third part of this machine was the letters of the alphabet, consisting of dots, lines, and spaces. If the paper-covered roller, moved by the clock-work, turns on its axis while the keeper of the electro-magnet presses the pencil against the paper, a line is made. If the power of the magnet suddenly forces the point of the pencil against the paper, and by a reverse action quickly raises it again, a dot is made. If while the magnet or a spring holds up the pencil, the paper moves forward, a space is the result. When the words and sentences are in one or more port-rules, each is run through the machine, and the message is sent to its destination at a distance. Such was the Morse telegraph when I first saw it, in the winter of 1836–'37. At this time, as Morse assured me, no man had seen the machine except his brother, Sidney E. Morse, the original proprietor of the *New York Observer.* Except the electro-magnet, all this machine is mechanical. This magnet was first described by William Sturgin, of England, in 1825, and was slightly modified by Professor Moll, of Utrecht; hence sometimes called the "Moll magnet." In the spring of 1827, I listened to a course of lectures before the New York Lyceum of National History, by Prof. James F. Dana, at Columbia College, New York, of which class Professor Morse and I were members, and where we for the first time saw the so-called Moll magnet. Nine years thereafter this magnet made part of the Morse electro-magnetic telegraph machine. Morse's machine was complete in all its parts, and operated perfectly through a circuit of some forty feet, but there was not sufficient force to send messages to a distance. At this time I was a lecturer on chemistry, and from necessity was acquainted with all kinds of galvanic batteries, and knew that a battery of one or a few cups generates a large quantity of electricity capable of producing heat, &c., but not of projecting electricity to a great distance; and that to accomplish this a battery of many cups is necessary. It was, therefore, evident to me that the one large cup-battery of Morse should be made into ten or fifteen smaller ones to make it a battery of intensity, so as to project the electric fluid through space. I said to Professor Morse, "I understand your difficulty, and will soon relieve your mind. I have a battery of forty cups, twenty of which will hold about as much liquid as your one cup, which will convert a battery of quantity into a battery of intensity." Accordingly, I substituted the battery of many cups for the battery of one cup.

The remaining defect in the Morse machine, as first seen by me, was that the coil of wire around the poles of the electro-magnet consisted of but a few turns only; while, to give the greatest projectile

, power, the number of turns should be increased from tens to hundreds, as shown by Professor Henry in his paper, published in the *American Journal of Science*, 1831, on the mutual relation of metallic conductors of electricity favorable to sending electric currents through long distances, and applicable, as the author stated, to " Mr. Barlow's project for a telegraph."   This paper by Professor Henry developed a broad principle in electricity, illustrating the fact that increasing the number of turns in a coil of insulated metallic wire carrying a current of electric fluid greatly increased the power of such current to project itself forward to greater distances.   And here let us point out the difference between a discovery and an invention.   Henry discovered a law of science not known till revealed by himself; Morse invented a machine which did not exist till produced by himself, which machine illustrated a law.   Henry does not claim the invention of a telegraphic machine.   Morse cannot and does not claim the discovery of a law of electricity.   There is in reality no conflict between the claims of these honorable gentlemen.

When Morse showed me his machine he had not seen Henry's paper, and knew not its purport till explained by myself.

After substituting the battery of twenty cups for that of a single cup, we added some hundred or more turns to the coil of wire around the poles of the magnet, and sent a message through 200 feet of conductors, then through 1,000 feet, and then through ten miles of wire, arranged on reels in my own lecture-room, in the New York University, in the presence of friends.   All these experiments were repeated with the original Morse machine, modified, as I have stated, by increasing the number of battery-cups, and the number of turns of wire around the magnet.

The main difficulties having been surmounted by the two modifications stated, Morse proceeded to operate the machine for general work.   The type and the port-rule, though good and effective, were found to be slow and heavy, and after a few weeks of trial he laid the types and the port-rule aside, and substituted therefor a key and key-board called the "correspondent," with which the telegrapher broke and closed the circuit between his own and a distant station, where his message is to be recorded.

I should here state, in connection with the type and port-rule, the labors and services of Mr. Alfred Vail, of Morristown, N. J., who was a pupil of mine in the New York University. He was greatly interested with the machine, and through him his father, Hon. Stephen Vail, ex-judge of Morris County, New Jersey, became interested in, and advanced funds to prepare and perfect the machinery of the invention. Young Vail invented a very ingenious machine to receive and distribute the type, which would have been of much value had not the use of the type been abandoned. Mr. Vail continued to be connected with the enterprise till the lines from Washington to New York and elsewhere were fully established. In July, 1843, he was associated with me, inspecting the first established line from Baltimore to Philadelphia. He was a good operator, and I believe was the first to read messages by the sound of the instrument that recorded them.

When the company devised means for setting up the lines they decided to lay the wires, five in number, from Baltimore to Washington, forty miles, in a leaden tube under ground. This was a favorite plan of Professor Morse. I objected to it on two grounds: *first*, that lead pipe, in acid soils, is liable to corrode, and let water in contact with the wires; and if any hole should be left in the soldering together of the ends of the pipe, in both cases water would get into the pipe and destroy insulation; and, *secondly*, if the insulation were once destroyed it would be difficult to find the defective point. But the company decided to proceed with the work. A plow was used with a share running 2½ feet deep, and carrying a coil of insulated wire inclosed in a coil of lead pipe which the plow deposited in the ground, and covered it as the plow progressed.

Forty miles of lead pipe were made in New York, in the autumn of 1843, and shipped to Baltimore in the end of November. Up to this date I had been engaged in New York inspecting the manufacture of the lead pipe and charging the same with the insulated wire, fed into the pipe by machinery while the pipe was drawn. I reached Baltimore in the early part of December, and learned that the party had nearly reached the Relay House. Nine miles had been laid, on inspection of which not one mile of wire was found to be sufficiently insulated to carry the electric current from end to end of the reach. Consultation being had, the apparatus and materials were taken to Washington, and by permission of Hon. H. L. Ellsworth, then Commissioner of Patents, stored in the basement of the Patent-Office, in the northeast corner, as the building was in 1843. Soon afterward a line of wires from the Patent-Office to the House of Representatives was stretched on poles, and the office for operating was soon after moved to the grounds of the city post-office, fronting then on Seventh street, where it remained several years.

Before lines of telegraph were set up, it was anticipated that in long lines, the ordinary current of electricity might not be strong enough to work the magnet at such distance so as to write, but would be so strong as to open and close a side or a local circuit, as suggested by Professor Henry. This mode of using one electric circuit and magnet to open and close another electric circuit, either for extending the main circuit to greater distances, or to operate any local circuit, although not in the machine when I first saw it, was discussed in an early part of 1837, before any lines had been constructed.

MORTUARY.

Died

In New York, on the second day of April, 1872,

Samuel Finley Breese Morse,

ÆT:

Eighty years, eleven months, and twenty-five days.

FUNERAL OF PROFESSOR MORSE.

The funeral of Professor S. F. B. Morse, who died on Tuesday evening, April 2, 1872, took place at the Madison Square Presbyterian Church, New York City, on Friday, the 5th April, at 11 o'clock. Before the hour arrived a vast concourse had assembled, not only filling the church, with the exception of the seats appropriated to the family, friends, and to the several delegations, but reaching far out into the street. All classes vied in testifying their respect to his memory.

The funeral procession, which reached the church soon after 11 o'clock, and entered during the rendering of a dirge by the organist, was headed by the Rev. William Adams, D. D., and the Rev. Francis B Wheeler, D. D., pastor of the Presbyterian Church of Poughkeepsie, of which Professor Morse was a member for the preceding twenty years. The pall-bearers were Gen. John A. Dix, Peter Cooper, William Orton, Cambridge Livingston, Daniel Huntington, Cyrus W. Field, Charles Butler, and Ezra Cornell. Following the bier and the members of the family were Governor Hoffman and staff, the legislative committee, members of the National Academy of Design, directors and operators of the Western Union Telegraph Company, members of the Evangelical Alliance, Chamber of Commerce, Stock Exchange, and Association for the Advancement of Science and Art, delegations from the common councils of New York, Brooklyn, and Poughkeepsie, and many of the Yale *Alumni*.

The exercises commenced with the anthem, "I heard a voice from Heaven," &c. Dr. Adams then read appropriate selections of Scripture, and the hymn, "Asleep in Jesus, blessed sleep," was sung to the tune of "Rest," both words and music being favorites of the deceased. An address was then delivered by Dr. Adams:

"The true value of a good life can never be lost; the good which men do, lives after them, and is not interred with their bones. Abel, the first one of our race who tasted death, being dead, yet speaketh.

He is the true Methuselah who originates good thoughts and projects, which live a thousand years after he himself has passed from
the world. Two days ago a funeral procession filed through our
streets with muffled drums, reversed arms, flags draped with black,
and with every sign of public woe, bearing the remains of one whom
we all loved and honored to their last resting-place. As the pageant
went by you said to yourselves, 'Such is the end of the life of the
body; like a vapor it vanisheth away; but the fidelity and loyalty of
the brave Christian soldier are not lost and cannot pass away; they
have entered as permanent properties into the life and history of this
country.'

" Pre-eminently true is this of the distinguished man whose death
has brought us together at this hour. If it be true, according to the
Scriptures, that no man dieth by himself, emphatically true is it that
the death of such a man as this is like the fall of an oak in a grove,
creating a wide chasm and bearing with it many trees, vines, and
boughs to the ground. Deep as are the sorrows caused by this
death in the home-circle and in private intimacies, it cannot but be
regarded as a public bereavement. We sorrow not alone; millions
share the shock. One is awed by the thought that no sooner had
death come to this dear and honored friend than, by means of that
instrumentality which his genius had effected, the intelligence was
throbbed beneath the billows of the ocean, across the continent east-
ward and westward, and simultaneously became the topic of remark
and the occasion of grief in London, Paris, Rome, Vienna, Berlin,
St. Petersburg, Syria, Egypt, India, China, Japan, and in every part
of the civilized world. We say, in familiar phrase, 'He is dead;' but
he lives still, and will live forever in forms of usefulness which are intimately related to the peace, welfare, and advancement of the whole
human race."

Dr. Adams then gave a sketch of the life of Professor Morse, and
of the great enterprise which his genius had originated, and drew a

beautiful portrait of his character, the crowning excellence of which was, that he was a humble and devoted disciple of Christ. He said :

"You remember a short time ago he was occupied with others of our fellow-citizens in acts of attention to a distinguished representative of the royal house of Russia. At the Holy Communion of this church next ensuing, (an occasion in which for domestic and personal reasons he felt an extraordinary interest,) at the close of the service he approached me with more than usual warmth and pressure of the hand, and, with a beaming countenance, said : 'O, this is something better and greater than standing before princes !' His piety had the simplicity of childhood. His household will never forget the purity and heartiness of his devotions.

"When his brother Sidney, last Christmas, died, he began to die also. Through fear of exciting alarm and giving distress to his own household, he did not speak so much to them as to some others, of his expected departure, but he used to say, familiarly, to some with whom he was ready to converse upon this subject : 'I love to be studying the Guide-Book of the country to which I am going; I wish to know more and more about it.' A few days before his decease, in the privacy of his chamber, I spoke to him of the great goodness of God to him in his remarkable life. 'Yes; so good, so good,' was the quick response; 'and the best part of all is yet to come.' Though spared more than eighty years, he saw none of the infirmities of age, either of mind or body. His delicate taste, his love for the beautiful, his fondness for the fine arts, his sound judgment, his intellectual activities, his public spirit, his intense interest in all that concerned the welfare, and the decoration of the city, his earnest advocacy of Christian liberty throughout the world—all continued unimpaired to the last."

Dr. Adams closed his eulogy as follows :

"To-day we part forever with all that is mortal of that man whom we have loved so much, and who has done so much in the cause of

Christian civilization. Less than one year ago his fellow-citizens, chiefly telegraphic operators who loved him as children love their fathers, reared his statue in bronze in the Central Park of this city. That venerable form, that face so saintly in its purity and refinement, we shall see no more. How much we shall miss him in our homes, our churches, our public gatherings, in the streets of the city, and in that society which he adorned and blessed! But his life has been so happy, so useful, so complete, that for him nothing remains to have been wished. He has left to his family, his friends, and his country a spotless name, beloved by all nations, and he died as a Christian, in the bright and blessed hope of everlasting life.

" Farewell, beloved friend, honored citizen, public benefactor, good and faithful servant! While your eulogy shall be pronounced in many languages, this, I believe, was your own highest aspiration, to have your name written as an humble disciple in the Lamb's Book of Life."

Prayer was then offered by the Rev. Dr. Wheeler, and the hymn, "Just as I am," was chanted by the choir. The remains were taken to Greenwood Cemetery and deposited in the receiving-vault. The burial-service was read, and prayer offered by the Rev. J. Aspinwall Hodge, pastor of the Presbyterian Church of Hartford, and son-in-law of the late Richard C. Morse. The benediction was pronounced by the Rev. Dr. Wheeler.

The morning after the death of Professor Morse, Governor Hoffman sent to the Assembly the following communication:

"STATE OF NEW YORK, EXECUTIVE CHAMBER,
"*Albany*, *April* 3, 1872.

" *To the Legislature:*

"The telegraph to-day announces the death of its inventor, Samuel F. B. Morse. Born in Massachusetts, his home has for many years of his eventful life been in New York. His fame belongs to neither, but to his country and to the world. Yet it seems fitting that this great State, in which he lived and died, should be the first to pay appropriate honors to his memory. Living, he received from Governments everywhere more public honors than were ever paid to any American private citizen. Dead—let all the people pay homage to his name.

"I respectfully recommend to the Legislature the adoption of such resolutions as may be suitable, and the appointment of a joint-committee to attend the funeral of the illustrious deceased.

"JOHN T. HOFFMAN."

PROCEEDINGS

OF THE

NATIONAL TELEGRAPH MEMORIAL MONUMENT ASSOCIATION.

A special meeting of the National Telegraph Memorial Monument Association was held at 2 o'clock p. m. on Wednesday, April 3, 1872, at No. 911 Pennsylvania avenue, Washington City, Vice-President Prof. B. T. Hedrick in the chair, and T. C. Connolly acting as secretary.

Dr. C. C. Cox, in appropriate terms, announced the death of Prof. Samuel F. B. Morse. "No ordinary occasion," he remarked, "has convened us in special session. A great man has fallen—a bright luminary in the firmament of science has become obscured by death! It is proper, therefore," he continued, "that this Association, organized to do him honor during his life, by constructing a permanent memorial to illustrate his expanding fame, should be the first, at the seat of Government, so inseparably identified with his early struggles, to arrange suitable honors to his memory, now that he lingers no longer among living men. Of course, wherever the tidings of his death have gone over the length and breadth of the land, suitable meetings will be convened expressive of the loss of a good citizen, a Christian gentleman, a profound philosopher, and a world-wide philanthropist. Eminently proper are such demonstrations of respectful regard; but the Republic—nay, the whole world—will expect that in this National Capital formal expression will be given to the admiration and gratitude of the people, and of their grief for the departure of this great benefactor of mankind."

On motion of Mr. A. S. Solomons, a committee of three were appointed to make preliminary arrangements for appropriate memorial services, and Messrs. Solomons, Hedrick, and Cox were designated as the committee.

Adjourned to meet at 3½ o'clock, Thursday afternoon, April 4, 1872.

T. C. CONNOLLY,
Secretary pro tem.

WASHINGTON, *April* 4, 1872.

An adjourned meeting of the National Telegraph Memorial Monument Association was held at 911 Pennsylvania avenue at 3½ p. m., Vice-President Prof. B. T. Hedrick in the chair.

The proceedings of the last meeting were read and approved.

The committee appointed at the last meeting to make preliminary arrangements for an appropriate demonstration of respect to the memory of the late Professor Morse, made the following report, which was adopted:

Your committee report that, in their judgment, proceedings of a public character should be had in the Metropolis of the nation in honor of the memory of the late Samuel F. B. Morse, and that arrangements should be made upon a scale commensurate with the fame of that great man, and the invaluable benefaction rendered to the world by his genius and labor; that, in order to make the proposed occasion as complete and impressive as possible, a meeting be held on the evening of Tuesday, the 16th instant, in the Hall of the House of Representatives, if said Hall can be secured; and further, that a committee of fifteen gentlemen be appointed to make all necessary arrangements, and a committee of five to draught and present suitable resolutions for the action of the meeting.

CHRIS. C. COX.
B. T. HEDRICK.
A S. SOLOMONS.

The committees, appointed by the chair, were as follows:

COMMITTEE OF ARRANGEMENTS.—A. S. Solomons, Richard Wallach, Samuel A. Duncan, Chas. F. Stansbury, M. G. Emery, Henry D. Cooke, D. W. Bliss, L. A. Gobright, Horatio King, T. W. Bartley, Albert J. Myer, John B. Kerr, O. E. Babcock.

COMMITTEE ON RESOLUTIONS.—J. W. Patterson, E. L. Stanton, T. C. Connolly, C. C. Cox, John Hitz.

Mr. Solomons stated that the Secretary of the Navy had tendered the services of the Marine Band for the occasion.

Mr. Davis, president of the Choral Society of Washington, was present, and said that the invitation to participate in the exercises had been received by the society, and it would afford them much pleasure to accept it and contribute, to the best of their ability, to the interest of the proposed memorial services.

Mr. Solomons offered the following resolution, which was adopted :

Resolved, That the people of the United States be requested to meet in their respective cities and towns on the evening of the 16th instant, at 8 o'clock, to give expression to their sense of the loss sustained by the world in the death of Samuel F. B. Morse, and to hold communication by telegraph with the assembly of the people's Representatives, and the citizens of Washington, and the District of Columbia, simultaneously convened, for the same purpose, in the capital of the nation.

A communication was received from Col. Leonard Whiteley, stating that he was authorized by President Orton, of the Western Union Telegraph Company, to tender the use of their wires for direct communication between the Morse memorial meetings proposed to be held.

Mr. Connolly offered the following resolution, which was adopted :

Resolved, That the liberal offer of President Orton, of the Western Union Telegraph Company, be accepted, and that the thanks of this Association be tendered him.

Mr. Connolly offered the following resolution, which was adopted:

Resolved, That the secretary give immediate notice to the chairmen of the several local branches of this Association, of the time and place of the proposed memorial meeting.

Adjourned.

H. AMIDON,
Secretary.

WASHINGTON, *April* 5, 1872.

A meeting of the committee of arrangements was held at 911 Pennsylvania avenue.

The chairman, Mr. Solomons, called the meeting to order, and H. Amidon was appointed secretary.

Present: Messrs. Solomons, M. G. Emery, General Myer, Horatio King, L. A. Gobright, Colonel Whitney, J B. Kerr, Charles F. Stansbury, Governor Corwine, and General Duncan.

Mr. Solomons reported that the United States House of Representatives had adopted a resolution granting the use of the hall of the House for the purpose of holding a meeting to commemorate the life and services of the late Samuel F. B. Morse.

On motion, ordered that a committee be appointed to select and invite speakers, and to arrange the entire programme of proceedings for the meeting.

Mr. Solomons, Mr. Stansbury, Dr. Cox, Mr. Kerr, Mr. Gobright, and General Myer were appointed such committee.

Mr. Stansbury offered the following resolution, which was adopted:

Whereas, the United States House of Representatives has placed its hall at the disposal of the National Telegraph Memorial Monument Association, for the purpose of holding a memorial meeting in honor of the late Samuel F. B. Morse, on Tuesday, April 16, and prominent members of both Houses of Congress, and other distinguished speakers, have consented to address the meeting; and

· Whereas, the telegraph has been freely placed at the disposal of this association for that evening to secure an exchange of sentiments with the meetings to be held in all portions of the country :

Be it resolved, That the municipal authorities of the cities of the United States are hereby invited to call meetings of similar character in their several localities, on the same evening, in order that the meetings may be in telegraphic communication, and thus a simultaneous expression be given to the national grief on the occasion of this irreparable loss.

Adjourned.

H. AMIDON,

Secretary.

WASHINGTON, *April* 8, 1872.

An adjourned meeting of the committee of arrangements was held at 911 Pennsylvania avenue, Dr. Cox presiding.

The proceedings of the last meeting were read and approved.

Present : Dr. Cox, Mr. King, Mr. Stansbury, Governor Cooke, Mr. Solomons, Dr. Bliss, and the secretary.

On motion of Mr. Stansbury, the chairman of the committee was requested to invite the Rev. Dr. Adams, of New York, to be present at the meeting on the 16th instant, and make the opening prayer.

The chairman was also requested to invite the family of Professor Morse to be present, and become the guests of the nation and this committee.

On motion, the Hon. Horatio King was authorized to complete the list of the speakers.

On motion of Dr. Bliss, it was ordered that a special committee of three on invitations be appointed.

Dr. Bliss, Mr. Stansbury, and Mr. King were appointed such committee.

On motion of Mr Solomons, it was

Resolved, That the Governors of the several States and Territories be invited to act as vice-presidents of the meeting, and in the event of their not being able to attend, to designate some one from their respective States or Territories to act in their place.

On motion of Mr. Stansbury, it was ordered that a committee of three be appointed to make arrangements for the accommodation of the press.

The Chair appointed Mr. Gobright, Dr. Bliss, and Governor Cooke.

On motion of Mr. Stansbury, it was ordered that a committee of three be appointed to superintend the necessary preparations on the floor of the House.

The Chair appointed Mr. Stansbury, Mr. Solomons, and Professor Hedrick.

Adjourned.

H. AMIDON,
Secretary.

WASHINGTON, *April* 9, 1872.

A meeting of the sub-committee of arrangements was held at 911 Pennsylvania avenue.

Present: Mr. Solomons, Mr. King, Dr. Cox, Dr. Bliss, Professor Hedrick, Mr. Stansbury, and the secretary; Mr. Solomons in the chair.

Mr. Solomons reported the passage of a resolution by the House of Representatives, authorizing the appointment of a committee of three of its members to act with the committee of arrangements of the Morse memorial services on the 16th instant, and that the Speaker had appointed Hon. William R. Roberts, of New York, Hon. Frank W. Palmer, of Iowa, and Hon. Francis E. Shober, of North Carolina, such committee.

Adjourned.

H. AMIDON,
Secretary.

WASHINGTON, *April* 10, 1872.

An adjourned meeting of the committee of arrangements was held at 911 Pennsylvania avenue, Mr. Solomons in the chair.

The proceedings of the last meeting were read and approved.

Present: Mr. Emery, Mr. Wallach, Mr. Kerr, Mr. Gobright, Dr. Cox, Mr. Stansbury, General Duncan, and the committee appointed by the House of Representatives, consisting of Messrs. Roberts, of New York, Palmer, of Iowa, and Shober, of North Carolina.

The Chair presented a communication from Messrs. Bogardus and Bendan Brothers, of New York, tendering the use of a life-size portrait of Professor Morse for the occasion of the memorial services on the 16th instant. The tender was accepted and a vote of thanks adopted.

The Chair also presented a letter from the Hon. J. S. Valentine, mayor of Wilmington, Del., stating that appropriate measures had been taken for a public meeting in that city at the same time as the meeting here.

On motion of Dr. Cox, it was

Resolved, That the secretary be directed to address a letter to the Rev. Dr. Wheeler, of Poughkeepsie, N. Y., inviting him to be present at the memorial services in honor of the late Professor Morse, to be held in the hall of the House of Representatives of the United States on the evening of the 16th instant, and that he be requested to make the closing prayer on that occasion.

On motion of Mr. King, it was ordered that the first message sent over the wires of the first magnetic telegraph—"What hath God wrought"—be placed as a legend over the portrait of Professor Morse, in the House of Representatives, on the occasion of the memorial services on the 16th instant.

On motion of Dr. Cox, it was

Resolved, That the Chairman be requested to report the programme and general arrangement for the memorial services to the committee appointed by the House of Representatives, on Monday morning the 15th instant.

Adjourned to Friday, the 12th instant, at 3 o'clock p. m.

H. AMIDON,
Secretary.

WASHINGTON, *April* 11, 1872.

An adjourned meeting of the committee of arrangements was held at the rooms, Mr. Solomons in the chair.

Present: Messrs. Bliss, Cox, Connolly, Duncan, King, Corwine, and Emery.

A letter was read from the Secretary of the Navy stating that the Marine Band had been ordered to be present at the memorial services on Tuesday evening next.

The Chair presented letters from the following governors of States, who had been appointed vice-presidents of the memorial meeting, and invited in the event of their not being able to be present to appoint some one from their respective States to act in their place:

Governor Hoffman, of New York, appointing the Hon. Fernando Wood to act as his proxy.

Governor Baker, of Indiana, appointing Senator Pratt.

Governor Geary, of Pennsylvania, appointing Hon. J. S. Negley.

Governor Padelford, of Rhode Island, appointing Hon. B. S. Edes.

Governor Caldwell, of North Carolina, appointing Col. John H. Wheeler.

Governor Scott, of South Carolina, appointing Hon. A. G. Mackey.

Governor Noyes, of Ohio, appointing Hon. A. F. Perry.

Governor Parker, of New Jersey, appointing Senator Stockton.

Governor H. D. Cooke, of District of Columbia, accepts the appointment in person.

The Chair also presented telegrams from Montreal and Philadelphia, stating that the mayors of those cities, respectively, would call meetings on the day appointed and communicate with this committee.

' Also, one from the Rev. Dr. Adams, of New York, stating that he would be present at the memorial services and take the part assigned him in the programme.

A telegram was also presented from Sidney E. Morse, esq., nephew of the late Professor Morse, stating that, accompanied by the sons of Professor Morse, he would leave New York on Monday night, to be present at the meeting.

A communication was also received from the New York Republican Association, accompanied by resolutions of regret, with a request that the officers of that association be permitted to represent the State of New York, and that they be assigned places on the occasion of the memorial services to be held in the Hall of the House of Representatives on the 16th instant.

Referred to committee on invitations.

Dr. Cox moved that officers having charge of public buildings throughout the country be requested to display the national flag at half-mast on Tuesday next, and that the trustees of churches be requested to toll their bells at sunset of that day.

Judge Corwine offered the following resolution, which was adopted:

Resolved, That the committee on invitations be requested to invite specially the following-named gentlemen: Professor Joseph Henry, of Washington, D. C.; Dr. J. M. Brodhead, of Washington, D. C.; Hon. John H. B. Latrobe, of Baltimore, Md.; Ezra Cornell, of Ithaca, N. Y.; Henry J. Rogers, of Brooklyn, N. Y.; Dr. L. D. Gale, of Washington, D. C.; Mrs. Vail and family; Rev. Geo. W. Samson, 491 Fifth avenue, New York.

Adjourned to 2 o'clock p. m. to-morrow.

H. AMIDON,
Secretary.

WASHINGTON, *April* 13, 1872.

An adjourned meeting of the committee of arrangements was held at the rooms.

The chairman not being present, Professor Hedrick was called to the chair.

Present: Dr. Cox, Mr. King, Mr. Emery, General Myer, Judge Corwine, Mr. Gobright, Col. J. S. Cunningham, Mr. Kerr, Dr. Bliss, and General Duncan.

A letter was received from the mayor of the city of Lynn, Mass., stating that at a meeting of the mayor and board of aldermen a committee was appointed to make the necessary arrangements for a mass-meeting on the 16th instant.

A communication was also received from the mayor of Buffalo, N. Y., stating that a similar meeting had been called in that city.

A similar letter was received from the mayor of Augusta, Ga., stating that he would call a meeting in that city.

The Chair reported that the following governors of States, in response to the invitation of this committee to act as vice-presidents of the meeting to be held in the Hall of the House of Representatives in honor of the late Professor Morse, had signified their acceptance of the position, and appointed the following proxies:

Governor Parker, of New Jersey, appoints Hon. J. P. Stockton.

Governor Whyte, of Maryland, appoints Lloyd W. Williams, esq.

Governor Washburn, of Massachusetts, appoints Hon. George F. Hoar.

Governor Scott, of South Carolina, appoints Hon. A. G. Mackey.

Governor Cooke, of District of Columbia, accepts in person.

Governor Brown, of Tennessee, appoints Hon. W. C. Whitthorne.

Governor Hadley, of Arkansas, appoints Hon. Powell Clayton.

Governor Brown, of Missouri, appoints Hon. James Craig.

Governor Carpenter, of Iowa, appoints Maj. O. Conner.

Governor Walker, of Virginia, appoints Hon. Jno. W. Johnston.

· Governor Leslie, of Kentucky, appoints General Jos. H. Lewis.

Governor Powers, of Mississippi, appoints Geo. C. McKee, esq.

Governor Baker, of Indiana, appoints Hon. D. D. Pratt.

Governor Hoffman, of New York, appoints Hon. Fernando Wood.

Governor Geary, of Pennsylvania, appoints Hon. James S. Negley.

Governor Padelford, of Rhode Island, appoints Hon. B. T. Edes.

Governor Caldwell, of North Carolina, appoints Col. Jno. H. Wheeler.

Governor Noyes, of Ohio, appoints Hon. A. F. Perry.

Governor Jacobs, of West Virginia, appoints Hon. J. J. Davis.

Governor Weston, of New Hampshire, appoints Franklin ———, esq.

Governor Campbell, of Wyoming Territory, appoints Hon. W. T. Jones.

Governor Harvey, of Kansas, appoints Hon. Fred. P. Stanton.

On motion adjourned.

H. AMIDON,
Secretary.

WASHINGTON, April 15, 1872.

An adjourned meeting of the committee of arrangements for the Morse memorial services was held at the rooms, the chairman, Mr. Solomons, presiding.

Present: Messrs. Hedrick, Bliss, Cox, Corwine, Stansbury, Duncan, Cooke, Kerr, Emery, Connolly, Kellogg, Myer, King, and the secretary.

The committee appointed to draught resolutions to be presented to the meeting in the hall of the House of Representatives on the evening of the 16th instant, submitted, as their report, the following resolutions:

Whereas, it has pleased Divine Providence to remove from the scene of his earthly labors our late illustrious citizen, Samuel Finley

Breese Morse, we, members of the National Morse Memorial Association, desirous of giving expression to our sentiments of esteem and
veneration for the deceased, do hereby adopt the following resolutions :

Resolved, That we share in the general sorrow pervading the country at the national loss of a great and good citizen, who has been and
will continue to be esteemed one of the brightest stars in the firmament of science, and among the most useful of human benefactors,
remarkable no less for his private virtues than for his public achievements; one who, in the light of the future, will be regarded by all
true admirers of genius and intellect as a grand and glorious model
of American character developed under the fostering care of republican institutions.

Resolved, That we recognize in the life of the late Professor Morse
an industry and perseverance in the prosecution of great purposes,
a variety and richness of intellectual culture and accomplishment, a
scholarly taste, a modesty of demeanor, and a purity of character,
upon which we look back with no common pride and satisfaction;
that in his death we experience, in connection with the whole civilized world, the loss of a colossal mind, whose faculties, rare in their
separate capacities, and still more so in their harmonious combination, have stamped upon the page of history the impress of a renown
imperishable as time itself.

Resolved, That as living he received the homage of all men, of
whatsoever clime and nationality, and was the recipient of distinguished honors from various institutions and governments of the
world, so, dead, he can be claimed by no mere locality; his fame is
no longer the peculiar property of any country, but belongs to the
whole earth, wherever science is appreciated and genuine worth honored.

Resolved, That the electric telegraph marks an important era in civilization; that, by contributing in a thousand ways to the industrial
agencies of the world, by the rapid diffusion of thought, the substitution of knowledge for ignorance, (thus arresting prejudice and unjust
estimate of character and conduct,) by quick and friendly interchange
of sentiment between nations, it may well be claimed to be the great
peace-maker, pointing in its results to a period of unity and univer-

sal brotherhood, when differences will be adjusted by the arbitration of reason and war rendered impossible; that, as the genius who, by the invention of the electro-magnetic telegraph, rendered practical the scientific discoveries of other eminent *savants*, Professor Morse is entitled to all the honors due from a grateful people to a splendid benefactor.

Resolved, That it is gratifying to reflect that Professor Morse lived to see the marvelous spread of his great invention around the entire circuit of the habitable earth, thus witnessing a triumph of his labors rarely vouchsafed to the living toiler in the paths of practical science; that ere he closed his eyes upon the great work of his life, Europe had completed nearly five hundred thousand miles of telegraphic communication, America one hundred and eighty thousand miles, India fourteen thousand miles, Australia ten thousand miles; that from the latest estimates the wires had penetrated the ocean for more than thirty thousand miles, the cables extending beneath the Atlantic and German Oceans, the Baltic, North Mediterranean, Red, Arabian, and China Seas, the Persian Gulf, the Bay of Biscay, the Straits of Gibraltar, and the Gulfs of Mexico and Saint Lawrence.

Resolved, That a copy of these resolutions be engrossed on parchment, signed by the officers of this association and the committee on resolutions, and forwarded to the family of the late Professor Morse, expressing our sincere sense of and profound condolence in the severe bereavement they have sustained by his death.

WASHINGTON, *April* 16, 1872.

Pursuant to adjournment the committee of arrangements met at the rooms, the chairman, Mr. Solomons, presiding.

Present: Messrs. Emery, Kerr, King, Stansbury, Cox, Corwine, and the secretary.

The Chair reported that two hundred additional tickets and invitations had been given to each member of the committee appointed on the part of the House of Representatives, and one hundred in addition to the chairman of that committee.

The Chair stated that the President of the United States, the Cabinet, judges of the Supreme Court, and other distinguished invited guests had been requested to meet in the room of the Speaker of the House of Representatives at 7 o'clock this evening.

The committee of arrangements was also requested to meet there at the same hour.

The following dispatch, to be sent to the various meetings throughout the country, was submitted and adopted:

CIRCULAR DISPATCH.

The National Morse Memorial Meeting is now in progress in the Hall of the House of Representatives, Speaker Blaine, assisted by the Vice-President of the United States, presiding, and the governors of the several States acting as Vice-presidents, and is now ready to receive communications.

The Chair reported that the following-named cities, through their mayors, had notified the chairman of the committee of arrangements that meetings in accordance with the circular sent out by the committee would be held in their respective cities on the evening of the 16th instant, and would communicate with the meeting held in the Hall of the House of Representatives: Worcester, Mass.; Augusta, Me.; Buffalo, N. Y.; Lynn, Mass.; Montreal, Canada; Wilmington, Del ; Concord, N. H.; Chicago, Ill.; Pittsburgh, Pa.; Indianapolis, Ind.; San Francisco, Cal.; Philadelphia, Pa.; Mobile, Ala.; Pensacola, Fla.; Salem, Mass.; Grand Rapids, Mich.; Vicksburgh, Miss.; Rochester, N. Y.

Adjourned to meet at the call of the chairman.

H. AMIDON,
Secretary.

WASHINGTON, *April* 18, 1872.

A called meeting of the committee of arrangements of the Morse memorial services was held at the rooms, Mr. Solomons in the chair.

Present: Messrs. Cooke, King, Hedrick, and the secretary.

On motion of Mr. King, it was

Resolved, That all the papers, dispatches, and addresses relating to the Morse memorial ceremonies be placed in the hands of Charles F. Stansbury, esq., to arrange for publication, with the request that he also prepare, to be published therewith, a brief sketch of the life of Professor Morse, including an account of his experiments and discoveries, and an obituary notice presenting the closing scenes of his eventful life.

On motion of Governor Cooke, Mr. Solomons, Mr. Stansbury, and Mr. King were appointed a committee to superintend the publication.

On motion of Mr. King, it was

Resolved, That the thanks of the committee be extended to the president and other officers of the Western Union Telegraph Company for their liberality and courtesy in placing the telegraph-wires at the service of the committee, free of charge, prior to and during the memorial services.

The same resolution was passed applying to the president and other officers of the Franklin Telegraph Company, and the resolutions were ordered to be engrossed and transmitted to the presidents of said companies respectively.

Governor Cooke offered the following resolutions, which were unanimously adopted:

Resolved, That the thanks of this committee are due to the chairman, A. S. Solomons, esq., who, by his indefatigable and judicious efforts, has contributed so much to the success of the memorial services.

Resolved, That our acknowledgements are also due to the secretary, H. Amidon, esq., for the very satisfactory manner in which he has kept the records of this committee.

On motion, adjourned *sine die*.

H. AMIDON,
Secretary.

ORDER OF MEMORIAL SERVICES IN HONOR OF THE LATE SAMUEL F. B. MORSE, IN THE HALL OF THE HOUSE OF REPRESENTATIVES, TUESDAY EVENING, APRIL 16, 1872.

Chairman, Mr. Speaker BLAINE.

Assisted by the Vice-President of the United States.

Prayer by the Rev. W. ADAMS, D. D., of New York.

Mr. Speaker BLAINE will announce the order of proceedings.

Music by the United States Marine Band.

Presentation of resolutions by Hon. C. C. COX, M. D., of Washington, D. C.

Address by Hon. J. W. PATTERSON, of New Hampshire.

Address by Hon. FERNANDO WOOD, of New York.

Vocal Music by the Choral Society of Washington.

Address by Hon. J. A. GARFIELD, of Ohio.

Address by Hon. S. S. COX, of New York.

Music by the United States Marine Band.

Address by Hon. D. W. VOORHEES, of Indiana.

Address by Hon. N. P. BANKS, of Massachusetts.

Vocal Music by the Choral Society of Washington.

Benediction by the Rev. Dr. WHEELER, of Poughkeepsie, New York.

COMMITTEE OF ARRANGEMENTS.

On the part of the Congress of the United States.—E. H. ROBERTS, New York; F. W. PALMER, Iowa; F. E. SHOBER, North Carolina.

C. F. Stansbury, D. W. Bliss, Richard Wallach, H. D. Cooke, L. A. Gobright, S. A. Duncan, M. G. Emery, O. E. Babcock, R. M. Corwine, C. C. Cox, A. J. Myer, B. S. Hedrick, J. B. Kerr, Horatio King.

A. S. SOLOMONS,
Chairman.

H. AMIDON, *Secretary.*

THE NATIONAL CAPITOL.

The large Hall of the House of Representatives of the United States was densely crowded on Tuesday evening, April 16, 1872, by the most distinguished people of the country, to take part in the ceremonies attendant on the Memorial services in honor of the great scientist and philosopher, SAMUEL FINLEY BREESE MORSE, LL. D., who tamed the fiercest, freest, and most powerful agent of nature to the chariot-wheels of triumphant science.

Under direction of the National Telegraph Memorial Monument Association, and the Committee appointed by the House of Representatives to confer and act with the former association, the arrangements to perfect a fitting tribute to the great scientist were of the most elaborate and complete kind, and seldom has there been an occasion which shone with greater splendor, or flashed upon a more dazzling or brilliant scene, ceremonies more affecting in memory of a great mind, than did this tribute to the immortal sage in whose memory the councils of the republic assembled to do honor.

From the parapet of the gallery, facing the Speaker's desk, a portrait of Professor Morse, (painted by Bendan, of Baltimore,) draped in mourning, and wreathed most beautifully with evergreens, bearing the legend "WHAT HATH GOD WROUGHT," looked down upon the Speaker and the honored guests around him, as the sage, conscious of his immortality and calm in his superiority might look upon the vanities he had long since cast aside from his heart and from his thoughts, yet with that satisfaction which we of human kind must ever contemplate the ceremonies offered in respect and love to his memory. The United States Marine Band occupied that portion of the gallery immediately behind the portrait, and at short intervals poured upon the audience the choicest strains of pathetic music, for which they are so famous.

Upon the floor, and in front of the Marine Band, were the Washington "Choral Society," who sang with marked effect several beautifully appropriate pieces; among them, the following, especially written for the occasion by Gen. William H. Browne:

> Immortal mind, now in heaven beholding
> The wondrous scenes all in glory unfolding,
> Thy Lord hath said, "LET THERE BE LIGHT!"
> And darkness dies in the radiance bright!
> Thou now canst speed like flashing thought,
> Again exclaim, "WHAT HATH GOD WROUGHT!"
> Thy toil hath rich fruition found;
> Glad soul, thou art a hero crowned!
>
> Thy fame goes forth on the wings of the morning,
> The lightning-steed the wide continent scorning.
> Thou spirit blest! thy toil is o'er;
> Thou art with God for evermore.
>> Hallelujah! hallelujah, for evermore,
>> For evermore!
>
> Come, raging storms!—but your fury is broken,
> For tongues of fire of your coming have spoken,
> And sons of toil, on land and sea,
> Defiant smile in security!
> O subtle power! the dream comes true
> Of him whose toy the lightning drew.
> O joy! all great colaboring minds,
> Your genius now all nations binds.
>
> Good-will, fly forth on etherial pinions,
> Fly! harnessed light, to remotest dominions,
> While thoughts sublime to heaven soar,
> O, GOD! be guide for evermore.
>> Hallelujah! hallelujah, for evermore,
>> For evermore!

. Speaker Blaine occupied the chair, and on his right Vice-President Colfax sat.   In the front row of seats, facing the Speaker's desk, were President Grant and his Cabinet, several members of the family of the late Professor Morse, and the Supreme Court of the United States and of the District of Columbia.   At the Clerk's desk, immediately beneath the Speaker, were placed the telegraph-instruments, the wires of which had been so successfully placed in connection with every part of the United States, and almost the entire world, by Messrs. Morell Marean, and James A. Gassaway, of the Western Union and Franklin Telegraph Companies, and by direct communication ticked ceaselessly on, receiving and sending messages everywhere, a tongueless mourner, but most eloquent in its inarticulate murmurings with requiems to the *manes* of the mighty dead.

PROCEEDINGS IN THE HOUSE OF REPRE-SENTATIVES.

Promptly at the appointed hour the Speaker's gavel fell, and the exercises were commenced with the following

PRAYER

by the Rev. W. Adams, D. D., of New York:

We adore Thee, O God, as the Maker of the heavens and the earth and " whatsoever passeth through the paths of the sea." Thou hast made of one blood all nations to dwell upon the face of the earth, and hast appointed the bounds of their habitation. As Thou hast taught us that all things were made " for Christ," we thank Thee that Thou hast revealed Thine own purpose in the " dispensation of the fullness of time to gather together in one all things which are in heaven and in earth, even in Him." Amid all that is seemingly incoherent and adverse, may we see more and more of order and harmony and the promise of that kingdom which is righteousness and peace and joy in the Holy Ghost. Accept our thanks for all the sons of science, enterprise, and faith, all events and achievements which have contributed to promote that kingdom upon the earth. Especially, on this occasion, do we thank Thee for the life and services of him in honor of whose memory we are now assembled. As Thou art the Author of all good thoughts, seating skill in the right hand, wisdom in the mind, and good intentions in the heart, we thank Thee for all which he was in the culture of Thy word and spirit, and for all which he did as the child and agent of Providence for the welfare of his country and the world. May that agency, associated with his name, be in all time, as it was at its inception, consecrated to concord, truth, and peace. As Thou hast removed Thy servant from this life, we thank Thee for the hopes of the glorious gospel, and that we may follow his ascending spirit to the society of good and faithful men in the kingdom of heaven. Comfort a bereaved family, the widow and the fatherless. Make them grateful for the treasure of his good name, of which death never can despoil them. Bless those over all the globe who, when we wake and when we sleep, manipulate the instruments whose words have gone forth to the ends of the world. Bless our beloved country; the President, and Congress of the republic. Make our officers just, and our exactors righteous. May our judges be as at the first and our counsellors as at the beginning. Let the glory of the Lord shine on our capital and in the homes of the people. May Thy kingdom come and Thy will be done in all the earth as in heaven. All which we ask through Jesus Christ, to whom be glory forever. Amen.

At the conclusion of the prayer Mr. Speaker Blaine addressed the audience as follows:

INTRODUCTORY REMARKS BY SPEAKER BLAINE.

Less than thirty years ago a man of genius and learning was an earnest petitioner before Congress for the small pecuniary aid that enabled him to test certain occult theories of science which he had laboriously evolved. To-night the Representatives of forty millions of people assemble in their legislative hall to do homage and honor to the name of Morse.

Great discoverers and inventors rarely live to witness the full development and perfection of their mighty conceptions. But to him whose death we now mourn, and whose fame we celebrate, it was in God's good providence vouchsafed otherwise.

The little thread of wire, placed as a timid experiment between the national capital and a neighboring city, grew and lengthened and multiplied with almost the rapidity of the electric current that darted along its iron nerves, until, within his own life-time, continent was bound unto continent, hemisphere answered through ocean's depths unto hemisphere, and an encircled globe flashed forth his eulogy in the unmatched eloquence of a grand achievement.

Charged by the House of Representatives with the agreeable and honorable duty of presiding here, and of announcing the various participants in the exercises of the evening, I welcome to this hall those who join with us in this impressive tribute to the memory and the merit of a great man.

The Marine Band followed with some excellent music ; after which Dr. C. C. Cox was introduced, and said :

ADDRESS OF DR. C. C. COX.

Mr. CHAIRMAN: In rising, as the organ of the National Morse Memorial Association, to present to the meeting resolutions expressive of their sentiments upon this commemorative occasion, I shall indulge in no extended preface. The fresh grave has an eloquence mightier than mere language. A great and good man, ripe in years and honors, has fallen from us. The scholar, the artist, the inventor is no more! It is fitting that in this city, where his brilliant career in practical science commenced, in the capital of the nation with which his name is inseparably associated, in this hall of Congress, the scene of his discouraging struggles and final success, his memory and achievements should be thus honored by appropriate ceremonies.

The presence of the electro-magnetic apparatus, which will to-night place us in communication with the telegraphic circuit of the whole world, revives scenes which transpired in New York ten months ago. I refer not so much to the event in Central Park, where the rare spectacle was presented of a living man beholding, amid the plaudits of an admiring multitude, the unveiling of his own monument, as to the ceremonies on the evening of the same day in the Academy of Music. There Morse's own fingers manipulated the interlocutory wires, amid the silence and emotion of a vast assemblage; and there, too, his voice, weak and tremulous, responded to the compliments and praises lavished upon him, deprecating in a spirit of self-abnegation all personal credit, and exclaiming, with an emphasis which thrilled every breast, "Not unto us, not unto us, but unto God be all the glory!" The fingers that made the wires talk on that memorable occasion have lost their cunning; the voice which gave utterance to the noblest of sentiments is hushed and echoless. Death has placed his seal upon Samuel Finley Breese Morse, and all that was great in intellect and pure in disposition has become fixed and permanent forever.

And what a character is left for our contemplation! What completeness of purpose! what graces of culture! what simplicity of temper! what intelligence, controlled by modesty, and sanctified by convictions of truth! Who better than Morse understood the value of life, comprehended its great mission, and illustrated to the latest syllable of time its true instincts, its personal discipline, its moral obligations, its godlike capacities? It is true he escaped not the penalty which almost invariably follows success. The specter envy confronted him more than once on his ascending path, but long ere death placed its impress upon him his eye read and his ear drank in words only of kindness, respect, and endearment.

There is something beautiful in the decline of his protracted and brilliant career. Like the gentle drawing to its close of a long summer-day came slowly and peacefully upon him the infirmities of age. His head had long borne the frosty honors of three-score years and ten, his gait had lost its elasticity, the eye its brightness—yet he still lingered. The old honored him, young men and maidens did him reverence. "When the ear heard him, then it blessed him; and when the eye saw him, it gave witness to him." The sun of life sank at last from mortal vision, but the twilight which followed that setting, embalmed and hallowed by his many virtues, is around us now, and will endure through all the ages of coming time.

Surely—

> "Ne'er to the chambers where the mighty rest,
> Since their foundation, came a nobler guest,
> Nor e'er was to the bowers of bliss conveyed
> A fairer spirit or more welcome shade."

Not in one land or in one language alone is his decease lamented. Wherever the humming wires stretch along lonely hill-sides, over far-extending prairies, through the streets of crowded cities, or flash and throb under ocean-tides from continent to continent the tidings of Morse's death have spread, awaking in the trapper of the western wilds, the fisherman on the northern banks, the shepherd in his Alpine fastnesses, and the dweller in far-off Indus a new and startling sense of loss. Wherever the message has reached, ample honors will be paid to his memory. The limner will adjust his easel, the sculptor take up the implements of his art, in order to trace once more the lineaments of the world's benefactor. Monuments of marble and bronze will adorn the marts of great cities and the halls of science and art. Though his remains have been laid away amid the shades of Greenwood, in the shadow of our great commercial metropolis, he belongs not to us alone. The whole world claims him. The pillars we raise do not appropriate him. He toiled not for himself, nor yet for his own country, but for the whole brotherhood of man. "This whole earth," said the Grecian orator, "is the sepulchre of illustrious men. Nor is it the inscriptions on their columns in their native soil alone that show their merit; but the memorial of them, better than all inscriptions, reposited more durably in universal remembrance than in their own tomb!" The fame of Morse will be enduring as the great principles upon which it is based. Everything in science, art, and nature will be tributary to his expanding renown.

> "The winds shall murmur of his name,
> The woods be peopled with his fame;
> The meanest rill, the mightiest river,
> Roll mingling with his fame forever!"

, Sir, I have nothing more to add.   The theme will be taken up by abler hands, and more eloquent tongues than mine will discourse of the departed; and, after eulogy shall have been exhausted, how far short must we still fall in appreciation of the great benefaction his genius has conferred upon the world—its untold results in modifying national intercourse and national prejudice, in diffusing knowledge far and wide, and hastening the coming era of "peace on earth and good will to men!"   How, then, can too much be uttered or done to keep alive in the memories of men the name and achievements of Morse?

> " Nothing can cover his high fame but heaven ;
> No pyramid sets off his memory
> But the eternal substance of his greatness,
> To which I leave him."

I have now the honor to read

THE RESOLUTIONS.

Whereas it has pleased divine Providence to remove from the scene of his earthly labors our late illustrious citizen, Samuel Finley Breese Morse, we, members of the National Morse Memorial Association, desirous of giving expression to our sentiments of esteem and veneration for the deceased, do hereby adopt the following resolutions:

Resolved, That we share in the general sorrow pervading the country at the national loss of a great and good citizen, who has been and will continue to be esteemed one of the brightest stars in the firmament of science and among the most useful of human benefactors, remarkable no less for his private virtues than for his public achievements; one who, in the light of the future, will be regarded by all true admirers of genius and intellect as a grand and glorious model of American character, developed under the fostering care of republican institutions.

Resolved, That we recognize in the life of the late Professor Morse an industry and perseverance in the prosecution of great purposes, a variety and richness of intellectual culture and accomplishment, a scholarly taste, a modesty of demeanor, and a purity of character, upon which we look back with no common pride and satisfaction; that in his death we experience, in connection with the whole civilized world, the loss of a colossal mind, whose faculties, rare in their separate capacities, and still more so in their harmonious combination, have stamped upon the page of history the impress of a renown imperishable as time itself.

Resolved, That as living he received the homage of all men, of whatsoever clime and nationality, and was the recipient of distinguished honors from various institutions and governments of the world, so, dead, he can be claimed by no mere locality; his fame is no longer the peculiar property of any country, but belongs to the whole earth, wherever science is appreciated and genuine worth honored.

Resolved, That the electric telegraph marks an important era in civilization; that, by contributing in a thousand ways to the industrial agencies of the world, by the rapid diffusion of thought, the substitution of knowledge for ignorance, (thus arresting prejudice and unjust estimate of character and conduct,) by quick and friendly interchange of sentiment between nations, it may well be claimed to be the great peace-maker, pointing in its results to a period of unity and universal brotherhood, when differences will be adjusted by the arbitration of reason, and war rendered impossible; that, as the genius who, by the invention of the electro-magnetic telegraph, rendered practical the scientific experiments of other eminent *savans,* Professor Morse is entitled to all the honors due from a grateful people to a splendid benefactor.

Resolved, That it is gratifying to reflect that Professor Morse lived to see the marvelous spread of his great invention around the entire circuit of the habitable earth, thus witnessing a triumph of his labors rarely vouchsafed to the living toiler in the paths of practical science; that ere he closed his eyes upon the great work of his life Europe had completed nearly five hundred thousand miles of telegraphic communication, America one hundred and eighty thousand miles, India fourteen thousand miles, Australia ten thousand miles; that, from the latest estimates, the wires had penetrated the ocean for more than thirty thousand miles, the cables extending beneath the Atlantic and German Oceans, the Baltic, North Mediterranean,

Red, Arabian, and China Seas, the Persian Gulf, the Bay of Biscay, the Straits of Gibraltar, and the Gulfs of Mexico and Saint Lawrence.

Resolved, That a copy of these resolutions be engrossed on parchment, signed by the officers of this association and the committee on resolutions, and forwarded to the family of the late Professor Morse, expressing our sincere sense of, and profound condolence in, the severe bereavement they have sustained by his death.

The following telegrams were then read:

[Telegram dated Boston, Mass., April 16, 1872.]

To A. S. SOLOMONS,

    Chairman, Washington:

I beg leave to transmit herewith a series of resolutions which have just been passed at a large meeting of the citizens of Boston, held in Faneuil Hall this evening:

Resolved, That the city of Boston, in common with the rest of the country and the whole civilized world, feels sensibly the loss which science has sustained in the death of Professor Morse, whose great invention has been of incalculable value to all the interests of of life, and has conferred lasting honor upon his country.

Resolved, That it is peculiarly incumbent upon us to express our sense of the loss which the world has sustained in the death of this eminent benefactor of the human race, from the fact that he was born among us, and that his early training was drawn from the institutions of New England.

                      WM. GASTON,
                        Mayor of Boston.

[Telegram dated Poughkeepsie, N. Y., April 16, 1872.]

To A. S. SOLOMONS,

    Chairman Committee National Morse

        Memorial Meeting, Washington:

The citizens of Poughkeepsie are now assembled to do honor to the memory of their late fellow-townsman, Samuel F. B. Morse, who was endeared to them not more by the brilliancy of his scientific discovery than by his benovelence and many Christian virtues. They unite with the whole nation and the world in giving expression to that spontaneous sympathy which is everywhere excited, and by his genius is made to vibrate this night through the nerves of his wonderful instrument to the uttermost parts of the earth.

S. M. BUCKINGHAM,
Chairman of Committee.

[Telegram dated Columbia, S. C., April 16, 1872.]

To Hon. JAMES G. BLAINE,

Chairman Morse Memorial Meeting, Washington:

The city council of Columbia joins with the grateful citizens of the civilized world in expressing its heart-felt commiseration at the incomparable loss to humanity of the great inventor of the magnetic telegraph, Professor S. F. B. Morse. His work is accomplished; he has been gathered to his fathers, but the great good which he wrought for civilization will live through countless ages to come.

JOHN ALEXANDER, Mayor.

[Telegram dated Pensacola, Fla., April 16, 1872.]

To A. S. SOLOMONS,

Chairman of the Committee of Arrangements, National
Telegraph Memorial Association, Washington:

I send you herewith a report of proceedings of a meeting of the citizens of Pensacola, held this evening.

C. LE BARON, Jr.,
President Pensacola Telegraph Company.

At a meeting of citizens of Pensacola, convened at the telegraph-office, for the purpose of testifying their respect for the memory of the late Prof. Samuel F. B. Morse, Mr. William H. Judot was called to the chair, and Mr. Charles Le Baron, jr., appointed secretary; when the following resolution was offered and, on motion, unanimously adopted, and ordered to be transmitted by telegraph, immediately, to the chairman of the Morse Memorial Association in session in the Hall of Representatives in Washington City:

Resolved, That we, the citizens of Pensacola, do cordially unite with our fellow-citizens of the United States in testifying our sorrow at the death of the late Prof. Samuel F. B. Morse, and our high appreciation of his character, and of the inestimable benefits which he has conferred upon mankind, annihilating time and space, encircling the earth with wires of instantaneous intercommunication, and drawing the different nations into the close communion of one great family. His wonderful genius has contributed to the prosperity and happiness of mankind, and crowned him with more unfading laurels than ever wreathed the brow of an illustrious conqueror. While we deplore his loss, we feel proud of him, as a citizen of our country, and tender this our tribute to his worth and memory.

WM. H. JUDOT,
Chairman.

CHARLES LE BARON, JR., *Secretary*.

[Telegram dated Council Chamber, Chicago, April 16, 1872.]

To A. S. SOLOMONS, *Chairman*

 National Morse Memorial Association, Washington:

A meeting of the common council of the city of Chicago is now in session at the City Hall, called for the purpose of paying their respects to the memory of the late Professor Morse, and send to you and other sister cities our condolence at the loss of a man who, by his genius, has proved himself one of the greatest benefactors of the human race; his memory will be cherished in every land where his wonderful invention is used. The names of Morse, Franklin, and Fulton will never be forgotten by a grateful posterity. The following resolutions were unanimously adopted by the common council:

Whereas the inventor, in the public estimation, is rapidly taking rank with the foremost of the world's benefactors; and whereas Samuel F. B. Morse ranks first in his class as an inventor and public benefactor: Therefore,

Resolved, That the city of Chicago, having largely received benefits from his labors in her prosperity and in her calamity; having through the instrumentalities devised by him reached the uttermost parts of the earth, vibrating the noblest chords of human sympathy, here adds her tribute of respect and honor to the genius and perseverance of the man who, overcoming all obstacles, gave to the world the wonderful magnetic telegraph, and thereby brought into close communion all nations, tongues, and people ; breaking down the clannish barriers that had divided men and made them enemies; that her citizens cherish the name of Morse, whose chief monument must ever be this high position in the hearts of the people, and that while we mourn his departure we will, as all the civilized world must, ever re-rejoice that he lived, and that his works remain with us.

Following the adoption of the resolutions, his honor, Mayor Medill, made some remarks on the utility and importance of the invention of telegraphy.

He said that Buckle, author of the History of Civilization, had said that to Adam Smith, the author of the science of political economy, was due the honor of conferring on mankind the greatest benefit, but he challenged this sentiment. To Morse should be given the palm of having made the discovery which yields in all respects the most to mankind. Alluding to the perfection of Morse's invention, he said General Stager, general superintendent Western Union Telegraph Company, who was present, would bear him out in the assertion that those who sought to improve telegraphs found the nearer they kept to the simple machinery and alphabet of Morse, the better. The mayor concluded with the following sentiment, which was received with applause: " Morse, one of the few names of the countless millions of the human race, was born not to die mortal in the flesh, but immortal in the memory of mankind."

Hon. A. H. Burley, comptroller, submitted the following sentiment: " Morse, with a thread, has bound all the nations of the earth and sealed the union with fire from Heaven."

General Stiles, city attorney, offered the following sentiment:

"Nature was personified in Morse, that one touch of his, will yet make the whole world akin."

Mr. William Henry Smith offered the following sentiment:

"The co-workers of Morse, though not recognized in monuments, nor mentioned in historical pages, yet worthy to be remembered; without whose skill and untiring industry the invention of Morse would have been robbed of half of its usefulness; but they are not without recompense, as the consciousness of a great work, modestly performed from the love of science and sense of duty, is a satisfaction which no power of man can take away."

JOHN H. McAVOY,

President of Common Council.

The Speaker then introduced the Hon. J. W. Patterson.

ADDRESS OF SENATOR J. W. PATTERSON.

In seconding the resolutions which have been read I will indulge in a few words only upon the life and character of him whose exalted fame is secure above the reach of eulogy. Samuel Finley Breese Morse, to whose memory we have met to pay a mournful tribute of respect, was the son of a distinguished Presbyterian clergyman, and was born on the soil of old Charlestown, which drank the blood of the first great battle of the Revolution. He received his primary education in the common schools of New England, and graduated from Yale College, at the age of 19, with a strong predilection for the natural sciences. From boyhood, however, he had a passionate love of art, and finally adopted it as a profession. Soon after graduating he went abroad to perfect himself in his chosen pursuit. Directed by the tutelage of West, Copley, and Allston, and inspired by the old masters, whose imperishable works he studied thoughtfully in the galleries of Southern Europe, he made rapid progress, and gave early promise of great eminence, both in painting and sculpture. Unfortunately, at the end of four years, poverty drove him from these Meccas of genius when his work was but half done, but in that brief period he exhibited powers as an artist, well illustrated in his Dying Hercules, which might have given him an immortality of fame had he been allowed to devote himself to the higher ranges of his calling. But Providence had reserved him for a special, if not a nobler, work; and so, on returning home, he was compelled by the "*res augusta domi*" to devote himself to the uncongenial drudgery of his profession. He could not enter those richer fields which lured and fascinated him from afar, and where the genius of the past had left in divinest forms, imperishable conceptions of beauty and grandeur. He was doomed to a great work of practical utility, and so was put to discipline in the schools of misfortune. After his return to America, Mr. Morse at first established himself, as a painter of portraits, in Boston. Not meeting the success he anticipated among his early friends, he removed, in 1818, to Concord, N. H. There he seems to have been more fortunate. Portraits painted at this period by the young artist are still to be found in the mansions of some of our oldest and best families.

Honorable mention is also made in the local papers of the time of a fire-engine invented by Mr. Morse, which was purchased, and, for a long time, used, by the citizens of Concord.

But painting and invention were not the only arts in which our hero won coveted trophies while a resident of New Hampshire. At an evening party he was introduced by a mutual friend to a Miss Lucretia P. Walker, one of the most beautiful and accomplished girls of the town. The result was fatal, for we read in the *Patriot*, under date of October 6, 1818, as follows: "Married, in this town, by the Rev. Dr. McFarland, Mr. Samuel F. B. Morse, the celebrated painter, to Miss Lucretia Walker, the daughter of Charles Walker, Esq." After that, however much men might deny his genius for art, they could not say he was not a man of taste.

Subsequently he established himself at Charleston, South Carolina, but in a few years removed to the city of New York. Soon after taking up his residence in the metropolis, he painted a full-length portrait of Lafayette, at that time the guest of the nation. This incident, though trivial, seems to indicate that he held a prominent place in his profession. We do not claim that he was a great or brilliant painter, but he was a thorough student of the theory and principles of art, and was the founder and first president of the National Academy of Design.

In 1829, his means having improved, he again went abroad to complete his professional studies ; but in 1832, being yet in Europe, he was chosen professor of the literature of the fine arts in the university of the city of New York, and returned at once to enter upon his duties.

During all these years, in which he had drifted from place to place, struggling manfully against misfortune, he had assiduously indulged his early love of study, and came to be recognized as one of the well-informed men of the country in matters of science, and especially on the subjects of magnetism and electricity. On his return voyage, in 1832, an account given by a Mr. Jackson of certain experiments made in Paris with the electrical magnet, showing that an electric spark could readily be obtained and diffused from the magnet, arrested his attention, and he profoundly pondered the practical possibilities of this imponderable and mysterious agent, which moved without perceptible friction or loss of time. Walking the deck and swinging in his hammock, he revolved the question, and at length reached the conclusion that it furnished the means of instantaneous communication between distant points, and, while yet on the sea, invented the electro-magnetic and chemical recording telegraph. Henceforth the "sightless couriers of the air," whom space could not weary, nor the seas stifle, were to be the servitors of the human will.

Professor Morse was two years in completing his recording instrument. It was at first rude, but afterward greatly improved. Two years more gave him the means to construct a duplicate to return replies to the messages sent through his experimental wires. When this was accomplished, he filed a caveat for a patent, but it was three years in going through.

In the mean time he came to Washington, and asked Congress to aid him in constructing a line between this city and Baltimore, in order to test the practicability of sending messages over long distances. He had already shown in his lecture-room that this could be done through a wire a mile in length.

The utility, or even the practicability, of the telegraph, now a universal instrument and an indispensable force of modern civilization, our predecessors of thirty years ago did not comprehend, and perhaps could not even foresee, and so the great inventor was laughed out of court.

He then turned to Europe, and traveled from capital to capital, soliciting the recognition and the aid he failed to secure at home. Here, too, he was baffled and ridiculed, and could not obtain even a patent. We cannot well realize the bitterness and anguish with which he turned away disappointed from this last refuge of his hope, for he was very poor, and, as a friend said, "had to coin his mind for bread." Conscious of the inestimable value to mankind of the boon he was proffering, and glowing with the anticipation of an honorable and enduring fame, the light seemed to vanish instantly and forever from his horizon, and he was left in Cimmerian darkness. But he would not despair of ultimate success. He returned home, and during the session of 1842 and 1843 presented a second petition to Congress for aid. Again the simple-hearted man of science had to endure the skepticism and wit of men who could not apprehend the inherent worth and potential grandeur of the gift of God to the civilization of the world which he was pressing upon their acceptance. There were a few kindred spirits who recognized the reach and value of his discovery and pressed his suit, but most pitied the enthusiasm and persistency of the man whom too much study had made mad, and seemed indifferent to its fate.

On the 21st of February, 1843, says the record, Mr. Kennedy, of Maryland, moved to take up the bill authorizing a series of experiments to be made in order to test the merits of Morse's electro-magnetic telegraph, and appropriating $30,000 to defray the expenses. The House was disposed to fun, and Cave Johnson said that as the present Congress had done much to encourage science, he did not wish to see the science of mesmerism neglected and overlooked. He therefore proposed that one-half of the appropriation be given to Mr. Fisk, to enable him to carry on experiments, as well as Professor Morse. Mr. Houston thought that Millerism should be included in the benefits of the appropriation. Mr. Stanley said he should have no objection to the appropriation for mesmeric experiments. provided the gentleman from Tennessee (Mr. Cave Johnson) was the subject. Mr. Cave Johnson said he would have no objection, provided the gentleman from North Carolina was the operator.

Several members called for the reading of the amendment, and it was read by the clerk, as follows : " *Provided*, That one-half of the said sum shall be appropriated for trying mesmeric experiments, under the direction of the Secretary of the Treasury."

The bill was unable to run the gauntlet of the wits of that day, and so slept over till the 23d, when it came up for final action. Mr. Morse stood in the back part of the hall, as the vote was being taken, and attempted to keep tally. but was too deeply moved by excitement to succeed, and when the result was declared, he was so overcome that his friend, the present Secretary of State, Mr. Fish, who stood near him, was obliged to support him to a seat.

The bill lingered in the Senate till the last day of the session and until he had exhausted his last dollar. Worn out by waiting, and being told by a Senator that there were a hundred and fifty bills to be disposed of before his would be reached, and that it could not be taken up out of its order, he left the Capitol in despair and retired to his lodgings, and brooded wakefully far into the night over his poverty and misfortunes. He awoke the next morning to learn from the daughter of his friend, Judge Ellsworth, that his bill, appropriating $30,000 to construct an experimental line of telegraphy between Baltimore and Washington, had passed during the last hours of the session. He sprang to his feet in amazement, and hastened to the Capitol to learn if it was true. It was true; and both his fortune and his fame were secure.

The first test of his invention was made on isolated wires, buried in a lead-pipe under ground. The result was not satisfactory. The wires were next elevated upon poles, and, as soon as the preparations were completed, Professor Morse placed himself at his instrument and dispatched to Baltimore, at the suggestion of Miss Ellsworth the expressive scripture, "What hath God wrought!" To the astonishment of the bystanders, a message was returned, and other telegrams passed and repassed with the greatest rapidity and accuracy over the wires. The triumph of the madman was complete, and abuse was turned into adulation.

It is difficult for us to realize how little the theory of telegraphy was understood thirty years ago, even by the most intelligent people. A distinguished functionary, who was present when the first successful experiment was made, is reported to have asked an assistant of Professor Morse, "How large a bundle could be sent over the wires, and if the United States mail could not be sent in the same way."

But the adoption and success of the telegraph was not owing wholly to the aid of the Government. Its establishment as a channel of public communication was largely due to the enlightened efforts of private citizens. I have before me a letter, which has been placed in my hands, showing that a resident of Washington, still living, and whose splendid benefactions will be long and gratefully remembered in 'this city, with the forecast of a statesman, gave his support to this great enterprise. It is as follows:

"WASHINGTON, *January* 7, 1869.

"W. W. CORCORAN, Esq.:

"MY DEAR SIR: Some time ago I promised, through my son-in-law, Mr. Fox, to send you the original list of subscribers to the stock of the first telegraph company organized in the United States, which I supposed to be in my possession. But as I have not, after much search, been able to find it, I think I was under a wrong impression as to its being left in my hands, to whom, in fact, it did not belong. The list embraced $15,000, deemed sufficient to construct a line of two wires between New York and Philadelphia, and was headed by you with a subscription of $1,000. It was gotten up after the failure of all our efforts to raise a dollar in New York or Philadelphia. Your example doubtless induced others to subscribe, and to your confidence in Professor Morse's invention and your kindness to him and his friends is ascribable the pecuniary means of testing the value of a mode of communication which now pervades the civilized world. And I do not appreciate your act the less because it was practically another of your many kindnesses to me, and a boon of inestimable value to the inventor of the American electric-magnetic telegraph, whom I had then the honor to represent.

"With enduring regard, your friend,

"AMOS KENDALL."

At last those long, weary years, crowded with hopes and fears, with struggles and disappointments, were crowned by a magnificent success. Mark with what rapidity the scene changed. The man who but yesterday was derided and vilified, who with constant anxiety eked out a scanty subsistence while he pressed through a thronging crowd of difficulties to the realization of his sublime conception, to-day is lifted upon the shoulders of the applauding multitude, and borne forward with paeons of victory. The necromancy of success has transformed the jeers of ignorant conceit into honors and wealth, lavished without measure by learned societies, statesmen, and rulers

of the earth. The grand invention is seized by capital, and a net-
work of cables girdles the globe, bringing the record of each day of
the world's history to the poorest and the humblest of all the people.

But the sagacity of the great inventor himself did not forecast the
full power and efficiency of his work, which has transformed every
pursuit of man, and changed the conditions, and bids fair to change
the character, of universal society; commerce now learns daily the
demands and the prices-current of all markets, and projects its colossal enterprises with a full knowledge of the policies and movements of nations. Through the electric diffusion of intelligence the
manufacturer is enabled to conform his fabrics to the varying fashions
of different peoples and production can keep pace with consumption,
and so avoid financial disaster from overstocked markets. Telegraphy
has revolutionized journalism, and given an open business directness
to the once tangled web of diplomacy; has brought a rapid interchange of national sentiments, and removed the jealousies and misunderstandings which have been the fruitful sources of strife; it has
given unity and precision to extended military operations, and so
shortened the duration of desolating wars; it has widened the area
over which republics may extend their jurisdiction, and given to mankind the advanced ideas and exalted faith of the most enlightened
nations.

But in the length of days vouchsafed to the honored dead, he saw
nobler and mightier results from his great discovery than even his
prophetic eye had forecast in the vistas of the future. I will read an
extract only from a letter which he wrote to Hon. Cyrus W. Field,
then at Rome, on December 4, 1871, which shows that he comprehended fully that the telegraph was one of the great forces of the
world's progress: "Could there not be passed in the great international convention some resolution to the effect that, in whatever
condition, whether of peace or war between nations, the telegraph
should be deemed a sacred thing, to be by common consent effectu-

ally protected, both on the land and beneath the water? In the interests of human happiness, of that 'peace on earth,' which, in announcing the advent of the Saviour, the angels proclaimed with 'good will to men,' I hope that the convention will not adjourn without adopting a resolution asking of the nations their united, effective protection of this great agent of civilization."

What honors are not due to one who has accomplished so much? The invention of written language by which thought is presented to the eye, by which it is accumulated and preserved for after generations, having been lost in the obscurity of ages, has sometimes been placed by philosophers, impressed with its value, among the immediate gifts of Providence; but is written language more marvelous than the electric telegraph, which, spurning all barriers of sea and land, transmits human intelligence to the antipodes without lapse of time, and renders thought omnipresent; which places at once the results of experience and noble endeavor and the best products of human intellect among the active resources of universal civilization, and without personal peril throws the light of knowledge and Christianity into the dark and cruel recesses of barbarism, and lifts the world to the level of revealed truth?

We are not ignorant of the fact that other parties, whose accomplishments we cannot question, have attempted to establish for themselves priority of invention of parts of the telegraph. We do not claim for Professor Morse the merits of a Henry or any other great discoverer in science; nor is it necessary that we should revive over the fresh grave of a departed benefactor the heated controversies of the past, for it will not be questioned, I apprehend, that he invented the telegraphic alphabet of the dot and dash, and that he first successfully applied the force of magnetism to a machine for the interchange of thought, and combined, if he did not discover, the elements of the telegraphic apparatus, which has enabled men to converse across the seas, and different nations to interchange thought without the impediment of tongues. It was he who first responded to the ancient seer who asked, "Can'st thou send the lightnings, that they may go and say unto thee 'Here we are?'"

When the voice of controversy shall be hushed, and the claims of all settled by the judgment of an impartial posterity, the fame of Morse will be linked forever with the history of human progress, and his name be handed down as a household word in after ages and in all tongues.

Such and so great is the story of this man's life. It seeks no eulogy from us, for it will survive, in characters of light, when our feeble words shall have perished from the memory of man; but the American people would dishonor themselves if they did not pause and express their gratitude for the great inheritance he has left to mankind.

The following additional telegrams were then received and read:

[Telegram dated Cincinnati, Ohio, April 16, 1872.]

To Hon. JAMES G. BLAINE, *Speaker*,
　　　　　　Washington:

The following resolutions were adopted by the Yale Club of Cincinnati, at its annual re-union this evening:

Whereas the death of Prof. Samuel F. B. Morse, of the class of 1810, which has been recently announced, has closed a long and illustrious life of scientific discovery and investigation; and whereas he was known and honored throughout the civilized world as the author of the most brilliant, useful, and purely scientific invention of modern times:

Resolved, That in the career of Professor Morse the world has beheld and acknowledged the highest triumph of national science, and that, while his death causes a profound sensation in all intelligent minds, his memory will be cherished with peculiar regard by the alumni of Yale College, as of one who, by a legitimate pursuit of the principles he had been taught as a student, has conferred unparalleled honor on their *alma mater*.

Resolved, That these resolutions be entered in the records of the proceedings of this club, be transmitted to the national meeting at Washington, and a copy be forwarded to the family of the deceased.

ALPHONZO TAFTS,

Of Committee.

[Telegram dated Harrisburgh, Pa., April 16, 1872.]

To Speaker BLAINE :

Washington:

The following resolutions were adopted at the Morse memorial meeting in this city :

Resolved, That the telegraphic fraternity of Central Pennsylvania will ever hold in grateful remembrance the memory of Samuel Finley Breese Morse, the able American who, undaunted by disaster, unchecked by the frowns of patronage and power, nor overcome by the jealousies of science, perfected and put in successful operation the system of telegraphic communication which not only challenges the world for its simplicity and power, but has been a potent agent in the rapid advancement of civilization.

W. B. WILSON,

H. A. CLUTE,

Committee.

[Telegram dated Savannah, Ga., April 16, 1872.]

To MEMORIAL MEETING :

Washington:

The citizens of Savannah, Ga., assembled to pay respect to the memory of Professor Morse, do unqualifiedly testify their regrets on the sad demise of the father of telegraphy, and tender their sincere condolence to the world that they have lost a great and good man.

His memory will always live and be cherished as one of the master minds of the world.

OCTAVUS COHEN,

Chairman.

JAMES STEWART, *Secretary.*

[Telegram dated Chamber of Commerce, Savannah, Ga., April 16, 1872.]

To A. S. SOLOMONS, *Chairman,*

Washington :

The Savannah Chamber of Commerce greet the Chambers of Commerce of the United States, and unite in mourning the national loss of a public benefactor.

OCTAVUS COHEN,

First Vice-President.

[Telegram dated Savannah, Ga., April 16, 1872.]

To Hon. JAMES G. BLAINE,

Chairman of Morse Memorial Meeting, Washington, D. C.:

The city council of Savannah, Ga., in meeting assembled, unites with the world in condolence and sympathy in the death of the great inventor of the magnetic telegraph.

ALFRED HAYWOOD,

Mayor pro tem.

[Telegram dated Cedar Rapids, Iowa, April 16, 1872.]

To MORSE MEMORIAL ASSOCIATION,

Washington :

A large meeting was held this evening at the City-Hall, in memory of Prof. S. F. B. Morse. Mayor Hill presided. Resolutions were offered by Col. B. F. Hutchins, and speeches were made by the mayor, Rev. Mr. Kendig, and others.

[Telegram dated Augusta, Ga., April 16, 1872.]

To MEMORIAL ASSOCIATION, *Washington:*

The great heart of humanity throbs with gratitude for the legacy left by Professor Morse to posterity. He has benefited his day and generation, and all future time. Though a sorrowing world mourns his loss, yet it cannot regret that He has said, "Come up higher."

[Telegram dated Syracuse, N. Y., April 16, 1872.]

To Hon. JAMES G. BLAINE,
  Speaker of the House of Representatives,
     Washington:

Syracuse is in full sympathy with your efforts to honor the memory of America's greatest genius, Samuel F. B. Morse. He annihilated time, and for all time his memory should be perpetuated. The central city of the Empire State, will rejoice to respond substantially in so noble and grand a cause.

      F. E. CARROLL, *Mayor.*

[Telegram dated Cincinnati, Ohio, April 16, 1872.]

To Hon. J. G. BLAINE, *Speaker,*
     Washington:

The people of Cincinnati send greeting to the friends of our illustrious fellow-citizen Professor Morse, in memorial meeting assembled, and unite with them in honoring the memory of one who has illumed the paths of science by his discoveries, and made his name honored and famous throughout the civilized world.

      S. S. DAVIS, *Mayor.*

[Telegram dated Charlestown, Mass., April 16, 1872.]

To PRESIDENT OF THE MEMORIAL MEETING AT WASHINGTON:

The city of Charlestown sends its tribute of honor and respect to the memory of her gifted son.

      WM. H. KENT, *Mayor.*

[Telegram dated St. John's, N. B., April 16, 1872.]

To Hon. JAMES G. BLAINE,

>*Speaker of the House of Representatives,*
>>*Washington :*

The citizens of St. John's desire to join you in honoring the memory of Morse.

>>THOS. M. REED, *Mayor.*

[Telegram dated Grand Rapids, Mich., April 16, 1872.]

To CHAIRMAN OF WASHINGTON MEMORIAL ASSOCIATION,

>>*Washington :*

At a meeting of our citizens held this evening pursuant to a call of our mayor, Hon. William Howard chairman, the following resolutions were unanimously adopted :

Resolved, That while we express hereby our sorrow in common with the civilized world over the death of Prof. S. F. B. Morse, we feel called upon to give expressions at the same time of gratitude and thankfulness to God for so useful and noble a life; that we recognize in him how God advances the peace, prosperity, and brotherhood of the world by such agencies. Like the telegraph by which intelligence and knowledge are more rapidly diffused, and commercial and national interests unified.

Resolved, That while we recognize the great truth that a philosopher is the birth of a thousand years, we remember with pride it required America only a century to produce a philosopher unsurpassed in genius and achievements. Whatever the world may have lost by his death, his life has been an unspeakable gain.

The meeting was addressed by many eminent citizens.

>>EBEN SMITH, *Secretary.*

[Telegram dated Indianapolis, Ind , April 16, 1872.]

To A. S. SOLOMONS,
>>*Washington :*

Meeting organizing in Board of Trade room at this time; will give report soon.

>>JNO. F. WALLICK.

[Telegram dated Mayor's Office, Hartford, Conn., April 16, 1872.]

To Hon. J. G. BLAINE,

Chairman, &c., Washington :

The city of Hartford joins cordially in the expressions of regret and pride which befit the memorial meetings for Professor Morse, whose fame is more than national, and whose invention will bless the most distant future.

HENRY C. ROBINSON, *Mayor.*

[Telegram dated Galveston, Texas, April 16, 1872.]

To A. S. SOLOMONS,

Chairman Committee of Arrangements,

Washington :

The city of Galveston, through its board of aldermen and mayor, beg herewith to transmit to you, as chairman of the committee of arrangements, their condolence in the great national loss sustained in the death of the late Samuel F. B. Morse.

ALBERT SOMERVILLE, *Mayor.*

[Telegram dated Reading, Pa., April 16, 1872.]

To SPEAKER BLAINE,

Washington :

A meeting of the citizens of Reading is now in progress, to join with her sister cities throughout the nation in paying tribute to the memory of the late Prof. Samuel F. B. Morse, father of the American telegraph system, and to tender their earnest sympathies to all who mourn the honored dead.

HENRY BUSHONG,
President Reading Board of Trade.

[Telegram dated Albany, N. Y., April 16, 1872.]

To Hon. JAMES G. BLAINE,
> *Speaker of House of Representatives,*
>> *Washington:*

From the depths of their hearts, the citizens of Albany add their tribute to the memory of one who combined in his person a pre-eminent genius with ail the moral and Christian virtues which constitute greatness, and who was second to none as a benefactor of mankind; such a man was Prof. Samuel F. B. Morse.

GEO. H. THATCHER, *Mayor.*

[Telegram dated New Haven, Conn., April 16, 1872.]

To NATIONAL MORSE MEMORIAL MEETING,
>> *Washington:*

A meeting of citizens in connection with city government is in progress. Resolutions are to be presented, and appropriate addresses made by Rev. Dr. Bacon and others. Copy of resolutions will be forwarded later.

HENRY G. LEWIS,
Mayor, presiding.

The Speaker then introduced the Hon. Fernando Wood:

ADDRESS OF HON. FERNANDO WOOD.

To say that we meet to-night to commemorate departed genius, would be as inaccurate as it would be an inadequate expression. The man may have gone, but the product of his genius still lives. It lives everywhere. It is to be found throughout and beyond the domain of civilization; upon the highest mountain-peak, and beneath the lowest depths of the ocean. The written history of mankind comprehends but a brief period of the world's existence, and within that period the Almighty has displayed His wonderful phenomena through but few human agencies. Force has had its conquests, which have been many; these were but the illustrations of the stronger against the weaker power. Reason has had its victories, in which the intellect has proved superior to force; while genius, a higher order of reason, has accomplished, through the sciences, much, if not all, that elevated our race to the highest altitude which mankind is capable of achieving consistent with the barriers of immortality.   But there is yet a power greater than force, a judgment deeper than reason, and an intellectual development higher than genius, and it has remained to this country and to this people to present it to the world in the brain of Morse.   Therefore it is that I repeat, that to say we meet to commemorate departed genius would be an inaccurate and inadequate expression.   We mourn the loss of the man, while bearing high appreciation of the ever-living and ever-present work he leaves behind.

To me, personally, this occasion is one of peculiar interest.   With Professor Morse I had relations of no ordinary kind.   A third of a century has intervened since I knew him first.   I was a witness to his early struggles, his hopes, and his anxieties.   After the failure of his first application to Congress for aid, in 1837, he visited Europe, where he conquered recognition against great opposition.   He returned strengthened in his convictions, though disappointed in his expectations.   I well remember the cheerful face, and quiet, unobtrusive manner, with which he renewed his application to Congress in the early part of 1842.   I was a member of that Congress; and as one of the Representatives from New York, where he lived, he made application to me, as one of my constituents, for assistance in obtaining Government aid.   I gave the little influence I possessed, more in consequence of my esteem for the man than from any knowledge of or confidence in the merit of the discovery he claimed to have made.   On the 11th of February, 1842, Mr. William W. Boardman, a member from Connecticut, introduced into the House a resolution in these words:

"*Resolved*, That the Committee on Commerce be instructed to inquire into the expediency of establishing a system of electro-magnetic telegraph for the use of the Government of the United States."

This was passed without opposition, and, indeed, without attention or discussion. Mr. John P. Kennedy, of Maryland, was the chairman of this committee, and while he had confidence in the practicability of the proposition many of the members did not favor it. Some doubted the propriety, others the constitutionality, of appropriating money for experimental purposes, while a number had no confidence in it whatever. The opposition was sufficiently strong to make it apparent that a favorable report could not be procured from the committee unless great efforts were made to effect it. It was at this moment that the propriety of giving some proof of the feasibility of his plans was suggested to Professor Morse. He established two batteries—one in each of the Committee on Commerce rooms of the two Houses, which were then in the basement of the old Capitol, before the present wings in which the House and Senate now sit were erected. He connected these batteries with wire, and by the aid of an assistant succeeded in transmitting messages, though very imperfectly. This experiment, although it did not remove the doubts of many, proved successful in justifying the proposed action in its behalf. On the 30th December, 1842, the committee, through Charles G. Ferris, of New York, reported the following bill:

"*Be it enacted, &c.*, That the sum of $30,000 be, and is hereby, appropriated out of any moneys in the Treasury not otherwise appropriated, for testing the capacity and usefulness of the system of electro-magnetic telegraphs invented by Samuel F. B. Morse, of New York, for the use of the Government of the United States, by constructing a line of said electro-magnetic telegraphs, under the superintendence of Professor Samuel F. B. Morse, of such length and between such points as shall fully test its practicability and utility; and that the same shall be expended under the direction of the Postmaster-General upon the application of said Morse.

"Sec. 2. *And be it further enacted*, That the Postmaster-General be, and he is hereby, authorized to pay out of the aforesaid $30,000, to the said Samuel F. B. Morse, and the persons employed under him, such sums of money as he may deem to be a fair compensation for the services of the said Samuel F. B. Morse, and the persons employed under him, in constructing and superintending the construction of the said line of telegraphs authorized by this bill."

This bill was accompanied by an elaborate report, prepared by my colleague, Mr. Charles G. Ferris, reviewing the history of electro-magnetism, and fully sustaining its adaptability to the transmission of messages. A letter from Professor Morse was attached to it, giving an interesting history of his previous efforts in this country and Europe to procure a practical official recognition of his invention. With this letter was another to him from Professor Joseph Henry, now of the Smithsonian Institution, and then president of Princeton College, indorsing and sustaining the application. Professor Henry was deemed high authority on all scientific subjects generally, and especially upon this, to which he had devoted much attention, and was himself a successful investigator in electro-magnetic science. On the 21st of February following, the bill, which had been referred to a Committee of the Whole House, was taken up for consideration, Robert C. Winthrop, of Massachusetts, in the chair. It met with opposition. Amendments intended to be ironical were offered with an intent to defeat its passage. It was finally adopted by the committee with an amendment striking out " the Postmaster-General," and inserting " Secretary of the Treasury." On the 23d of February, on motion of Mr. John P. Kennedy, of Maryland, the House took up the bill, and it was passed under the operation of the previous question by a vote of 89 to 83. Of the eighty-nine members who voted in the affirmative there are but eleven now living. Among these are Millard Fillmore, Caleb Cushing, Robert C. Winthrop, Henry A. Wise, Richard W. Thompson, Hiland Hall, and myself. I am the only member of the present House who was a member of that Congress, and, with the exception of Senator Garrett Davis, of Kentucky, the only member of either House. The bill was received by the

Senate on the same day, and referred to the Committee on Commerce. February 25, Silas Wright, of New York, reported it back from that committee favorably. March 3 the bill passed the Senate without either opposition or debate.

It may not be out of place to relate incidents in connection with this interesting moment in the final passage of the bill, pregnant with such important results to Morse himself. These were not within my own knowledge at the time, but come to me with so much credibility that I incorporate and adopt them as entirely reliable. It is said that, after waiting and watching for the Senate to reach the bill in regular order, at a late hour of the night, almost in despair, he approached one of the Senators and asked him the probabilities of its passage.

The Senator replied, " Professor Morse, if I were you I would go back to New York and abandon this idea. It is now 10 o'clock, as you see, and there are forty-three bills before yours. But if it were possible for yours to be reached it would be defeated, because Congress has no sympathy with your bill."

Morse, with a heavy heart, went to the hotel, bought his ticket to New York, paid his bill until after breakfast, kneeled down, opened his heart to God and committed all his affairs to Him. He said: " I had then but thirty-seven and a half cents in the world." This, however, was when he had done everything possible to be done. He felt that he had been anxious to benefit the world by an invention which he knew needed only a trial, and he retired and slept like a child.

In the morning he arose early to take the train, and then came a rap at the door, with a message that a lady wished to see him.

" It must be a mistake," he said to the waiter: " the message is for some other person."

The waiter, however, insisted. He descended and found it to be the daughter of the Senator, who, as he entered, exclaimed:

" Professor Morse, I come here this morning to congratulate you on the passage of your bill."

" How can that be ?" he replied. " I was there until 10 o'clock last night, and there were then forty-three bills ahead of mine."

" Ah, but, Professor Morse," she said, " father watched there until five minutes before midnight, and then saw the President put his signature to your bill. And I asked of him the privilege of bringing you the news."

" If that is true," said the Professor, " the first message that ever passes over those wires shall be yours."

And when those wires were all ready, the first electric telegraph, he forbade that they should be used until he gave the signal, and then he called upon the young lady to give her message, and that first message is still preserved among the archives at Washington. It was taken from the Bible : " What hath God wrought."

This is the history of the legislation which authorized the construction of the first telegraph in the United States. It was established by the Government between Washington and Baltimore. A salary of $2,500 a year was allowed Professor Morse for his services. The wires were laid originally along the sleepers of the railroad, encased in leaden tubes, and underground. This mode was adopted in consequence of its economy, but it proved a failure and an impediment in the transmission of electricity. Subsequently, the present plan of extending the wires on poles was adopted. It took about one year for the completion of the line, it being opened to the public for the first time in May, 1844. And this was the first practical demonstration of the success of the Morse system of telegraphy. I do not assert that the principle was new or original with him, but that he was the first to make it practical and utilitarian, and adapted it to the great purposes to which it is now put, is beyond question ; for it has received universal acceptance everywhere where a knowledge of science exists. Nor do I pretend that without the aid which Congress gave him at the time to which I refer, the world would have lost its benefits; yet it is certain that though for eight years preceding he had fully and successfully completed his invention and proven its merits, both here and in Europe, he had not been enabled to establish it as a practical accomplishment by actual operation. How much longer he would have been compelled to wait, or whether, borne down by disappointments and deferred hope, he would have lived to see it accomplished at all, (he was then fifty years old,) are questions which, to say the least, are subject to doubt. Hence, I am disposed to attach importance to the action of Congress in extending the aid it did at that particular juncture. Professor Morse never ceased to recognize this fact. He never met me without recurring to it. Last year, upon the unveiling of the Morse statue erected by the city of New York, and now standing in the Central Park of that city, he addressed to me a letter written in his usual kindly spirit, eloquent in the appreciation of the aid I had extended to him in the Congress referred to.

Alas! he is now no more! Aside from his intellectual endowments, Professor Morse was no ordinary man. Throughout life he maintained the same placid spirit. I have seen him in the palace of the Tuileries, and at the court of St. James, surrounded and admired by royalty, and venerated by the *savants* of Europe, the same gentle, and modest citizen that he was when he trod the streets of Washington poor, and obscure, an humble suppliant for additional pecuniary assistance to enable him to convert mankind to the faith that was within himself! Let us pass him to posterity and to fame, conscious that as he was eminent in life so is he happy in death. He has bequeathed to the world his own monument, that will live throughout all ages, while among the benefactors of mankind he will stand with the highest and greatest of all.

The following additional telegrams were then received and read:

[Telegram dated Ottumwa, Iowa, April 16, 1872.]

To CHAIRMAN MORSE MEMORIAL ASSOCIATION,

Washington:

The city of Ottumwa, through her city council, unites with Burlington in testimony in respect to the memory of Prof. S. F. B. Morse, one of America's greatest benefactors.

W. L. ORR, *Mayor.*

[Telegram dated Leavenworth, Kansas, April 16, 1872.]

To Hon. JAMES G. BLAINE,

President &c., House of Representatives,

Washington:

The city of Leavenworth, the youngest of the sisterhood, joins with the universal voice of the nation in mourning the loss of the great Morse, and begs to add an humble flower from the prairies of the West to the garland that decorates his honored bier.

D. R. ANTHONY, *Mayor.*
W. W. CREIGHTON, *Clerk.*

[Telegram dated Columbus, Ga., April 16, 1872.]

To NATIONAL TELEGRAPH ASSOCIATION, *Washington,*

Columbus joins the rest of the country in doing honor to the memory of Professor Morse.

JNO. McILHANNY,
Mayor, and Chairman of Citizens' Meeting.

[Telegram dated Vicksburgh, Miss., April 16, 1872.]

To A. S. SOLOMONS,

Chairman, Washington:

A memorial meeting is in session here, Governor Powers presiding. Hon. Geo. F. Brown addressing the meeting.

BENJ. A. LEE, *Mayor.*

[Telegram dated hall of the House of Representatives, State Capitol, Columbia, S. C., April 16, 1872.]

To Hon. JAMES G. BLAINE,

Chairman Morse Memorial Meeting, Washington, D. C.:

The State of South Carolina, at the city of Columbia, as represented by the citizens assembled in the hall of the house of Representatives, in this city, tender to their fellow-citizens the expression of their profound sympathy in the world-wide loss sustained in the death of Prof. S. F. B. Morse. The immense concourse now assembled are moved with the deepest emotion as they recall the value and extent of the gift which he has bestowed. Patriotism, gratitude, national fame, and personal esteem combine to do him their sincerest honor.

M. LABORDE,
Chairman.

[Telegram dated San Francisco, Cal., April 16, 1872.]

To Hon. JAMES G. BLAINE,
President of Morse Memorial Meeting, Washington :

The citizens of San Francisco unite with you in homage to the memory of Samuel F. B. Morse. They mourn that all of him that was mortal has gone to its rest. With you, they rejoice that his great discovery remains to bless the world and raise his honored name higher on the glorious list of its real benefactors. To us of the Pacific Coast, his achievements are of priceless value. Through him we are at this hour united with you; and for all mankind he has annihilated space and outstripped the very wings of the morning. As his triumphs over nature were splendid, so shall the fruits of his victory endure forever.

WILLIAM ALVORD,
President of Morse Memorial Meeting.

[Telegraph dated Loudon, Tenn., April 16, 1872.]

To the BOARD OF MANAGERS OF THE MORSE MEETING,
                                        Washington:

We, the citizens of Loudon, Loudon County, Tenn., deeply deplore the necessity of assembling to pay a tribute of respect to the late Prof. S. F. B. Morse. We cannot hope to add one scintillation of brightness to his illustrious name, which is already bedecked with the richest jewels that honor can lavish upon the chosen few.

"*Resolved*, That we condole with science in the death of so distinguished a son.

"*Resolved*, That we deplore the loss of him who has placed our nation first on the catalogue of science by uniting the world in electrical converse.

                                        JAS. MAHONEY,
                                              Chairman.
                                        S. L. BLAIR,
                                              Secretary.

[Telegram dated Rochester, N. Y., April 16, 1872.]

Speaker BLAINE,
            Chairman Morse Memorial Meeting, Washington:

The city of Rochester sends greeting to your assemblage at the national Capitol. She claims prominence among the early promoters of Morse's great invention.

                                        M. B. ANDERSON,
                                              Chairman.

[Telegram dated Charleston, S. C., April 16, 1872.]

To the Hon. JAMES G. BLAINE,
            Chairman of the Morse Memorial Meeting, Washington:

Whereas this council, representing the citizens of Charleston, S. C., feel, in common with the people of the entire civilized world, the great loss occasioned by the death of Professor Morse, the father of telegraphy in the United States, would respectfully beg to unite their sympathy with the Morse Memorial Association Meeting, now being held in the city of Washington, D. C., this evening, in the following telegram :

The late Professor Morse : May his memory ever live in the hearts of his countrymen ; by his genius and his discovery the innocent has been protected, the guilty has been punished, merit has triumphed, crime has perished, trade, commerce, manufactures, and mechanism have flourished.   May his invention of the electric wires never more bring to this generation the sad and unwelcome message of war, but that all messages may have for their groundwork peace, freedom, prosperity, and happiness.   We deeply deplore his loss.

JOHN A. WAGANER,

Mayor.

W. W. SIMMONS,

Clerk.

[Telegram dated Charlotte, N. C., April 16, 1872.]

To the MORSE MEMORIAL COMMITTEE,

Washington :

We ask a place in the front rank of those who do honor to the genius of our country.   Among those born of woman the scientific achievements of no one has entitled him to more honor among men than he whose memory you commemorate.

Mecklenburgh County, N. C., where America's first Declaration of Independence was made, through the voice of her daughter, Charlotte, remembers him whose light lives, though he has passed away. If he taught us not by precept, he did by "line upon line."   We will ever reverence his memory.

JOHN A. YOUNG,

Mayor.

[Telegram dated Milwaukee, Wis., April 16, 1872.]

To Mr. SPEAKER BLAINE,
House of Representatives,
Washington:

The common council of the city of Milwaukee, in joint convention assembled, this afternoon, unanimously adopted the following resolutions :

Resolved by the common council of the city of Milwaukee, That this city, in common with the whole country have heard with deep and lasting regret of the death of the late Samuel F. B. Morse, to whom the country and the whole civilized world owe that wonderful development of modern science, the electric telegraph. Accustomed as we are to all the multitudinous benefits of the electric telegraph, we should recall them upon the occasion of the death of its illustrious inventor. It has not only been an almost miraculous convenience, personally, to every intelligent human being within the limits of human civilization, but it has wrought a revolution in all commerce which has brought together the nations of the earth in a closer alliance of friendship and business than the world ever saw before. The great achievements and wonderful benefits of this invention are so numerous and so vast that it would fill volumes to detail them, and it is far beyond the limits of a resolution even to glance at them. We limit ourselves to a general acknowledgment, to lay as a garland upon the tomb of the great inventor who has just passed from the scene of his earthly labors to the presence of the Almighty Being, the secrets of whose laws he was in life so far successful in discovering.

Resolved, That his honor the mayor be requested to communicate these resolutions to Hon. James G. Blaine, Speaker of the House of Representatives, at Washington, to be by him placed before the memorial meeting to be held this evening in the House of Representatives.

D. G. HOOKER, *Mayor.*

The Speaker then introduced the Hon. J. A. Garfield.

ADDRESS OF HON. J. A. GARFIELD.

The grave has just closed over the mortal remains of one whose name will be forever associated with a series of achievements in the domain of discovery and invention the most wonderful our race has ever known. Wonderful in the results accomplished; more wonderful, still, in the agencies employed; most wonderful in the scientific revelations which preceded and accompanied its development.

The electro-magnetic telegraph is the embodiment, I might say the incarnation, of many centuries of thought, of many generations of effort to elicit from nature one of her deepest mysteries.

No one man, no one century could have achieved it. It is the child of the human race, "the heir of all the ages." How wonderful were the steps which led to its creation! The very name of this telegraphic instrument bears record of its history—"Electric, Magnetic!"

The first, named from the bit of yellow amber whose qualities of attraction and repulsion were discovered by a Grecian philosopher twenty-four centuries ago; and the second, from Magnesia, the village of Asia Minor, where first was found the loadstone, whose touch turned the needle forever to the north. These were the earliest forms in which that subtle, all-pervading force revealed itself to men. In the childhood of the race men stood dumb in the presence of its more terrible manifestations. When it gleamed in the purple aurora, or shot dusky-red from the clouds, it was the eye-flash of an angry God, before whom mortals quailed in helpless fear.

When the electric light burned blue on the spear-points of the Roman legions it was to them and their leaders a portent from the gods beckoning to victory. When the phosphorescent light, which the sailors still call St. Elmo's fire, hovered on the masts and spars of the Roman ship, it was Castor and Pollux, twin gods of the sea, guiding 'the mariner to port, or the beacon of an avenging God luring him to death.

When we consider the many startling forms in which this element presents itself, it is not surprising that so many centuries elapsed before men dared to confront and question its awful mystery. And it was fitting that here, in this new, free world, the first answer came revealing to our Franklin the great truth that the lightning of the sky and the electricity of the laboratory were one; that in the simple electric toy were embodied all the mysteries of the thunderbolt. Until near the beginning of the present century the only known method of producing electricity was by friction. But the discoveries of Galvani in 1790, and of Volta in 1810, resulted in the production of electricity by the chemical action of acids upon metals, and gave to the world the Galvanic battery and the Voltaic pile, and the electric current. This was the first step in that path of modern discovery which led to the telegraph. But further discoveries were necessary to make the telegraph possible.

The next great step was taken by Oersted, the Swedish professor, who, in 1819–'20, made the discovery that the needle when placed near the galvanic battery was deflected at right angles with the electric current. In the four modest pages in which Oersted announced this discovery to the world the science of electro-magnetism was founded.

As Franklin had exhibited the relation between lightning and the electric fluid, so Oersted exhibited the relation between magnetism and electricity. From 1820 to 1825, his discovery was further developed by Davy and Sturgeon, of England, and Arago and Ampère, of France. They found that by sending a current of electricity through a wire coiled around a piece of soft iron, the iron became a magnet while the current was passing, and ceased to be a magnet when the current was broken. This gave an intermittent power, a power to grapple and to let go, at the will of the electrician. Ampère suggested that a telegraph was possible, by applying this power to a needle.

In 1825, Barlow, of England, made experiments to verify this suggestion of the telegraph, and pronounced it impracticable on the ground that the batteries then used would not send the fluid through even two hundred feet of wire without a sensible diminution of its force.

In 1831, Joseph Henry, now secretary of the Smithsonian Institution, then a professor at Albany, New York, as the result of numerous experiments, discovered a method by which he produced a battery of such intensity as to overcome the difficulty spoken of by Barlow in 1825.

By means of this, his discovery, he magnetized soft iron at a great distance from the battery, pointed out the fact that a telegraph was possible, and actually rang a bell by means of the electro-magnet acting on a long wire.

This was the last step in the series of great discoveries which preceded the invention of the telegraph.

When these discoveries ended, the work of the inventor began. It was in 1832, the year that succeeded the last of these great discoveries, when Professor Morse first turned his thoughts to that work whose triumph is the triumph of his race. He had devoted twenty-two years of his manhood to the study and practice of art. He had sat at the feet of the great masters of Europe, and had already, by his own works of art, achieved a noble name from the work of interpreting, and he now turned to the grander work of interpreting to the world that subtle and mysterious element with which the thinkers of the human race had so long been occupied.

I cannot here recount the story of that long struggle through which he passed to the accomplishment of his great result; how he struggled with poverty, with the vast difficulties of the subject itself, with the unfaith, the indifference, and the contempt which almost everywhere confronted him; how, at the very moment of his triumph, he was on the verge of despair, when in this very Capitol his project met with the jeers of almost a majority of the National Legislature. But when has despair yielded to such a triumph? When has such a morning risen on such a night? To all cavilers and doubters, this instrument and its language are a triumphant answer. That chainless spirit which fills the immensity of space with its invisible presence; which dwells in the blaze of the sun, and follows the path of the farthest star, and courses the depths of earth and sea—that mighty spirit has at last yielded to the human will. It has entered a body prepared for its dwelling. It has found a voice through which it speaks to the human ear. It has taken its place as the humble servant of man; and through all coming time its work will be associated with the name and fame of Samuel F. B. Morse.

Were there no other proof of the present value of his work, this alone would suffice that, throughout the world, whatever the language or the dialect of those who use it, the telegraph speaks a language whose first element is the alphabet of Morse; and in 1869, of the 16,000 telegraphic instruments used on the lines in Europe, 13,000 were of the pattern invented by Morse. The future of this great achievement can be measured by no known standards. Morse gave us the instrument and the alphabet. The world is only beginning to spell out the lesson, whose meaning the future will read.

The following additional telegrams were then received and read:

[Telegram from Worcester, Mass., April 16, 1872.]

To CHAIRMAN MORSE MEMORIAL COMMITTEE,

Washington:

At a special meeting of the city government, held this evening in the council chamber, which was largely attended by prominent citizens of this city, the following resolutions were unanimously adopted:

Resolved, That while we recognize the hand of an all-wise Providence in the removal of Professor Morse from the scene of his early labors and triumph, we render thanks for his illustrious life, prolonged in tranquillity and happiness to the full limit of human days, and crowned with imperishable honor.

Resolved, That as Americans we rejoice in the well-earned fame of our countryman; and as sons of Massachusetts claim a closer relation to that fame, while as citizens of a community which is a chosen home of invention and the industrial arts we are peculiarly called upon to pay to his memory our tribute of admiration and gratitude; and recognizing in the honors so freely bestowed upon our countryman by imperial courts, the deserved rewards of exalted and successful genius, we perceive their still higher reward in the consciousness that his invention was accepted as one of the greatest, if not the greatest, of benefits to humanity; that it was asserted with every modern triumph of commerce and civilization, and that by it the terror of the sky has become the harbinger of peace and good will to the nations.

Resolved, That we commend to the youth of our country the life of Professor Morse as a noble example of high resolve, determined purpose, and patient courage, undismayed by temporary failure and defeat.

The skepticism of less enlightened spirits could not make him doubt, nor their ridicule make him ashamed, nor the hardships of poverty drive him to despair, but strong in faith and steadfast amid discouragements, he triumphed at length over every obstacle, and has left a memory which a grateful world would not willingly let die.

GEORGE F. VERRY,
Mayor of Worcester, Mass.

[Telegram dated Mayor's Office, Saint Paul, Minn., April 16, 1872.]

To Hon. JAMES G. BLAINE and SCHUYLER COLFAX, and gentlemen composing the memorial meeting in honor of the late Professor Morse, Washington:

GENTLEMEN: The city of Saint Paul greets you, and heartily unites with your memorial meeting in showing respect to the memory of the late Professor Morse. The world honors him as its great benefactor, but our nation mourns him as her well-beloved son and as the worthy compeer of Franklin. The mantle of Franklin was, indeed, cast upon him, but with a double portion of his spirit. May the names of both be ever held in a nation's remembrance in sacred fellowship.

J. H. STEWART, Mayor.

[By telegraph from Salem, Mass., April 16, 1872.]

To A. S. SOLOMONS,

Chairman of the Committee of Morse Meeting, Washington:

At the meeting in Salem, Mass., in memory of Professor Morse, the following preamble and resolution, offered by Dr. George B. Loring, one of the vice-presidents of the National Telegraph Memorial Monument Association, were adopted:

Whereas, under the providence of God, Samuel F. B. Morse, one of the most distinguished Americans of this age, having completed a long and honorable and useful life, has been gathered to his fathers, like a shock of corn fully ripe, leaving a proud record behind him: Therefore,

Resolved, That, in common with all the enlightened communities of the civilized world, we recognize the high value of the services of Professor Morse in the work of advancing the intellectual and physical well-being and prosperity of mankind, by his great invention; and that the heartfelt gratitude of the American people is due to God for having bestowed upon them the supreme blessing of a life endowed with great faculties, through whose instrumentality all the nations of the earth have been provided with that constant and immediate communication which may unite them in one brotherhood, for their elevation and refinement.

SAMUEL CALLEY, Mayor.

[By telegraph from Chicago, April 16, 1872.]

To the MEETING IN HONOR OF PROFESSOR MORSE,

Washington:

The officers and employés of the Great Western Telegraph Company unite in the testimonial of respect to the memory of the author of the system.   Nothing but the direct inspired teaching which unites God and man surpasses the value of his discovery.   Franklin in drawing electricity from the clouds only demonstrated a scientific fact.   *Our* saint of science drawing electricity from the earth sent it around the world, and with a click made all the knowledge of the world instantaneously common and useful—the first grand approach to that dream of Schiller, of an age when all nations will live united, brother-like, together.   May his electric spark of life which has passed from earth to Heaven ever be near us, and inspire all who are engaged in working out the future of his grand discovery with a true appreciation of their novel profession.

D. A. GAGE,

President.

N. REEVE,

Assistant Secretary.

[Telegram dated Council Chambers, Savannah, Ga., April 16, 1872.]

To MORSE MEMORIAL MEETING,

Washington :

To the memory of Professor Morse.   Nations deplore his loss.   To his memory are due the benefactions of generations still to come.

JAMES STEWART,

Clerk of Council, City of Savannah.

[Telegram dated Toledo, Ohio, April 16, 1872.]

To the COMMITTEE OF ARRANGEMENTS OF THE

NATIONAL TELEGRAPH MEMORIAL MONUMENT ASSOCIATION,

Washington :

At the Morse Memorial Meeting held this evening, presided over by Mayor W. W. Jones, the following preamble and resolutions were unanimously adopted:

Acknowledging our indebtedness to the discoveries of the late Prof. Samuel Finley Breese Morse, and desirous of expressing our

'grateful homage to his transcendent genius, and our sincere tribute
to his memory we, the people of Toledo, in council assembled have

Resolved, That in common with the inhabitants of the globe who par-
take of the civilization and the progress of the age, recognize in
the career of one who has made to science a contribution of the
most benefit of any that can be traced upon the pages of history.

Resolved, That the pure life and unsullied character of Professor
Morse, together with his invaluable services to the cause of science,
entitle him to be regarded as one of the most illustrious of America's
sons, and one of the greatest of the benefactors of his race.

W. W. JONES,
Mayor and President of the Meeting.
C. T. WALLS,
Secretary.

The speakers were Lieut. Governor Lee, J. R. Osborn, esq., and
Rev. R. M. McCune.

[Telegram dated City Hall, Lynn, Mass., April 16, 1872.]

To CHAIRMAN MORSE MEMORIAL MEETING,

House of Representatives, Washington:

Assembled to-night by invitation of the Representatives of the nation,
in common with her sister cities throughout the land, to tender her
tribute of respect to one who, born in Massachusetts, became, in
grateful recognition of his services to mankind, by adoption, a citizen
of the world; who, fortunate among men, was the admiration of man
kind; by his success in two distinct professions, adding to the fame of
the finished artist the renown of the accomplished scientist; who,
grasping the facts which others had wrought out, combined them in
that wonderful invention which has utilized the lightning which
Franklin drew from the clouds, and made it the swift messenger of
man, putting that girdle round the world which shall bind in one
the nations of the earth; who, passing the ordinary bound of human
existence, lived to see every nation of the earth share the fruits of his

beneficent labor, and to receive from all the recognition of honor so justly his due, and who has left the record of his labors and his life, rounded and completed by every Christian grace, as a precious legacy to his family, his nation, and the world.

The city of Lynn, through her Representatives, inscribes upon her official record the profound appreciation of the life-work of Prof. Samuel Finley Breese Morse, and especially of those years of toil and privation which resulted in the invention of the magnetic telegraph, whose effect upon the peace and prosperity of the world has conspicuously illustrated the truth that " Peace has her victories, no less renowned than war."

Resolved, That a copy of the above be sent to the family of the deceased, to the press, and to the Representatives' meeting convened, at the National Representatives' Hall at Washington.

For the committee:

B. B. BREED,
Chairman.

[Telegram dated Frederick, Md., April 16, 1872.]

To the NATIONAL TELEGRAPH MEMORIAL ASSOCIATION,

Washington:

The following preamble and resolutions were offered by Dr. Lewis H. Steiner, senator, of Frederick County, and unanimously adopted by the Morse Memorial meeting at Frederick, Md.:

Whereas, the practical applications of the principles of science to the wants of mankind have contributed largely to the advance of civilization, and to the increase of enterprise and prosperity among all nations which have been favored with a knowledge of the same; and

Whereas, the names of those who have made themselves conspicuous by teaching the world how to utilize the treasures of science ought to be held in grateful remembrance by the citizens of the land that gave them birth: Therefore,

Resolved, That we herewith join with the citizens of the United States assembled this evening in their different cities and towns, in recording our sincere regret at the loss experienced by the world in the death of Prof. Samuel F. B. Morse, the inventor of the magnetic telegraph, who first made known the fact that electricity could be transmitted through great lengths of wire without any material diminution of its power, effective as a means of communication between distant points, thereby annihilating distance and bringing all parts of the world in close proximity; who lived to see his invention introduced in all nations and all climes, and who has just been called to his eternal rest, covered with honor and rewards as one of the greatest benefactors of his age.

Resolved, That the name of Morse will be esteemed, along with that of Franklin and Fulton, as among the most honored names in the galaxy of our country's great men.

Resolved, That a copy of these resolutions be transmitted to the National Memorial Telegraph Association, signed by the officers of the meeting.

L. J. BRENGLE,
President.

F. M. MILLER,
    Secretary.

[Telegram dated Principal Office Western Union Telegraph Company, New York, April 16, 1872.]

To Hon. JAMES G. BLAINE,
    Speaker House of Representatives, Washington:

While watching the service of the telegraph to-night, not only in conveying to you the many heartfelt greetings of great and good men most widely separated, but in the vast number of commercial and domestic messages flying in every direction over our wires, I desire to send on behalf of this, the largest of all American telegraph offices, and the last I believe which Professor Morse ever visited, a sincere tribute to his immortal memory.

A. S. BROWN,
Manager New York Office.

The Speaker then introduced the Hon. S. S. Cox.

ADDRESS OF HON. S. S. COX.

It is difficult, ladies and gentlemen, to be eulogistic and at the same time be just and discriminating. To speak fairly, one must distinguish between the men who find ideas and found principles, and those who adapt them to practical ends.

There are original forces, uncreated by man, but discovered by his science, which man modifies into varied forms of beauty and utility. They are a source of wonder and awe; but to the ordinary mind only such when symbolized into forms and machines. Man clothes these forces with a vesture, made of rude material, like iron and wood, and they are most useful and beautiful when benign and civilizing. He who harnesses matter by the "invention" is like him who does the fighting in war, when perhaps he never had an adequate idea of the real issues of the conflict. But still the fighter is the hero; the thinker must wait for some "great hereafter." Your Newtons and La Places in the celestial mechanism; your Aragos, Ampéres, and Henrys in electro-magnetism, are not the temporary but the eternal heroes. The lesser but more useful intellect carries off the chaplet and sometimes the lucre. I would rather discover the law which rules the molecule than the law which adapts its force and gravity to a water-wheel or steam-engine. The beautiful and hidden genii which reside in nature, the sprites of the river, the spirit of the vapor and lightning—the inner forces—are almost ideal; but the actual lives in the loom and spindle, the mill-stone, the thrashing-machine, and the telegraph!

Jacquard, the inventor of the loom—the poet of matter—awoke one morning with a machine out of his dream. He only desired to make better tools for his trade. Levers, pulleys, springs, and wheels made music to him in his sleep. He made the loom which paints our fabrics of silk, and all human nature, especially woman nature, recognizes him as its friend. [Laughter.] He had another dream—this Jacquard. His punctured cards changed the labor of one-third of our race. He made by his genius a portrait or a landscape on a shawl or a ribbon; but his other and costly dream was a machine to make nets. He desired to catch fish, this simple apostle. For this he was arrested, and there was no *habeas corpus* for him. He was brought from Lyons to Paris. The powers were afraid he would go to mercenary England with his invention. He was confronted with Napoleon and Carnot. The great war-minister startled him by screaming: "Are you the man, sir, who can do what God Almighty cannot, tie a knot in a stretched string?"

If such a simple invention could startle Carnot into such an expression, what would he have said, then, if the invention of Morse had flashed across his mind? Is there not a closer kinship between the supernatural and the telegraph than between the "stretched string" and the Almighty power? Magic pretended to control spirits, to read the future, to provide talismans, to sway the will, to make men invulnerable, to raise tempests, to master the devil, to create an elixir, and to give perpetual youth. Yet even these fables are as froth beside the substantial magic of the telegraph.

Men like Napoleon and Carnot did not understand the Lyons weaver. They were bent on other objects. He was simply bent on his dream and its realization. He was an illustration of the Oriental word: "He came to his own, and his own received him not." From the time of our Saviour to the time of Columbus this word has been verified. But Morse is an exception. He came with his grand thought to his own; notwithstanding jeers and irony, his own—his own nation—received him kindly. It is the special honor of America that they first received and encouraged him in his hour of trial. It received this marvel, only next to the realization of a spiritual agency— this wonderful and magical art—this other miracle of a new gospel— the instantaneous transmission of missives to the "afar" by the lightning. [Cheers.] The world is full of these mysterious agencies, which outdo the miracles of magic. We do not know but that the magnetic electric element is the viewless vinculum between our bodies and souls. I am no materialist, but I wonder if this element be not the cord—infinitely finer than the silken gossamer on the looms of the East—which binds spirit to matter. Miss Browning has said, and I give it for the young people here to ponder, that—

> "Leave two clocks
> Wound up to different hours, upon one shelf,
> And slowly, through the interior wheels of each,
> The blind mechanic motion sets itself
> Athrob to feel out for the mutual time."

I have never tried this experiment, but there is something strange, something magnetic in the tremulous experiences of the lover, even if husband or wife, which are in harmony with all law, and which no law can sever—not even the divorce law of Indiana. [Laughter.] I am the more persuaded of this by the philology of the French word, magnetism. It is the word *aimentation;* from the word *aimer*, to love. It is attraction—a load-stone—the mysterious power by which hearts, even at a distance, and by missives, under oceans and over mountains, may commune and love.

Not to the poetic fancy, or to the *a priori* reasoner, do we owe the application of the mysterious agencies which surround and influence us. We owe it to such practical men as Samuel F. B. Morse.

How best can the American people memorize his achievement? No friend of the great inventor will claim that he found the magnet, much less the subtle element that pervades it. No candid man can believe that the discovery of the magnetic circuit or the exclusive origin of the telegraphic machine belongs to him. He never claimed it. The truths of science, briefly narrated, will illustrate his claim. It is enough to complete his fame, to state some of the truths of his gentle and laborious life.

May I be permitted briefly to rehearse his history, without injustice to his predecessors or contemporaries?

FACTS ABOUT PROFESSOR MORSE.

There was never a man who so took the world by the storm of contraries as Samuel Finley Breese Morse. His fame was his own rounded achievement. His greatness was not thrust upon him. It was not stumbled into by lucky accident. It was the legitimate and necessary result of his grandly co-ordinated powers, working to sublime ends. It is the peculiar felicity of his memory that due and sufficient credit can be given to every one connected with his discovery without detracting an iota from his own claims to greatness. When Volta experimentally demonstrated that electricity was a result of chemical action, and the regular product of the forces eliminated by decomposition, he not only made the electric telegraph possible, but he revealed to the world the existence of a new principle and source of power, the tenth part of whose wonderful functions has not been discovered or utilized.

It was in the winter of 1819 that the great Oersted made his discovery of the regularity of the electrical currents and the affinity between the spark elicited by the friction of amber and the current induced by the voltaic pile. Almost immediately Schweigger was enabled to invent the galvanometer, and Arago to demonstrate the wonderful facts of magnetic induction.

These were among the beginnings in electric progress. What may in the future be the consummation of such efforts? In the judgment of those who know, who are scientists, electro-magnetism may not only be used as a motive power, but put to other uses, which will again startle our race. [Cheers.]

The faculty of increasing to an unlimited degree the intensity of the magnet and the tension of the current, by simply adopting a horseshoe form for the soft iron of the magnet and wrapping it about with an abundant coil of wire, was the next discovery made in electro-magnetism. It was the discovery of our own illustrious Henry. This done, the electro-magnetic telegraph became possible; nay, probable; nay, necessary. The great electro-magnet made by Henry in 1828, and set up in the museum of Princeton College, still asserts its miraculous powers by dragging a great mass of fifty-sixes, such as no magnets are called upon to lift in these degenerate days.

It was now that Ampère and Faraday came in, and, discovering a new branch of science, showed how the magnetic needle could be made to oscillate east and west in a regular and determinate fashion, to record, repeat, and perpetuate its vibrations at the dictation of the same coil which Henry had shown to be so powerful. Like the elephant's proboscis, it could draw a cork and pick up a pin with the same ease and grace that it could lift a ton.

Immediately, almost simultaneously, and out of the very necessities of scientific progress, we have a dozen, a hundred, telegraphic suggestions.

It detracts nothing from Morse's merits—it adds very largely to his claims to real greatness—that he was not strictly a man of science, but a man of art. He went from the field of practice into the field of speculation, and accomplished more by his gleaning than the whole tremendous array of reapers had found there. He was a man accustomed to deal peculiarly with results; for the tools and materials of the artist are all of them the results of applied intelligence and the products of human manufacture.

It is, of course, hyperbolical to say that if electric telegraphy had not been already invented, Morse would have certainly discovered it; but it is sure that if this career had not opened before him he would have won eminence in some other career equally great, even if not equally conspicuous.

It is curious to notice how often this power and possibility to instantaneously transmit intelligence had been the subject of debate and experiment before the idea of it crossed Morse's practical brain. We have instances that extend through the long course of two centuries, in respect to electric systems alone.   As for other sorts of experimenting in telegraphy their name is legion, and their enumeration tediousness.

In electric telegraphy we have the attempts of Strada, in 1617, which are almost contemporary with the great and initial treatise of William Gilbert de Magnete, and long before the experiment of Caboeus and Boyle, and the discoveries of Otto Gueriche.

If you must take Oersted, Ampère, Henry, and Faraday into the account of Morse, we must go further. We must not reject or neglect either Gilbert or Newton, Boyle or Hawksbee, Grey or Desaguliers, Nollet or Monnier, or Franklin.

Senor Salva built a telegraph in 1798, from Madrid to Aranjuez, 26 miles, which enabled messages to be sent by the means of frictional electricity.

Unlike almost every other discovery of science the electric telegraph was developed in advance of the methods necessary to perfect it.   Hence the inadequacy of its earlier methods and later materials. In this respect our great Morse was like Kepler. He invented his methods before he was sufficiently informed to be able to rationalize his laws. His genius transcended his skill. His single brain compassed more than his studies had enabled him to derive from all the world that had lived before him.

Bain's electro-chemical telegraph is vastly more original, vastly more ingenious than Morse's. But Morse has succeeded and Bain has not succeeded. The practical world has pronounced in Morse's favor; in fact, has dogmatically declared that it will have Morse's system and none other. You may like Wheatstone's best, or Vail's, or Bain's, but the world, which pays the cost of telegraphy, chooses to have Morse's. The Morse system, if we are not misinformed, enables its operators to transmit one thousand words, while the Bain, the House, and the other systems give facilities for only about two hundred. Consequently, Morse's plan is at least five times as profitable to the companies as other plans are.

The simplest facts of science are the confusion of wonder, and the shame of the searchers for prodigies. When Puck announced that he would put a girdle about the earth in forty minutes, how could he have imagined that Morse would come after him, and would develop a system by means of which a man may send a message to-day to Hong-Kong or Yokohama, which, after traveling thirty thousand miles, and being translated into a dozen languages, would reach its destination *yesterday* morning, while he was still enjoying his morning slumbers, and before he had even dreamed of the necessity that would presently devolve upon him of altering the currents of electricity and intelligence that flow through the straits of Malacca, and rousing from sleep the quiet oysters of Chittagong. [Cheers.]

These facts and conclusions, hastily collected, show that the man whose genius we celebrate deserves all that America, or the world outside of our hemisphere, has done to honor his memory. He has accomplished more than Franklin to realize the sublime verse:

"Eripuitcœlo fulmen, sceptrum que tyrannis."

He gave to the universal people the means of speedy and accurate intelligence, and so stormed at once the terrible castles of Giant Doubt and Giant Despair. He has saved time, shortened the hours of toil, accumulated and intensified thought by the rapidity and terseness of the electric messages. He has celebrated treaties. He makes war; for no battle can be fought without his instant aid. Go to the uttermost parts of the earth; go beneath the deep, deep sea; to the land where snows are eternal, or to the tropical realms, where the orange blooms in the air of midwinter, and you will find this clicking, persistent, sleepless instrument ready to give its tireless wing to your purpose. [Cheers.]

In a volume which I have read on the *Telegraphie Electrique*, by Moigno, I find a splendid dedication to the great Arago.   While it honors the names of Volta, Œrsted, Ampére, and Faraday, and makes Arago the first to give certain effect to the "*Alimentation Momentanée*," it fails to note the name of Morse.   But since then the French, more generous than the English, have led the world to honor him, whose special honor to us is that we have the grace and thoughtfulness to honor him.

We honor him not alone for his achievement in mechanism, but for his beautiful and unselfish life.   I hold in my hand a letter from Mr. A. G. Vermilye, of New York, to Dr. Prime, of the Observer, which shows that when the $80,000 was voted him by foreign powers he refused it, until persuaded by his friends that it was an honorary testimonial.   He did not care nor expect to be rich.   He only wore the badges and diamonds with which he was decorated in deference to the custom, as he was wont to say; for he was a simple man, of true American mold.

I am proud to say that the heart of this man was as big as his mind.   He gave much more in proportion than he received.   His charities had no limit outside of his means, and sometimes were not even restricted there.   All who knew him loved him.   Those who knew him best not only honored him most, but loved him best.   Our great Allston was his preceptor in art, but his debtor in friendship.   Leslie looked up to him, honored, loved him.   He was not soured by disappointment, nor did he lose his genial spirit nor his liberal hand by the force of detraction or long waiting.   He brought the amenities which art had acquainted him with into the severe field of science, and, even when old, gray, and solicited by the strongest temptations that ever assailed a man, he refused to forget and ignore the principles he had learned to love.   Whether in early life, painting, perhaps, for a living; or modeling a statue in England, under the eye of Allston; or plying his magnetic experiments in the University building at New York; or testing the daguerreotype; or supervising a Sunday-school in Paris; or contesting the British and other claimants of his invention; or asking a reluctant Congress for aid; or, at last, unveiling the statue of Franklin in Printing-House Square—in whatever sphere, under all skies and in all moods, he was a peerless man. In presence, he is comparable with our ideal of the patriarchal days; in character, as pure as the unspotted snows of the north; and in all aims, scientific, social, and Christian, as lofty as his faith in truth was resolute and devoted.

True, he was surrounded in life by anxieties and trials. The clouds of obscurity and adversity were about him, year after year, while he struggled; but he signally illustrated the verse of Festus:

> "The clouds which hide the mental mountains,
> Rising nighest heaven are full of finest lightning."

Now that he has gone above the clouds and mountains of earth; now that his spirit, perhaps, by intuitions as instant as his electric current, communes with the angels and beings of another sphere— those fleet messengers of the Almighty—may not the imagination be allowed to picture his reception in the Eternal City! May we not believe that, for one who has done so much to bind the earth in unity, there was new occasion on his advent for the choral welcome:

> "Peace on earth, good will to men!"

The address was followed with music by the Marine Band; after which Speaker Blaine announced that the telegraph on the Clerk's desk was in direct communication with London, and read the following message which had just been transmitted:

The following additional telegrams were then read:

LONDON, ENGLAND.

[Telegram dated London, April 16, 1872.]

To CYRUS W. FIELD, *Washington :*

Barely ten months have elapsed since I participated as representing the Anglo-American Telegraph Company in doing honor to Professor Morse, and it is with sincere regret that I now tender to the people of the United States the heartfelt condolence of the directors of the Anglo-American and French Atlantic Telegraph Companies for the loss of one who occupied so eminent a position among men of science, and whose name will be recorded in the history of the world as that of one of the pioneers of that marvelous road by means of which the inhabitants of the two hemispheres are brought into instantaneous relation with each other.

HAMILTON, Chairman.

LONDON, ENGLAND.

[Telegram dated London, April 16, 1872.]

To the MORSE MEMORIAL MEETING:

The operators of England, Ireland, and Scotland join with their American brethren in paying a tribute of respect to the memory of the founder of the Morse system, and offer their sympathies to the Morse Memorial Association in mourning the founder of their craft.

WETHERBEE,
Chairman of Committee.

MONTREAL, CANADA.

[Telegram dated Montreal, April 16, 1872.]

To A. S. SOLOMONS, Esq.,

Chairman Committee of Arrangements Morse Celebration,

House of Representatives:

Montreal joins the distinguished assembly now at Washington, in tendering its tribute to the memory of the immortal Morse, whose spirit hovers in our midst, and whose genius discovered the means of uniting with electric fire the world in one common brotherhood.

CHAS. J. GOURSOL,
Mayor.

HONG-KONG, CHINA.

[Telegram dated April 16, 1872.]

To CYRUS W. FIELD:

The Hong-Kong Chamber of Commerce learns with most unfeigned regret the death of Professor Morse, and mourns this great loss to telegraphy and science.

FULLER.

BOMBAY.

[Bombay Chamber of Commerce; received at New York, 2 p. m., April 15, 1872.]

To CYRUS W. FIELD, *New York:*

This Chamber of Commerce heard with great regret of Professor Morse's death, and records its sense of the great loss to the scientific world caused thereby.

[Telegram dated April 16, 1872.]

To CYRUS W. FIELD, *Washington:*

The superintendents and staffs of submarine telegraphs in Bombay, Madras, China Straits Settlements, Java, and Australia express their sincere regret at the death of Professor Morse, to whom telegraphy owes so much, and whose memory will always be dear to the large army of telegraphists spread all over the globe.

STACEY,
Bombay

BATAVIA, JAVA.

[Telegram dated April 16, 1872.]

To CYRUS W. FIELD:

Batavia Chamber of Commerce regrets to learn of the death of Professor Morse.

VANDENBURG, *President.*

INDIA—CHINA—AUSTRALIA.

[Telegram dated April 16, 1872.]

To CYRUS W. FIELD, *Washington:*

The directors, officers, and staff of the Associated Submarine Companies to India, China, and Australia, unite in deepest sympathy with America for the loss of her great citizen, Professor Morse, whose genius has done so much to extend the benefits of electrical science among all classes and all lands of the civilized world.

JOHN PENDER.

EGYPT.

[Telegram dated April 16, 1872.]

To CYRUS W. FIELD:

The telegraphic staff in Egypt deplore the loss of the eminent Professor Morse, who has rendered such valuable service to the telegraphic extensions all over the world.

GIBBS.

SINGAPORE, ASIA.

[Telegram from Singapore; received at New York April 15, 1872.]

CYRUS W. FIELD, *New York:*

This Chamber of Commerce learns with deep regret the great loss telegraphy and the scientific world has sustained in the death of Professor Morse.

UNITED STATES CONSULATE, HALIFAX, N. S.

[Telegram dated United States Consulate, Halifax, N. S., April 16, 1872.]

To Hon. J. G. BLAINE,
Speaker of the House of Representatives, Washington:

Permit me as Consul of the United States, and on behalf of the American citizens residing in Halifax, to unite with the Representatives of American people in paying deserved honors to the memory of the the immortal inventor of the Morse system of telegraphy, which now encircles the globe and unites distant nations in one common bond of brotherhood.

M. M. JACKSON,
United States Consul.

[Telegram dated New Orleans, La., April 16, 1872.]

To A. S. Solomons,

Morse Memorial Meeting, Washington :

I regret that circumstances prevent the holding of a public meeting in the city of New Orleans to express our appreciation of the great service rendered to science and civilization by the late Professor Morse; but, in the name and on behalf of the city of New Orleans, I beg to assure you of our deep sense of the loss which the country has sustained by his demise, and our sympathy with the object of your present gathering.

BEN: F. FLANDERS,
Mayor.

[Telegram dated San Francisco, April 16, 1872.]

To the Chairman of the Morse Memorial Meeting,

Washington, D. C.:

A Morse Memorial Meeting was held this afternoon at the City Hall, Mayor Alvord president, James Gamble, general superintendent Western Union Telegraph, secretary. Eulogistic speeches were made by several prominent citizens. Series of resolutions adopted. Meeting well attended.

JOHN FOLEY.

[Telegram dated Des Moines, Iowa, April 16, 1872.]

To the Morse Memorial Association:

> "'Twas Franklin who, with simple strand,
> Caught the lightning in his hand ;
> 'Twas Morse who, with a little wire,
> Taught it to speak the heart's desire.
> May their souls together dwell in glory,
> While their names live here in song and story."

G. ORWIG.

[Telegram dated Salt Lake, Utah, April 16, 1872.]

To Hon. CHAIRMAN OF THE MORSE MEMORIAL MEETING,

Washington:

Honor is due to the wise and the great. Professor Morse was both. My affections follow him to the spirit world.

BRIGHAM YOUNG.

[Telegram dated Salt Lake, April 16, 1872.]

To the Hon. CHAIRMAN OF THE MORSE MEMORIAL MEETING,

Washington, D. C.:

Utah cordially joins the fraternity of States and nation in expressing sorrow at the demise and irreparable loss the world has sustained in the decease of Professor Samuel F. B. Morse. Each successive year developed through the genius of Morse additional gems of electrical science, to the great benefit of mankind. In each development he recognized the finger of Divinity, and in his unostentatious manner is expressed the sentiment of his first telegram, "What hath God wrought!" His name will shine in letters of living light throughout all coming ages.

DANIEL H. WELLS, *Mayor.*

[Telegram dated Topeka, Kansas, April 16, 1872.]

To Hon. A. S. SOLOMONS,

Chairman Morse Memorial Meeting, Washington:

The citizens of Topeka extend to you their hearty co-operation in all your proceedings, and mourn with you the nation's loss.

TERRIN F. WELCH, *Mayor.*

[Telegram dated Saint Augustine, Fla., April 16, 1872.]

To A. S. SOLOMONS,

Chairman of the Committee of Arrangements

National Telegraph Memorial,

Washington:

The oldest city in the United States to her sister cities throughout the world, greeting:

We unite with you in deploring the loss and honoring the memory of Professor Morse, who by his genius has annihilated the space that separates us.

WM. J. WATKINS,

Mayor of Saint Augustine, Fla.

[Telegram dated Council Chamber, Detroit, Mich., April 16, 1872.]

To A. S. SOLOMONS,

> *Chairman of the Committee of Arrangements,*
>> *Morse Memorial Meeting, Washington:*

We beg to submit the following report of our special committee:

To the honorable the COMMON COUNCIL, of Detroit:

GENTLEMEN: Your special committee, to whom was referred at the last session of your honorable body the communication of Hon. A. S. Solomons, of Washington, relative to the memorial meeting invited to be held simultaneously in the cities of the United States on the evening of the 16th of April, respectfully report that the subject and papers were referred on such short notice as to render a call for a general meeting of citizens for such purpose impracticable, and therefore, as this is the evening designated for the manifestation of the respect and admiration of a people for the memory of Prof. Samuel F. B. Morse, it respectfully recommends the adoption of the following resolutions:

Resolved, That this Council, as the representatives of the people of the city of Detroit, unite with their fellow-citizens throughout the United States to-night in the expression of the highest appreciation of the services and genius of the late Professor Morse, in invention and application to public purpose and benefit of the system of electric magnetic telegraphy, which, in the twenty-eight years since 1844, has united cities, states, countries, and continents; reduced months to minutes, thereby resulting in the gain of valuable time in communication with each other.

Resolved, That this Council sympathize with the feelings that have invited this simultaneous manifestation of respect for the memory of this gifted man, and cheerfully participate in it as a just and well-earned tribute, due not only from this country and people, but from all nations of the civilized world.

Resolved, That the city clerk be instructed to transmit a copy of these resolutions to the Chairman of the committee of arrangements of the National Telegraph Monumental Association, for the meeting now in simultaneous session with our own, in the city of Washington, D. C.

F. RUBELE.
PHILO PARSONS.
FRANCI ADAM.

[Telegram dated New York, April 16, 1872.]

To the MEMORIAL MEETING, HOUSE OF REPRESENTATIVES,
Washington:

The *Alumni* of Yale College, assembled in New York, unite with the meeting in Washington in all that can be said or felt of love, honor, and veneration for the late Professor Morse. Yale will ever be proud to claim as hers a name, than which there is none brighter on the rolls of the Universities of the world.

[Telegram dated Petersburgh, Va., April 16, 1872.]

To A. S. SOLOMONS,

Chairman Committee of Arrangements, Washington :

At a meeting of the citizens of Petersburgh, held on the night of April 16, in Merchants' Hall, Mr. Letmeyer stated that it was desired to introduce resolutions of respect to the memory of the late Professor Morse, and called the mayor to the chair. Mayor Wood paid a brief tribute to the services and character of Professor Morse, and announced that the meeting was ready for business.

On motion, a committee of five was appointed to draught resolutions.

The following committee was appointed : E. S. Gregory, Wm. H. Baxter, S. H. Owens, S. M. Cox, and A. L. Archer, who, after retiring, reported the following resolutions :

Resolved, That whereas the long, laborious, and eminent life of Prof. Samuel F. B. Morse, of New York, the inventor of the magnetic telegraph, has been recently brought to a close, surrounded by many illustrious evidences of the triumphs he accomplished in the field of useful science: Therefore, be it

Resolved by the citizens of Petersburgh, in public meeting assembled, That they unite with the people of the United States in the testimonial of respect which is to-night being paid throughout the country to the memory of the lamented dead.

Resolved, That to his patient, arduous, and long-unrewarded labors in behalf of scientific discovery, the fortitude with which he bore reverses and discouragements, the energy with which he urged the cause of truth, the modesty with which he recognized success and wore the lavish honors that were showered upon him; and his simple, blameless, and patriotic life, entitle his memory to our highest regard and respect, and should recommend his name to conspicuous distinction among the benefactors of mankind.

Resolved, That the qualities by which he deserved and secured success render him worthy the imitation of all who labor for sublime results of public utility, and civilized progress in the fields of scientific exploration.

Resolved, That while the magnificent consequences of the invention of Professor Morse, rising eminent everywhere throughout the world, render any tribute to his honor unnecessary, and are in themselves the best and richest monuments to his name, we must be permitted to accord to him the praise which belongs to a career of eminent public service, and to recognize in him one of the noblest sons of whom America may well be proud.

[Telegram dated Indianapolis, Ind., April 16, 1872.]

To Hon. J. G. BLAINE, *Washington:*

The citizens of Indianapolis, convened at the chamber of commerce, the mayor presiding, join in the universal expression of sorrow occasioned by the death of the illustrious servant and friend of mankind, Samuel F. B. Morse, and mingle their voice with that of

the whole civilized world, now simultaneously speaking, in expressing
their sense of the grand achievement of genius which has made the
world one.

DANIEL MACULEY,
Mayor.

[Telegram dated Cleveland, Ohio, April 16, 1872.]

To MORSE MEMORIAL COMMITTEE, *Washington:*

Samuel F. B. Morse having departed this life, ripe in years, and
clothed with honor and renown, and the council of the city of Cleveland desiring in appropriate terms to express its sense of the loss
sustained in his death by this country and the whole world: Therefore, be it

Resolved, That we deplore the loss of one who, in his pure and
noble life, his determined industry, his great intellect, his firm and
unyielding belief in the ultimate success of the discovery made by
him, causing him to press its claims in spite of the opposition and
jeers of a people having no faith in human progress, and that we will
ever hold in grateful remembrance his name and deeds.

The above resolution was unanimously adopted by the city council
of the city of Cleveland.

THEO. VOGES,
City Clerk.

[Telegram dated Wilmington, Del., April 16, 1872.]

At a meeting of the citizens of Wilmington, Del., the following
resolutions were unanimously adopted:

Whereas, it has pleased the allwise Disposer of the events of men
and nations, in the order of his providence, to bring to a close the
earthly existence of one of the greatest citizens of our republic, Professor S. F. B. Morse, it seems peculiarly fitting, as is at this moment
being done in all parts of our country, to make a national and public
expression of the sentiments of respect to his memory which are
entertained by the people: Therefore, it is

Resolved, That in the eminent services of the late Professor Morse, in perfecting and establishing the magnetic telegraph, he has not only distinguished himself and our republic, but has also conferred one of the greatest blessings ever effected by any one in civil life, by the rapid diffusion of intelligence, thus bringing into close proximity the whole brotherhood of mankind, and contributing greatly toward the elevation and civilization of the race and the establishment of peace and good-will over all the earth.

Resolved, That this meeting not only approve of, but heartily subscribe to, the praiseworthy object of the National Telegraph Memorial Association, in their effort to erect a national monument at Washington to the memory of a man so justly entitled to our respect and veneration.

Resolved, That a committee be appointed to execute a plan for the collection and transmission of the contributions of the people of this city and State to the said Monument Association at Washington.

J. S. VALENTINE,
Mayor, Wilmington, Del.

[Telegram dated Nashville, Tenn., April 16, 1872.]

To A. S. SOLOMONS, *Chairman, Washington:*

The citizens of Nashville, in common with the whole civilized world, desire to pay all proper respect to the memory of the late Samuel F. B. Morse, LL. D., and therefore send to the National Telegraph Memorial Association an expression of their deep and ardent respect for the distinguished inventor; their undying admiration for one who has done more for the progress of art and science than any other scientist, and their hope that all will be done that is possible to perpetuate the memory of the greatest man that the world has ever produced.

K. J. MORRIS, *Mayor.*

The Speaker then introduced the Hon. D. W. Voorhees.

ADDRESS OF HON. D. W. VOORHEES.

Honors paid by the living to the dead are as old and as universal as the races of mankind. They follow the bereavements of the cabin and the palace. Simple ceremonies attend the humble and the lowly, and frail memorials mark their resting-places; while the long procession, the solemn and lofty dirge, the crowded assemblage, and the voice of eulogy all wait on departed eminence and glory. The barbarian chants a requiem over the grave of his fellow-mortal, and the Christian celebrates the virtues of his fallen comrade. No one ever dies all forgotten, and no one ever wholly perishes from the face of the earth. The influences of a life, even in this world, are eternal. The tomb cannot inclose them. They escape from its portals, and continue to pervade the daily walks of men, like unseen spirits, guiding and controlling human thought and action. Who is free from their touch? Whose life and destiny have not been colored and fashioned by the influences of those who have passed away, even unknown to fame? The greatest actors on the broad stage of human affairs have pointed back from the loftiest points of their elevation to the mother with her prayers, to the father with his toil and devotion, to unselfish kindred, to self-sacrificing friends, and bowed with reverence before the living power associated forever with their names and memories. Every mind and heart reproduces some of its achievements and some of its qualities in the minds and hearts of others after it has gone to far-off spheres and realms. And this is the average of human influence—the silent, but mighty, stream of causes producing effects, on which mankind, from its birth, has been borne gradually and steadily forward in its vast career of progress and development. Now and then, however, the current of this stream receives a new and startling velocity. Some intellectual force, towering over all others of its period, occasionally imparts to all the world at once an impulse which condenses the ordinary advancement of centuries into the thrilling compass of a single day. Then nations and generations, and not merely individuals, become the subjects of an irresistible and everlasting influence. A new era is then noted on the page of the historian, and new gateways are opened for the onward movements of humanity. Such an event happened in this capital when only twenty-eight years ago a single wire was drawn through the air as a messenger of thought, as swift and unfailing as the light of the sun. It was a period of mental activity and pride, and men were boastful of the light and knowledge which the world already possessed; but the results which followed this achievement were as the awakening of dawn after long and heavy darkness. A revolution forward and upward in the progress of the world was at once accomplished, of greater practical consequence to the human family than any other known in history. The toils, the penury, and the hopes deferred, which had darkened many years of the life of the student and the philosopher, were succeeded by a triumph whose proportions will continue to swell and expand until time shall be no more. The influence of this one man has taken to itself the wings of the morning, and visited the uttermost parts of the earth. It dwells in all the four quarters of the globe, and shapes the destinies of men and nations with a power second only to the omnipresent omnipotence of God himself. Professor Morse in one sense is dead. His body, after its labors of four-score years, has laid down to rest and to sleep until the voice of the Master shall awaken it again. But, even in this world, his life has but just begun. As his great soul enters upon its new career in the regions of immortality, so does the influence which he left behind him here move forward each day to new developments of glory and of power. We are here to-night because he lives in his works, and because his undying genius still sways and governs our conduct. Forty million people, whose representatives we are, bow reverently at his tomb for the same reason. All the civilized races of the earth are his mourners, because his great discovery has testified of him in their midst. Memorial services, however, cannot reach him. He is beyond the sounds of praise or the fragrance of its incense.

> " Can honor's voice provoke the silent dust,
> Or flattery soothe the dull, cold ear of death ?"

No, we simply honor ourselves on this occasion by recognizing the gigantic power of the mighty dead, and attesting his immortality here on earth. Thus I interpret the meaning of these imposing national solemnities.

If we pause here for a moment to reflect upon the class to which the discovery of Professor Morse belongs, we find it in that field which has produced nearly all there is of useful knowledge. The physical sciences alone can place man in his true relation to the material universe. He arose from the dust in the hour of his creation, a master and a conqueror by divine right in the world of nature. Dominion was given to him over all. Power was granted him as the lord of a domain and all it contained, but it was a power which had to be reduced to possession by knowledge. He who is ignorant of the properties and laws of the physical world can have no control of its tremendous agencies. The most polished nations of antiquity, therefore, rose to no higher fame than that which is acquired in wars and conquests. The shape and motion of the earth; the movements and the functions of the heavenly bodies; the electricity of the clouds; the magnetism of metals; the qualities and powers of steam, were to them almost entirely sealed mysteries. If they sometimes caught a glimpse of an element of science they applied it to no useful purpose. Cicero, it is true, with that universal wisdom which distinguished him, admits the importance to the human understanding of physical investigation. " Est animorum ingeniorumque nostrorum naturale quoddam quasi pabulum consideratio contemplatique naturæ." But in this he stood almost, if not quite, alone, and it was left for modern ages to produce those wonderful results which attend a revelation of the secret forces and principles of nature. They are numerous and beneficent to the wants and comfort of the human family; but the discoveries which caused the steamer to plow the deep in safety, and the railroad-train to fly across a continent, and which led to the instantaneous transmission of thought to the opposite regions of the globe, stand unrivaled in the history of mental triumphs over the elements of physical creation. And these sublime achievements are American! Fortunate and glorious as our history has in many things been, it has no page so bright as this. Fulton and Franklin and Morse are American names. We have lived as a nation less than a century, and yet, in the realms of useful philosophy, practical art, and beneficial science, all the centuries of all the past furnish no parallel to our glory. The American mind has contributed more in these walks to the elevation and happiness of mankind than all the other nations and ages of the world combined. All else may fail us, but this will never fail. Our liberties may be lost, our free form of government may fall to the ground, our very name be blotted from the map of nations, but the inventions of American genius will continue to illuminate the world with a light as imperishable as the stars in the heavens.

There is another reflection, however, which presents itself for brief mention on this occasion. In the brilliancy of the discoverer's fame, after his success is complete, the world is apt to forget the price he paid for his immortality. It is often a most melancholy task to trace the weary and painful struggles which men of science have made, in order to be permitted to bless mankind. Looking behind the sweet hour of their triumphs, we usually behold a dismal plain of poverty, and an almost friendless life of vigilant, unremitting, and exhaustive labor. The feverish, throbbing brain; the anxious, sleepless nights; the longing, sick, and disappointed heart—all are there. The sneers of dullness, the opposition of envious intelligence, and the cold and stinted patronage of the timid and doubting also attend the efforts of every daring explorer in unknown regions after new truths. Columbus was fifty-seven years old when he at last sailed on the fulfillment of his long and troubled dream. In the prosecution of his vast design he had begged bread and water at the gates of the convent of Santa Maria de Rabida, and encountered the malevolent superstition of

Spain in the fifteenth century before the council at Salamanca. He followed the camp of Ferdinand and Isabella for years, and fought in their bloodiest battles against the Moors, in order to be near the court and solicit its aid in the discovery of a new world. He borrowed money to buy suitable apparel in which to appear in the presence of his sovereigns. He journeyed, foot-sore and travel-stained, with the peasants on the highways; but in the midst of it all, whether in want or in humiliation, in fatigue or in danger, whether battling under the cross against the crescent or lingering in the ante-chamber of royalty for an audience, he never for an instant lost sight of the mission on which he had embarked his life. He was present when the last Moorish king surrendered the keys of the Alhambra, and he was a spectator when the whole court and army of Spain were abandoned to jubilee; when the air resounded with shouts of joy, with songs of triumph, and hymns of thanksgiving. Yet at this great moment an old Spanish writer thus describes him: "A man obscure and but little known followed at this time the court. Confounded in the crowd of importunate applicants, feeding his imagination in the corners of ante-chambers with the pompous project of discovering a world; melancholy and dejected in the midst of the general rejoicing, he beheld with indifference, and almost with contempt, the conclusion of a conquest which swelled all bosoms with jubilee and seemed to have reached the utmost bounds of desire." So, too, perhaps, might the great American, whose deeds we commemorate to-night, have been seen in the halls of this Capitol, when, at the age of fifty-two years, he witnessed general rejoicings over the success of small events in comparison to that which was so clear and so immeasurably great to his view. In some niche or corner or gallery he watched and waited for the succor he had so long sought in vain. It came at last, as did the three small ships to Columbus; and similar results followed, to a certain extent, in both instances. Success was immediate and glorious. One delivered a new hemisphere to the knowledge of mankind, and the other compelled the lightning to carry instant communication between both hemispheres. They rose from adversity, and culminated in conquests alike, but their fates and fortunes there diverged. The mighty Genoese admiral realized the anguish of those who hang on princes' favors. He drained the cup of his country's ingratitude to its dregs. His great heart was broken in prisons and in chains. He was three hundred years in advance of the powers whom he served. He died in sorrow, and with the unpropitious clouds of his early life again lowering over his head.

Not so with Professor Morse. Happy and bright was the age in which he achieved his triumph. He was shorn of none of its honors or its profits. He took his place permanently in the temple of fame, and received the well-earned rewards of his toils and his genius. He lived with the affections of the world clustering about him, and died honored, revered, and mourned by the human race. The world has advanced, and it still advances.

The following additional telegrams were then read:

[Telegram dated Mobile, Ala., April 6, 1872.]

To A. S. SOLOMONS,

Chairman, House of Representatives, Washington:

At a meeting of the citizens of Mobile, Ala., held April 16, 1872, the following preamble and resolutions were adopted:

Whereas, the recent death of Professor Samuel Finley Breese Morse has called forth the sympathy and regret of the whole civilized world; and

Whereas, it has been determined to give expression to that sympathy and regret by simultaneous action in the principal cities and towns of America: Therefore, it is hereby

Resolved, That we, the citizens of Mobile, cordially unite in the expression of our admiration for the services rendered mankind by the late Professor Morse, especially for his invention of the electric-magnetic telegraph; the most brilliant, and at the same time one of the most useful achievements of human genius.

Resolved, That while we can scarcely sorrow for the death of one who has attained a ripe old age, whose work has been so well and so thoroughly done, and who leaves to his family and his country the fragrance of the memory of a well spent, beneficent, and illustrious life, yet we feel that this country and this age have sustained an irreparable loss—the loss of one who has conferred upon them benefits beyond the achievements of the warrior, the statesman, or even in ordinary cases of the scholar and the philosopher.

Resolved, That these resolutions be published in the city papers, and that a copy of them be forwarded to the Telegraph Memorial Monumental Association at Washington.

[Telegram dated Louisville, Ky., April 16, 1872.]

To Hon. JAMES G. BLAINE, *Chairman, Washington :*

Message of the Board of Trade and citizens of the city of Louisville, Ky.:

The thought is impressive and beautiful, that in the deep stillness of this evening's gliding hours shall run along the electric wire from all parts of our country, and from lands beyond the wide seas, heart-prompted messages of admiration and gratitude in reverent commemoration of the great and good man, to whose clear, pure spirit and searching mind was given the magic word at which nature opened her inmost recesses, and bade her subtlest power become man's obedient messenger. The Board of Trade of Louisville, in behalf of its members and of all their fellow-citizens, feeling the beauty and impressiveness of this consecrating service, would add their loving tribute to the myriad offerings, not in formal resolution, but in a sentiment expressive of their fervent hope that the world, remembering the first message sent by Professor Morse, "What God hath wrought!" remembering, too, the telegraphic greeting sent by him when the crowning honor was placed on his brow, " Glory to God in the highest, peace on earth and good-will to all men !" may always attest its gratitude to the father of the magnetic-telegraphic system, and its reverence for his memory, by faithfully employing this finest of material agencies; this noblest, grandest of inventions, in promotion of the great interests of commerce, civilization, and religion, to the honor of God and to the welfare of humanity.

W. S. BULLOCK,
Chairman of Committee.

J. J. PORTER,
President.

W. H. MERRIWEATHER,
Secretary.

[Telegram dated Davenport, Iowa, April 16, 1872.]

To A. S. SOLOMONS,
Chairman of Committee of Arrangements
of Memorial Meeting, Washington:

At the call of the city council, a large meeting of the citizens of Davenport have assembled, and just organized, for the purpose of uniting with you and other meetings of similar character throughout the country in giving simultaneous expressions to their feelings and sentiments in view of the great loss which this nation and the world have sustained in the death of Professor Morse.

Whereas this meeting has been called for the purpose of joining in a national memorial to the late S. F. B. Morse: Therefore,

Resolved, That while we lament the death of Professor Morse, even at a ripe old age, we have special pride in cherishing the memory of a fellow-citizen who, by the unanimous verdict of the world, has been acknowledged one of its greatest and most illustrious benefactors.

Resolved, That it is good in this public manner, and through the electric agency which his intellect evoked, to testify our esteem and veneration of the departed, whose discovery has conferred honor on our native land and blessings on the world.

Resolved, That the foregoing be signed by the officers and published.

A. H. BENNETT,
Mayor.

[Telegram dated Trenton, N. J., April 16, 1872.]

To the National Telegraph Memorial Association,

Washington:

A public meeting of citizens of Trenton express their deep sorrow at the death of Professor Morse, as follows:

Whereas, in the course of nature, Prof. Samuel F. B. Morse, one of the great benefactors of the human race, has been removed from the scenes of his early labors and triumphs, entailing an irreparable loss not only upon his immediate countrymen, but upon the citizens of the whole civilized world as well; and whereas, in response to the invitation of the National Telegraph Memorial Association, we are here to-night to join with them in doing honor to his memory: Therefore, be it

Resolved, That we, the citizens of Trenton, N. J., have a common interest in the name and fame of Prof. Samuel F. B. Morse, enjoying as we do the results of his genius as the great discoverer of practical magnetic telegraphy, and mourning as we shall hereafter the loss of one who, as a man of genius, had few equals and no superior.

Resolved, That the action of this memorial meeting be at once telegraphed to the meeting of the National Telegraph Memorial Association now being held in the Hall of Representatives, Washington City.

JOHN BRIEST,

Mayor.

[Telegram dated Saint Louis, Mo., April 16, 1872.]

To His Excellency Vice-President Colfax,

and Hon. J. G. Blaine,

Presiding Officers of the Memorial Meeting

in honor of the late Professor Morse,

Washington:

Every human soul in this city, without distinction of age, color, sex, or condition, pays tribute at the shrine of immortal genius, the shrine of one who attained to the knowledge of the gods, to command the thunderbolt, not to destroy, but to save. Well did he perform his mission.   Language fails to speak his praise; his name shall live through endless days.

JOSEPH BROWN,

Mayor of Saint Louis.

[Telegram dated Pittsburgh, Pa., April 16, 1872.]

To Hon. J. G. BLAINE,

    Washington :

At a meeting of citizens of Pittsburgh, held this afternoon, to express regard for the memory of the late Professor Morse, the following were adopted as the expression of those present:

Resolved, That in the death of Professor Morse the entire civilized world has suffered an irreparable loss, and a loss that nations yet to be civilized will in time appreciate.

Resolved, That we of the Iron City have special cause to mourn the death of one to whose invention so much of our greatness and prosperity is due.

Resolved, That we unite with other cities of the country in sincere expression of regret at our common bereavement.

J. A. BLACKMORE, *Mayor.*

[Telegram dated Burlington, Iowa, April 16, 1872.]

To CHAIRMAN NATIONAL MORSE MEMORIAL MEETING,

    Washington :

The following resolutions were unanimously adopted at the Morse memorial meeting held here this evening:

Whereas it has pleased the Divine Ruler of the Universe to call hence Professor Samuel Finley Breese Morse, America's most distinguished citizen, who has gone to the heavenly garner, like a ripe sheaf in its season, crowned with his reward: Therefore, be it

Resolved, That we honor the memory of Professor Morse as one of the greatest benefactors of the human race, in subjecting the powers of nature to human control, so as to combine the inhabitants of the globe as one family.

Resolved, That we praise the Lord that it is permitted to us to control the powers of nature, and to make them obedient to our use:

and that we regard the past triumph of Professor Morse as the herald of new and further advancements in the field of science.

Resolved, That his rare attainments, accurate judgment, and comprehensive intellect, that enabled him to grasp and utilize these mobile, elastic, imponderable forces of nature, to make them subservient to man, with all their quickening powers upon trade, commerce, and human progress, command our grateful admiration and regard.

Resolved, That a copy of these resolutions be transmitted by telegraph to the Central Morse Memorial Association at Washington, D. C.

D. ROVER,
Chairman.
A. T. HAY,
H. W. STARR,
Committee on Resolutions.

[Telegram dated Union Hall, Burlington, Iowa, April 16, 1872.]

To the CHAIRMAN OF THE

NATIONAL MORSE MEMORIAL MEETING, *Washington:*

The citizens and telegraphers of Burlington, here assembled, to the National Morse Memorial Association, Washington, greeting: We mourn with you the irreparable loss of one of America's greatest public benefactors.

GEO. W. ROBERTSON,
Chairman.

[Telegram dated Portsmouth, N. H., April 16, 1872.]

A. S. SOLOMONS, *Washington:*

PORTSMOUTH MEETING.—Mr. Hackett offered the following resolutions, which were unanimously adopted:

Resolved, That the citizens of Portsmouth have received with deep regret the intelligence of the death of Samuel Finley Breese Morse, a benefactor of his race and age, whose genius and perseverance have brought the world into instantaneous intercourse and sympathy; extended the borders of civilization, and provided a medium and influence for making a brotherhood of the whole family of man.

Resolved, As a token of our respect to the memory of such a public benefactor, and of our appreciation of the blessings he has conferred upon the world, that the mayor be requested to cause the national flag to be displayed at half-mast over the City-Hall for one week.

[Telegram dated Concord, N. H., April 16, 1872.]

To A. S. Solomons, *Chairman, &c., Washington:*

Concord, New Hampshire, once the residence of Professor Morse, rejoices in his fame, and meets to-night to honor the memory of the inventor of the electric telegraph.

[Telegram dated Omaha, Nebr., April 16, 1872.]

To National Morse Memorial Association,

Washington:

Resolutions passed by the city council of Omaha, assembled in regular session, on Tuesday evening, April 16, 1872, in memory of the late Professor S. F. B. Morse:

Whereas, the National Morse Memorial Association meet in the National House of Representatives at Washington this evening, to commemorate by some appropriate ceremonies the life and fame of the late Professor S. F. B. Morse, the inventor of the system of telegraphy; and,

Whereas, it has extended an earnest invitation to all the municipalities in the land to join in this great and worthy service, placing all the telegraphic lines in the country at their disposal for the transmission of messages, that there may be a simultaneous expression of reverence and respect from one end of the land to the other: Therefore, be it

Resolved, by the city council of Omaha, the chief commercial city of Nebraska, that the city of Omaha recognizes with profound respect and gratitude the inestimable service which the late Professor Morse performed for the world by the invention of the great and wonderful system of electro-magnetic telegraphy; an invention whose influence is daily felt, not alone in the sphere of business, but through every phase of humanity.

Resolved, That Omaha reverently joins in the great memorial services in which the whole nation is engaged to-night, and tenders its tribute of affectionate regard to the august memory of the great man who, by the evident inspiration of Almighty God, has done more than any other to conquer the wildest elements of nature, and to demonstrate the superiority of the human intellect over all material things.

Adopted.

J. H. MILLARD,
Mayor.

Speaker Blaine said that Professor Morse was born on the slope of Bunker Hill, and he had the honor to introduce General N. P. Banks, in whose district Bunker Hill is located, and who would deliver the concluding address of the evening, and whose voice was always welcome to an American audience.

REMARKS OF HON. N. P. BANKS.

It is only by compulsion that I trespass upon your time at this hour. The earliest messages by the telegraph are among the most striking illustrations of its power in promoting the interests of Christian civilization and the unity of nations. "What hath God wrought!" These words, which involuntarily spring to the lips when the telegraph is named, were the first that flashed over the wires established by the wise munificence of the American Government. How well they express the emotions that are excited by the contemplation of this weird mechanism! We cannot question the authenticity of this first dispatch, since it is known that a woman was present to suggest it. Since the construction of the line from Washington to Baltimore, what progress has been made in the transmission and extension of the sphere of human intelligence! Thoughts of domestic affection, the decrees of public administration, protocols of peace and war, the feverish pulsations of finance, the startling revelations of life and death, the terrible transformations of earth and air are received and judged at the same instant from the center to the circumference of the earth. Time has no duration, distance no space, the physical world no barrier, the impalpable air no capacity to bar or delay the magic messenger. Over what mountains, through what subterraneous caves of unfathomed ocean, by what dark defiles, past what crowded cities and States, with what lightning speed, by what incomprehensible power, our most secret thought flashes onward, silent as the ecstatic bliss of souls that by intelligence converse, gathering sustenance and strength from its courses through fire, water, earth, and air, until it reaches its goal at the utmost parts of the earth, ere we can say, "It is gone!" Whoever received intelligence from this source without a thrill? Who has been served by it without a new and imposing sense of the divinity of man? And yet how little we know of it! To what great changes in the destiny of nations it may hereafter lead! Whoever would know the ultimate power of the telegraph must seek wiser men than any of this generation. To discover its limits we must be able to solve the mysteries of the great hereafter. It is not given to the reason, nor the imagination, nor the divination of man to anticipate its triumphs. We can estimate the future only by what we know of the past. Our comprehension is limited to the recognition of each successive wonder as it may be revealed to us, and then we can do no more than repeat the inspired language incorporated in the first telegram: "What hath God wrought!"

Capitalists did not favor the enterprise, but they soon learned to avail themselves of its advantages. Intelligent and practical men, however, were satisfied by other dispatches that the telegraph might prove, after all, in business affairs, what a Yankee would call "handy."

One early return-message, if not the first from Baltimore, was addressed to President Tyler, whose name is borne upon the statute authorizing the construction of the telegraph. Its author must have been of the masculine gender. The President did not then enjoy that untroubled repose which innocent minds now accord to the possessor of Executive power. His political relations were infelicitous.

His correspondent comprehended the situation. "How is the President?" said he. "Better," said the President, "since Congress adjourned." There may be some virtue still left in that medicine; but I doubt if magnetic, electric, or telegraphic power could ever satisfy the permanent occupants of these classichalls of that fact.

A more signal exhibition of its general utility was lately given at an evening party in London, upon the completion of the cable between England and India, through the Bay of Biscay, the Mediterranean and Red Seas and the Indian Ocean. The ordinary parlor furniture was re-inforced by a temporary telegraphic connection with the great London lines, and the lady of the house, as a substitute for music and cards, allowed her guests to shower compliments and congratulations upon their friends in different parts of the world. Mr. Lesseps, the projector of the Suez Canal, called up the Khedive of Egypt, at Cairo. The Viceroy of India entered into conversation with the President of the United States, at Washington, a distance of 8,443 miles or more, a third of the circumference of the globe. The President congratulated the Viceroy, in return, on having established communication with the rest of the world. The conversation lasted forty minutes. The countess of Mayo called up her husband at Simla, to know how her boys were. The King of Portugal responded to an inquiry in five minutes—less time than any question was ever answered in Congress. The Prince of Wales sent a message to President Grant, which was received three hours earlier than it was sent, that being the difference in time between London and Washington. The Pesident is often ahead of time, and occasionally a little in advance of some younger people. Having thus honored the principal dignitaries of the earth, the ladies and gentlemen found a novel source of amusement in making late evening calls upon their friends in different parts of the world.

What has been done can be repeated; and if the ladies and gentlemen present are disturbed by unexpected messages from Europe,

Asia, Africa, America, or, to use a parliamentary phrase, " another place," they must attribute it to the sensitive and excited condition of telegraphic elements upon this memorable occasion, that calls together, in all parts of the world, those who desire to honor its immortal founder.

The occasion justifies some personal consideration of the great man who is now universally recognized as the creator of the telegraph. The honorable gentlemen who preceded me have portrayed his character with felicitous and generous fidelity. I am grateful that they left me the privilege of presenting one or two observations upon the subject.

The touching recital which Colonel Strother, his pupil, gave a day or two since of the struggles through which Professor Morse worked out his great destiny, the poverty and hunger which paralyzed his energies even in the opulent and generous city of New York, reveals to us the evidence it furnishes of his confidence in the great conception which filled his soul, of his patience in suffering, his manly pride, his integrity of character, his devotion to the duty that his own genius imposed upon him! It is another deathless name to be inscribed upon the list of benefactors of the human race, who, like the poets, learned in suffering what is told in song.

There is, doubtless, some connection between the profession of Mr. Morse and the invention which gave him renown. The cultivation of the imagination, which naturally resulted from his studies in art, imparted a clearer insight into the nature of things than another course of life might have given. It revealed to him affinities, and led him to conclusions not obvious to other minds. Genius is, in truth, the capacity to discern the relation of things and events to each other which apparently have no connection. This quality of mind Mr. Morse exhibited throughout his career. In the intervals of professional labor he suggested mechanical improvements with facility, but improvements did not satisfy him; the creative power had greater fascination. It was what he learned in conversation with Dr. Jackson and Professor Henry of experiments in magnetism and electricity, and the possibility of transmitting intelligence by electricity, that permanently aroused the dormant energies of his soul.

It is said that he had very little knowledge of the general principles of electricity, magnetism, or electro-magnetism. If the civil-service commission had tested his capacity to solve the great problem which had long occupied the thoughts of scientific men, it would undoubtedly have reported him imcompetent for the work. It was not his ambition to learn what other people knew, but to discover what they did not know. He had heard that an electric current would pass instantaneously through a length of wire, and his passion was to discover how intelligence could be transmitted by means of these electric forces. His success is one of innumerable proofs that the greatest of all fallacies is the saying that "a little learning is a dangerous thing."

One of the finest passages in Shakespeare is found in the account of the tragedy of Bottom, the weaver, and Snug, the joiner, the players that, in the "Midsummer Night's Dream," assembled to celebrate the nuptials of the prince—those hard-handed men of Athens, that never labored in their minds till then. "Ah!" said the court chamberlain to the prince, at the opening of the tragedy, "It is not for you. I have heard it over, and it is nothing, nothing in the world." They have very little knowledge of the great principles of magnetism, electricity, or electro-magnetism. But the prince said, "Let them come in. The best are but shadows, and the worst none the worse if imagination can amend them."

The best of the men of science are but shadows, and Mr. Morse was but the shadow of a shadow. Yet he had "imagination" to "amend" their deficiencies. Had he devoted his life to the study of the sciences it is possible he might never have discovered the telegraph. To coin uncommon images you must avoid common currents of thought.

It is probable that the plan of his telegraph struck the inventor the instant he gave his mind to the subject, and that the years of harrowing care that crossed his path were spent in devising the machinery to execute his conception. He fixed to a short bar of iron, attracted by an electro-magnet, a lever with a pencil attached, which marked paper moving upon a cylinder, made to revolve by clock-work. It was this "method of recording" that constituted his invention. We can now see that there was "imagination" in his ignorance.

There had been many imperfect plans, but Morse had the "imagination" to "amend" them. One hundred and forty-three years had been spent in vain efforts to accomplish the result. Twenty different telegraphs had been constructed without success. Grey, Bishop, Watson, Franklin, Lesage, Lomond, Reusser, Boeckman, Salva, Betancourt, Ronald, Dyer, Somering, Steinheil, Professor Henry, Dr. Jackson, Ampère, Gonon, Servell, St. Amand, Schelling, Gauss, Weber, Cooke, Wheatstone, and others—Englishmen, Frenchmen, Germans, and Americans—contended for the mastery of the electro-magnetic forces and the secret of transmitting intelligence by their occult power.

At last, after nearly a century and a half of unsatisfied though not fruitless labor, came our great countryman, whose triumphs as an inventor, united to the simplicity of his character and the spotless purity of his life, have won for him the admiration and respect of mankind.

"The world moves!" Galileo said it long since, when he was compelled to retract his theory of the planetary system: "*E pur se muove.*" It moves nevertheless. It was his only protest, and it traversed the centuries like the cry of oppressed truth protesting against ignorance and persecution.

' Fifty years ago the prominent nations were organized upon ideas of family, dynasties, and artificial forms of political society, dictated by accident or custom. Mountains and seas interposed, made enemies of nations that ought, like kindred drops, to have mingled into one. The great nations of the earth are now established upon the recognition of races that represent ties of consanguinity and blood,—the great stem—families created by God

Social organizations now struggling into existence, disregarding the ties of nationality and of race, are pressing the world forward to a more elevated and expansive unity. Christianity, commerce, literature, art, science, discovery, invention, are agents of a nobler civilization than the world has yet attained. The great business corporations which control the principal industrial interests of mankind are breaking down the barriers that have obstructed communication between States. The Asiatic nations have thrown off the traditions of isolation and exclusion that characterized their history for centuries.

These stupendous changes have been accomplished in a great degree by the remarkable discoveries and inventions of the present century, most of which have been of American origin. The steamship and the railway, which is the steamboat applied to land navigation, afford limitless facilities for international communication. The photograph, the discovery of Daguerre, familiarizes all nations with the portraiture, customs, traditions, and the prominent incidents in each day's history of the world. The sewing-machine is gradually bringing all people to one common standard of dress. And the telegraph affords the whole human race the means of instantaneous communication with all parts of the globe. We have but to establish a uniform system of coinage and currency, a common standard of weights and measures, an approximation to a common language, to found governments upon the basis of public opinion in order to bring the world to a common brotherhood—that universal democracy, founded upon justice, and recognizing the Creator as the father of all, for which philosophy, philanthropy, and Christianity, have been so long seeking. Of these agencies the telegraph is first in importance and power. It is the point of union between the improvements of the past and the progress of the future; no single achievement of man surpasses it in importance since it was said, "Let there be light, and there was light!"

The mysterious connection between art and invention, as manifested by Fulton, Daguerre, and Morse, deserves at our hands a recognition that shall adequately express our appreciation of their great importance to modern civilization. It is not for me to suggest what this shall be; but I cannot forbear to express the opinion that the telegraph—the invention of that illustrious American whose life we honor and whose memory we revere—ought not to be monopolized for personal interests or prostituted to the aggrandizement of gigantic speculative corporations. It is the duty of the Government to place this power—the greatest ever wielded by man—within the reach of the humblest citizen, and to dedicate it forever to the commonest necessities of each day's life. We owe this to the memory of the illustrious American who left it as his legacy to mankind. It will constitute at once the noblest monument to his genius and the greatest benefit to his race.

I have the honor to represent the city which gave him birth. He drew his first breath from the pure atmosphere of Bunker Hill. The city of Charlestown, in Massachusetts, honored as his birth-place—the home of his youth, to which he turned his thoughts near the close of his career—still cherishes the products of his genius which distinguished his earlier profession. It was just that Charlestown, the first to resist the oppression of a foreign government, should have given to the world the grand promoter of universal intelligence. They revere the memory of those who secured to them civil and religious liberty, and they will honor the memory of their fellow-citizen who has closed his career as one of the noblest benefactors of the age in which he lived. They will still hope to receive from him the benefit of his inspiration, as of his example and his works. Death is but a step in life. One who achieved such distinction by such sacrifices and such triumphs in this world, we may hope, at least, will find a place of dignity among the divinities of another, from which he will keep watch and ward over those whom he knew and loved so well. There is nothing absurd or sinful in our aspirations for a closer uniting between a mortal and an immortal existence.

What if the rose were born a lily, and by force of heat and eagerness for light grew late and fair! Then 'twere a true type of the first fiery name that makes a low name honorable. They who take it by inheritance alone, adding no brightness to it, are like stars seen in the ocean that were never seen but from their bright originals in Heaven.

The following additional telegrams were then read:

[Telegram dated Philadelphia, April 16, 1872.]

To Hon. JAMES G. BLAINE, *Chairman :*

Philadelphia unites with the rest of our continent in doing homage to the memory of the illustrious deceased, and to-night a large assemblage has come together in the hall hallowed by memories of Franklin, the great discoverer, to pay tribute to the genius of Morse, the great inventor.

WILLIAM S. STOKELY,
Mayor of Philadelphia.

Resolved, That, in grateful remembrance of the services that he rendered humanity through the power of his genius of invention, which has united by electric currents the people of the whole world, it becomes us, the citizens of Philadelphia, to join with the nations of the earth to recognize in an appropriate manner an event of such solemn significance as the removal by death, from his long-time

sphere of honor and usefulness, Professor Samuel F. B. Morse.   His
fame is of all future time; his works, wrought by God, as he said, are
for all people, but the daily beauty and excellence of his eminent
Christianity, his generous culture, abiding gentleness and broad sympathy, are chiefly the remembrance and the loss of his own countrymen, among whom he lived, wrought, suffered, and died.   As representatives of the city of Philadelphia, wherein Franklin first
proclaimed man's power over the lightning; who brought it from
the clouds, bound servant to the earth, it is especially proper that
we should unite in expressions of regret and sorrow for Professor
Morse, who at a later day gave to the lightning voice; caused it
to speak the language of all lands, and to carry hither and thither, as
on the wings of the wind, messages of little and great moment.
That, while recognizing the mortal death of Professor Morse, we also
know that he still lives, not alone in the infinite peace of the blessed,
but in the daily usefulness of the invention he gave to mankind and
in the grateful remembrances of humanity, whom his genius helped
forward to a higher plane of enlightenment.   With those who were
near and dear to him we desire to sympathize and to offer them such
condolence as their great loss demands, and our sorrow and regret
can convey.

W. S. STOKELY, *Mayor.*

[Telegram dated Harper's Ferry West. Va , April 16, 1872.]

To A. S. SOLOMONS,

National Telegraph Memorial Monument Association,
Washington:

Maryland and Loudoun Heights unite to mourn the death of him
whose name will never die, and whose genius gave practical effect
to the promptings of nature, and made all the world akin.

J. J. KENN,
Representing Municipality of Harper's Ferry, West Va.

[Telegram dated Augusta, Me., April 16, 1872.]

To the PRESIDENT OF THE NATIONAL MEMORIAL MEETING.
House of Representatives, Washington:

At a mass-meeting of the citizens of Augusta, called in conformity with the resolves of the National Telegraphic Memorial Monument Association, the following resolution was unanimously adopted:

Resolved, That the people of this city unite with the people of the United States and of the civilized world in expressing their reverence for the memory of the great inventor of the telegraph, Samuel F. B. Morse.

J. J. EVELETH,
President.

S. W. LANE, *Secretary.*

[Telegram dated Moberly, Mo., April 16, 1872.]

To A. S. SOLOMONS,

     Chairman, Washington :

We beg leave to express our deep regret at the loss of him whose genius developed a new field of service; made our profession what it is, and gave to commerce its most valuable auxiliary.

EMPLOYÉS

Saint Louis, Kansas and Northern Railroad of Missouri.

[Telegram dated York, Pa., April 16, 1872.]

To Hon. Speaker J. G. BLAINE,

     Washington, D. C.:

At a meeting of ladies and gentlemen assembled here in the Court-House, under the auspices of the *York County Historical Society,* the Hon. Adam J. Glossbrenner was called upon to preside. Mr. Heiges, who proposed Mr. Glossbrenner, made mention that he was for thirteen years a trustee of the first telegraph company organized in the country, and also, while a member of Congress, gave his active and zealous support to the schemes of Professor Morse to establish his system. Mr. Glossbrenner on taking the chair expressed his gratification on being called on to preside over a meeting called to do honor to the greatest inventor of the age. David Small, esq., and James Kell, esq., were elected vice-presidents, and Levi Maish, secretary.

Rev. Mr. Baum made a beautiful and impressive prayer.

M. J. Eichelberger, esq., Capt. W. H. Laniur, Prof. S. B. Heiges, Hiram Young, and Joseph Rool, were appointed to draught appropriate resolutions.   During the absence of the committee, Rev. H. E. Niles made a very interesting address.   He narrated a number of personal recollections of Professor Morse's early struggles in Congress, in his efforts to get assistance from the general government, and mentioned the names of some of the public men through whose zealous support he was enabled to introduce his great invention. He also mentioned the fact that a young lady, a favorite of Professor Morse, Miss Ellsworth, was permitted to dictate the first message transmitted over the first line established, and that she gave the Scripture quotation, "What hath God wrought!"   The committee on resolutions reported a series of resolutions expressive of the deep veneration in which Professor Morse was held for his great inventive genius and moral worth.   They were directed to be deposited in the archives of the Historical Society, and published in all the papers of the borough.   Interesting and appropriate remarks were also made by George W. Heiges, esq., and Prof. S. B. Heiges.   After a benediction by the Rev. Charles West Thompson, the meeting adjourned.

A. J. GLOSSBRENNER,

President.

[Telegram dated Memphis, Tenn., April 16, 1872.]

To Hon. J. G. BLAINE,

Speaker House Representatives, Washington:

A meeting of citizens was held this evening at the office of the telegraph-superintendent, when, on motion, Col. James Coleman, superintendent of the sixth district, was called to the chair, and Charles A. Stearns appointed secretary.   The chairman explained the object of the meeting, which was to pay appropriate honors to the late Professor S. F. B. Morse, inventor of the telegraph.

On motion of Mr. C. McCarthy, a committee was appointed to draught a paper expressive of the sentiments of the meeting. The committee was composed of Col. Leon Trousdale, II. A. Montgomery, and Barney Hughes, who reported the following, which was adopted by acclamation:

A quarter of a century ago, through the invention of S. F. B. Morse, intelligence was flashed between cities, along the telegraph-wires, and space was annihilated. So far as the communication of ideas are concerned, mankind were naturally astonished, if not incredulous, at the announcement and successful working of an experiment so remarkable in its character and so beneficent in its results; a contrivance so promotive of civilization and enlightenment spread throughout the Union, almost as rapidly as the spider in a summer night weaves her shining webs over the fields and forests. The other continents soon joyfully accepted the call to electric communication, until far along, from peak to peak the rattling crags among them, leaps the live thunder, not from one lone cloud, but every mountain, found a tongue, and not only the mountains but the watery plain has been subjected to the touch of a genius which seems almost an inspiration, or a miracle, so vast was the conception; and it can no longer be said that man's steps are not upon ocean's paths, for continents, kingdoms, empires, and republics are linked in the embrace of instant communication through the pathless waves, by the sublime genius of him who has connected his name with the most wondrous invention, which circles the earth daily with one continuous and unbroken strain of intelligence and intercommunication. There are but four inventions to which that of Morse is comparable: the printing-press, which disseminates thought through multitudinous leaves day by day; the telescope, which draws nearer to our vision the heavenly bodies, and enables man to calculate their magnitudes and view their phenomena; the mariner's compass, which has given him the power to sail safely through all seas and mark out highways on the fields of ocean ; and the steam-engine, that swift messenger of locomotion on land and sea : but above all these, the invention of the telegraph, towers like the highest peak above neighboring mountains of the same chain. The death of Professor Morse, at the ripe age of eighty-one years, crowned as he was with the princeliest honors that could be conferred on a man by admiring mankind, excites the liveliest sensibilities in us, who have been associated with a profession of which he was the creator, and we therefore unite with our brethren who are assembled this evening at Washington City, and in every important city on the continent, in bearing our emphatic and sincere testimony to the grandeur of such a character, which was illustrated no less by the highest genius than the gentlest virtues of a great and good man.

The chairman of the committee, Col. Leon Trousdale, secretary of the Chamber of Commerce and secretary of the Agricultural and Mechanical Association, made very appropriate remarks, setting forth the eminent service to mankind which had been rendered by Professor Morse in the invention of the telegraph, placing him above Galileo, Fulton, and other great benefactors of mankind. Colonel Coleman, chairman of the meeting, paid a beautiful tribute to the pre-eminent services of Professor Morse. The Signal-Corps was represented by Mr. Samuel W. Rhode.

[Telegram dated Baltimore, April 16, 1872.]

Hon. A. S. SOLOMONS,

    Chairman, Washington :

The citizens of Baltimore and the friends of the late Professor Morse are now assembled in the " Morse building," and send the following:

To the MORSE MEMORIAL ASSOCIATION,

      Washington, greeting :

The city of Baltimore, between which and Washington, in 1843, the first electric telegraph was laid by S. F. B. Morse, and which transmitted from one to the other the glad tidings, as well as the convincing proof, of the success of his great invention, unites through the same wonderful agency to-night with the National capital in doing honor to his memory and in celebrating, while illustrating, the triumph of his genius. The limited circle first quickened by the electric fire has reproduced itself in multiplied and enlarged circles till they have embraced the circumference of the earth. The spark then kindled survives the great inventor's death, and, like the spirit that conceived it, still lives, keeping pace with that spirit in its immortal circuit, radiating through day and night, and through all seasons and climes, imparting currents of light and beneficence to mankind. Thus hath God wrought!

Resolved, That this meeting shares with the world in regretting the loss which mankind has sustained in the death of Professor Morse.

Resolved, That it is some consolation that, although dead, he "still lives." His great invention, which can neither be fully appreciated nor exaggerated, will forever give him a place in the hearts of his fellow-men.

Resolved, That proud as Massachusetts may be of having given him birth, she will admit that the whole country has a right to claim him.

Resolved, That Maryland would seem to have some peculiar title in his fame, from the fact that the first practical experiment of his invention was made by wires between Washington and Baltimore, and that the material aid which enabled him to make such experiment was an appropriation by Congress, adopted at the instance of one of her sons, the late John P. Kennedy, then Secretary of the Navy.

JOSHUA VANSANT,
Chairman.

CHAS. G. KERR, A. WILSON, Jr., *Secretaries.*

MEMORIAL MEETINGS.

MEMORIAL MEETINGS.

The following is a record of memorial meetings held in different parts of the country:

IN THE CONGRESS OF THE UNITED STATES, WASHINGTON.

In the House of Representatives, Hon. Mr. Cox, of New York, offered a concurrent resolution, which was agreed to, declaring that Congress has heard with profound regret of the death of Professor Samuel F. B. Morse, whose distinguished and varied abilities have contributed more than those of any other person to the development and progress of the practical arts, and that his purity of private life, his loftiness of scientific aims, and his resolute faith in truth render it eminently proper that the Representatives and Senators of the United States should solemnly testify to his worth and greatness.

The National Academy of Design, of which he was the founder and the first president; the New York Chamber of Commerce, and various societies and corporations of the city of New York have adopted resolutions of respect.

A large meeting of citizens of Washington was held in that city, on Thursday evening, to take action in relation to the death of Professor Morse. Arrangements were made for the use of the hall of the House of Representatives for imposing memorial services in honor of the late Professor, which took place on Tuesday evening, April 16, at which distinguished gentlemen delivered addresses.

The following resolution was unanimously adopted:

"*Resolved*, That the people of the United States be requested to meet in their respective cities, towns, and villages, on the evening of the 16th day of April, at 8 o'clock, to give expression to the loss sustained by the world in the death of Professor Samuel Finley Breese Morse, and to hold simultaneous communication by telegraph with the assembly of the people's representatives and the citizens of Washington convened for the like purpose in the Capital of the nation."

To this the Western Union Telegraph Company sent a prompt response:

To A. S. SOLOMONS, Esq.

Chairman:

MY DEAR SIR: I am authorized by Mr. Orton, our president, to say to you that the Company will cheerfully grant the use of our wires for direct communication between the simultaneous Morse Memorial meetings which it is proposed to hold. Please advise me of the date fixed upon for the meeting.

Very truly yours,

LEONARD WHITNEY,

Manager.

A committee of five on resolutions, with Senator Patterson as chairman, and a committee of arrangements of fifteen, with Mr. A. S. Solomons as chairman, were appointed with full power to act.

MEETING AT BOSTON, MASS.

A public meeting was held at Faneuil Hall, Boston, on the evening of April 16. under the auspices of the Mayor and the city council, to afford an opportunity for a public expression of respect for the memory of the late Samuel F. B. Morse. The attendance was quite as large as could have been expected at a meeting of this kind. Previous to the opening of the exercises the Germania Band performed funeral marches in the musicians' gallery. The speakers of the evening were greeted with applause when they entered. Among those who took seats on the platform were his honor the Mayor, the Hon. Josiah Quincy, the Hon. R. H. Dana, the Hon. George S. Hillard, Collector Russell, ex-Mayors Wightman, Norcross, and Lincoln, E. P. Whipple, esq., M. G. Farmer, esq., of Salem, the inventors of the fire-alarm telegraph, the Hon. Peter Harvey,

Professor Horsford, the Hon. C. W. Slack, Aldermen Little, President Dickinson of the Common Council, and several other distinguished gentlemen.

OFFICERS OF THE MEETING.

After calling the meeting to order the mayor called upon Mr. Wood, the New England superintendent of the Western Union Telegraph, to read a list of the gentlemen who had been selected to be the vice-presidents of the meeting. Mr. Wood read the following names :

Vice-Presidents.—His Excellency William B. Washburn, Hon. William Claflin, Hon. H. H. Coolidge, Hon. Josiah Quincy, Hon. John E. Sanford, Hon. Alexander H. Rice, Hon. F. W. Lincoln, Hon. Otis Norcross, Hon. Marshall P. Wilder, Hon. Emory Washburn, Hon. John H. Clifford, Hon. J. M. Wightman, Hon. N. B. Shurtleff, Hon. Thomas Russell, Hon. George B. Upton, Hon. E. R. Mudge, Hon. Harvey Jewell, Hon. Alpheus Hardy, Hon. George S. Hillard, Professor Samuel Eliot, Professor J. D. Runkle, Hon. S. H. Walley, Hon. B. R. Curtis, Hon. William Gray, Hon. George C. Richardson, Hon. Albert Fearing, Hon. R. A. Chapman, Hon. Horace Gray, jr., Hon. John Wells, Hon. J. D. Colt, Hon. Seth Ames, Hon. Marcus Morton, Hon. George B. Loring, Hon. Lorenzo Sabine, Homer Bartlett, esq., Col Thomas Aspinwall, William Perkins, esq., J. M. Forbes, esq., Gardner Brewer, esq., Nathan Carruth, esq., Amos A. Lawrence, esq., James L. Little, esq., Francis Bacon, esq., James M. Beebe, esq., Edward Austin, esq., J. Ingersol Bowditch, esq., Roland Worthington, esq., Henry L. Pierce, esq., Benjamin E. Bates, esq., Benjamin T. Reed, esq., James T. Fields, esq., Samuel Little, esq., M. F. Dickinson, jr., esq., Hon. E. S. Tobey, William B. Spooner, esq., Col. Charles G. Greene, Hon. Henry W. Paine, Hon. William Whiting, Hon. George Lewis, Hon. H. O. Houghton, Hon. William H. Kent, Edward Atkinson, esq., Charles W. Slack, esq., Hon. S. N. Stockwell, Delano A. Goddard, esq.,

George L. Ward, esq., Joseph J. Ropes, esq., William Parsons, esq., Avery Plumer, esq., J. C. Converse, esq., Nathaniel H. Emmons, esq., F. B. Crowninshield, esq., N. J. Bradle, Charles F. Jenkins, Weston Lewis, W. W. Greenough, T. C. Amory, Charles H. Allen, Samuel C. Cobb, George B. Nichols, Charles W. Wilder, Alvan Adams, R. B. Forbes, Edward Whitney, Hamilton A. Hill, Nathaniel Adams, Nathan Crowell, George B. Faunce, S. D. Warren, Nathan Mathews, Cyrus Wakefield, Nehemiah Gibson, G. W. Pope.

Secretaries.—Charles F. Wood, William G. Blanchard, M. P. Kennard.

The Mayor then read the letter and resolution from the Chairman of the National Telegraph Memorial Monument Association, suggesting that the meeting be held simultaneously with meetings in other parts of the country, and said :

LADIES AND GENTLEMEN : Several distinguished citizens have consented to appear here to-night and address you. They are gentlemen known here and everywhere in the country, and there will therefore be no occasion to announce them otherwise than by their names. I will first introduce to you the Hon. Josiah Quincy.

Mr. Quincy read the following :

Resolved, That the city of Boston, in common with the rest of the country and the whole civilized world, feels sensibly the loss which science has sustained in the death of Professor Morse, whose great invention has been of incalculable value to all the interests of life, and has conferred lasting honor upon his country.

Resolved, That it is peculiarly incumbent upon us to express our sense of the loss which the world has sustained in the death of the eminent benefactor of the human race, from the fact that he was born among us, and that his early training was drawn from the institutions of New England.   (Applause.)

LETTER FROM ROBERT C. WINTHROP.

The secretary next read the following communication :

BROOKLINE, April 16. 1872.

DEAR MR. MAYOR : I am sincerely sorry that a previous engagement for this evening will prevent my attendance at the meeting to which you have so kindly invited me. It would have given me peculiar satisfaction to take part in the proposed tribute to the memory of Professor Morse. I could hardly, indeed, have said much of " the loss sustained in his death." Spared, as he was, to a venerable old age, with his great work fully accomplished and universally recognized, nothing remained for him but to " put on that immortality" to which he had ever looked forward with a Christian's hope and faith. There is no loss in such a death. But the gain and the glory which the nation has derived from his life would have furnished such a subject of remark as has rarely been presented at any public commemoration.

When Professor Morse first appealed to the Government of the United States for aid in his telegraphic experiments, thirty years ago, it was my fortune not only to be a Representative in Congress from the city of Boston, but to be a member of the Committee on Commerce, to which his appeal was referred, and by which the first appropriation in his behalf was reported. I rejoice to remember that I supported that appropriation both in committee and in the House, though not a few around me were either leaving their seats to avoid the responsibility of the measure, or remaining only to deride and oppose it. Boston may thus claim to-night to have contributed at least one vote to the original success of the great enterprise.

Two years afterward I stood in the throng on the steps of the Capitol, while the first formal messages were passing along the magic chords between Washington and Baltimore; and when the announcement of Mr. Polk's nomination for the Presidency, a few seconds only after it had been decided upon by a convention, forty or fifty miles off, with the tender of the Vice-Presidency to **Mr. Silas Wright**, refused in our presence as soon as made, gave us all the earliest and most vivid impression, not merely that a new kind of *wire-pulling* had entered into politics, but that a mysterious and marvelous power of the air had at length been subdued and trained to the service of mankind.

Since then I need not say the triumphs of the electric-telegraph, over land and over sea, have made themselves felt in every sphere, public and private, throughout the world, and have literally come home to every man's fortunes and fireside.

We of Massachusetts do not forget that Morse, like Franklin and Count Rumford, pursued his researches and achieved his successes far away from the place of his birth. But we cannot forget, also, that the native soil of them all is contained within the same narrow boundaries which include Lexington and Bunker Hill and Faneuil Hall.

We have thus something of a peculiar right and duty to unite in doing honor to the name and fame of Professor Morse, and to count them and cherish them among our own historical treasures.

Regretting once more my inability to be with you,

I am, dear sir, with great respect and regard,

Yours, faithfully,

ROBERT C. WINTHROP.

His Honor WILLIAM GASTON,

Mayor of Boston.

A TELEGRAPHIC DISPATCH FROM WASHINGTON.

The secretary announced that the following dispatch had been received:

WASHINGTON, D. C.,

April 16, 1872—7.45 p. m.

TO MEETINGS NOW IN SESSION AT:

Chicago, Milwaukee, Saint Paul, Saint Louis, Pittsburgh, Cincinnati, Indianapolis, Louisville, San Francisco, Memphis, Charleston,

Savannah, Mobile, New Orleans, Montreal, Worcester, Mass., Portland, Augusta, Me., Lynn, Mass., Boston, Warrenton, Mass., Concord, N. H., New Haven:

The National Morse Memorial Meeting is now in progress in the Hall of the House of Representatives, Speaker Blaine, assisted by the Vice-President of the United States, presiding, and the Governors of the several States acting as vice-presidents—and is now ready to receive communications.

A. S. SOLOMONS,
Chairman.

REMARKS OF PROFESSOR HORSFORD.

The Mayor then introduced Professor Horsford, of Cambridge, who read a long and admirable sketch of the development of the magnetic-telegraph, and of Professor Morse's connection therewith. He first gave an account of the discovery of electricity, and the attempts that were made to utilize it before his time. The following portions of his address were of especial interest:

In 1832, Professor Samuel Finley Breese Morse was returning from France on board the packet-ship *Sully*. Among the topics of conversation on that memorable voyage was the possibility of the practical electric-telegraph, in view of the recent discoveries in the departments of electricity, magnetism, and galvanism; and during that voyage the resolution was formed by him to enter upon and prosecute the necessary experimental researches required to produce a working telegraph. It may be fairly presumed that Professor Morse, whose previous life had not been devoted to scientific pursuits, on that occasion gathered from all with whom he conversed on the subject all they were in condition to impart. It cannot be doubted by any who know him, that Dr. Charles S. Jackson, of our city, who was a fellow-passenger in the *Sully*, cheerfully imparted his conviction of the possibility and practicability of the telegraph in the light of the discoveries that had recently been made.

But "the testimony to the paternity of the idea in Morse's mind and to his act and drawings on board the ship is ample."

This possibility was recognized by electricians generally, "but to perfect it, ingenuity of a high order was called into play, together with much study and perseverance." Before completing the voyage, Professor Morse had, according to his own account, worked out and committed to paper the general plan of his *registering telegraph*.

Of the progress of Professor Morse's invention from 1832, to September 27, 1837, when he exhibited his registering telegraph, those who are familiar with the difficulties of invention generally can form some idea; how many devices he had tested and thrown aside, the world will probably never know. He experimented at great length in the direction of a chemical telegraph, but was not satisfied with his results. His mind settled upon the idea of a mark or succession of marks requiring pressure. I am not aware that at this early period he had any idea of employing, as the medium of transmitting intelligence, the sound which accompanies each mark as made in the modern Morse instrument. It was my privilege to be shown by Professor Morse in 1840, (and I shall never forget the charm with which he invested the two hours he gave to me, an utter stranger) the original instrument first exhibited by him in 1837. It resembled in external appearance a small melodeon, having a key-board on which were the letters, the figures, periods, commas, &c. These keys were levers. The ends of the levers, distant from the seat of the operator, were attached to segments of brass circular disks, upon the rims of which were prominences and depressions of unequal length, so arranged that the prominences would close, and the depressions open the magnetic circuit, and thus magnetize and demagnetize a bar of soft iron. When magnetized, the bar of iron drew to itself one end of an iron lever, to the other end of which a pencil or pen was attached, the point of which, by this action of the magnet, was pressed against a moving ribbon of paper; when the bar was demagnetized, the lever was restored to its original position by a spring, and the pencil lifted from the paper. It is easy to see that an arrangement of prominences and depressions on the brass segments might be so contrived that each key should produce its own particular set of dots, lines, and spaces. This was the first practical registering telegraph, if we except possibly the experimental results of Steinheil—which were to Professor Morse absolutely unknown—which traced lines and dots upon a ribbon of paper, as well as produced sounds upon a series of bells, but which never came into practical use. Steinheil's paper was not published till 1838, and he abandoned his own device and adopted Morse's in its place. Cooke, of England, when a student at Heidelberg in 1836, conceived the idea of a telegraph from an experiment which he witnessed at the university, in which the deflection of the magnetic needle was caused by the electric current. He produced in that year an instrument illustrating his plan, and associated himself with Professor Wheatstone, and they together applied for a patent, which was issued to them on the 12th of June, 1837. They employed at that time five magnetic needles and coils, and either five or six wires. Morse used only one. The telegraph of Cooke and Wheatstone, in its greatest perfection, addresses itself to the eye for the interpretation of its signals. It makes no record. Morse's telegraph records its message in permanent characters.

It rarely happens that all the stages of an important and useful discovery of this class are presided over by one mind. More frequently the earlier and later stages fall into different hands. In this event the rewards are divided. The nearer one is to the conclusion of the series, the larger uniformly is his measure of material return. Where all have been the offspring of one mind, the honors and pecuniary emoluments enter alike into the reward. Where the naked speculation or suggestion only can be claimed, or where a crude device merely had been proposed and success predicted, the author will be assigned a place in the world's esteem, distinguished in some degree in proportion to the chances and detail of his plans and predictions. If it be not as high as the man of suggestion sometimes deems his due, it is because the applause of mankind seems to be reserved for its heroes—the men who have not only encountered difficulty, but made its conquest—rather than for its men of speculation, whose influence on the well-being of the race is more transient, or, if lasting, less direct.

The common sense of the world has made a uniform and, we must believe, a just discrimination in its award of merit to him who, patiently following the lead of a conception, has brought to successful issue and recognition new agencies for advancing civilization, rather than to them who equally with the former had the same happy conception, and had it even at an earlier date, but neglected the duties nature prescribed as the condition of fruition. The step from the first more or less vague conception of a new truth to its conclusive demonstration, is a matter of far more importance and difficulty than the happy and sometimes, to all appearances, intuitive guesses which have invariably preceded every great discovery. Newton formed a right estimate of his own claims when he ascribed his success to the patient and laborious pertinacity with which he kept fast hold of an idea until, by long thinking and varied experiment, he has proved either its truth or its falsehood." (*Quarterly Review:* Newton as a scientific discoverer.)

The public journals of the time and of recent date have made us familiar with the details, the jeers, the buffetings, the struggle, the self-sacrifice which attended the effort to procure the appropriation by Congress of the money necessary to construct a line of telegraph between Baltimore and Washington. It is not my province on this occasion, however grateful such a task might be, to dwell upon them, nor upon the plaudits and honors and fortune that came at last to crown the noble life which has so recently closed.

' I will occupy but a moment further in defining what I conceive to be the more important of the just claims of Professor Morse as an inventor.   What was *his own?*

1st. The *idea*, the *conception* of a registering telegraph by chemical changes effected by the electric current, and by intermittent mechanical presence, seem both of them to have been absolutely original with Professor Morse.

2d. The *plans* by which the discoveries in electro-magnetism could be made serviceable to produce a registering telegraph were committed to paper by Professor Morse in 1832, and a portion of the actual apparatus which he had planned was completed in that year.

3d. In 1835, he had completed a single transmitting and receiving apparatus and exhibited it in successful operation to many witnesses.

4th. In 1837, he had completed an apparatus for transmitting and receiving and registering intelligence at both ends of the line.   He discovered and demonstrated that his conception of registration could be realized.

Now, Mr. Wheatstone's attention was *first* drawn to the matter by Cooke, and Cooke received his first notions from a lecture at Heidelberg in 1836; and in 1837, Cooke and Wheatstone obtained a patent. The invention patented by Cooke and Wheatstone was, at the best, but an improvement and simplification of the invention of Ampère in 1830, of Schilling in 1832-'33, and Gauss and Weber in 1833-'34, in which advantage was taken of the electro-magnet of Professor Henry.   Cooke and Wheatstone's was not a *registering* telegraph, but was dependent upon the deflections of a needle, the movements of which required the attention of the eye and a clerk to translate and write them out.   In point of time, Morse's transmitting and registering telegraph preceded Cooke and Wheatstone's transmitting and receiving telegraph.

Professor Morse was not satisfied with his attempts to produce registration by the chemical effects of the electric current.   *Visible* chemical phenomena were produced by Soemmering in 1809, and by Harrison G. Dyer in 1827, but the effects they produced did not permit *registration*.   It was reserved for Mr. Alexander Bain to carry to its fulfillment the idea of the registering chemical telegraph, which he patented in 1846.   [Davy obtained a patent for a similar but more complicated device as early as 1838.]

5th.   A great merit of the Morse apparatus is its extreme simplicity.   Time will not permit me to attempt to present the combination of various elements that enter into the Morse working telegraph, even if I were fully competent to such a task.   He is entitled to the honor of having *combined* all these various elements, to render possible and practicable the evolution of an original idea.

6th.   He is entitled to the further honor of having fought and conquered the difficulties which this effort of combination encountered. The strength, and faith, and patience, and courage with which he pursued his invention to its completion are the attributes which men honor.   If we do not credit to Professor Morse individual discoveries in electro-magnetism—which he never claimed—we ascribe to him the greater honor of having cast previous discoveries into the alembic of his own mind, and evolved the first practical registering telegraph, and so made those discoveries, by fusion with his own discoveries and inventions, subservient to the highest interests of civilization.

MORE DISPATCHES.

The secretary then read a dispatch from Hong-Kong, signed Fuller, and another from Egypt, signed Gibbs, together with some domestic dispatches.

REMARKS OF HON. R. H. DANA, JR.

The Mayor next introduced the Hon. R. H. Dana, jr., who said:

Mr. MAYOR AND LADIES AND GENTLEMEN: After such an event as the announcement of these dispatches from all parts of the world, any attempt to impress upon our own minds the value of this discovery seems to me to be more than useless.   Can we really bring it home to our minds that China and Egypt are conversing with Boston and Washington, and expressing their sympathy in the loss and their admiration of the character of this great discoverer?   Why, a few years ago, Mr. Mayor, when I went to China and to Japan, they seemed to me to be places very far off. I thought I never should get to Japan, and when I got there I didn't know that I should ever get away.   The Japanese embassadors now in Washington converse with their government daily by the wonderful invention of that man whom we are called together to honor to-night.

[Mr. Dana then paid Professor Horsford a very high compliment for his address, and continued:]

It is an honored custom of Boston, Mr. Mayor, that the Chief Magistrate of the city should call together the citizens whenever any great event has occurred in which we are all interested.   Especially has it been our custom to assemble together to mingle our sympathies and express our regrets when the community is deprived by death of the services of an illustrious citizen.   There are some upon this platform here, I know, who can remember when Faneuil Hall was filled to commemorate the death of the elder Adams.   There are some who can remember when Faneuil Hall was again filled to hear the eloquent notes of Everett on the death of the younger Adams, and again of Lafayette; and, sir, yesterday those flags, drooping from half mast, mourning the untimely fate of him who had upheld them, and the republic of which they were the symbols, in their darkest hours—they remind us, sir, of the days when this hall wore the symbols of mourning for the death of our great Chief Magistrate, patriot, and martyr.   As we are looking about this hall at these pictures that adorn its walls, we are reminded that it is mainly to the heroes, and patriots, and sages, and statesmen of the land that the honors of these occasions have been given.   But, sir, I am sure you will say—I am sure that all here present will say—that we are met to-night on an occasion worthy of this place, worthy of our best efforts, and appealing to the deepest feelings of every American. We are met to pay honors to one of the heroes of peace. It is right, eminently right, that the citizens of a republic should bear testimony—that the citizens of a republic more than those of any other government should give a generous recognition—to great public merit. Under the old systems in other parts of the world they have their modes of remunerating great public benefactors. There are orders of merit that are conferred upon them; there are titles of nobility and pensions to them and their descendants. To the latest generation, the descendant bears a title which everywhere and to all persons recalls the great benefactor upon whom that title was first conferred. Now, we citizens of a democratic republic have discarded all these methods of encouraging effort and rewarding success. We consider them to be unreasonable and unnecessary, and inconsistent with the fair rights and interests of the greatest number. But it has always seemed to me that for that very reason there is a ten-fold obligation resting upon the citizens of a republic to give the freest and most generous expression of gratitude and admiration to their fellow-citizens who have been the benefactors of their race. [Applause.] We confer upon Morse no title of nobility. We enroll his name in no legion of honor; but we give him the admiration of our understandings, and the warmest affections of our hearts. Mr. Mayor, I can contribute nothing like that which has been contributed by Professor Horsford of a scientific character respecting Mr. Morse. What little I can say of a humbler sort I respectfully submit to my fellow-citizens. In my boyhood I knew him; in my earliest manhood I knew him. I had the honor I may not truly say of his friendship, but certainly of his most friendly acquaintance. He was connected with those I most loved and honored in the world by ties, not of blood, but of affection and common pursuits and common studies; and I know from the earliest period, before he was known to the world as the great inventor, the marked affection and respect which was entertained for him by all persons who came within the range of his acquaintance. He was a youth of remarkable personal beauty, of very attractive manners, of a most enthusiastic temperament, a pure heart, and a blameless life. There are no drawbacks in the eulogies which we can pronounce upon Mr. Morse. All these characteristics he had ; and I am reminded to-night, by seeing upon the platform one of the war of 1812, and '14, whose vacant sleeve carries with it always the memory of the sortie of Fort Erie—I am reminded that Mr. Morse with two or three other Boston citizens was, unfortunately, overtaken and detained in London by the unexpected breaking out of the war. I have frequently heard these gentlemen, his companions, speak of this characteristic—the ardent and enthusiastic patriotism of Mr. Morse. It knew no bounds. So great was it that it sometimes endangered his personal safety. Why, he loved the old frigate Constitution, launched within sight of his father's house, as he loved his brother. When the news came that she had captured the Guerriere, and brought her into Boston ; and then again the Java, his enthusiasm rose higher and higher. His spirits sank or rose, like a thermometer, with the tidings of good or ill success of his country. Had he been at home, every faculty of his ardent nature would have been given to her service. But, Mr. Mayor, there are many others whom you have kindly invited to say a word to the citizens of Boston this evening. and I must not trespass upon these sacred hours. I wish simply to join with my fellow-citizens, for one moment, in the expression of gratitude which we owe, and which all portions of the world owe, to this great discoverer. There is not a spot of habitable earth that might not well respond to-night in tones of sympathy and gratitude. The dispatch says " Egypt." Well, sir, that is not all. I am not an enthusiast, I am sure, when I say that not many years hence, certainly not many generations hence, there will be the magnetic telegraph across the deserts of Africa. It

will wake into life that vast silent continent, and Ethiopia will stretch
forth her hands for the grasp of her brethren throughout the world.
[Applause.]   But of all the places which may well respond to-night,
there is none that has a better claim to be heard, none upon whom
the duty of speaking with the heart and with the understanding in
his memory presses more heavily than upon Boston and this hall.
For, Mr. Mayor, Boston is the capital of the State of his birth; and
he was born in one of those valleys that lie between Bunker Hill and
Faneuil Hall.   [Applause.]

ADDRESS OF MR. E. P. WHIPPLE.

Mr. E. P. Whipple, who was received with considerable applause,
said :

Mr. Mayor : I have been attracted specially to this meeting from
the fact that its purpose is to commemorate an inventive mind. The
government of the city of Boston, in calling a meeting in Faneuil
Hall to do honor to the dead inventor, whose invention can never
die, has shown itself to be on a level with the science and the humanity of the age. [Applause.] Our civilization, sir, depends for
its progress upon the ever fresh supply of those intellects who wrest
from reluctant nature the secrets she so jealously hoards and hides.
Certain inventions do not merely extend the dominion of human
intelligence, but they at the same time are the beneficent creators of
new wealth to satisfy human needs. Why, it is computed that Henry
Cobb, the mechanic, whose machine created the iron manufactures
of Great Britain, added six hundred millions of pounds sterling to
its national wealth; and Bessemer's recently-discovered process of
making steel has already, it is said, added two hundred millions of
pounds sterling to the nation's riches.   Here, you see, is a sum equal
to the whole vast amount of the English national debt, which can be
traced to two inventive brains.   [Applause.] Great Britain spent a
thousand millions of pounds sterling—five thousand millions of dol-

lars—in her twenty years' war with revolutionary and imperial France. Now, who supplied the sinews of that long and terrible war? Is not the answer plain? They were supplied by James Watt and Richard Arkwright, two men who gave to their country labor-saving machines, which were equivalent to the manual labor of five hundred millions of men. English statesmen and English generals, with all their blunders, could not waste wealth as fast as Watt and Arkwright created it. And the first Napoleon was at last overwhelmed, not by Pitt, Percival, Liverpool, or Wellington, but by two illustrious inventors, one of whom began life as a mathematical-instrument maker, and the other as a common barber; these were the men who overthrew Napoleon. And I doubt whether we, with all our familiarity with the worth of industrial invention, can still realize the enormous, the unutterable debt of gratitude we owe to such of our countrymen as Whitney, Fulton, Howe, McCormick, and Morse. [Applause.] As to Morse, we know that at one time in his career he gained a precarious livelihood in New Hampshire, a very precarious one, indeed, by painting portraits, at fifteen dollars a head. Who would have supposed that from such an artist would have sprung such an artisan? But as to his particular invention, you of course all remember the well-known lines of Byron as he witnessed a thunder-storm among the Alps. He wished he might speak with lightning, but Morse made that lightning not only converse, he made it to write, also; he has forced it not only to flash terror, but to flash intelligence; he has made it to be the obedient humble servant of the meanest as well as of the greatest of men and women. Under his control it condescends even to be careless or insipid, a retailer of gossip, or thrall of scandal mongers. You all recollect the remark of the old lady, when she saw a telegraph-pole, with its wires, set up before her country cottage. "Now," she spitefully said, " I suppose no one can whip a child without its being known all over creation!" Certainly not, my good woman; the press of Calcutta and St. Petersburg will hear every slap you give, and hold you to strict account for all unnecessary infantile castigation. Even the restive Yankee, who, asking the operator in the early days of telegraphy "how long it would take to send a message to Washington?" and on being told "five minutes," replied he "could not wait," even he can now be satisfied. By the blessed difference in time, he can be consoled by the assurance that this telegram from Liverpool will arrive several hours before the operator sent it. In short, Franklin drew the lightning from the skies; Morse sent it over the earth, and commanded it to do the behests of his fellow-men. But this taming of the seemingly untamable lightning has wrought noble as well as brilliant results. It enables great nations to communicate with each other in a minute of time, and prevents error by the transmission of thoughts in the minds of individual statesmen to statesmen of other countries. It enables the merchant who is rusticating at Newport or Saratoga, to direct the course of his ships, separated from him though they be by ten or twenty thousand miles; and it equalizes prices by the transmission of intelligence that prevents monopoly. It enables the press to annihilate space, and bring every morning Europe, Asia, and Africa to your very doors; and last, though not least, it makes every throb of the human heart, every tear and tender anxiety for absent friends, kinsmen, parents, lovers, known everywhere ; and unites Boston, London, Paris, Berlin, Rome, Naples, and even Hong-Kong into one great metropolitan city. [Loud applause.]

OTHER DISPATCHES.

At this point dispatches were read by Mr. Wood, from Lynn, Salem, Portsmouth, N. H., Augusta, Me., and other places. From Providence came the intelligence that "forty street-lamps in the park have just been lighted by electricity." The following message was received from Washington: "Indications of regret, respect, and sympathy for the late Professor Morse are now being received by the memorial meeting in progress at Washington from all parts of the civilized world. It will be impossible for us to give a copy of them all, for they are without end. Let it be understood that not a country or State is missing."

The chairman next introduced the Hon. George S. Hillard to the audience. On rising he was greeted with applause. He spoke as follows:

ADDRESS OF HON. GEORGE S. HILLARD.

Mr. MAYOR, LADIES, AND GENTLEMEN: It is an honorable fact in the history of our country that at this moment all over the land, men are met together to do honor to the man whose claims to distinction and memory rest upon the fact that he was eminently successful in applying the laws of science to the arts of life. With peculiar propriety it belongs to us to do honor to Mr. Morse, because he was of us. He was born but a rifle-shot from the spot on which I stand; he was reared under influences indigenous to this soil. We have a right to a local pride in Mr. Morse. A just national pride is a thing to be indulged in; we have a right to be proud of our great men. Every great man is a product of two facts: one is original capacity, and the other the institutions under which he was reared. I suppose Mr. Morse would hardly have invented the electric telegraph if he had chanced to have been born in Mexico or Peru.

Now, fellow-citizens, I do not propose to travel over the ground my predecessors have gone over. Who is he that cometh after three such kings as have addressed you? Allow me to deflect a little, seemingly, from their path of thought here, and yet in so doing I trust I shall observe a law which, after a short space, shall bring me back again. I am thinking here to-night of two other men, between whose lives and that of Mr. Morse there is a peculiar parallelism seen, as has been already mentioned—Franklin, born at the beginning of the last century, a Boston boy, our own, and all ours; the next was Count Rumford, born about ten miles off, in Woburn; and the next was Morse, born in the next city. The dates of the birth of these three men are separated about forty years from each other. One marks the beginning of the century, another the middle, and the other the close; and these three men have secured their title to immortality by discoveries in invention in heat, in light, and electricity, and in electro-magnetism, those airy sciences which seem more like thought transmitted through matter than matter itself. These were all practical men; they made their science subserve the wants and uses of man in his daily life. We associate with Franklin the lightning-rod and the " Franklin stove;" with Rumford, the " Rumford oven " and the " Rumford fire-place." These, you may say, are simple things, but the man that economizes fuel, that enables us to meet what is the great and first thing in life during eight months of the year—to keep ourselves warm—the man who lightens to one-half of creation the daily burden of cooking, is surely entitled to be held in honored remembrance. But Franklin and Rumford were practical men; they were great scientific discoverers. Franklin's discovery of electricity in the lightning was a great discovery which is still bearing fruit. Rumford's discovery that heat was a mode of motion was of great value in the history of science, and, if I mistake not, I think the reputation of Rumford among men of science is to-day rather on the increase than otherwise. Now, these three men were alike in other respects: each reached a good old age, each had the rare good fortune, which all inventors and discoverers do not have, of having success come to them while alive; they had honors, they had recognition, they had success, they had wealth itself delivered to them, and did not die before they had a sight of the promised land to which their thoughts and their action tended. Now, there is another point in which these men were alike, and that was, patience and perseverance; that power of taking hold of an idea and never letting it go until success was achieved; that power of taking a subject and holding it up, and never allowing the glass to be deflected to the right or to the left; that power which Sir Isaac Newton said, so far as he knew, was the only thing in which he excelled other men.

Mr. Morse did not pretend to be an original discoverer of science. He was a modest man; he would have disclaimed all honors of that kind. His merit, as Professor Horsford has already told you, was the skill and ingenuity with which he devised an instrument more expeditious, more simple, more cheap than any other, for doing that thing which a great many others, in other parts of the world, at the same time were trying to do with him: and in the second place, his perseverance in knocking at the door of Congress; in holding on to his invention and not letting it go, until at last, as the iron is made hot by repeated blows of the hammer, apathy and indifference and opposition were overcome, and he lived to see the complete triumph of his idea. Now, many men have ideas, many men have brilliant guesses, striking suggestions and smart surmises, which they give utterance to in their speech or in their books; but it is the man who puts the idea into shape, who gives it form and drapery, it is he, and he alone, who writes his name on the undying tablets of fame. [Applause.] Another remarkable thing about Mr. Morse was, that he was forty years old before he began to think of being a man of science. He was an artist, a painter, up to the age of forty, and an artist of no mean rank; in some points of view an artist of high merit. Now, in the sixteenth century there were men who were great artists and also great men of science. Michael Angelo was one of them, and Leonardi da Vinci was another. He was one of the most eminent men of science that ever lived, and it was only because he was so great an artist that the world throws into shadow his reputation as a man of science. But for the last hundred years I do not happen to recollect anybody that had these two professions in combination; that was eminent as an artist, and that was, as Mr. Whipple so felicitously expressed it, a king as an artisan, a creator of beauty for forty years, and then leaving the flowery paths of beauty and taking hold of the stern realities of practical life, and achieving such marvelous results! It is never too late, my friends, to turn over a new leaf in the great book of knowledge.   [Applause.]

Nor should we forget here the man Morse, not merely as an artist or artisan, but the man Morse. You know that behind what a man does there always stands out the fact of what he is. Now, Mr. Morse will bear the strictest scrutiny here. There have been artists of very high rank whose lives their biographers are willing to leave in shadow, and there have been men of science who have shown certain infirmities of temper and character which historian and biographer are willing to forget. Now, Mr. Morse was from the beginning a man remarkable for character, a man as an artist who never yielded to any of the peculiar seductions and temptations to which the impressionable temperament of artists sometimes yields. He was simple in his habits, he was laborious, he was pure in his life and conversation. His love of beauty—the beauty which he worshiped—was the pure, high-ideal beauty, not sensual or debasing. So as a man of science the same elements are seen, self-respect, dignity of character, self-control, not getting into any unseemly controversy, maintaining always a calm, equable and serene mind, showing his to be a noble life to consider in both those parts. To him Heaven gave not merely success, but gave him old age without infirmities, an old age with the possession of all those faculties that make life attractive. It is a going down of a great light in a calm and serene horizon. It is, as I said, an honorable thing for us that we come here to do honor to the memory of this eminent, of this pure, this good man. It is a thing that marks our progress in civilization when men come together, not merely to do honor to the great statesman or the great soldier—all honor to them in their sphere and place—but also to the artist, who places the use of beauty at the service of common life; to the scientific discoverer, who brings a new law to light, who wrests from coy and retiring nature some of those secrets she is always anxious to hide from investigating minds, and from the skillful applicant of discoveries conferred upon humanity. These men are heroes; they are soldiers; they are soldiers in that great battle that has been going on ever since the world was a world, between ignorance and knowledge, between truth and error. Their triumphs are pure, in them there is no alloy; their victories are without bloodshed; with them there mingle not the wail of the widow or the tear of the orphan. [Loud applause.]

The resolutions were put to the meeting by the chairman, and unanimously carried, and the meeting adjourned.

MEETING AT CONCORD, N. H.

CONCORD, N. H., *April 16.*—The services in memory of the late Professor Samuel F. B. Morse were held this evening in Phœnix Hall. Mayor Kimball presiding. The Rev. D. W. Faunce opened the meeting with prayer, and was followed by Joseph B. Walker, esq., who gave a short history of Professor Morse as connected with Concord. The Rev. Dr. Bouton and Asa McFarland gave brief and interesting personal recollections of the deceased, and the Hon. George G. Fogg presented a serious of resolutions, which were read and unanimously adopted. Brief remarks were made by the Rev. J. J. F. Lovering and Samuel B. Page, esq., and a poem was read by Rossiter Johnson, esq. A telegraphic communication was received from the meeting at Washington and answered. The services closed with a benediction by the Rev. Dr. Bouton. The attendance was very large. Several portraits of old residents, painted by Professor Morse, were hung upon the walls of the hall.

MEETING AT AUGUSTA, ME.

AUGUSTA, ME., *April 16.*—In compliance with the call of the National Telegraph Memorial Association, a memorial meeting of the citizens was held this evening in honor of the late Professor Morse. The following resolution was adopted:

Resolved, That the people of this city unite with the people of the United States and of the civilized world in expressing their reverence for the memory of the great inventor of the telegraph, Samuel F. B. Morse.

MEETING AT NEW HAVEN, CONN.

In response to a call from his honor Mayor Lewis, a meeting of the members of the city government and of citizens was held at the chamber of the board of councilmen, in the City Hall, New Haven, on the evening of April 16, 1872, to take action upon the death of the late Samuel F. B. Morse, LL. D.

The meeting was called to order at 8 o'clock by Alderman Johnson T. Plate; and upon motion, Hon. Henry G. Lewis, Mayor of New Haven, was elected chairman, and John S. Fowler, esq., assistant city clerk, secretary. The mayor, upon taking the chair, made some remarks upon the distinguished attainments of the deceased, and his former intimate relations with New Haven.

Upon the conclusion of the mayor's address, the following resolutions were introduced by Hon. Francis Wayland:

Whereas, it has pleased Divine Providence to remove by death, Samuel F. B. Morse, LL. D.: Therefore,

Resolved, That we recognize in this sad event not only a national bereavement, but the loss of one who has done more to unite the human race in the ties of a common brotherhood than any other man of modern times.

Resolved, That in the success which has crowned the scientific services of the deceased, we see a signal instance of merit promptly and properly rewarded, and a gratifying proof that public benefactors are not always neglected by the generation which enjoys the fruits of their inventive genius.

Resolved, That the career of our distinguished fellow-citizen affords ample encouragement to our countrymen to persevere in all efforts for extending the domains of useful science, and widening the area of human knowledge.

Resolved, That New Haven is especially called upon to commemorate this afflictive dispensation, from the fact that the honored father of Professor Morse found here in his later years a welcome home, and in our cemetery his final resting-place; also, because the deceased was an eminent alumnus of Yale College; was long connected with one of its departments; was a generous contributor to its gallery of paintings and stautes, and to the funds of the Theological Seminary, and was for a considerable time a resident of our city.

Addresses were then made by Rev. Leonard Bacon, D. D.; Prof. J. H. Niemeyer, of the Yale School of the Fine Arts; and Prof. William H. Brewer, of the Sheffield Scientific School.

Telegraphic apparatus had been placed in the chamber, under the direction of Mr. J. M. Fairchild of the Western Union Telegraph Company, and communication was had with the meeting held simultaneously at Washington, and the meetings held at the same time in other cities throughout the United States.

After adopting the resolutions the meeting adjourned.

MEETING AT TRENTON, N. J.

A large meeting was held on the evening of April 16, in the rooms of the Board of Trade, for the purpose of joining in the general sorrow expressed by the nation for the death of his eminent scientific gentleman

The meeting was called to order by Mr. O. D. Blackfan, who read the call, and then nominated Mayor Briest to preside. The mayor accepted the honor with a few remarks.

William C. Taylor was appointed secretary.

Colonel Freese moved that a committee of five be appointed to draught resolutions expressive of the sense of the meeting at the death of Professor Morse.

Adopted.

The following persons were appointed: J. R. Freese, O. D. Blackfan, Dr. J. B. Coleman, A. S. Livingston, and Mr. Kennedy.

The committee retired.

Dispatches were read from Saint Paul, Milwaukee, Philadelphia, Syracuse, Harper's Ferry, Galveston, San Francisco, Des Moines, Pittsburgh, Halifax, N. S., Concord, Saint John, N. B., New Orleans, Nashville, Cincinnati, Indianapolis, &c.

The Western Union Telegraph Company had carried their wires into the rooms, and Mr. Jesse R. Mills, the operator, furnished the meeting with the dispatches during the progress of the meeting.

Rev. J. C. Brown made the first speech, and spoke of the advantages of the telegraph. He mentioned the fact that the first wires ever put up were put up in the University of New York, by Professor Morse. The first daguerreotypes were taken in the same institution, by Professor Draper. Two hundred thousand miles of wire are now stretched over the different parts of our country. He showed the cheapness of the telegraph over old letter-postage. It has annihilated distances, and, in many respects, blessed mankind. He spoke of the advantages to the intellectual world, the mighty revolutions which the electric wire has made all over the world in disseminating thought, and in bringing people together from distant parts.

General Rusling spoke of his experience in witnessing the first operations of telegraphing in Trenton, and particularly in the Army, and mentioned some stirring incidents.

The committee on resolutions reported the following:

Whereas, in the course of nature, Professor Samuel F. B. Morse, one of the great benefactors of the human race, has been removed from the scenes of his labors and triumphs, entailing an irreparable loss, not only upon his immediate countrymen, but upon the citizens of the whole civilized world as well; and

Whereas, in response to the invitation of the National Telegraph Memorial Association, we are here to-night to join with them in doing honor to his memory : Therefore,

Resolved, That we, the citizens of Trenton, New Jersey, have a common interest in the name and fame of Samuel F. B. Morse, enjoying, as we do, the results of his genius, as the great discoverer of practical magnetic telegraphy, and mourning, as we shall hereafter, the loss of one who, as a man of genius, had few equals and no superiors.

Resolved, That the action of this memorial meeting be at once telegraphed to the meeting of the Washington National Memorial Association, now being held in the Hall of Representatives at Washington City.

The resolutions were read.

General Rusling continued his remarks.

Mr. Kennedy said he commenced his acquaintance with Professor Morse, when he was constructing the telegraph between Capitol Hill, Washington, and Baltimore. He explained the progress that had been made in telegraphing, and how the ground or independent circuit was discovered by Mr. Morse.

He gave an interesting account of the attempted introduction of the telegraph in the island of Cuba—Professor Morse and himself having received the royal charter. Part of the line was erected through the South and on its way to Cuba, but upon the breaking out of the war it was surrendered, and finally their charter was covered by subsequent grants.

Mr. Freese spoke of his acquaintance with Professor Morse in Paris. He found him an American of large heart, always taking a deep interest in everything American, and especially in explaining the numerous articles of American genius in the Paris Exposition. He was also a good man. Not only was he devoted to science, but to his God, and was a regular attendant at church, and, he believed, connected with a Sunday-school.

Mr. F. S. Mills mentioned the circumstance of meeting Mr. Morse in Baltimore, in 1844, when he was engaged in his first grand experiment in laying a telegraphic line between Baltimore and Washington. He was communicative, and took a great interest in explaining this new and important invention to all who visited his little office. He also referred to the enthusiastic manner in which Mr. Morse and his great invention were received in the Democratic convention then in session in Baltimore, when he appeared there in person and read the first dispatch from Silas Wright, congratulating the convention upon the nomination of James K. Polk. The delegates were wild with excitement, and threw their hats and handkerchiefs in the air, cheering Mr. Morse fully five minutes without cessation.

Dr. J. B. Coleman followed with some remarks, and called upon Mr. Wright to explain the difference between the Bain and the Morse mode of communicating by telegraph.

Mr. J. A. Wright then spoke of the difference in the several modes of telegraphing.

Mr. A. S. Livingston, Mr. Buchanan, and others followed with remarks, and the meeting closed with interesting conversations.

MEETING AT SAVANNAH, GA.

In pursuance of proclamation from the Mayor, a number of citizens assembled in the council chamber on the evening of the 16th April, to testify in a public manner their regret at the death of the late Prof. S. F. B. Morse.

Messrs. Turner and Brown, of the Western Union Telegraph Company, established connection with the meetings at Washington and elsewhere, having their apparatus placed in the council-room.

Shortly after eight o'clock, Hon. Alfred Haywood, mayor *pro tem.*, proposed that the meeting be organized by the election of Octavus Cohen, esq., as chairman.

The motion was seconded and adopted, and Mr. Cohen took the chair.   Dr. James Stewart was then unanimously elected secretary.

The Chair stated the object of the meeting as announced in the proclamation, and requested Secretary Stewart to read the communications from the National Memorial Telegraph Association and the Western Union Telegraph Company of Savannah in reference to the subject.

This being done, the Chair announced that the meeting was prepared to hear any suggestions.

Hon. Alfred Haywood, mayor *pro tem.*, offered the following:

The city council of Savannah, in meeting assembled, unites with the world in condolence and sympathy at the death of the great inventor of the magnetic telegraph.

ALFRED HAYWOOD,
Mayor pro tem.

The message was immediately sent over the wires.

The following was received and read by the secretary:

WASHINGTON, *April* 16, 1872.

To the MAYOR *of Savannah:*

The National Morse Memorial Meeting is now in progress in the Hall of the House of Representatives.   Speaker Blaine, assisted by the Vice-President of the United States, presides.   The Governors of the several States are acting as vice-presidents.   The meeting is now ready to receive communications.

A. S. SOLOMONS, *Chairman.*

NEW YORK, *April* 16, 1872.

To the MAYOR *of Savannah:*

The lines of the Southern and Atlantic Telegraph Companies will be open to the use of yourself and the committee, in connection with the Morse Memorial services to be held in Washington to-night. Any telegrams from you and said committee will be cheerfully forwarded to Washington, or to and from any of the principal cities in the country.

JAS. R. CRENSHAW, *President.*

The chairman then presented the following in behalf of the Chamber of Commerce:

CHAMBER OF COMMERCE,
Savannah, April 16, 1872.

To A. S. SOLOMONS,
Chairman, Washington:

The Savannah Chamber of Commerce greets the Chambers of Commerce of the United States in mourning the national loss of a public benefactor.

OCTAVUS COHEN,
First Vice-President.

After this message was dispatched, the following telegrams were received and read by the clerk:

CYRUS W. FIELD, *Washington:*

Batavia Chamber of Commerce regret to learn the death of Professor Morse.

VANDENBURG,
President, Batavia, Java.

CYRUS W. FIELD, *Washington:*

The telegraphic staff in Egypt deplore the loss of the eminent Professor Morse, who has rendered such valuable service to the telegraphic extensions all over the world.

GIBBS.

MONTREAL, *April* 16, 1872.

A. S. SOLOMONS, Esq.,
Chairman Committee of Arrangements Morse Celebration,
House of Representatives, Washington:

Montreal joins the distinguished assembly now at Washington in tendering its tribute to the memory of the immortal Morse, whose spirit hovers in our midst, and whose genius discovered the means of uniting, with electric fire, the world in one common brotherhood.

CHAS. J. COURSAL,
Mayor.

Cyrus W. Field, Washington:

Barely ten months have elapsed since I participated as representing the Anglo-American Telegraph Company in paying honor to Professor Morse; and it is with sincere regret that I now tender to the people of the United States the heart-felt condolence of the directors of the Anglo-American and French Atlantic Telegraph Company, for the loss of one who occupied so eminent a position among men of science, and whose name will be recorded in the history of the world as that of one of the pioneers of that marvelous road by means of which the inhabitants of the two hemispheres are brought into instantaneous relations with each other.

HAMILTON, Chairman.

Saint Louis, April 16, 1872.

His Excellency Vice-President Colfax,
and Hon. James G. Blaine,
Washington:

Every human soul in this city, without distinction of age, color, sex, or condition, pays tribute at the shrine of immortal genius—the shrine of one who attained to the knowledge of the gods, and commanded the thunderbolt not to destroy, but to save. Well did he perform his mission. Language fails to speak his praise. His name will live through endless days.

JOSEPH BROWN,
Mayor.

CHARLESTON, S. C., *April* 16, 1872—8 p. m.

The Hon. JAMES G. BLAINE,

Chairman of the Morse Memorial Meeting, Washington:

Whereas, this council, representing the citizens of Charleston, S. C., feel, in common with the people of the entire civilized world, the great loss occasioned by the death of Professor Morse, the father of telegraphy in the United States, respectfully beg to unite their sympathies with the Morse Memorial Association Meeting, now being held in the city of Washington, D. C., this evening, in the following telegram:

"The late Professor Morse: May his memory ever live in the hearts of his countrymen. By his genius and discovery the innocent has been protected, the guilty has been punished, merit has triumphed, crime has perished, trade, commerce, manufactures, and mechanics have flourished. May his invention—the electric telegraph—never more bring to this generation the sad and unwelcome message of war, but may all messages have for their groundwork peace, freedom, prosperity, and happiness. We deeply deplore his loss."

JOHN A. WAGENER,
Mayor.

W. W. SIMONS, *Clerk.*

The next message sent was as follows:

SAVANNAH, April 16, 1872.

The citizens of Savannah, Ga., assembled to pay respect to the memory of Professor Morse, do unqualifiedly testify their regrets at the sad demise of the father of telegraphy, and tender their sincere condolence to the world that we have lost a great and good man. His memory will always live and be cherished as one of the master minds of the world.

OCTAVUS COHEN,
Chairman.

JAMES STEWART, *Secretary.*

The next message sent was as follows:

SAVANNAH, *April* 16, 1872.
To the NATIONAL MEMORIAL TELEGRAPH ASSOCIATION,
                              Washington:

The Savannah Press yields full tribute to the mighty genius of the lamented Professor Morse, through whom its greatness and usefulness have in a large measure been derived. As the exponent of public opinion, the Press, in its regrets at the demise of one of the greatest public benefactors the world has ever known, but reflects the grief of the entire country.

The SAVANNAH PRESS, through

OCTAVUS COHEN,
                              Chairman.

The meeting then adjourned.

MEETING AT WORCESTER, MASS.

Both branches of the city government met on Tuesday evening, April 16, 1872, in their respective chambers, in regular session, by adjournment from Monday evening. The usual routine business of roll-call having been disposed of, an order was passed to assemble in joint convention at 7.45, for the purpose of listening to a memorial address prepared by the Rev. George Allen. Promptly at that hour the Mayor called the convention to order, and John D. Washburn, esq., read the following address:

Mr. PRESIDENT: The century to which this day belongs, is, above all that have gone before it, an age of wonders. Art, science, government, the intercourse of nations, and even humanity itself have met and mingled on a broader platform, with more glowing and more generous manifestations than the face of day had ever smiled upon.

This memorial-day, Mr. President, is itself a glorious anomaly—

an unexampled expression of grateful sentiment to one of its largest and most generous benefactors. This day bears willing witness to the onward and upward progress of civilization. It gives assurance of international good-will; it relieves the discouragement of mournful ages; it animates the hope that the natural brotherhood of man, instead of being a disputed theory, will become a manifest, an accepted, and a practical truth.

It is right, Mr. President, all history proves it right, and conscious nature feels it to be right, that we meet as we do this day to contribute our measure of sentiment to the conflux of thought and heart which mingles from the four quarters of the globe at the decease of the world's benefactor. The sentiment of gratitude is common to humanity, and the time never was when that sentiment was wholly left without expression. The fruit of the olive-tree, time out of mind, has been the staff of life, the necessity and the luxury of the limited climates that favored its production. By nature, except in some rare freak, it is neither palatable nor wholesome. By some seeming accident, as if nature were untrue to herself, an individual tree produced a better fruit whose seed did not reproduce its like, and if I do not misconstrue mythology, some woman, by design or accident, or perhaps both, found out the art of grafting a scion of the good olive-tree into the wild, to feed the nation and light a lamp in every dwelling. A grateful sentiment, in a rude age, deified the sagacious woman, and Minerva, the goddess of wisdom, was called the inventress of the olive, as well as the presiding genius and protector of Athens.

But thick as may be the darkness which still covers many nations, or whatever superstition yet lingers even where the true light now shineth, the grosser forms of idolatry are already gone from a large part of the world, and distinct signs come thick and fast to give assurance that the rest of the world will soon cast such idols to the moles and the bats.

Nevertheless, men must look at men, compare men with men, take their dimensions, and set the small in the shadow of the great till the all-seeing Judge shall reverse human decisions, making those that were first last, and the last first.

The controlling purpose of this meeting, Mr. President, is to honor the memory of Samuel Finley Breese Morse for what he was, as made known by what he did. It certainly becomes this city, as the heart of the Commonwealth, to mingle our respect with the world's contribution of honor to so illustrious a benefactor to mankind. In a city not unkown for its enterprise, industry, skill, and thrift in mechanic arts, as well as for its general intelligence; in a county which, perhaps, has no rival on this continent in the contributions of its sons to inventions that have changed the movements and condition of the world; in a State where so many useful inventions and discoveries have first seen the light,—a Commonwealth that enrolls as her sons the names of Franklin, Whitney, Perkins, Morton, Blanchard, Bigelow, Whittemore, Howe, and Morse, besides others, who, by their inventive genius, have contributed to lift the world to an elevation never known before. In such a community as ours, Mr. President, it would be out of place and out of character not to render signal honor to the memory of him who has commanded, by his beneficent genius, the best homage of the world.

But though I thus speak, I recognize the truth that no man's birth, nor the place of it, has any merit of its own. They are jointly and severally mere incidents, having of themselves neither honor nor shame, whether in the palace or in the hovel. True honor is never an accident. The real honor of a man is that which he himself makes. His shame is not less his own doing. The world may forget, or never know the birth-place of Professor Morse, but they will always see the man in his work. They will see his genius in the invention he found out—in what it has already done, and what it will keep doing to the end of time. They will consider the globe as his whereabout, and mankind as his owner. They will contemplate with growing admiration, from century to century, the wonders which one mortal man has accomplished for his race.

The invention of Professor Morse has caused a double surprise. Indeed, it is hard to tell which has been the greater marvel, the invention itself, or the sudden work it has already done. In this it has had no predecessor, nor is its equal soon, if ever, to be looked for. All other inventions have gone with a comparatively slow and lazy gait about the world. The progress and wide diffusion of this, all abroad, have come, partly from its own character and partly from the period of its origin. It was too great a necessity for delay. The invention told its own story to the world as no other ever did or can hereafter do.

That we may more wisely estimate the services of Professor Morse, it will be profitable to ourselves, as well as just to his memory, to linger a few moments in contemplation of what his invention has already done, as suggestive of what it will hereafter accomplish.

In respect to its past achievement, it is only a contrast to whatever had been done before. As a rule, in all past time, the greatest and most useful inventions were slow in gaining the favor they deserved, and in doing the good they intended. Cadmus, whoever he was, if indeed he was at all—Cadmus, the reputed inventor of letters, a meager alphabet—could not forecast its future, nor could his own age appreciate what was present. In its benign errand to the world, it crept lazily along the shore, from city to city, till at length, after a weak and struggling infancy, it gained the favor of the wise, and became a power among the nations.

Whether the story be a myth or a history, it correctly represents the ignorance of ages, and forecasts the fate of most inventions for long centuries thereafter.

Even at a recent period, genius has been buffeted by ignorance, and rewarded with contempt. Its greatest success has been little

less than a failure, compared with the sudden and world-wide triumph
of the magnetic telegraph. Before it came of age it traversed continents, spread its net-work over nations, stopping not at the broadest
river, and leaping over mountains with the same instant bound as
over the most level plain. And to accomplish what?

What has it not accomplished already? Let every interest, every
calling, every passion, every enterprise, yea, let the whole nature of
man in all its real or imagined realities answer the unlimited question.
Literature, science, art, agriculture, navigation, commerce—let them
all reply. Let fashion in all its modes, let the appetite in all it cravings,
let joy and grief, let all human anxieties, let the bride and the bride-
groom, let birth and death tell their hopeful and mournful stories, let
the policy of civil governments, let the camps and battle-fields, let
impatient, hungry office-seekers, stock-jobbers, money-changers, let
every ring of ambition and avarice tell all they dare tell ; let religion
lift up her voice, telling both her glory and her shame ; let the hopes
of civilization, the mingled cries of justice and humanity, the patient
labors of every mission-field and station—let each and all these mis-
cellaneous groups tell what they know of the doings of the telegraph in the past, and you will have an intimation, a presentiment, of
what will be in the untold centuries of the future.

But wonderful as is the invention and amazing its doings, and grat-
ified as must have been the inventor at the success of his patient and
persevering labors, he saw in that machine and its numberless, measureless doings, that the maker and itself were but as the smallest
bubble on the broadest ocean, compared with the mechanism and
the Maker of the Universe, and that, however truthfully that filmy
globule might reflect the handiwork of the visible heavens bending
over it, it was less than nothing and vanity. So, these are a part of
His ways, but the thunder of His power who can understand ?

The address was listened to with close attention by the audience, consisting of the City Council and some twenty-five or thirty prominent citizens.

The following resolutions were presented by the committee appointed to prepare them, and were unanimously adopted:

Resolved, That while we recognize the hand of an all-wise Providence in the removal of Professor Morse from the scene of his earthly labors and triumphs, we render thanks for his illustrious life, prolonged in tranquillity and happiness to the full limit of human days, and crowned with imperishable honor.

Resolved, That, as Americans, we rejoice in the well-earned fame of our countryman; as sons of Massachusetts, we claim a closer relation to that fame; while as citizens of a community which is a chosen home of invention and the industrial arts, we are peculiarly called upon to pay to his memory our tribute of admiration and gratitude, and recognizing in the honors so freely bestowed upon our countryman by imperial courts the deserved rewards of exalted and successful genius, we perceive its still higher reward in the consciousness that his invention was accepted as one of the greatest, if not the greatest, of benefactions to humanity; that it was associated with every modern triumph of commerce and civilization; and that by it the terror of the sky has become the harbinger of peace and goodwill to the nations.

Resolved, That we commend to the youth of our country the life of Professor Morse, as a noble example of high resolve, determined purpose, and patient courage, undismayed by temporary failure and defeat. The skepticism of less enlightened spirits could not make him doubt, nor their ridicule make him ashamed, nor the hardships of poverty drive him to despair; but, strong in faith, and steadfast amid discouragement, he triumphed at length over every obstacle, and has left a memory which a grateful world would not willingly let die.

Hon. Henry Chapin, in a graceful and complimentary manner, moved a vote of thanks to Rev. Mr. Allen for his address; which was unanimously tendered.

Councilman Towne moved that a copy of the resolutions be furnished to Mr. J. G. Tobey, manager of the Franklin line, for transmission to the central memorial meeting at Washington, and it was so voted.

MEETING AT WORCESTER, MASS.

A number of prominent citizens assembled in the common-council chamber on the evening of April 12, 1872, by request of the mayor, to confer with the city council in relation to a communication recently received by him in regard to the death of the late Samuel F. B. Morse, and to take suitable action to express the sorrow of the citizens of Worcester at this sad event.

His honor Mayor Verry called the meeting to order, and spoke as follows:

Prof. Samuel F. B. Morse was born in the city of Charlestown on the 27th day of April, 1791. He was the son of Rev. Jedediah Morse, the author of Morse's Geography, and was graduated at Yale College in 1810. Possessing a talent for art, he devoted himself to the study of painting and sculpture, both in this country and in Europe, and acquired very considerable celebrity. After a successful course of study abroad he returned to his native land, and established himself in his profession as a painter of portraits. In 1832, he conceived the idea of the electro-magnetic-recording-telegraph. For twelve years he struggled against the skepticism, and even ridicule, of his countrymen, to give them practical demonstration of the feasibility of his magnificent conception. In 1844, after many discouragements, he completed the first line of electro-magnetic telegraph, and demonstrated to the world its utility and value.

This man, whose name the world will always cherish, and whose fame should be recorded on imperishable tablets, died at his residence in New York on Tuesday, the 2d of April, 1872, at the advanced age of 81 years, loved, honored, and respected as an upright and worthy citizen. It is common to die—

> "All that live must die,
> Passing through nature to eternity."

But though it is the common lot of all, it is well that survivors should for a moment pause from the busy cares of time "to do obsequious sorrow" at the portals of the grave; and when one has gone, from the fruits of whose great life the world has garnered a harvest of benefactions, each man and woman is his heir, sharing the benefits of the great legacy he has left behind him. Especially to us, who share the pride that Massachusetts was his birth-place, it must be a melancholy pleasure, by some suitable memorial exercises, to join the nation in honoring the name and embalming the memory of Samuel F. B. Morse.

On Wednesday last I received the following communication :

WASHINGTON, D. C., *April* 15, 1872.

To the Hon. GEORGE F. VERRY,

Mayor of the City of Worcester, Mass. :

SIR: I have the honor to transmit to you herewith a resolution adopted by this association, inviting the co-operation of the friends and admirers of the late Professor Samuel F. B. Morse throughout the country, in holding meetings on Tuesday evening, the 16th instant, simultaneously with the great National Memorial meeting to be held in the House of Representatives at the National Capital.

On behalf of this Association, I respectfully and earnestly request you to take appropriate measures, at the earliest moment possible, for holding such a meeting in your city at the time named. The telegraph-wires will be freely open on the occasion for an exchange of sentiments between the several meetings and the one held here. The favor of an early reply is requested.

Very respectfully, yours,

A. S. SOLOMONS,

Chairman of the Committee of Arrangements
for the National Telegraph Memorial Monument Association.

Desiring that our citizens should have an opportunity, in such manner as they should deem proper, to express their gratitude, admiration, and respect for this great man, just departed, I have thought it proper to invite a conference of the citizens with the city council, that by consultation, it might be determined what action should be taken to appropriately commemorate the sad event.

I, therefore, cordially invite all who are present to participate in the proceedings of this meeting, and, if your deliberations shall result in the adoption of some appropriate memorial exercises, I think I may pledge the hearty co-operation of the city council in carrying them out.

The meeting was then organized by the choice of Mayor Verry as chairman, and H. L. Shumway as secretary. The mayor announced that two plans had been proposed for an appropriate recognition of the event: the first was, to hold a special meeting of the city council on Tuesday evening, at which appropriate resolutions shall be adopted and telegraphed to the central meeting at Washington; the other, to hold a mass-meeting of citizens, at which memorial addresses shall be delivered and resolutions adopted.

Mr. J. D. Washburn eulogized the character of Professor Morse, alluding to him as one of the most illustrious men America has ever produced. During his life he probably received more honors from foreign nations than were ever conferred upon any other private citizen. Professor Morse was not only the inventor of the system of land-telegraphing, but also originated the idea of submarine cables.

Mr. Washburn favored the first plan proposed, and offered the following resolution:

Resolved, That the city council be requested to hold a meeting on Tuesday evening next, and pass appropriate resolutions on the death of Professor Morse, and transmit the same to Washington as the sentiment of the citizens of Worcester.

Mr. Joseph Mason favored the resolution. He spoke of the great benefits which Professor Morse had conferred upon the world, classing him with Franklin and Fulton as a public benefactor. The inventor is frequently forgotten in the results of his labors, and the speaker thought that it would be impossible to gather an audience sufficiently large to make a mass-meeting a success.

Judge Chapin spoke of Worcester as a central point of art and industry, and thought, if a suitable person could be procured in the short time between this and Tuesday evening, a mass-meeting should be held; but as this seemed impossible, he should favor the resolution. All feel an admiration for the life and genius of Morse, but many of us know too little in regard to his personal history.

Hon. Isaac Davis did not want to see the occasion passed by with simple resolutions. He spoke of Massachusetts as the home of inventors, and thought that Worcester, at all events, should notice the death of her distinguished son with proper tokens of respect. He also spoke of the celebrity of the deceased as an artist, and closed by calling on Rev. George Allen, who was in college with Professor Morse, to give expression to his views.

Mr. Allen spoke feelingly of the geniality and nobleness of character which marked the college-life of the deceased, and said these qualities had always distinguished him through life. He combined a mechanical skill with a noble intellect, and had all the elements of character which go to make up a true man. The speaker alluded to the fact that Franklin and Morse, whose names are joined together in the science of electro-magnetism, were born within two miles of each other. Both were Massachusetts men, as were also the inventors of the cotton-gin, the turning-lathe, and the sewing-machine. He regretted that the history of the inventions and personal lives of these men were not better known.

Judge Williams said that if there was any probability that Mechanics' Hall could be filled, and that a suitable person could be found to address the meeting, he would be glad to go there, with other citizens of Worcester, to do honor to the memory of this distinguished man; but, as such was not likely to be the case, he favored the resolution.

Mr. Washburn briefly stated his reasons for offering the resolution. In the first place, he thought that if a mass-meeting was held in Mechanics' Hall it would not be satisfactory in point of numbers, and he preferred a dignified memorial from the city council to a poorly-attended meeting of citizens. Another objection was that the time is too short for any gentleman to collect the proper materials for the exhaustive address which would be expected.

Mr. J. G. Tobey, manager of the Franklin telegraph line, of Worcester, eulogized Professor Morse as the true inventor of the electric-telegraph, in spite of the efforts made recently to detract from his deserved honors. He extended the free use of the line to the citizens to transmit any resolutions or messages they may see fit to the central meeting at Washington.

Mr. A. P. Marble thought that one of the objects of the proposed meeting should be to hand the name of Professor Morse down to posterity, and suggested that it should be held in the high-school-house hall, and that the teachers and older pupils of the public schools be invited to be present.

After further discussion Mr. Washburn's resolution was adopted.

The Mayor thought that a committee of five citizens should be chosen to unite with a like committee of the city council in preparing a set of resolutions, to be adopted at the special meeting of the city council to be held on Tuesday evening. Rev. Mr. Allen, Isaac Davis, Judge Chapin, J. D. Washburn, and Joseph Mason were chosen as a citizens' committee, and his honor the Mayor, Mr. Reed, president of the common council Alderman Marble, and Councilmen Pratt and Goddard on the part of the city government.

The meeting was then dissolved.

MEETING AT MILWAUKEE, WIS.

A meeting of the common council of the city of Milwaukee was held to take into consideration suitable honors to be paid to the memory of the late Professor Samuel F. B. Morse, whereupon the the following resolutions were unanimously agreed to:

Resolved, by the common council of the city of Milwaukee, That this city, in common with the whole country, has heard with deep regret of the death of the late Samuel F. B. Morse, to whom the country and the whole civilized world owe that wonderful development of modern science, the electric-telegraph. Accustomed as we are to all the multitudinous benefits of the electric-telegraph, we should recall them upon the occasion of the death of their illustrious inventor. It has not only been an almost miraculous convenience personally to every intelligent human being within the limits of human civilization, but it has wrought a revolution in all commerce, which has brought together the nations of the earth in a closer alliance of friendship and business, than the world ever saw before. The great achievements and wonderful benefits of this invention are so numerous and vast that it would fill volumes to detail them, and it is far beyond the limits of a resolution to even glance at them. We limit ourselves to a general acknowledgment, to lay as a garland upon the tomb of the great inventor who has just passed from the scene of his earthly labors to the presence of the Almighty Being, the secrets of whose laws he was in life so far successful in discovering.

Resolved, That his honor the Mayor be requested to communicate these resolutions to Mr. Speaker James G. Blaine, of the House of Representatives, at Washington, to be by him placed before the memorial meeting to be held this evening in the House of Representatives at Washington.

MEETING AT MONTREAL, CANADA.

The Chairman of the committee of arrangements having telegraphed to the Rev. Prof. Dr. De Sola, inviting the Municipal 'authorities of the city of Montreal to unite in the Memorial services which are to take place on the 16th April, 1872, in the House of Representatives at Washington, his Worship the Mayor sent the following dispatch:

MONTREAL, *April* 16, 1872.

To A. S. SOLOMONS, Esq.,

Chairman Committee of Arrangements Morse Celebration,

House of Representatives, Washington, D. C.:

Montreal joins the distinguished assembly now at Washington in tendering its tribute to the memory of the immortal Morse, whose spirit hovers in our midst, and whose genius discovered the means of uniting, with electric fire, the world in one common brotherhood.

CHAS. J. COURSOL, *Mayor.*

MEETING AT OMAHA, NEBR.

RESOLUTIONS PASSED BY THE CITY COUNCIL OF OMAHA CITY, NEBR., ASSEMBLED IN REGULAR SESSION ON TUESDAY EVENING, APRIL 16, 1872, IN MEMORY OF THE LATE PROFESSOR SAMUEL F. B. MORSE.

Whereas, the National Morse Memorial Association meets in the National House of Representatives at Washington, D. C., this evening, to commemorate, by some appropriate ceremonies, the life and fame of the late Professor Samuel F. B. Morse, the inventor of the system of telegraphy; and

Whereas, they have extended an earnest invitation to all the municipalities in the land to join in this great and worthy service, placing all the telegraphic lines in the country at their disposal for the transmission of messages, that there may be a simultaneous reverence and respect from one end of the land to the other: Be it

Resolved, by the city council of Omaha, the chief commercial city of Nebraska, that the city of Omaha recognizes with profound respect and gratitude the inestimable service which the late Professor Morse performed for the world by the invention of the great and wonderful system of electro-magnetic telegraph, an invention whose influence is daily felt, not alone in the sphere of business, but in every department of human life.

Resolved, That Omaha reverently joins, by this act, in the great memorial service in which the whole nation is engaged to-night, and tenders its tributes of affectionate regard to the august memory of the great man who, by the evident inspiration of Almighty God, has done more than any other to conquer the wildest elements of nature, and to demonstrate the superiority of the human intellect to all material changes.

J. H. WILLARD, Mayor.

Attest: J. M. McCune,
    City Clerk.

MEETING AT SAN FRANCISCO, CAL.

San Francisco, Cal., April 16, 1872.

A number of citizens met in the chamber of the board of supervisors to take some appropriate action in respect to the memory of the late Professor Morse. Owing to the short notice given, the meeting was not as well attended as it otherwise would have been by our citizens to do honor to the memory of the distinguished deceased. Among those present were Mayor Alvord, Colonel J. Middleton, E. L. Goold, James Gamble, George S. Ladd, F. Mac-Crellish, Col. W. H. L. Barnes, J. MacDermot, J. Benton, Gen. H. A. Cobb, J. S. Hittell, Supervisors King, Kenny, Goodwin, and Barrett.

The time having arrived for the meeting to be called to order, Colonel Middleton nominated his honor Mayor Alvord as chairman. Geo. S. Ladd was nominated and elected secretary.

In taking the chair, his honor the Mayor stated all knew the object of the meeting; which was, to place themselves in conference with the memorial meeting to be held in the evening in the National House of Representatives.

Colonel Middleton then briefly addressed the meeting. They all honored the great man of science, and they had assembled to let the public know that they were in sympathy with the people of the United States at the great loss. He (the speaker) had the honor of having aided to inaugurate the first telegraph-line in the State of California, and hoped that appropriate resolutions would be adopted.

Mr. MacCrellish moved that a committee of five be appointed, to draught suitable resolutions expressive of the sense of the meeting, and that the resolutions be telegraphed to the House of Representatives in time for the meeting to be held during the evening. In making the motion, he proposed, with the consent of the chair, to name Colonel Barnes as chairman of the committee.

The motion was adopted. The chair named Colonel Barnes, F. MacCrellish, James Gamble, Colonel Middleton, and General Cobb as the committee, who immediately retired for deliberation.

THE RESOLUTIONS.

After an absence of a few minutes the committee returned, when Colonel Barnes presented the following resolutions:

Whereas, Professor Samuel F. B. Morse died in the city of New York on the second day of April, A. D., 1872; and

Whereas, in the Capitol of the United States there is to be held, on the evening of this day, a Memorial meeting in his honor; and

Whereas, the citizens of San Francisco desire to unite with such meeting in its expression of national gratitude for the great discoveries of Professor Morse and of the national regret at his death, and to that end have now assembled together: Therefore, be it

Resolved, That, on behalf of the citizens of San Francisco and of the people of California, we recognize the inestimable services of Professor Samuel F. B. Morse to the American nation and the whole civilized world. His genius has united the intelligence of all mankind, strengthened and extended the commercial relations of all nations, annihilated otherwise insuperable barriers of deserts and mountains, and made the silent depths of oceans thrill with the progress and history of continents. His vast conception of enlisting electricity in the work of civilization was the grandest thought of time, and he lived to see it developed to ultimate and complete success. In every personal and social relation of life the humblest individual has cause to bless his name. In the political relations of the government to the States of the Union, the results of his labors have powerfully aided to bind each to the other, by furnishing a means of thorough, universal, and simultaneous knowledge of events, necessities, and policy, bringing all to act for the common good and with a common impulse. They have borne a signal part in guiding the diplomatic relations of all nations, and in peace and war alike have been of inestimable value.

Resolved, That, as the sense of this meeting, the Mayor of the city of San Francisco be, and is hereby, requested to forward to Hon. J. G. Blaine, Speaker of the House of Representatives and President of the Memorial meeting to be held this evening in the National Capitol, at Washington, D. C., the following telegram:

To Hon. JAMES G. BLAINE,

> *President of the Morse Memorial Meeting, Washington, D. C.:*

The citizens of San Francisco unite with you in homage to the memory of Samuel F. B. Morse. With you they mourn that all of him that was mortal has gone to its rest. With you they rejoice that his great discoveries remain to bless the world and raise his honored name high on the glorious list of its real benefactors. To us of the Pacific coast his achievements are of priceless value. Through him we are this hour united with you, and for all mankind he has annihilated space and outstripped the very winds of the morning. As his triumphs over nature were splendid, so shall the fruits of his victories endure forever.

WILLIAM ALVORD,
President Morse Testimonial Meeting.

On motion, the resolutions were adopted.

Mr. J. Gamble, superintendent of the Western Union Telegraph Company, was requested to immediately transmit the resolutions; whereupon the meeting adjourned.

MESSAGE FROM THE MAYOR.

The following message was also sent by the mayor:

MAYOR'S OFFICE, *San Francisco, April* 16, 1872.
To the MORSE MEMORIAL MEETING,
Washington, D. C.:

The citizens of San Francisco are in unison with you this evening heart and soul. Morse's honored name will not be forgotten so long as telegraph-wires are stretched across our house-tops and streets, for our children will be so taught that they may tell their children of the great man who first transmitted thought at lightning speed around the globe. The electric telegraph is his monument, and, should books and manuscript be destroyed, tradition will keep his name and memory fresh in the hearts of the people.

WILLIAM ALVORD, *Mayor*

CORRESPONDENCE BETWEEN THE COMMITTEE OF ARRANGEMENTS AND MAYOR ALVORD.

The following correspondence between Mayor Alvord and the Chairman of the committee of arrangements of the Morse Memorial meeting, which was held at Washington this evening, was telegraphed direct over the Atlantic and Pacific line:

WASHINGTON, D. C., *April* 16, 1872.
Hon. WM. ALVORD,
Mayor of San Francisco:

The National Morse meeting now assembled, is honored by the presence of the President of the United States, and other distinguished men now at the Capitol, and greetings and respects to all the people of the Pacific slope.

A. S. SOLOMONS,
Chairman Committee of Arrangements.

SAN FRANCISCO, *April* 16.

A. S. SOLOMONS,

Chairman of Committee of Arrangements, Washington, D. C.:

San Francisco returns your greetings. She deplores with you the death of the illustrious inventor. But our regrets are tempered by the reflection that his work was accomplished, his highest aspirations attained. He died in the fullness of years, the benefactor of mankind.

WM. ALVORD, *Mayor.*

MEETING AT BURLINGTON, IOWA.

The meeting for the purpose of expressing the feeling of the citizens of Burlington, Iowa, in regard to the death of Professor Morse was a large and sympathetic one. The speaker's stand, in front of the hall, was draped in mourning, and on the stand was a telegraphic sounder, accompanied, for ornament rather than use, by a beautiful "register." Mr. Ludwig, the manager of the Western Union line in Burlington, had made connections in the hall with all the prominent points in the United States.

Mayor Robertson called the assemblage to order, and stated the object of the meeting.

Upon motion, the mayor then appointed as a committee on resolutions Messrs. David Rorer, A. T. Hay, and H. W. Starr.

The committee reported the following resolutions, which were unanimously adopted:

BURLINGTON, IOWA, *April* 16, 1872.

CHAIRMAN NATIONAL MORSE MEMORIAL MEETING,

Washington:

The following resolutions were unanimously adopted at the Morse Memorial meeting, held here this evening:

Whereas, it has pleased the Divine Ruler of the Universe to call hence Professor Samuel Finley Breese Morse, America's most distinguished citizen, who has gone to the Heavenly Garner like a ripe sheaf in its season, crowned with his reward: Therefore, be it

Resolved, That we honor the memory of Morse as one of the greatest benefactors of the human race, in subjecting the powers of nature to human control, so as to combine the inhabitants of the globe as one family.

Resolved, That we praise the Lord that it is permitted to us to control the powers of nature, and to make them obedient to our uses, and that we regard the past triumph of Morse as the herald of new and further advancements in the field of science.

Resolved, That his rare attainments, accurate judgment, and comprehensive intellect, (that enabled him to grasp and utilize these mobile, elastic, imponderable forces of nature, and make them subservient to man, with all their quickening powers upon trade, commerce, and human progress,) command our grateful admiration and regard.

Resolved, That a copy of these resolutions be transmitted by telegraph to the Central Morse Memorial Association at Washington. D. C.

D. RORER, Chairman.

A. T. HAY,
H. W. STARR,
    Committee on Resolutions.

The mayor then called upon Dr. Harvey, who spoke at length in regard to the telegraph and Professor Morse's connection therewith, referring especially to the fact of his having established a universal compass and brought the whole human race into brotherhood by means of this telegraphic alphabet and machinery.

Dr. Harvey was followed by the Rev. Dr. Salter, whose address was as follows:

On the day and at the very hour in which the first President of the United States was inaugurated in his high office in the city of New York, a youthful minister of the gospel was installed pastor of one of the most ancient churches of New England. It was then more than a century and a half since the founding of that church,

during the whole of which long period it had remained the only
church in the town.   There had been fought the first great battle of
the Revolution, in which the meeting-house of the church, in common with the town, was burned by the enemy.   "At this time," say
the records of the church in Charlestown, Mass., "upwards of 380
dwelling-houses and other buildings, valued at £156,660 18s. 8d.,
were consumed, and 2,000 persons reduced from affluence and medi-
ocrity to the most aggravated exile."

With the achievement of the national independence this church
rose from its ashes, and by a happy coincidence saw Jedediah Morse
installed in office as their pastor and teacher, at the very time
when General Washington was taking the Chief Magistrate's oath to
preserve, protect, and defend the Constitution of the country.   Previous to this, Mr. Morse had made the acquaintance of General
Washington, and had conversed with him upon his favorite subject
of study, the geography of America and of the world.

At the close of the second year of his ministry, a son was born to
the Massachusetts pastor, who was named after his mother's family,
Samuel Finley Breese, his mother being a granddaughter of the
fifth president of the College of New Jersey, Samuel Finley.   Born
within about a mile of the spot where Benjamin Franklin first
breathed the vital air, and a year and ten days after his exit from
earth, Morse early acquired the habits of observation and study
which had marked the great American philosopher; and favored with
richer advantages, and enjoying the ripest academical culture of the
time, set before his mind some lofty ideals of an honored and useful
life that should conquer fresh spoils from nature and art, and add
new wealth and glory to man's earthly state.   The fine arts, and the
sciences of chemistry and electricity, especially aroused his enthusiasm,
and in the former he won distinction by the originality and boldness
of his designs, and rendered signal service in securing dignity and
commanding eminence for studies in art by the "National Academy,"

of which he was one of the chief founders, and president for sixteen years. It was, however, in the application of the subtle agencies of the electric fluid that Morse was destined to render the most memorable service to the advancement of knowledge and the progress of human society. He saw the first experiments in electro-magnetism exhibited in the United States, and pursued through patient years the great idea of harnessing the mysterious power into the service of human intelligence and making it a vehicle for the transmission of thought. He had fully matured the problem in his own mind in 1832, but more than ten years elapsed before the public men of the nation were convinced of its practicability and value, or Congress could be induced to make an appropriation for carrying a telegraphic line from Baltimore to Washington.

It was among the felicities of my youth to have seen Professor Morse, when a student in the University of the City of New York, in 1837, and to have witnessed his first successful experiments made in a public manner, with several thousand feet of wire, in one of the rooms of the University. The spectacle was novel and startling, but a freshman was too immature to look on with more than vacant wonder and amazement. Several years' patient and industrious waiting was necessary to assure the country that here was one of the greatest agents of modern civilization.

For more than thirty years this great invention has now held its place among the proudest monuments of human art, and during this period its illustrious author was permitted to live and behold its successful working around the earth and under the depths of ocean.

This memorial, therefore, is one only of joy and congratulation, and calls the people of America, and especially the youth of the United States, to tread the same paths of study and observation, and aspire after the discovery of mysteries yet hidden in nature, and toil on through whatever fortune and whatever embarrassments, to bring new life upon the pathways of home-life, and new forces and helps for the heavy work of man's earthly lot in regaining his predestined dominion over nature.

Professor Morse was a Christian, a son of the Puritans, and gave the triumphs of his genius to the cause of public charity, to the advancement of humanity, and to the work of the world's redemption.

The mayor then called upon the Hon. David Rorer, who said:

Mr. PRESIDENT: In speaking of the present it is profitable to revert to the past.

Time was when beacon-fires gleamed from hill-top to hill-top as bearers of intelligence well understood. This was in the rude ages, when few could read and still fewer could write. Thus Scotland rallied her hostile bands, and thus our own more cultivated forefathers of modern times rallied the hosts of liberty in revolutionary days.

Next came post-horses and post-coaches as carriers of news. Then the winding of the post-boy's or stage-driver's horn was the signal, all over the land, for anxious crowds to congregate and hear the news. Hence mail-day, once a week, became a sort of gala-day in many a village of our great West. Thus it was, or else by the still more tardy pack-horses and wagons, all the way from Philadelphia, New York, or Baltimore, the news came over the mountains from our former homes in the East. The still more tardy flat-boat carried our letters to the South. The shores of our rivers re-echoed the quaint songs of the boatman, "Away down the river—Long time ago," and the hills were enlivened with merry wagoners, jingling their bells along over the mountains and back; bearers of luxuries, letters, and news from "O'er the hills and far away," to gladden or sadden our hearts.

Scaling the mountains and floating down the river, in those days, were manly vocations, and the hearts of the people, instead of repining, warmed with gratitude and pride at the magnitude of our country.

When this old country was new, and the great west was in our valley, thirty days was the ordinary time in which to hear from a mother, a brother, a sister, or a father, or a business transaction east of the mountains.

Next came Fulton with his steamboat upon our waters; then the old "river-gods" were at a discount, and months were shortened into weeks, and shouts of gratitude went up along the shores of our rivers wherever a steamboat ruffled their waters.

Close upon the heel of Fulton came the steam-car of Stephenson and of Grey. The iron horse took up his course toward the great West, and then was realized the language of the sacred writer: "The chariots shall rage in the streets; they shall jostle one against another in the broad places; they shall blaze like torches and run like the lightnings." But ere he reached the great west, the great west had moved onward to the western sea, and the once great west was now the central power of the nation. So now, again, the great west was "Over the mountains and far away." But the car of science, driven by genius, still moved on. In this emergency came Morse, to whose great name no words can add renown. He taught the lightnings how to go, and how to come, and how to speak. Yes, Franklin chained the lightnings, but Morse it was who taught them how to speak; gave ubiquity to their speech; anticipated time and annihilated space. In the language of inspiration, he made a "way for the lightnings," and answered the Divine inquiry put to Job, "Can'st thou send the lightnings that they may go, and say unto thee *Here we are?*" How great are the works of Providence, who has "put all things in subjection to man." Wonderful invention! "Its sound is gone out into all lands—its words to the end of the world." It more than realizes the fairy language of Shakespeare, "I'll put a girdle round the earth in forty minutes." It directs embassies, regulates commerce, commands armies, raises and depresses the stocks, regulates the running of trains, gives warning of coming storms, heralds victories, and announces defeats; it conveys the stern language of defiance, and the soft whisperings of love. So long as the lightnings traverse the heavens, the telegraph will be the monument of Morse.

At the conclusion of Judge Rorer's address, the mayor read the following message from Ottumwa:

OTTUMWA, *April* 16, 1872.

CHAIRMAN OF THE NATIONAL MORSE MEMORIAL ASSOCIATION,

Washington:

The city of Ottumwa, through the City Council, unite with Burlington in testimony of respect to the memory of Professor Samuel F. B. Morse, as one of America's greatest benefactors.

W. L. ORR,
Mayor.

Hon. T. W. Newman was called for, and delivered an address.
Professor Pearson then read a short and very tasteful poem.
The following message from the mayor of Milwaukee was read as it passed over the wires through the hall:

MILWAUKEE, *April* 16, 1872.

Speaker JAMES G. BLAINE,

House of Representatives, Washington:

The Common Council of the city of Milwaukee, in joint convention assembled this afternoon, unanimously adopted the following resolutions.

D. G. HOOKER,
Mayor.

Resolved, by the Common Council of the city of Milwaukee, That this city, in common with the whole country, have heard with deep and lasting regret of the death of Samuel F. B. Morse, to whom the country and the whole civilized world owe that wonderful development of modern science, the electric telegraph. Accustomed as we are to all the benefits of the electric telegraph, we should recall them upon this occasion of the dispensation of the Almighty Being, the secret of whose laws he was in life so far successful in discovering.

Resolved, That his honor the Mayor be requested to communicate these resolutions to Mr. Speaker James G. Blaine, of the House of Representatives at Washington, to be by him placed before the Memorial meeting to be held this evening in the House of Representatives.

The following dispatches from San Francisco were also received and read by the mayor:

SAN FRANCISCO, *April* 16, 1872.

Hon. JAMES G. BLAINE,

President of the Morse Memorial Meeting, Washington:

The citizens of San Francisco unite with you in homage to the memory of Samuel F. B. Morse. With you they mourn that all of him that was mortal has gone to its rest. With you they rejoice that his great discoveries remain to bless the world, and raise his honored name high on the glorious list of its real benefactors. To us of the Pacific coast his achievements are of priceless value. Through him we are this hour united with you, and for all mankind he has annihilated space and outstripped the very wings of the morning. As his triumphs over nature were splendid, so shall the fruits of his victories endure forever.

WILLIAM ALVORD,
President.

MAYOR'S OFFICE,
San Francisco, April 16, 1872.

To the MORSE MEMORIAL MEETING, *Washington:*

The citizens of San Francisco are in unison with you this evening heart and soul. Morse's honored name will not be forgotten so long as telegraph-wires are stretched across our house-tops and streets, for our children will be so taught that they may tell their children of the great man who first transmitted thought at lightning speed around the globe. The electric telegraph is his monument, and, should books and manuscripts be destroyed, tradition will keep his name and memory fresh in the hearts of the people.

WILLIAM ALVORD,
Mayor.

The following message was received in reply to one sent by the meeting:

GEORGE ROBERTSON,
Chairman of the Morse Meeting, Burlington:

There was a meeting of the committee from the city council and the telegraph-operators, at the Ballingall House, to mourn and sympathize with you in the loss of one of America's most esteemed benefactors.

P. G. BALLINGALL,
Chairman.

Gen. A. C. Dodge, being called for, delivered an address, referring especially to the fact of Professor Morse receiving by telegraph in Washington the news of the nominations at the presidential conventions in 1844, and to the conferring of the Cross of Isabella upon him by the Spanish government at the time that General Dodge was minister to Spain.

On motion, the speakers of the evening were requested to furnish copies of their remarks, to be forwarded to the Morse Memorial Association at Washington.

The citizens and telegraphers of Burlington here assembled, to the NATIONAL MORSE MEMORIAL MEETING,
Washington, greeting:

We mourn with you the irreparable loss of one of America's greatest public benefactors.

GEORGE ROBERTSON,
Mayor.

MEETING AT NASHVILLE, TENN.

A meeting of citizens was held at the mayor's office, at 6 o'clock on the evening of April 16, 1872, to pay a tribute to the memory of the late Professor Morse.

Mayor Morris was called to the chair, and the representatives of the press were appointed secretaries.

The mayor presented the following documents, received by him a day or two since:

NATIONAL TELEGRAPH MEMORIAL MONUMENT ASSOCIATION,
Washington, D. C., April 5, 1872.

To the Mayor of the City of Nashville:

SIR: I have the honor to transmit to you herewith a resolution adopted by this association, inviting the co-operation of the friends and admirers of the late Professor Samuel F. B. Morse throughout the country in holding meetings on Tuesday evening, the 16th instant, simultaneously with a great National Memorial meeting to be held in the House of Representatives at the National Capitol.

On behalf of this association, I respectfully and earnestly request you to take appropriate measures at the earliest moment possible for holding such a meeting in your city at the time named. The telegraph-wires will be freely open on the occasion for an exchange of sentiments between the several meetings and the one held here.

The favor of an early reply is requested.

Very respectfully, yours,

A. S. SOLOMONS,
Chairman of Committee of Arrangements.

Whereas, the United States House of Representatives has placed its hall at the disposal of the National Telegraph Memorial Association for the purpose of holding a memorial meeting in honor of the late Samuel F. B. Morse, on Tuesday, April 16, and prominent members of both Houses of Congress and other distinguished speakers have consented to address the meeting; and

Whereas, the telegraph has been freely placed at the disposal of this association for that evening to secure an exchange of sentiment with the meetings held in all portions of the country: Be it

Resolved, That the municipal authorities of the cities of the United States are hereby invited to call meetings of similar character in their several localities on the same evening, in order that the meetings may be in telegraphic communication, and thus a simultaneous expression be given to the national grief on the occasion of this irreparable loss.

H. AMIDON, *Secretary*.

After consultation, the mayor was requested to forward the following dispatch:

To A. S. Solomons,

 Washington, D. C.:

The citizens of Nashville, in common with the whole civilized world, desire to pay all proper respect to the memory of the late Samuel F. B. Morse, LL. D., and therefore send to the National Telegraph Memorial Association an expression of their deep and ardent respect for the distinguished inventor, their undying admiration for one who has done more for the progress of art and science than any other scientist, and their hope that all will be done that is possible to perpetuate the memory of the greatest man the world has produced.

K. J. MORRIS,
Mayor.

The meeting then adjourned.

MEETING AT PORTSMOUTH, N. H.

At a memorial meeting held on Tuesday evening, April 16, 1872, in honor of Professor Morse, Mayor Walker presided, and A. F. Howard, esq., acted as secretary.

On taking the chair, the mayor spoke substantially as follows:

Professor Morse was the son of Rev. Jedediah Morse, a Congregational minister, who settled in Charlestown, Mass. Professor Morse was born in Charlestown, April 27, 1791; graduated at Yale College in 1810, and went to England to study painting, under the famous artist Benjamin West. He returned to this his native land in 1815, but again visited Europe in 1832; and, in crossing the Atlantic, he conceived the idea of the electric telegraph and the identity or relation of electricity and magnetism. In 1837, and 1838, he went to Washington to procure aid from the Government to assist him in the furtherance of his plans; but, from the suspicions of some and the ridicule of others, he failed in his attempt, and was obliged to wait four long years, when, on the morning of the 4th of March, 1843, he was startled at the information that Congress had appropriated the sum of $30,000 to aid him in this great enterprise. In 1844, the great fact was demonstrated, and the enterprise was successfully completed between Washington and Baltimore. Professor Morse married the accomplished daughter of Judge Charles Walker, of Concord, N. H., who, it was said, was the handsomest lady in the city of Concord, beautiful in person, and still more beautiful in spirit.

Among his other accomplishments, Professor Morse excelled in portrait-painting. He once resided in Portsmouth, and it is but right and proper that we, the citizens of Portsmouth, should, in common with other cities and towns throughout our entire country, unite in tendering our tribute of respect to the honored dead. No one enterprise has contributed more to the advancement of civilization and Christianity than the electric telegraph. It has brought together the East and the West, the North and the South, in one common brotherhood.

At the conclusion of his remarks the mayor called upon Hon. W. H. Y. Hackett, who said:

Professor Morse's experience was much like that of other great and good men who had struggled through difficulties to benefit the world. He encountered opposition, neglect, and derision. It was the penalty that he and others had paid for being in advance of their age, and for insisting upon blessing the world in spite of their ignorance and prejudice.

Coming together to indicate our respect for the memory of one of the benefactors of our country and the world, we should be reminded of how much our comfort and convenience have been augmented by him, and by the toil, perseverance, and genius of other great and good men.

In enjoying the benefits of their labors we are prone to forget our debt to them. We are in the daily enjoyment of the results of steam as a producing and transporting agent, and electricity as a swift-winged messenger, as a matter of course, without remembering our benefactors. We go to the telegraph-office and order an article from any part of the world, as we go to the provision-store and order our dinner; and we go home and find the article in our dwellings, without any grateful recollection of the toils and struggles of Watt, who gave us the steam-engine, or of Stephenson, who gave us the railway, or of Morse, who gave us a messenger as swift as light.

In the morning paper we read what was done in our Congress the night before, and side by side we see the doings of the British Parliament at the same time, and what was done the same day by governments and on the exchanges in the capitals of Europe and the world. In a word, this morning's paper gave us a synopsis of the world's history for yesterday. And we regard it as a matter of course that all this should be done for us.

How appropriate it is that the civilized world should, this evening, manifest and exchange their tokens of respect for the memory of him who has given us the telegraph, without which the steam-engine and the railroad would not have been complete. It makes us wiser and better men, occasionally to give public and united expression of our gratitude to public benefactors. Besides, it may convey comfort and encouragement to some neglected child of genius who, like Watt, Stephenson, and Morse, may be struggling to benefit the world.

Who has read the life of Watt without involuntarily trembling, at points in his history, with apprehension that the steam-engine might be lost to the world? Who can know the history of Stephenson's labors to obtain the privilege of giving to the world the railway, without admiring that genius and perseverance which was stronger than the ignorance and prejudice of England? And Morse's twelve years' struggle to give to the world an equal blessing, shows equal power and perseverance.

It is now forty years since Samuel Finley Breese Morse, while crossing the Atlantic, conceived the idea of telegraph-wires, substantially as they are now in operation.

Soon after reaching home he verified his theory. He exhibited to the learned and the wealthy proof that his theory was true. But few believed, and none aided. At length, six years afterward, in 1838, he applied to the Congress of the United States for aid and encouragement to give his great discovery to the world. He was treated much as Stephenson was treated when he went before the British Parliament asking for an opportunity of giving the railway to the world. When Stephenson said that he could build a railway that would obtain the speed of twelve miles an hour, he met more men inclined to send him to the hospital for the insane than to give him a charter or encouragement. When Morse asked Congress to give him the means to make his discovery available, members ridiculed him as visionary. One member, soon afterward a cabinet-officer, moved to connect with the telegraph, mesmerism; another, moved to include Millerism; and another member, thinking Morse's lunacy pointed in another direction, moved to add to the appropriation sufficient to establish a line of telegraph to the moon. Thus treated in his own country, and by his own government, Morse went to

England and to France—but returned without any aid or encouragement. In 1843, he again applied to the United States Congress, and at the close of the session, by a fortunate incident, $30,000 was included in a bill to aid in this great enterprise, and in 1844, Morse's success flashed over the world like an electric shock.

Since then the whole civilized world have admitted their obligations to this great and good man. Honors have been showered upon him, and the contributions of money from Europe to Professor Morse have been large.

Besides the general grounds upon which Mr. Morse is entitled to our gratitude and respect, he has local claims which we gladly recognize. He resided for some time in Portsmouth, and he married a New Hampshire lady—a descendant of a Portsmouth family.

He died at a good old age, and the civilized world will honor his memory.

At the close of his remarks Mr. Hackett offered the following resolutions, which were unanimously adopted :

Resolved, That the citizens of Portsmouth have received with deep regret the intelligence of the death of Samuel F. B. Morse, a benefactor of his race and age, whose genius and perseverance have brought the world into instantaneous intercourse and sympathy; extended the borders of civilization, and provided a medium and influence for making a brotherhood of the whole family of man.

Resolved, As a token of our respect for the memory of such a public benefactor, and of our appreciation of the blessing he has conferred upon the world, that the mayor be requested to cause the national flag to be displayed as a flag of mourning over the City-Hall for one week.

The meeting was also addressed by E. M. Brown, esq., and T. E. O. Marvin, esq., after which it was adjourned.

A. F. HOWARD,
Secretary.

MEETING OF THE COMMON COUNCIL, CHICAGO, ILL.

In accordance with the action of the Council, on the recommendation of the mayor, had at the regular meeting held April 15, 1872, his honor the Mayor, the aldermen, and other city officers, assembled at the council-chamber to pay respect, in their official capacity, to the memory of the late Professor Samuel F. B. Morse, with Mr. President McAvoy in the chair.

The president, in opening the proceedings, said the object for which the present meeting had been called was well known. They were assembled to pay their respects, in an official capacity, to the memory of one of the greatest benefactors of the human race, Professor Morse, the inventor of the electric telegraph.

It was proper that Chicago should contribute its mite of respect to the memory of Mr. Morse. Every city in the United States brought into communication with the electric telegraph was engaged in the task of paying similar tributes of respect. Chicago had received as great benefits from the electric telegraph as any other city, and it was fitting they should assemble in this manner. He suggested that a committee on resolutions should be appointed.

Alderman Bond moved that the Chair appoint a committee of three, together with his honor the mayor, to prepare and submit appropriate resolutions.

The Chair appointed his honor the Mayor, Aldermen Bond, Bateham, and McGenniss as such committee.

The committee, through Alderman Bond, presented the following preamble and resolution, which were unanimously adopted, and transmitted by telegraph to the National Morse Memorial meeting, in session in the hall of the House of Representatives at the national capital :

Whereas, The inventor, in the public estimation, is rapidly taking a rank with the foremost of the world's benefactors; and

Whereas, Samuel F. B. Morse ranks first in his class as an inventor and benefactor: Therefore

Resolved, That the city of Chicago, having largely received benefits from his labors in her prosperity, and in her calamity having through the instrumentality devised by him, reached the uttermost parts of the earth, vibrating the noblest chords of human sympathy— here adds her tribute of respect and honor to the genius and perseverance of the man who, overcoming all obstacles, gave to the world the wonderful magnetic telegraph, and thereby brought into close communion all nations, tongues, and peoples, breaking down the clannish barriers that had divided them and made them enemies; that her citizens cherish the name of Morse, whose chief monument must ever be his high position in the hearts of the people, and that while we mourn his departure we, with all the civilized world, must ever rejoice that he lived, and that his works remain with us.

His honor Mayor Medill offered as a sentiment: " Morse, one of the few names of the countless millions of the human race born not to die; mortal in the flesh, but immortal in the memory of mankind," and addressed the meeting as follows:

Mr. President: It is proper on an occasion of this kind to offer a few thoughts or observations on the work of this great man. His name has been so long a household word among us that it is hard to realize he has departed from this life. His work has been of such character that it seemed to have given him an immortality that has been spiritual, so to speak. He has successfully grappled with the most subtle of all material substances and reduced it to the highest use which it is possible for the mind to conceive, to which it could be put. Previous to this invention of Morse, the human race had never, with all its inventive effort, and all expenditure of thought and money and labor, been able to project thought in advance of the body. It had never been able to transmit the feelings, sentiments, ideas, and wishes of each to the other, beyond the reach of the sound of the

voice or the glance of the eye. Morse was the first of all the countless millions of the human race who was able to separate mind—or
thought, rather—from the mortal body, and send it round the world,
and annihilate time and space at the same time. The highest effort
of mechanical genius carried thought no faster than it carried the
body. Men had employed the carrier-pigeon; they had employed
beacon-lights, and various contrivances which to us now seem of
trivial character; but to convey an idea between men, it was necessary to send a man with it to deliver it, and hence the speed of the
delivery was measured by the speed with which the messenger could
travel. Morse changed all that. He has stretched, by his genius,
over the world a net-work of wires, under the oceans, and across the
rivers and seas, to operate on this globe as the nervous system of the
body acts in the individual.

Franklin first discovered the nature of the electric element, and I
have often thought that had he lived a little longer, had his mind
not been engrossed with the cares of state, with the birth of a republic, and with the philosophies which he was teaching mankind,
that he would have robbed Morse of his immortality. I have
thought that Franklin at times almost made the invention that Morse
made, but he had too many great things on hand to engross his
time, and was unable to prosecute his own great discovery. Others
took up the matter where Franklin left off, in Europe and America,
and groped in the dark for two generations; but Morse was the fortunate mortal who discovered the secret of employing this subtle fluid
as a messenger to bear thought from man to man and from nation to
nation, and round the earth. We have become so accustomed to
the use of the telegraph that it seems now almost as if we always had
it, as if it had come down to us from the days of the ancients; and yet
there are several gentlemen now in this hall who remember very distinctly those embarrassing and discouraging struggles of Professor
Morse to induce Congress, after capitalists had refused to let him

have a dollar, to advance him a little money to demonstrate and prove the utility of his invention! I remember it vividly. I watched the progress of that struggle for several years, and everything that was printed and said about it. My heart was interested in it. I was then a young man, just coming out of boyhood, but I wrote letters to such members of Congress as I knew, urging them to let him have the money he asked to make his experimental wire, for, from what I had read of Morse's explanations, I was satisfied that what he claimed was correct.

Very soon after that I became publisher of a daily newspaper, and since then I have always been a patron of the invention. It would be very hard for the press to give up Morse's work. It would be very hard for an editor to feel that he had made a newspaper in which he did not present to his readers the world's news, fresh, as fast as it fell from human lips or was thought by human brains, put into type and then into the paper, and then put into the hands of its patrons. If we want to estimate the value of this great discovery or invention, let us consider how much we would take, in money or other valuable things, to surrender it forever. How much, gentlemen, would Chicago, America, or the civilized world take to give up the electric telegraph, and have it blotted out, with the knowledge that it never could be recovered? Why, you might almost as well ask a man to give up his life or the bread that he eats; to separate himself from home, country, wife and family, as to separate himself from the uses of the subtle, spiritual agency which has brought him in contact with the entire race. Here we sit, this evening, talking with the American people, and, if it were necessary, the representative of this invention here to-night, General Stager, would have placed us in communication with Europe, Asia, Africa, and the islands of the ocean, taking no more time to bring the utterances of the people at the antipodes to us here, and to tell the sentiments in return, than it does to transmit this news to the nearest police-station across the street.

This invention was needed to perfect human communication. There are limits to the velocity of bodies, governed by fixed mechanical laws, that can never be exceeded. I suppose we have nearly reached the limit of physical locomotion. If we go much beyond that we have already achieved, we do it at the peril of life and limb. We increase in a geometrical ratio the danger of death. But in this invention of Morse's we have accomplished the whole at a bound. Distance is annihilated, and time with it, and mortal man here on this crowded earth, through the genius of this great man, has grasped and enjoys one of the attributes of Divinity, proving the truth of the Bible statement, that man is created in the image of his Maker.

The great philosopher, Buckle, says that, in his opinion, perhaps the man who conferred the greatest amount of benefit on the human race was Adam Smith, the discoverer of the science of political economy. I am inclined to challenge even so high an authority as Buckle. I believe that the meed of praise belongs to Morse rather than to Smith. I believe that Morse has done, and will do, more for the good of mankind, materially, morally, and intellectually, than Smith, who gave us those great rules of political economy. Smith dealt with material things. He showed the ignorant men, and the wise men who were ignorant on this subject, the value and necessity of freedom of trade, and the true laws of commerce, and the principles upon which exchanges should be conducted throughout the world among men, but it was a gross invention in comparison with this ethereal one of Morse. If America had never produced another inventor than S. F. B. Morse, she would be in danger of no other nation, ancient or modern, or of future times, snatching from her the palm of invention, for I can conceive of no triumph of genius over material things that ever can eclipse the use of electricity in the transmission of thought.

And, as the resolutions that have been adopted set forth, he is one of the very few men who ever lived to see his own monument erected by a grateful people. Morse lived to the full age allotted to man, and the people were so impatient to erect a memorial to his memory that they could not wait for him to pass to "that bourne from which no traveler returns," and so the benefactor saw his own monument, and heard the verdict of posterity in the flesh, before he had been gathered to his fathers.

I shall never, as long as I live, forget my introduction to Mr. Morse. I had never seen him until two years ago. I was in the city of New York, in the office of the Western Union Telegraph Company, conferring with the president of that great company in regard to an increased service of news for the West. While talking with Mr. Orton, a venerable, fine-looking, benevolent old gentleman, with long, silvery locks, came into the room and sat down. Mr. Orton, observing that I was not acquainted with him, introduced me. I spent ten or fifteen minutes in very agreeable conversation with him, with a great many more thoughts passing through my mind than I uttered to him, as I sat in the presence of this man, who had placed in possession of his race this wonderful magnetic telegraph. His eye was clear, his form erect, and his voice was strong, and he seemed to be in sound health. I did not dream that he was then approaching four-score years.

Mr. President, it is impossible to eulogize the memory of Morse. His works are superior to any tribute of praise that it is possible for us to bestow. As the resolutions you have adopted set forth, he has gone from us in the flesh, but his works remain with us, and will remain with us so long as the human race exists. They will remain to bless mankind, and to promote "peace and good-will among men." For, in proportion as this system of telegraphic communication is extended among the nations of the earth, in that proportion will the causes of alienation, and all misunderstandings and prejudices, be broken down by its means. Nearly all the misunderstandings among men grow out of prejudice and ignorance, and the mission of the telegraph is to abolish ignorance of one another among men, and to enable one to know what all know, and to know it at the very moment that utterance is given to the thought, and to enable the whole earth to realize day by day what all parts of it are doing, thinking, and saying, and intending to do. It enables the thousand millions of the human race to think in unison, and to speak with one voice, and there only remains, in my opinion, the perfection of this system, and the cheapening of transmission, to yield to the world more good than it ever entered into the hearts of men to expect from it.

REMARKS OF ALDERMAN L. L. BOND.

Alderman Bond said he felt like saying a few words regarding Morse as an inventor. He had long believed the inventor had not been accorded the position he deserved. When we compare the works of Shakespeare with the labor of that poor collier, George Stephenson, we find the practical utility of the works of the latter the greatest. Jefferson and all the other great statesmen of the nation have done much, and from their records we would not take one jot of credit, but how the Declaration of Independence and state documents pale into insignificance beside the inventions of Fulton and Morse. Some people have tried to rob Morse of the honor of inventing the magnetic telegraph, but when it is conceded that his work remains, in all essential points, as it came from the masterbrain, the greatness of the man cannot be denied.

SENTIMENT AND REMARKS OF GENERAL STILES.

General Stiles, city attorney, offered the following sentiment:

Nature was personified in Morse. That one touch of his will yet make the whole world kin.

General Stiles added: The discovery of Morse—and it was a discovery, I think, rather than an invention—made the whole civilized world neighbors. Had it been made a thousand years ago, and had the discoverer dared to claim that its operations were in obedience to natural law, he would have been burned at the stake. Had he claimed it as a miracle, he would have had an army of believers, and he could have founded a great and still-enduring religion. His discovery was not an accident. With a heart full of faith he had long sought for it; not with the feverish faith of a religious enthusiast, but with the nobler faith of a man of science.

How touchingly were its uses illustrated during our great calamity, when over the wires, from minute to minute and from hour to hour, flashed that which touched a world of hearts, whose pulsations of sympathy, coming back to us, we heard and felt as plainly as one feels the heart-throbs of a near friend in anguish.

The discovery and the discoverer will go together, and both will be remembered so long as mind shall communicate with mind.

Mr. W. H. Smith, of the Western Associated Press, offered the following sentiment:

The co-laborers of Morse: Though not recognized in monuments, nor known in the historic page, yet worthy to be remembered; without whose skill and untiring industry the invention of Morse would have been robbed of half its usefulness; but they are yet not without recompense, as the consciousness of a great work, modestly performed through a love of science and sense of duty, is a satisfaction which no power of man can take away.

Mr. Smith said that there was a class of men greatly concerned in the science of telegraphing who should not be forgotten on this night, when this great inventor of the telegraph is being honored. —He referred to those who had co-operated with Professor Morse in his great work, without whose assistance he would have failed in accomplishing the work in all its perfection as we behold it to-day. He meant those who had employed themselves, and given their money in the perfection of instruments, and who had made valuable suggestions from time to time in regard to the science of telegraphing. Personal allusion was made to Gen. Anson Stager, to whom the honor of establishing long circuits was principally due. By means of long circuits, Chicago could be connected not only with the principal cities of the country, but with the whole world. Long circuits were never believed to be possible in the infancy of the telegraph. To Chicago was also due the credit of the duplex-instrument, which could send a message in opposite directions at the same time over a single wire, and which was used with great success during the late severe storm in working off the great accumulation of dispatches at Chicago and Buffalo.

MR. BURLEY'S SENTIMENT.

Mr. A. H. Burley, city comptroller, offered the following sentiment:

Morse, with a thread, has bound all the nations of the earth, and sealed the union with fire from heaven.

PRESIDENT McAVOY'S MESSAGE.

Mr. McAvoy sent the following message:

COUNCIL CHAMBER, CHICAGO,
April 16, 1872.

To A. S. SOLOMONS,

Chairman National Morse Memorial Association,

Washington, D. C.:

A meeting of the Common Council of the city of Chicago is now in session at the City-Hall, called for the purpose of paying their respects to the memory of the late Professor Morse, and send to you and other sister cities our condolence at the loss of a man who by his genius has proven himself one of the greatest benefactors of the human race. His memory will be cherished in every land where his wonderful invention is used. The names of Morse, Franklin, and Fulton will never be forgotten by a grateful posterity.

JOHN H. McAVOY,
President of the Common Council.

After which the meeting adjourned.

C. T. HOTCHKISS,
City Clerk.

MEETING AT AUGUSTA, ME.

In compliance with the request of the Chairman of the Committee of Arrangements at Washington, a public meeting of our citizens was held on the 16th of April, 1872, at 8 p. m., in the city rooms. The Mayor was called to the chair, and Hon. Samuel W. Lane chosen secretary.

A statement of the object of the meeting was made, and appropriate remarks were offered by several gentlemen.

The following resolution was then read and unanimously adopted:

Resolved, That the people of Augusta, Me., unite with the people of the United States and of the civilized world in expressing their reverence for the memory of the great inventor of the telegraph, Samuel F. B. Morse.

After directing the resolution to be forwarded to the assemblage at Washington, the meeting adjourned.

J. J. EVELETH.

MEETING AT CHARLESTON, S. C.

[Official.]

CITY-HALL, OFFICE OF CLERK OF COUNCIL,
Charleston, S. C., May 3, 1872.

On the 16th day of April, 1872, the City Council of Charleston, S. C., met at 7 o'clock p. m. to unite with the National Morse Memorial meeting then being held in the Hall of the House of Representatives, at Washington, D. C., in sympathy with the nation, on the death of its honored son, Samuel F. B. Morse, when the following preamble was unanimously adopted, and ordered to be forwarded immediately to Washington:

Whereas, this Council, representing the citizens of Charleston, S. C., feel, in common with the people of the entire civilized world, the great loss occasioned by the death of Samuel F. B. Morse, the father of telegraphy in the United States, respectfully beg to unite their sympathies with the Morse Memorial Association meeting now being held in the city of Washington, D. C., in the following telegram:

The late Professor Morse: May his memory ever live in the hearts of his countrymen. By his genius and his discovery, the innocent have been protected, the guilty have been punished, merit has triumphed, crime has perished, trade, commerce, manufactures, and mechanism have flourished. May his invention—the electric telegraph—never more bring to this generation the sad and unwelcome message of war, but that all messages may have for their groundwork, peace, freedom, prosperity, happiness. We deeply deplore his loss.

MEETING AT POUGHKEEPSIE, N. Y.

ROOMS OF THE BOARD OF TRADE,
Poughkeepsie, N. Y., April 10, 1872.

Immediately after the meeting of the Board of Trade the members present resolved themselves into a citizens' meeting to make arrangements to act in concert with other towns and cities in the United States in bestowing honors to the memory of the late Professor Samuel F. B. Morse.

Mayor Eastman was elected president, and Alderman Webb secretary.

The following committee of arrangements was appointed: Chairman, Rev. Francis B. Wheeler; S. M. Buckingham, W. Hinckley, John I. Platt, W. W. Hegeman, E. Killey, E. B. Osborne, O. H. Booth, E. Ellsworth, George Innis, John F. Winslow, Philip Hamilton, De Witt Webb, Matthew J. Vassar, Otis Disbee, and President Raymond of Vassar College.

Arrangements were made to hold a general meeting on Tuesday evening, the 16th inst., and at that time, to be in telegraphic communication with similar meetings throughout the United States.

MAYOR'S PROCLAMATION.

CITY OF POUGHKEEPSIE,
State of New York, April 10, 1872.

In accordance with a resolution adopted by the National Telegraph Memorial Association inviting the co-operation of the friends and admirers of the late Professor Samuel F. B. Morse throughout the country in memorial exercises on Tuesday evening, the 16th instant, simultaneously with a great National Memorial meeting to be held in the House of Representatives, at the national capital, I respectfully suggest that appropriate measures be taken for holding such a meeting in this city, which has been his residence for a quarter of a century.

I earnestly request that citizens unite with an appropriate committee of arrangements in such action as shall evince our estimation of the man, and the loss our city and the world has sustained.

H. G. EASTMAN,
Mayor.

MEETING OF CITIZENS.

Poughkeepsie's tribute to the memory of Samuel Finley Breese Morse was placed on record at the Presbyterian church, in this city, on Tuesday evening, April 16, 1872. That large edifice was crowded with hundreds of the best citizens of Poughkeepsie and their families, every one of whom sincerely mourned the loss of so distinguished a citizen. Care had been taken to decorate the church, or at least a portion of it, with flowers. Vines of ivy were entwined about the pulpit, while directly in front of it, resting upon a table, was a beautiful cross of white flowers, surmounted by a floral crown, and having at its base a circlet of roses. To the right and left, about ten feet away, were two small stands, each covered with a fountain of flowers, the odor from which permeated the air, imparting a fragrance which spoke of spring. At the head of each aisle, also, were tables filled with floral offerings neatly and artistically arranged. The sixth pew from the front, on the north side of the center row, was hung in black and was vacant. It was the one formerly occupied by Professor Morse when alive, he being a member of the Presbyterian Church. It was the only vacant spot in the church, and with its somber surroundings spoke volumes.

The exercises were made to have a more intimately personal bearing upon the life of the illustrious inventor by the fact that three of the speakers were his pastor, his physician, and his lawyer; the three persons who, of all others, must have been best acquainted with his private life. Of course their remarks were listened to with the greatest interest, as each from his own point of view helped to make the assembly acquainted with Professor Morse as a man, a Christian citizen, and a near friend.

At 7.30 p. m. the board of trustees and faculty of Vassar College arrived, together with the board of directors of the Board of Trade, and the Mayor and Common Council, all taking seats reserved for them in the front of the body of the church. Rev. Francis B. Wheeler, Rev. Wm. H. Wines, and Dr. Parker arrived next and took seats upon the platform, when the organist, Prof. E. O. Flagler, played as a voluntary a selection from Stabat Mater. Every seat in the beautiful church was at this time occupied. Before the close of the voluntary, his honor Mayor Eastman, President Raymond, of Vassar College, and Hon. John Thompson came upon the scene. At the proper time, Mayor Eastman stepped upon the platform in front of the pulpit and spoke as follows:

We have assembled here to-night to pay a tribute of respect to one of the most illustrious of the nation's dead, and to dwell upon the good that has been done upon earth by the one we mourn. Wherever the electric telegraph is known—and that is wherever there is civilization—the intelligence of the death of Professor Samuel F. B. Morse, the man who taught lightning to speak the language of men, has been received with profound regret.

The glory of his achievements and eminent services to the world are recognized in every part of the globe, and millions of slender shafts everywhere bordering the great highways of travel are significant monuments to his genius and fame.

For more than a quarter of a century he was an esteemed resident of this community, revered and honored by all this vast people, and much of the remarkable history of his checkered life passed under our own observation. While other assemblages are convened at this hour in all parts of the land in Memorial exercises for the illustrious dead, we, his neighbors and friends, are permitted to come to the very altar where he worshiped, to pay our last tribute to his genius and virtue, and to bow with reverence around his vacant seat, while he who was his beloved pastor, and others who have been his associates, tell us the interesting story of his eventful life, of his humble beginnings, his early struggles, then his trials and persecutions, and finally his glorious success and achievements.

For such a purpose are we assembled, and may the impressive exercises of the occasion furnish an instructive lesson to mankind. In accordance with the published announcement, the Rev. Mr. Wines will now open the exercises.

Rev. William H. Wines read a portion of the Scriptures, commencing, "The heavens declare the glory of God, the firmament showeth His handiwork."

The scriptural reading was followed by prayer, also by Rev. Mr. Wines. The choir then sung an anthem,

> "Why lament the Christian dying,
>   Why indulge in tears or gloom?"

The opening address of the evening was made by Rev. Francis B. Wheeler, pastor of the Presbyterian Church, and also an intimate pastoral and social acquaintance of the dead electrician. Mr. Wheeler's remarks were listened to with profound attention. He spoke as follows:

We meet to-night in memory of a great and good man, who was and still is—though our eyes are holden that we cannot see him—a man whom God richly endowed, greatly ennobled, making his hoary head a crown of glory. For it must be remembered that the place Professor Morse held, and holds to-night, though out of the world, is not the result of accident, but the outgrowth and product of providential investment and personal culture. The son of a New England clergyman, poor in the beginning, thoughtful, studious, resolute, persistent, and God-fearing, he pushed his way through hard toil, against opposition and ridicule, up to that commanding eminence from whose summit, as a mount of transfiguration, he passed into glory.

Some of the salient points of his life may be given. Born in 1791, graduated at Yale in 1810, he passed under the instruction of Washington Allston and Benjamin West, then, abroad and at home, occupied in the study of art, modeling and painting in Paris, in Charleston, S. C., in Boston, Mass., and Concord, N. H., and in the city of New York, where he founded the Academy of Design, becoming its first president, filling also a professorship in the University. His life thus far, up to 1829, though honored and useful, had nothing of remarkable interest. At that time he crossed the sea again, and was absent three years, in intimate relations with European *savants*, investigating with Daguerre the marvels of light and the pictures of the sun. In 1832, as the packet-ship *Sully* sailed out from the port of Havre, we find Professor Morse a passenger, and the great thought of his mind on the homeward voyage was that of electricity and magnetism. This was revolved continually in his berth, as he paced the deck, as he conversed with his fellow-passengers, and there, on the wide, open sea, the telegraph was born, and as the sea touches all shores and belongs to all people, so it, with such birth-place, was born for all lands and for every tongue; like the angel of the Apocalypse, with one foot on sea and the other on land, proclaiming that time should be no longer.

Arriving in New York, he prosecuted his investigation with enthusiasm, in poverty and under the imputation of being a visionary and fanatic; in the chamber of the University, where, in 1837, he demonstrated the practicability of his invention to hundreds of persons, the whole apparatus, except a clock, having been made by himself. But it was not until 1844, that he compelled the attention of mankind, by telegraphic communications between the two cities of Washington and Baltimore. After this. there was no lack of success and no want of honor. Kings delighted to do him service, and everywhere his name was spoken with profound admiration and respect. In 1846, he became a resident of Poughkeepsie, connecting himself with the Presbyterian Church in January, 1848, where he has spent a large portion of his time for 26 years. And it is a matter of gratulation, fellow-citizens, that the child of his invention, born on the sea and rocked by the storm, reached its maturity here. Our noble river is immortalized by the name of Fulton, while its banks and our city have been rendered illustrious by the name of Morse.

But why speak of the scholar and the philosopher, and these headlands that lie along the shore of his life, albeit "*forsan et hæc olim meminisse juvabit,*" when there are other and greater attractions in the man and the Christian ? Simple and unaffected in his manners, warm and generous in his nature, sunny in all the aspects of his life, unsuspecting in his thoughts, noble in his aims, a marvelous magnetism in his eye and words that drew all hearts to him, no man ever bore so large and such accumulating honors so meekly. But his highest excellencies were manifest in his Christian life, his loyalty to God, his affection for Jesus Christ, his reverence for truth, his profound and child-like submission to the word of God; always recognizing himself as an instrument in God's hands for perfecting God's praise and advancing the interests of humanity. How well I remember the look of humility that covered his face, the hushed utterances of his lips, when allusion was made to some of his proudest triumphs. "Not unto me, not unto me, but to God be all the glory. Not what hath man, but what hath God wrought? I am but a little child doing the work of my heavenly Father." Never was there a man more positive in his opinion, more clear in his religious convictions. Some one in Brooklyn said, last Sabbath, "He was little or nothing in his religion. He was a member of a Presbyterian Church, and in this regard he allowed others to think for him." Whoever said this did not know Professor Morse, for his whole life was one burning, brilliant refutation of this. Whatever he was in art, in science, and in letters, he was greater, as a disciple of his Lord; a profound religious thinker, sharply defined in his religious statements, clear, bold, vigorous, outspoken, there could be no uncertainty as to what he thought and what he believed. In this regard he was in striking antagonism with many scientific men of the age, who have divorced themselves from a pure, simple, Biblical faith. He knew what he believed, whom he believed, why he believed. This belief was his own, thought out and settled for himself. He had no Master but one, and that one was Jesus Christ, the Lord. As the rounding touch and beautiful finish of the years came upon him, there was a more thorough and earnest committal of himself, at every point of his being, in this direction. His death was but the bright coronal of the

Christian's hopes and the Christian's faith. To know such a man is a rare privilege; to be with such a man, is to stand almost at the gate of heaven. I deem myself fortunate in knowing him; that I have been permitted to look upon that brow, beneath which throbbed that active, restless, creative brain; into those eyes that kindled and flashed into such inspiration; to hear that voice that summoned the lightnings from the skies, and their answer came, "Lo, here we are;" to grasp that hand that harnessed them and sent them forth on messages of peace; the man who so faithfully served his own generation, and now, by the will of God, has fallen asleep. They hung upon his person princely badges of high, distinguishing honors; they reared to him a statue of bronze. Countries and cities vie with each other in commemorating his greatness and his virtues. But he needs no such memorials; every sheaf of wires that pulses in the sea; every line of telegraph on land that hums in the wind—all bring honors. All trades, all arts, all sciences, all commerce will perpetuate his memory, and coming generations shall rise up and call him blessed. The name Morse, in the old Celtic, is said to be hero—this its meaning. "Peace hath her triumphs as well as war," and as they of old lifted their heroes to the skies, and wrote them there among the stars, so we will lift our Morse on high, and as the aurora blazes there in sheets of flame and pillared light, so his name shall brighten with the years, while his commanding genius and living heart shall move on in the high emprise of God, in the broad fields of light beyond the flood and above the cloud. The body sleeps, and we laid it lovingly away, "where the wicked cease from troubling and the weary are at rest." We shall miss his venerable presence in our streets; in the home of "Locust Grove," where he welcomed so warmly his friends; in this house of God, where his seat to-night is so mutely eloquent. But,

> After the burden and heat of the day,
> The starry calm of night;
> After the rough and toilsome way,
> A sleep in the robe of white.

The journey is over, the fight is fought,
  He hath seen the Home of his love;
And the smile on the dreamer's face is caught
  From the land of smiles above.

O sweet is the slumber wherewith the King
  Hath caused His weary to rest,
For, sleeping, he hears the angels sing,
  And leans on the Master's breast.

His very name is as ointment poured
  On the moonlight pale to-night,
And the chamber is sweet to Thy servants, Lord,
  For the scent of his raiment white.

The silent chamber faceth the east,
  Faceth the dawn of the day,
And the shining feet of the great High Priest
  Shall break through the shadows gray.

The golden dawn of the day of God
  Shall smite on the sealed eyes;
The trumpet sound shall thunder around,
  Our dreamer shall wake and rise.

The night is over—the sleep is slept,
  He is called from his shadowy place;
OUR MORSE shall stand on the glorious land
  And look on the Master's face.

The next speaker was Rev. John H. Raymond, president of Vassar College, who said:

There surely never was a commemorative occasion on which panegyric was so little called for as on this. When a whole nation, when (I may say) two continents are in joint session to do honor to an individual, brought into communication by that very invention which gave him his world-wide fame—the voice of private eulogy seems gratuitous indeed. So far as his praise is concerned, silence appears the most fitting thing.

It is natural to ask what was the secret of Professor Morse's splendid career? The completeness of it was wonderful. A life so long, a character so well balanced, a culture so varied and rounded out, have seldom been granted to any man. Few have touched society at so many points. As an artist, an inventor, an educator, a scholar, a loyal member of a Christian church, there is little in his life to regret; abundant occasion for commendation and praise.

In such a career we feel that there is nothing accidental. This man did not stumble into greatness, nor was it thrust upon him from without. It was the outcome of something within. Nor did he reach it by any single leap of genius or sudden flash of inspiration. It was wrought out by a steady, healthy, systematic process. It co.t him effort; it taxed all the resources of a cultivated intellect, and proved the energy of his will.

He was no exceptional genius—no brilliant meteor flashing athwart the view of men, and extorting exclamations of wonder and admiration, but the law of whose movement defied calculation and baffled imitation. He was a fair representative of what may be accomplished by a broad education, an earnest purpose, and persevering endeavors. Brilliant as is his fame, it is what thousands may reasonably hope to share—at least to earn—by making the same wise and faithful use of their faculties and their opportunities.

He gained nothing by indirection, by short cuts, by random guesses. For every pound of success attained, he was willing to pay his pound of honest labor expended—labor of muscle or labor of brain. He meant to succeed by first thoroughly understanding what he had taken in hand, measuring exactly the amount of resistance and difficulty to be overcome, then collecting the necessary forces and holding on till all the necessary conditions of accomplishment were fulfilled. His triumphs were the triumphs of intelligence—of knowledge hardly earned and persistently applied. And we have a right to be proud of such a man as a neighbor and a fellow-countryman. We are willing to have him presented to the world as a representative American—a specimen fruit of our institutions, our system of education, and of the national spirit.

Dr. Jedediah Morse, the geographer, and the father of Professor Morse, was a man of prodigious vitality, and fathered a large amount of brain in his sons, all of them in different ways. While thus, in his organization, he represented the best New England breed of men, his training showed the best style of New England education at the beginning of this century. But thousands have sprung from as good a stock, and had as favorable surroundings, and yet brought nothing to pass. Thousands have had like chances, but did not secure them— happy junctures unperceived, frequent suggestions never brought to the birth—tides in their affairs—

> "Which taken at the flood might have led on to fortunes;
> Omitted, all the voyage of their life
> Was bound in shallows and in miseries."

And apart from all the benefits flowing from his great works, Morse will not have lived in vain if he may stand to succeeding generations as an illustrious example of fidelity to opportunities.

Among many characteristics which contributed to Professor Morse's grand success, I think tenacity of purpose will be found to hold a prominent place. From the moment when the dim idea of an electro-magnetic and chemical recording telegraph rose before his mind, on shipboard in 1832, till the establishment of the trial line from Washington to Baltimore, in 1843, he never relinquished it for a moment, and every month contributed something to the advancement of the enterprise. By persistent reflection, the first dim suggestion wrought itself out into a definite plan. The crude approaches were steadily improved and the alphabet perfected, until the invention stood complete, and he could demonstrate its effectiveness by ocular proof to all who would give him attention. His task was only just begun. Unless he could convince the world of its availability, he had produced nothing but a toy. Public opinion must be conquered, governments were to be won. Morse paused not, but he found it an herculean and disheartening labor. A whole winter at Washington brought him nothing but disappointment. Some respected his intelligence and admired his enthusiasm; more laughed at him for his dreams. On the adjournment of Congress in the spring of 1838, he hastened to England to meet a like result; thence to France, where he obtained only an empty recognition; thence back to his own country to renew his efforts here. Four weary years of fruitless labor wore away, and another seemed before him. What a winter of heart-sickness must have been that of 1842–'43, which he spent at Washington, amidst the seething crowd of hungry suitors for the nation's bounty, pressing his modest request for the public trial of an invention which promised measureless benefits to the country, and had now borne triumphantly every scientific test? The last evening of the session came, and he relinquished again the hope of success. But he had already done the work—the end was nearer than he imagined. He had left the Capitol in disgust, had packed his trunk for home and retired to rest, when at midnight of that 4th of March, the last hour of the session, news was brought him of the unexpected passage of his bill, and the victory was won. It was the triumph of persistent purpose.

It may be expected that I should say something of Professor Morse's relations to education. These were numerous and important, but time forbids me to enlarge. On the one side we may claim him as the fruit of education, and in a special manner of that old New England system—which has of late been so sharply questioned, accused of narrowness and barren of practical results, but which may proudly point to such men as the legitimate product of its influences and the proud vindication of its methods.

He was, during much of his life, a practical educator. While yet an artist, he was largely instrumental in the founding of the National Academy of Design, of which he was president for the first sixteen years, and which still survives—a noble monument of his enlightened devotion to the highest human culture. He also held a professorship in the University of the City of New York, where he lectured

on the philosophy of his favorite arts.   He was one of the men first
selected by Mr. Vassar as trustee for his College for Women, and
held a place in its board until his death.   At all times and in all
places he has manifested a cordial sympathy with every institution
and instrumentality which promised to aid in the enlightenment of
mankind.   If he owed much to education he has nobly acknowledged and generously repaid the debt, and not the least by that
great invention which will preserve his name to the latest generations, and is and will be, the universal illumination of the race, whose
great function is the swiftest and widest diffusion of knowledge among
all the nations of the globe.

DR. E. H. PARKER'S ADDRESS.

Never before did the civilized world take pause in its bustling,
hurried life, at the death-bed of one who, neither potentate nor
prince, neither king nor kaiser, neither warrior nor statesman, had
made himself more famous than all, and bestowed an unspeakable
boon upon the peoples and the nations.   It was fitting that civilization
should breathlessly wait for the least indication that gave a half
promise of improvement till hope had gone, and should now bow in
united sorrow at his grave.   Into what occupation and into what
circle has not the great invention of him, whom we commemorate, brought constant use and benefit?   Tamed by his genius, the
lightning is ever carrying swift messages of love and sorrow, of trade
and of statecraft, of the greatest and of the smallest events of life,
blessing families and speaking peace to nations.   Hence it is that
the high and the low, the great and the humble, individuals and
governments unite to commemorate his loss and to reciprocate messages of condolence from the frozen North to the torrid South, across
continents and beneath oceans.   But while others mourn the great
benefactor, acknowledging the indebtedness of the world to his patient
labors and unwearied perseverance, we feel that which is more per-

sonal. We see that the world has lost another of its great men, but we feel that we have been touched more deeply, and have bid a long farewell to a respected fellow-citizen, a valued neighbor, a dear friend. It is not necessary that we should indulge in sounding eulogy, however merited. His memory needs not that with us; rather let us talk together as friends of him who was one of us, the current of whose life mixed with ours, and whose absence will long leave with us an aching void. It is now more than thirteen years since I had the honor of an introduction to Professor Morse. It was upon the occasion of a rather formal and yet spontaneous reception given to him on his return from Europe by his friends and neighbors. Many of you will remember that we met him at the station and escorted him, in a long cavalcade, to his beautiful residence at Locust Grove. I was presented to him by that elegant gentleman the late Dr. Roosevelt, than whom it would be difficult to find a more delightful example of the refined courtesy and ease of the older and better school. At that interview I was especially struck by the fact that Professor Morse was deeply touched by this cordial and unexpected demonstration, so much indeed as to be unable to find more than the simplest words in which to thank his friends for their kind attention. After that time I had frequent occasion to see him and to know him; and that is the same as to say that I had learned to admire and to love him; how much and how deeply I scarcely knew till the last of his life's sands were just running out. It is doubtful if any class of men see others as they are, so clearly as physicians. Admitted to the innermost penetralia of families; confided in more absolutely than the father confessor; seeing people in those moments when the shadow of death falls across their path, and the mask of appearance drops and is forgotten; appealed to almost as a god to save a life trembling in the balance, and sometimes thanked almost as if a god, when that life has been restored; witnesses of the most unreserved and sacred joy as a new life springs into being, and sharers of the deep and unaffected grief breaking forth as the last breath passes the long-loved lips—it is no wonder if they know men thoroughly. If they find few who are absolutely perfect, they find few in whom there is not much that is good. A man may be great to others and yet ill bear this close scrutiny, and that Professor Morse bore it well is to my own mind one of the most complete proofs of his real greatness; that greatness which is excellence. The more one saw him the more he was admired, and one forgot the discoverer, the inventor, in the man. His checkered and eventful life had made him know the bitterness of poverty, and taught him that the world is full of men struggling against adverse circumstances; and when wealth crowned his labors he never forgot the lesson, but gave his sympathy and aid to those less fortunate. As an artist he always clung to his first love, and was interested in those who still followed art. Those who can best judge him in this regard, his fellow-artists, say: " Early devoted to art, he brought to its pursuit a cultivated mind, conscientious study, and sound practice, leaving works of high excellence, and proving that he was only withdrawn from the greatest success as an artist by the absorbing claims of his famed invention." The Academy of Design largely owed its foundation to him, and, if I am not mistaken, he contributed to its aid not only by advice but gifts. I have heard him relate the particulars of his early acquaintance with Daguerre, the father of photography, which gave him a permanent interest in the rapid progress and improvement of this art. Professor Morse himself was one of the first, if not the very first, in this country to attempt to take portraits by this process, and although his devices for overcoming the various difficulties were ingenious and scientific, he early abandoned his studies in this direction, either because he was too much occupied to pursue them, or, as I always fancied, because his artistic taste was repelled by the inherent defects and faults of such pictures. Physical science was always attractive to him, and he kept himself well informed as to its progress. Although I knew this, I confess it was with some surprise that I found, last summer, that he had provided himself with an elegant binocular microscope, for it is not often that one takes up these minute studies at fourscore years. In this respect he resembled his elder brother—whom he too soon followed to the grave—who almost to the day of his death was busy in devising an improved method of obtaining soundings from the deep seas. In the politics, both of our own and foreign countries, his interest was constant and sometimes intense. A mere politician, a self-seeker, a manipulator, a wire-puller, he was not and could not be. But the fires of true patriotism burned strong within him, and I have no doubt of his entire truthfulness when he said, in his last public address, while speaking of his invention : " It was nursed and cherished, not so much from personal as from patriotic pride. Touching its future, even from its birth, my most powerful stimulus to perseverance, through all the perils and trials of its early days, (and they were neither few nor insignificant,) was the thought that it must inevitably be world-wide in its application, and moreover that it would be everywhere hailed as a grateful American gift to the nations." The recent civil war in our country had in him a close observer of its events and of its leaders, and of those he spoke to me freely and unreservedly, knowing that we had in our ideas much that was common. But upon those who differed with him he never obtruded his views, though if discussion rose he knew how to hold both his argument and his temper. Sometimes when annoyed, perhaps by public attacks, made upon him with more zeal than judgment, he would say, with a smile, " They will see things differently one of these days." His anxiety was for his country, his whole country ; in the first place that it should not be torn asunder, and afterward, lest all public virtue should be buried in the threatening waves of corruption and peculation. Into his religious life I did not intrude, though in the many familiar conversations which he held with me this greatest of subjects would often crop out. His faith was simple—child-like, shall I say, or rather manly—believing, not because his intellect could grasp these greatest mysteries, but because they were announced by God and taught in His Holy Word. But the thing which always impressed me most was the light in which he looked upon his own invention and his personal relations to it. He knew that he had toiled at it year after year, and that it was the legitimate result of his studies and labors. So far, it was thoroughly and completely his own. But he had at the same time a profound impression of the fact that it was by the Divine favor that he had been selected to bestow upon man this great boon. Thus, while he was properly proud of his invention, it was with something akin to awe that he regarded it. I do not know if I convey my idea distinctly, but you will, perhaps, understand me if I compare his feelings to those which we may imagine to have been experienced by the inspired writers of Holy Scriptures, conscious on the one hand that it was only by quiet, intellectual toil that they wrought out their arguments and reasoning; and yet unconscious, on the other, that they were moved by the in-breathing of the Spirit. Full of years and full of honors, with his natural forces unabated, he has entered into his rest, without the trial of long and weary days of illness and failing strength. With sorrowing hearts we turn from his grave, not with the hopeless wail of the classic heathen, " *Vale, Vale, longum Vale*," but placing over his remains the inscription used by the early Christians, " *In pace Domini dormit.*"

HON. JOHN THOMPSON'S ADDRESS.

When the wires a short time ago announced the dangerous illness of Professor Morse, public attention was at once awakened, and public anxiety could not be satisfied without knowing from hour to hour his condition; and when at last we learned that all was over, one universal expression of regret was heard from all parts of the land. Public sympathy and admiration would have made him immortal.

When Henry Clay died he had sincere mourners, but nearly half of the nation were not admirers of his principles or his course. When Webster died many who bowed before the grandeur of his genius did not approve of his policy, or the tenor of his personal or political career; but when Morse passed among the immortals, one universal expression of grief burst from all ranks of society and all grades of men. Never since Washington died has such sympathetic unanimity been witnessed. Even Lincoln, martyr as he was to a great idea and a great cause, had not such universal tokens of honor and regret. And now, in thinking of what Morse has accomplished, we are led in retrospect over a few years agone, to consider the inventions which have so changed the face of society and given to us the agencies of modern civilization. We behold men, rude, savage, fierce, cruel, hewing each other down with broadsword and battle-ax, in close personal encounter. Gunpowder is invented, and the savagery is abated; and we have, beside, a force to level our mountains and bring out our mineral wealth from the bowels of the earth. We see, again, the small craft of commerce creeping cautiously, by the sight of woodlands and the stars, from one near shore to another, the sailors shuddering at the terrors of Scylla and Charybdis. The magnetic needle is put in the binnacle, and the ship of 5,000 tons plows the Atlantic and Pacific Seas without sun by day or star by night, reaching unerringly her haven. We see in the lone cell or study the pale monk or student slowly transcribing the annals of his nation, or the revelations of God, which few, alas! can read in the wild, weltering chaos of society. The type is set, the press throws off its myriad leaves full of the treasures of science, literature, history, and revelation, so that all ranks may learn the wonderful works of God. We see nations hostile, segregated, with no intercourse, no community of feeling or interest. And lo! the vapor is caught, imprisoned, condensed, and reveals the strength of a thousand giants, propelling us by land and by sea until time and space is comparatively annihilated, and men pass from State to State as on the wings of the wind. It wanted, to complete the circle, an agent and vehicle of thought; that intelligence should be winged with lightning; that this agency of a spiritualized civilization, this closing link in the beautiful chain of Divine benefactions, should come to finish the series, and, lo! the telegraph was born, and stands to-day the crown and consummation of all. Not that we can say that this one or that is more important than the other; like rays of the prism their harmony so blends as to form the glorious sight in which society lives and moves and has its being. And is this the end? Who can tell? It has been said that society has gained nothing by these scientific changes and inventions; that the men of ancient times manifested more stalwart virtues, more heroism, self-sacrifice, and devotion, when they lived, as in the immediate presence of God, without the knowledge of the laws of matter or the agency of second causes. It would be sad to think so. We must remember, moreover, that these specimens of our early heroes were few and far between, and became the divine gods of antiquity, colored by the imagination of after times, giving a charm to poetry as well as pathos to devotion. Moreover, we can hardly tell whether humanity has suffered most from its ignorance or its depravity. Wars and fightings and misunderstandings have come from ignorance, or misapprehension of a rival's views or policy, or engendered by fear; facility of intercommunication, and a truer knowledge of each other's interests, tends to peace, amity, and good neighborhood; universal brotherhood must be preceded by universal intercourse. We are not here to mourn over the demise of our friend; as well mourn that he was born, that he lived and labored, as that he died. If immortality be not the dream of imagination, he still lives, enthroned amidst the worthies who have preceded him, in wider spheres of usefulness and amidst the unfolding splendors of a limitless career. He and all of us are born into eternity; for what is eternity but the great deep sea of God's immensity, on which empires, nations, men are but as the froth of the tumbling billow, or the ships that, dotting its bosom, leave scarce a ripple as they float, or a bubble as they sink into the measureless profound? Let us learn from this hour that although we can never rival Professor Morse in the wealth of his achievements, or the glory of his renown, we may yet imitate him in the consecration of life and genius to the good of humanity and the service of Heaven, and in passing by all human applause, to sit with a filial faith and affection, like a little child, at the foot of the Savior's cross.

When Mr. Thompson finished, Mayor Eastman said the tune to which the next hymn would be sung was a great favorite with Professor Morse, and was brought by him to this country from Germany.

The choir then sung a hymn commencing—

> "Come, glorious Hope, bid Faith arise,
> Till on our path, the day shalt dawn."

That concluded, at the request of the mayor the entire audience joined in singing the doxology, when Dr. Wheeler pronounced the benediction, and the vast assemblage filed slowly out.

The following was the programme for the evening:

IN MEMORIAM.

SAMUEL FINLEY BREESE MORSE, LL. D.

Born April 27, 1791. Died April 2, 1872.

Hon. H. G. EASTMAN, presiding.

ORGAN VOLUNTARY.

Reading the Scriptures: Rev. WILLIAM H. WINES.

Prayer: Rev. A. P. VAN GIESEN.

ANTHEM.

Addresses: Rev. FRANCIS B. WHEELER, D. D., Rev. JOHN H. RAYMOND, LL. D.,
EDWARD H. PARKER, M. D., Hon. JOHN THOMPSON.

HYMN.

DOXOLOGY.

Praise God, from whom all blessings flow;
Praise Him, all creatures here below;
Praise Him above, ye heavenly host;
Praise Father, Son, and Holy Ghost.

Benediction: Rev. P. K. CADY, D. D.

Why lament the Christian dying,
Why indulge in tears or gloom?
Calmly on the Lord relying,
He can greet the opening tomb.

What if death, with icy fingers,
All the fount of life congeals?
'T is not there thy brother lingers,
'T is not death his spirit feels.

Though for him thy soul is mourning,
Though with grief thy heart is riven,
While his flesh to dust is turning,
All his soul is filled with Heaven.

Scenes seraphic, high and glorious,
Now forbid his longer stay;
See him rise, o'er death victorious;
Angels beckon him away.

Hark! the golden harps are ringing,
Sounds unearthly fill his ear;
Millions now in heaven are singing—
Greet his joyful entrance there.

Come, glorious Hope, bid Faith arise,
Till on our path the day shall dawn
That lights the plains of Paradise,
Where those we loved and lost, are gone.

Though visions sweet our souls surprise,
We dare not look t'ward yonder throne,
Where incense veils the dazzling skies
Around the ever-blessed One;

But gaze with quickly-beating heart
Where in our dreams the palm-trees rise,
And seem, in some fair bower apart,
To catch the gleam of loving eyes.

Where haply stands, with clasped hands,
Some angel, whispering, "Cease to mourn.
The love ye lost, of priceless cost,
A thousand-fold shall yet return."

Love, Hope, and Faith, stronger than death,
Help us to say "Amen, Amen,"
To work and wait the voice that saith,
"Lo! all is lost and found again."

E. A. D.

MEETING AT DAVENPORT, IOWA.

The Morse Memorial meeting at Le Claire Hall on Tuesday evening, April 16, 1872, was a credit to the city of Davenport, Iowa. It was composed of the most intelligent citizens, and evinced the feelings of sincere respect and deep gratitude which are cherished for the inventor of the electric telegraph, and the all-pervading regret for his loss.

The meeting was called to order by Mayor Bennett, who stated its object, and then gave a glowing description of the benefit derived from telegraphy. He eulogized the character of Professor Morse, and gave an account of his early struggles in this country and in Europe. It was in 1843, that he obtained a grant of money from Congress to assist in testing his discovery and invention. In 1844, his first forty miles of wire were run from Baltimore to Washington. Its extensive use since that time is one of the marvels of the age. The mayor also spoke of the private character of Professor Morse in terms of high praise.

On motion, a committee on resolutions, consisting of Messrs. George E. Hubbell, J. T. Lane, H. Lischer, and Colonel Berryhill, was appointed, who after consultation reported the following:

Whereas, this meeting has been called for the purpose of joining in a national Memorial to the late Samuel F. B. Morse: Therefore,

Resolved, That while we lament the death of Professor Morse, even at a ripe old age, we have special pride in cherishing the memory of a fellow-citizen who, by the unanimous verdict of the world, has been acknowledged as one of the greatest and most illustrious benefactors.

Resolved, That it is good in this public manner, and through the electric agency which his intellect invoked, to testify our esteem and veneration for the departed, whose discovery has conferred honor on our native land and blessings on the world.

Resolved, That the foregoing resolutions be signed by the officers, and published in the daily papers.

Colonel Berryhill related incidents of Professor Morse's experience in the early days of telegraphing. He was personally acquainted with Professor Morse, who, he said, was a modest, unassuming man, a thorough scholar, and a constant laborer in behalf of art and science. The first telegraph erected by him had two wires for completion of the circuit; and when one of the wires broke, the Professor discovered that the earth "would form the other wire." The colonel also related some interesting incidents in Professor Morse's early career, and then stated that the Bible itself foreshadowed the telegraph—Job, xxxviii, 35th: "Canst thou send lightnings, that they may go, and say unto them, 'Here we are?'"

The resolutions were adopted. Manager Matlock, of the Western Union Telegraph office, had extended wires to the hall, and connecting them with the instrument, telegraphed the resolutions to the Chairman of the National Telegraph Memorial Monument Association at Washington. Previous to this, on the opening of the meeting, Mayor Bennett sent a telegram to A. S. Solomons, esq., Chairman of the committee of arrangements for the Memorial meeting at Washington, informing him of the assembling of the people of Davenport, and also one to the Mayor of Chicago, to the same effect.

Addresses were then delivered by several gentlemen. George E. Hubbell, esq., read a brief paper concerning the wonderful changes wrought by telegraphy in modes of business in the commercial world, the benefits conferred upon humanity in various ways by it, and of the well-won honor the civilized world paid the inventor.

Rev. Mr. Goodhue mentioned his personal experience with Mr. Morse. He spoke of his religious character as one worthy of emulation; his first message over the first line, "What hath God wrought?"

evidenced this.   Mr. Goodhue drew an interesting comparison between the benefits of telegraphy and those of steam.   He instanced some of the personal characteristics of Professor Morse, and said that his equal in service to mankind was produced but once in ten generations.

Hon. J. T. Lane also eulogized the service Professor Morse had rendered mankind in bringing electricity under control for the transmission of intelligence.   He gave facts in the growth of electrical science, from the first discoveries till Professor Morse utilized them all in his inventions.   He referred to his six years' struggle in getting aid from Congress.   For instance, Cave Johnson moved that half the $30,000 be devoted to the development of mesmerism, which motion was favored by the Speaker of the House, and other members moved amendments for the construction of lines to the moon.   Mr. Lane drew a lesson from the early career of Professor Morse as an incentive to the young men of to-day.   Most all great inventors had died without witnessing the full triumph of the work of their hands and brain, but Professor Morse had lived to enjoy the rewards of his life-work, and receive the world's honors.

Bishop Henry W. Lee, after speaking of Professor Morse as a discoverer and inventor, referred to his Christian character, and of his making the Bible the basis of science, as all true science must be founded on the word of God.   The bishop elaborated this idea with his usual ability, and with marked effect.

Rev. Mr. Seaver made a few eloquent remarks concerning Professor Morse's services, introducing them with an allusion to feelings often experienced by himself in observing a light ahead when wandering at night; he felt then that others had preceded him, and there were safety and friends ahead.   Professor Morse was a torch-bearer for the human race.   He then made a plea for "visionary men" as the leaders in science and invention; for really all the discoverers who have benefited mankind have been treated as "visionary men." He spoke of the grand work of the telegraph in effecting a union of the human race. He said he would agree with Bishop Lee in basing science upon the Bible, but he would test all religions by science as well.

Brief but interesting addresses were also made by Mr. Ingham and Rev. Mr. Miller.

A dispatch from Chicago announced that the wires were so burdened that responsive dispatches would not be received, probably, before morning, and the meeting adjourned.

MEETING AT COLUMBUS, GA.

MAYOR'S OFFICE,
Columbus, Ga., April 13, 1872.

In compliance with the request of the National Telegraph Memorial Monument Association, the friends and admirers of the late Professor Samuel F. B. Morse are requested to meet in the council-chamber Tuesday evening, the 16th instant, at 8 o'clock, to give expression to the honor and esteem we hold for the memory of Professor Morse.

Distinguished speakers are expected to address the meeting.

JNO. McILHENNY,
Mayor.

In response to the above call of Mayor McIlhenny, a number of citizens of Columbus, Ga., assembled in the council-chamber on Tuesday evening, April 16, 1872, to give expression to the general feelings of regret at the death of Professor Morse.

Mayor McIlhenny was called to the chair, and M. M. Moore requested to act as secretary.

Mayor McIlhenny stated that the meeting had been called in pursuance to a request of the National Telegraph Memorial Association, and met his hearty approval. He alluded briefly to the great benefit to mankind resulting from the discovery of Professor Morse, his worth as a man, and the general regret at his death, manifested by meetings held in all portions of the country on this evening, all communicating with a common center simultaneously, through the medium of the invention of the lamented dead, to whose memory to-night we have met to pay tribute.

Maj. A. M. Allen eloquently eulogized the character of the deceased; he spoke of his discovery as of infinite value—the greatest discovery of the age—and moved that a committee of three be appointed to prepare a suitable tribute to his memory.

Maj. A. M. Allen, G. A. Miller, and Dr. T. F. Brewster were appointed such committee, and after consultation reported the following resolutions, which were adopted:

Resolved, That in the death of Professor Morse the civilized world has been bereaved, while the cottage of the poor and the palace of the rich, the crowded city and the solitary hamlet, the illiterate and the cultivated, the artisan and the millionaire have all alike lost a friend and a benefactor, who by his magic touch bound continents together, annihilated distance, and held the surging sea subservient to his word.

Resolved, That to his mighty genius the commercial and agricultural, the mechanical and manufacturing, the literary and scientific interests of mankind are indebted for the most wonderful invention of this or any other age; and long after his body shall have moldered into dust, will succeeding generations rise up to do honor to his name.

Resolved, That no monument, however rare and costly, can compare with that which his own intellectual power has unconsciously erected over his new-made grave—a monument that shall defy the ravages of time and the alternatives of fortune.

Major Miller, in seconding the resolutions, took occasion to refer to the difficulties incurred by Professor Morse in perfecting his invention, and his reward after success—a great incentive to the youth of the country.

After preparing the following telegram for transmission to the National Telegraph Memorial Monument Association, the meeting adjourned.

"COLUMBUS, GA., *April* 16, 1872.

"Columbus joins the rest of the country in doing honor to the memory of Professor Morse.

"JNO. McILHENNY,
"*Chairman Citizens' Meeting.*

"M. M. MOORE, *Secretary.*"

MEETING AT CONCORD, N. H.

In accordance with the request of the National Telegraph Memorial Monument Association of Washington, D. C., a goodly number of ladies and gentlemen of Concord, N. H., assembled at Phenix Hall, on Tuesday evening, April 16, 1872, to honor the memory of the late Professor Samuel F. B. Morse. While the audience was assembling, the Concord Brass Band discoursed some stirring music, and part of the people inspected some excellent portraits, hung in the hall, which were painted by Professor Morse in 1817. These were of Rev. Dr. Asa McFarland and wife, and Mrs. John Bradley, mother of the late Richard Bradley, esq. They are about 10 by 12 inches in size, and in an admirable state of preservation.

At 7.45 o'clock, Mayor Kimball, president of the meeting, accompanied by the gentlemen who were to participate in the exercises of the evening, entered the hall. The exercises opened with music by the band, after which Mayor Kimball announced the object of the meeting, and the selection of Mr. A. H. Robinson, of the associated press, as secretary, which was followed with prayer by Rev. D. W. Faunce, at the conclusion of which Hon. Geo. G. Fogg offrede the following resolutions:

Resolved, That the discovery and application of the electric tele-graph to the instantaneous transmission of intelligence from and to the remotest parts of the earth, annihilating space and time, and bringing into immediate relations of neighborhood the inhabitants of the farthest isles of the sea, is the grandest miracle science has ever revealed to the world.   For that miracle the world is indebted to the labors and genius of Professor Samuel F. B. Morse, whose memory a nation honors to-night, whose name is a household word in all civilized lands, and will be as imperishable as human language and human thought.

Resolved, That, while uniting with his grateful and admiring coun-trymen of other cities in this evening's Memorial tribute to the genius of one of America's most illustrious sons, and one of the world's greatest benefactors, we, the citizens of Concord, do the more heartily join in this tribute on account of the peculiar relations Professor Morse sustained to this community; and we gratefully recognize the good providence of God that brought him to us in the morning of his professional life, where he won the heart and hand of one of Concord's loveliest daughters, lovely in person not more than in spirit, and eminently worthy to share his affections and honors. Held to us by this bond, he never ceased to cherish the recollec-tions of his early struggles and triumphs here, and even after the world had showered down its honors and decorations at his feet, he found no purer satisfaction than in a return to the place whose mem-ories continued dearer to his heart than the world and all its honors.

Resolved, That the subject of this Memorial service was scarcely happier in his life than in his death.   No man ever did better life's great work, and no man could better wait or more trustingly obey the summons to "come up higher."

Joseph B. Walker, esq., was first introduced, and spoke as follows :

Mr. Mayor and Friends: The nation meets to-night in simulta-neous gatherings, in all sections of its wide domain, to honor the memory of one who has placed the world under obligations to him that must continue through all time.   While the incalculable benefits which his genius has bestowed upon us, in common with all others, render it fit that we join in this general acclaim, his former connection with Concord furnishes an additional reason for our action in this direction. Our fair city is one with which he formed a pleasant acquaintance in his early manhood, and which he continued to regard with deep interest to the very last days of a long life.

Quite a number of our elderly people remember distinctly Mr. Morse's temporary sojourn here, more than fifty years ago. He came first in the spring of 1817, bringing a letter of introduction from his father, the Rev. Dr. Jedediah Morse, of Charlestown, Mass., the renowned geographer, to Rev. Dr. Asa McFarland, at that time pastor of the church and minister of the town. He had graduated at Yale College, seven years before, and prompted by a strong preference for painting, had chosen it as his profession, and for four years had been studying it in London, under the instruction and encouragement of Washington Allston, Benjamin West, and other eminent masters in art of the time. Since his return to this country he had been seeking employment as an artist, at such points as seemed most likely to afford it, and it was as a painter of portraits that he first visited Concord. The place was at that time a small one, containing less than three thousand inhabitants, yet there were gathered within its limits quite a number of persons ready and competent both to appreciate and encourage the efforts of an artist possessing the high merits of Mr. Morse.

His pencil found, consequently, ready employment, and to it, and to it alone, we are indebted for the vivid likenesses we now have of Dr. and Mrs. McFarland, of Mrs. John Bradley, of Deacon John Kimball and Mrs. Kimball, as well as of several others, which I will not now particularize. These are all in oil, and admirably done; presenting not only faithful delineations of physical features, but portraying with wonderful accuracy the general mental and psychological character of each individual. The posture, the tone, the expression, and all the indefinable somethings, easy to appreciate but impossible to express, of these early efforts of Mr. Morse, give undoubted evidence of an artistic genius, capable and sure, if exercised, soon to raise him to an equality with Stuart and Peale, with Copley and West and Allston.   These little paintings, now cherished by their possessors as faithful transcripts of the forms and features of dear friends long dead, are also of high value as works of art, and particularly so as illustrative of its early history in America.

There are still other works of his pencil yet remaining in New Hampshire.   Among them is a life-size portrait of Hon. William Pickering, of Greenland, painted a little later than the ones just mentioned, which would do honor to the best living artist of to-day, and another of Lucretia Pickering Walker, afterward his wife, the superiority of which to all others produced by him while here is doubtless due in part to the loveliness of the subject and the personal attachment of the artist.

But his more pretentious pictures were painted elsewhere.   A curious little history attaches to one of these, which was detailed to the speaker a few years since, at Poughkeepsie, by Mr. Morse himself. He was located, he said, at one time in Charleston, S. C., and was there received with great kindness, and was given valuable and important orders.   Prompted by a feeling of gratitude for the favor shown him by a family whose acquaintance he had there made, he presented to them, upon leaving, a painting by himself, the subject of which was a scene in the Iliad of Homer.   Some time afterward misfortune befell this family, and the picture went out of their possession, but whither, he could not learn.   Just as the mother follows with interest the wanderings of her children, the artist watches over, with solicitude, the more cherished works of his pencil, for these are his children, creations of his brain and heart.   Having sought long and earnestly for traces of this one's fate, but all in vain, he finally mourned it as lost.

Calling, however, one day, a few years since, at the house of his brother, the late Sydney E. Morse, of New York, he was struck almost dumb with astonishment at finding the long-lost painting upon the parlor-wall. It had been recently purchased in Europe by a friend of his brother, brought home with him upon his return, and presented to the brother, as a friendly gift, with no knowledge whatever, on the part of either, of its paternity or former history. The emotions of such a moment an artist only can appreciate.

But great as was the genius of Mr. Morse in this direction, his largest fame was not destined to rest upon his achievements as a painter. He gave early evidence of the possession of unusual inventive powers. These he was continually strengthening by study, and while in college had given much attention to chemistry, under Professor Silliman, and to natural philosophy, under Professor Day.

We must not therefore be surprised to learn that during one of his earliest visits to Concord he exhibited to such persons of his acquaintance as he thought might take an interest in it, the model of an improved fire-engine which he had himself invented; and Dr. Bouton's invaluable History of Concord informs us that in April, 1818, the town purchased "an additional fire-engine," constructed upon this model, and which is well remembered by persons now resident among us.

Thus early we find struggling up to increasing power and wider grasp the splendid genius whose inventions were destined ere long to annihilate distance, and unite the scattered nations of the whole earth into one family, with power of simultaneous converse with each other, however remote and wherever situated many of them might be.

It is a fact, of which Concord has a right to be proud, that two great men whose names will never die, and whose fame is common to both hemispheres, have formed here alliances of marriage. Just before the Revolution, Benjamin Thompson sought here a residence, and soon after found here a wife. When, in after years, among the honors lavished upon him at foreign courts, the Elector of Bavaria, in consideration of distinguished services, bestowed upon him the title of Count of the Holy Roman Empire, there was appended to it, at his request, the addition of Rumford, the early name of Concord, the birth-place of his wife and child.

Soon after his advent to Concord Mr. Morse was introduced to its society, at an evening party assembled at the house of Mr. Samuel Sparhawk, which then, and until quite recently, stood a few feet north of and next above the building of the New Hampshire Historical Society, and which was subsequently, for many years, occupied as his residence by the Rev. Dr. Bouton. Here had gathered, upon a pleasant evening in the year 1817, a good representation of the beauty and the youthful manhood of the town. That the accomplished artist should have made a marked impression upon the company, now meeting him for the first time, is by no means strange. He was in the very prime of his early manhood, being then about twenty-six years old. To a tall and handsome figure and fine features, illumined by piercing black eyes, was added the charm of pleasing manners, polished by frequent minglings in choicest circles and by foreign travel. His mind, previously well disciplined by a collegiate course, had been greatly enriched by large stores of elegant as well as useful information, gathered both at home and abroad.

In reply to the warm request of a friend, a few hours previous to the gathering of the company just alluded to, that he would accept the invitation sent him and be present, Mr. Morse playfully remarked that, inasmuch as he felt quite sure that he might do so without detriment to his affections, he would go. And it would seem but reasonable to suppose that a man who had, for seven years, withstood the blandishments of the *salons* of New Haven and Boston, and of New York and London, might venture with entire safety into the simple circles of a remote country village, such as Concord then was. But dangers often arise where we least expect them, and there are periods in a man's life when too much confidence in his heart's impregnability may lead to consequences more serious than he anticipates.

It so happened that there was present, on this occasion, a young lady of whom our native-born people, remembering her well, speak in terms of the most enthusiastic admiration, all assuring us that the gracefulness of her figure and the exceeding beauty of her features were more than matched by the graces of her manners and the sweetness of her disposition. Then and there Mr. Morse met her for the first time. The acquaintance thus began soon grew to a mutual attachment, that was confirmed by a betrothal, and crowned by a marriage on the 29th day of September, 1818. Mr. Morse and his wife took up their residence at New Haven, where were born to them three children, all of whom have survived them, the eldest being Mrs. Edward Lind, of Porto Rico, in the West Indies, and the others, Mr. Charles W. Morse, of Brookline, and Mr. Finley Morse, of Poughkeepsie, N. Y.

Never existed a happier union, but it was terminated by a calamity as unexpected as it was terrible. While, in apparent health, Mrs. Morse was caressing her youngest child, then an infant, the angel who bears the inverted torch beckoned to her from on high, and her spirit followed him instantly. This was on the 7th day of February, 1825.

The care with which Professor Morse has ever guarded the spot where her ashes repose, and the touching memorial he has carved upon her monument, are but two among a thousand evidences of an affection that was immortal. The tie thus severed, but now re-united, has ever preserved in his heart a lively interest in the welfare of Concord. From time to time he has returned here, and revisited the localities and friends associated with this period of his early life. His last visit was in August, 1864, when he called upon old friends, and passing up and down our streets pointed out to the cherished companion of his maturer years localities he had known and loved for more than half a century.

Thus imperfectly, Mr. Mayor and gentlemen of the committee of arrangements, I have discharged the duty your kindness has forced upon me. The incidents which I have been able to present of Professor Morse's early connection with Concord are few and simple, but they are a part, nevertheless, of the history of a great life that will be remembered through all time. Would that I could have done it better. But the recent closing of the portals of his tomb and the regrets which a long friendship inspires are but poor stimulants to powers which at best are unequal to a task like this. Happily, to others here present attaches the higher privilege of recounting the loftier achievements of his later life. Yet, I cannot close this brief record without bearing personal testimony to the splendor of his genius, to the enthusiasm he ever manifested in the great subjects to whose study he has devoted a long life, and to the patience with which he wrought, through weary years, upon the great problems he has so successfully solved. He has gained a victor's wreath, but it is a bloodless one. Through his instrumentality God has unfolded mysterious secrets of nature never before unveiled, and blessed our age as few ages have ever been blessed before. And he has also earned a brighter crown than any of ivy or of laurel, for Morse, the philosopher, has always been and has died an humble Christian man.

Rev. Dr. Bouton followed, with interesting personal reminiscences of Professor Morse and his father, Rev. Jedediah Morse, of Charlestown, Mass., whom he remembered once to have seen while the speaker was a student at Yale College. The senior Morse was then a venerable man, tall in figure, gray-haired, and gentle in manner. Almost the first thing he heard talked about when he came to Concord was Professor Morse and the excellent lady he here selected for his wife—a lady who was regarded as the belle of Concord, if not

of the State.   After alluding to some of the distinguished men who
had reflected honor upon Concord by reason of their residence
here, such as Count Rumford, Professor Morse, Judge Levi Wood-
bury, and Senator Wilson, the first two of whom were remarkable for
their personal beauty and inventive genius, he gave a brief account
of the invention of the telegraph, as narrated to him by Professor
Morse, on one of his visits to Concord, and in his own house, and of
the discouragements he met before it was practically applied between
Washington and Baltimore, and the first message, "What hath God
wrought!" was transmitted, in 1844.

Asa McFarland, esq., was introduced, and spoke as follows :

Mr. MAYOR AND FELLOW-CITIZENS: The only contribution I can
offer this evening will be meager in quantity, and I fear unsatisfactory
in character, for it is nearly fifty-five years since Professor Morse
became a sojourner in Concord, and a guest in the family of my
father; and I, then a lad, looked upon him as boys regard those who
have reached man's estate.   I have no recollection of him outside of
the house in which I then dwelt and still reside.   I do not remember
seeing him in the streets with other men, or in any public assembly;
but his personal appearance and address are distinct upon my
memory.

At the table one day, I believe in May or the early part of the
summer of 1817, my father said to my mother that he had received
a letter from their mutual friend, Rev. Jedediah Morse, D. D., of
Charlestown, Mass., invoking a kind office in behalf of his son, the
late Professor Morse, who had returned from a residence of several
years in London as a pupil of the celebrated portrait-painter, Benjamin West.   My mother had often heard Rev. Dr. Morse in the
pulpit of the Old South Church, Boston, in exchange with her pastor,
Rev. Joseph Eckley, and was, beside, a frequent visitor in the
family of Dr. Morse.   The request of the father found a ready, nat-

ural, and cheerful response in my parents, and the young artist made his appearance in due time; how long after this conversation I am unable to say.

My parents were, I think, the first subjects of his pencil in Concord, and his studio was the habitation in which they dwelt, as were the houses of others whose portraits were taken; that is to say, I think he had no single apartment where he performed his work. The young painter was to me an object of greater interest than many other equally meritorious guests at our house; for he was genial, accessible, and communicative, and, what especially enhanced him in my youthful fancy, he had dwelt in the great European capital, and frequently talked of it during the hours my parents were seated near his easel. I was much in the room, and became deeply interested by hearing him mention the wonderful objects and notable people he saw when abroad.

The eminent man whose life and works we this evening commemorate was, at the time here under consideration, about twenty-six years of age, elegant in person, and pleasing in address. He was tall and symmetrical; eyes and hair black or very dark, and complexion, I think, of the Italian cast, neither dark, light, nor florid, but somewhat swarthy. He treated the people of this settlement, then of only about twelve hundred inhabitants, to three surprises: First, (what had not been done by the one or two painters who preceded him,) to portraits which were recognized at sight wherever exhibited; second, by securing as his prize and conveying from town as his wife, and in the face of the young gallants of Concord, a lady remarkable above all others of her sex then here for her beauty, and estimable for her excellencies, Lucretia P. Walker, daughter of Charles Walker, esq., whose parents dwelt in a house now owned and occupied by Cyrus W. Paige, esq., then one of the best habitations in Concord; and, thirdly, he surprised the town by the munificence of the fee bestowed on the clergyman who performed the marriage-rite. My next-door neighbor, Rev. Dr. Bouton, informs me that he was once surprised by a marriage-fee of twenty dollars; that of my father consisted of twenty-five dollars, in five golden half-eagles, coin now rarely seen by the mass of people.

At this or a subsequent visit in Concord, Mr. Morse brought to our house the model of a fire-engine of his invention, which was several times filled and discharged. One of the enlarged machines was purchased and used here, the second machine in use for a corresponding purpose. The only significance in this fact is, that it affords proof of the early inventive genius of him upon whom we this evening bestow public honor as one worthy not only of the most profound regard and gratitude of his countrymen, but the equally deep gratitude of the civilized world.

At the conclusion of Mr. McFarland's speech the band played America.

Rev. Mr. Lovering followed with a short and eloquent address upon the influence of great men upon mankind, especially great inventors, and said that much of the greatest heroism of the world had been manifested by persons in the practical walks of life, and prominent among them were the names of Franklin and Morse; the former snatched the lightning from the heavens, and the latter taught it to articulate in speech. He briefly alluded to the progressive steps taken in electrical science by the predecessors of Morse, for whom it was reserved to make a practical and tangible use of the hints of others, not only by laying wires upon the land, but under the waters of the ocean.

Rossiter Johnson was next introduced, and read the following poem, written for the occasion:

THE VICTORY.

When Man, in his Maker's image, came
To be the lord of the new-made earth,
To conquer its forests, its beasts to tame,

To gather its metals and know their worth—
All readily granted his power and place,
Save the Ocean, the Mountain, and Time and Space;
And these four sneered at his puny frame,
     And made of his lordship a theme for mirth.
Whole ages passed while his flocks he tended,
     And delved and dreamed, as the years went by;
'Till there came an age when his genius splendid
     Had bridged the rivers, and sailed the sky,
And raised the dome that defied the storm,
And mastered the beauties of color and form;
But his power was lost, his dominion ended,
     Where Time, Space, Mountain, or Sea was nigh.
The mountains rose in their grim inertness
     Between the nations, and made them strange,
Save as in moments of pride or pertness
     They climbed the ridge of their native range,
And, looking down on the tribe below,
Saw nothing there but a deadly foe;
Heard only a war-cry, long and shrill,
     In echoes leaping from hill to hill.
The Ocean rolled in its mighty splendor,
     Washing the slowly-wasting shore,
And the voices of nations, fierce or tender,
     Lost themselves in its endless roar.
With frail ships launched on its treacherous surge,
And sad eyes fixed on its far blue verge,
Man's hold of life seemed brittle and slender,
     And the Sea his master for evermore.
And Space and Time brought their huge dimensions
     To separate man from his brother man,
And sowed between them a thousand dissensions,
     That ripened in hatred and caste and clan.
So Sea and Mountain and Time and Space
Laughed again in his lordship's face,
And bade him blush for his weak inventions,
     And the narrow round his achievements ran.
But one morning he made him a slender wire,
     As an artist's vision took life and form,
While he drew from heaven the strange, fierce fire,
     That reddens the edge of the midnight storm;
And he carried it over the Mountain's crest,
And dropped it into the Ocean's breast;
And Science proclaimed, from shore to shore,
That Time and Space ruled man no more.

> Then the brotherhood lost on Shinar's plain
> Came back to the peoples of earth again.
> "Be one!" sighed the Mountain, and shrunk away.
> "Be one!" murmured Ocean, in dashes of spray.
> "Be one!" said Space, "I forbid no more."
> "Be one!" echoed Time, "till my years are o'er."
> "We are one!" said the Nations, and hand met hand
> In a thrill electric from land to land.

Samuel B. Page, esq., made the closing speech, and spoke of Professor Morse as the embodiment of the sentiment, "Whatever you do, do with your might," his life being one of persistent and well-directed efforts for the good of the world. He lived to wear the crown of his own glory, and his name and memory are part of the history of the past, the present, and for all time to come.

After the "Russian Anthem" by the band, the resolutions were unanimously adopted, and the meeting closed with a benediction by Rev. Dr. Bouton.

MEETING AT FREDERICK CITY, MD.

In response to the proclamation of the honorable Mayor of Frederick City, a large number of gentlemen assembled at the court-house on the evening of April the 16th, 1872, to pay a last tribute to the memory of that illustrious personage, Professor Samuel F. B. Morse, whose great gift to the world numbers him among its greatest benefactors.

On motion of Mr. Thomas Gorsuch, Maj. Lawrence J. Brengle was called to the chair; and on motion of Capt. H. Clay Haill, Mr. F. B. Miller was appointed secretary.

The following preamble and resolutions were offered by Dr. Lewis H. Steiner, State senator, of Frederick County, and unanimously adopted:

RESOLUTIONS.

Whereas, the practical applications of the principles of science to the wants of mankind have contributed largely to the advance of civilization, and to the increase of enterprise and prosperity among all nations which have been favored with a knowledge of the same; and

Whereas, the names of those who have made themselves conspicuous by teaching the world how to utilize the treasures of science ought to be held in grateful remembrance by the citizens of the land that gave them birth: Therefore,

Resolved, That we herewith join with the citizens of the United States, assembled this evening in their different cities and towns, in recording our sincere regret at the loss experienced by the world in the death of Professor Samuel F. B. Morse, the inventor of the magnetic telegraph, who first made the fact that electricity could be transmitted through great lengths of wire, without any material diminution of its power, effective as a means of communication between distant points, thereby annihilating distance, and bringing all parts of the world in close proximity; who lived to see his invention introduced in all nations and all climes, and who has just been called to his eternal rest, covered with honors and rewards, as one of the greatest benefactors of his age.

Resolved, That the name of Morse will be esteemed, along with that of Franklin and Fulton, as among the most honored names in the galaxy of our country's great men.

Resolved, That a copy of these resolutions, signed by the officers of this meeting, be transmitted to the National Telegraph Memorial Monument Association at Washington.

In presenting the foregoing preamble and resolutions, Dr. Steiner said, in substance:

Rarely has such an event occurred as the assembling of the citizens of a great nation simultaneously in its cities and principal towns, to express regret at the death of a private citizen who had never borne office at the hands of his country, and whose life had been wholly given up to the cultivation of letters, the fine arts, and the practical applications of science. We know how the death of the statesman or the warrior sends a thrill of sorrow through the body-politic, and how the sad feelings that fill the breasts of those who have learned to lean upon their strong arms will find expression in words that teem with the eloquence of sorrow. But the private citizen is mostly lamented in the home-circle; he passes into the shadow-land, only with the lamentations of his family and immediate neighbors accompanying him. Yet, to-night, the strange spectacle is presented of meetings held throughout the length and breadth of the land to honor the memory and regret the departure of a private citizen. The National Congress pauses in its political discussions and its legislative deliberations, and with eloquence and burning words of praise weaves a garland to lay upon his fresh-made grave; the great cities silence for a while their busy quest for gain, to pour forth tributes of thanksgiving to God for the blessings He gave us through the instrumentality of this citizen; and emulating the spirit that actuates our brethren, we are also assembled this evening to do honor to his memory.

Samuel Finley Breese Morse has been gathered to his fathers, after having attained the good old age of fourscore years. An artist by profession, he attained a prominence that made him an object of attraction in the city of New York, where he located himself in 1822, and speedily secured such patronage as showed the high esteem in which he was held. In 1827, his attention was directed to electro-magnetism, a science then in its infancy. Eight years before that, Oersted of Copenhagen, had shown that when a current of electricity was passed through a wire it would cause a magnetic needle to deflect from its natural position, and to stand at right angles to the current; and only two years before, Sturgeon, of London, had found if a current of electricity were passed through a copper wire wound about a piece of soft iron, bent into the form of a horse-shoe, that the iron would become temporarily magnetic; losing this power, however, when the current ceased to flow. In 1828, Henry, now the honored head of the Smithsonian Institution, found that by increasing the number of coils about a soft-iron bar, its magnetism could be greatly increased, and that the electric current could be transmitted through great lengths of wire without any great loss of its intensity. The problem then began to present itself to scientific minds, how these facts could be employed so as to transmit information in words between distant points. Von Schilling of St. Petersburg, Steinheil of Munich, Gausso Weber of Göttingen, Wheatstone of England, and others made more or less successful attempts to solve this problem; but it was left to Morse to invent the most practical method of using the facts discovered by science, for the purpose of communicating words and sentences through great lengths of wire. To him was given the high honor of being the father of telegraphy throughout the world.

* * * * * * *

The first telegraph was laid between Washington and Baltimore, and was first employed May 27, 1844; now the whole country is covered with a net-work of telegraph wires, requiring more than fifty thousand miles of wire to meet the demands of business, and involving the outlay of more than fifty millions of capital. The telegraph visits every civilized nation on the globe, spans the bosom of the ocean, and binds the world together with the strongest possible cords. It is not only devoted to the uses of gain, and of the sterner realities of life, but also to messages of love and pleasure, as well as to those of death and sorrow. It has become the necessity of an age unsurpassed in history for its rapid marches over the plains of scientific discovery. It has become the means of instantaneous communication between mankind in their hours of business and pleasure.

> Speak the word, and think the thought,
> Quick 'tis as with lightning caught,
> Over, under, lands or seas,
> To the far antipodes;
> Now o'er cities thronged with men,
> Forest now, or lonely glen;
> Now where busy commerce broods,
> Now in wildest solitudes;

> Now where Christian temples stand,
> Now afar in Pagan land;
> Here again as soon as gone,
> Making all the earth as one.
> Moscow speaks at twelve o'clock,
> London reads ere noon the shock;
> Seems it not a feat sublime ?—
> Intellect has conquered Time!
> Sing who will of Orpheus' lyre,
> Ours the wonder-working wire.

Addresses eulogistic of the life and character of Professor Morse were delivered by Francis Brengle, B. F. M. Hurley, and Milton E. Smith, after which the meeting adjourned.

MEETING AT LYNN, MASS.

A message was received from the Common Council, proposing a convention of the two branches for Memorial services in honor of the late Professor Samuel F. B. Morse, agreeably to resolutions passed at the last meeting. The board concurring, the mayor and aldermen, together with invited guests, proceeded to the council-chamber for the above purpose.

IN CONVENTION.

Mayor Buffum, upon taking the chair, proceeded to deliver the following address :

GENTLEMEN OF THE COUNCIL AND FELLOW-CITIZENS: I am happy to meet you on this occasion, to do honor to one of those great heroes of science whose achievements have contributed to the advancement and civilization of mankind. It is a great sign of progress when the nation joins in celebrating the praise of those who have won victories over nature, in the interest of peace and civilization. As mankind advances, mind will prevail over matter, reason will overcome prejudice, and we shall no longer hold up to the world as heroes those who have achieved their greatness through physical strength. These will sink into insignificance before the higher and better civilization that is to come. When we look back over the ages that are past and mark the progress of the races, and witness how many have labored and toiled and struggled to bring us up to where we stand to-day, our hearts swell with gratitude to those who have achieved for us so much of greatness, and given us so many advantages over those who have lived before us. Among the many inventions of our day, the telegraph may be regarded as the greatest of all.

"Not if ten tongues were mine, ten mouths, an unbroken voice and a breast of brass, could I relate all that is to be told," said Homer. "Not if a hundred tongues were mine, a hundred mouths and an iron voice, could I relate all that is to be told," said Virgil. This they said in the ages when it was the office of the poet to recite as well as compose his verse. They said this under the limitations of the ages that gave to thought such spread as it could have by recitations of the human voice, in the ears of the people assembled in the banquet-hall, the camp, the market, the street, at best in the theaters and public games, or by copies laboriously made by the hand and pen. Those ages are past. The invention of the press and telegraph has made actual the wish of the poets, and gone a flight beyond that; it leaves human thought now almost as free in the elements of outward matter as it is in the motions of the mind within. The telegraph has transmitted thought with a rapidity which has almost outrun thought itself. These inventions, together with the steam-engine, have given to every genuine author the power to speak to all nations whatsoever the mind within moves him to say. For him now all elements labor as subjects in actual service. Stone and lead and brass and iron obey his call, and come forth from the bed where they sleep in the bowels of the earth, in darkness and chaos, into light and form, to receive his impress and creative word.

> "God said, Let 'there be light;'
> Grim Darkness felt His might
> And fled away."

The lightning along the telegraph has become our errand-boy, and the sun—in photograph—has became our sketcher. Ours is the land, and ours the boundless barren sea; we compass them both in our sphere. We yoke the steam to our ships and cars, as well as to our press, and harness the lightning in our service.

Such dominion has thought now; such agencies now in the telegraph and press; such promises in the future—the like was never before seen, never before dreamed of by any mind, without the impeachment of insanity. We can never know what a debt we owe to those who have toiled and labored in the past. We can never realize how much they softened and inclined the nations to peace and amity, by bringing them into near and more intimate relations to each other. The dreams of the insane have now become realities through these great inventions. There was never a day since the world began when mankind enjoyed more equally the blessings of life than now. New inventions, redeeming time, are giving to all the means of culture and refinement. Knowledge is covering the earth as the waters cover the sea. Time and space no longer separate mankind. Coliseums of equal magnitude to those built in the palmiest days of Rome are now reared among us, but no human sacrifices are given to gratify a brutal and blood-thirsty populace. Our coliseums are reared in the interest of the arts, and of peace— peace, presided over by the geniuses of our age, who minister to the higher and nobler faculties of the soul in strains of music sweet as those sung by angelic voices on creation's morn. Let us, then, rejoice in whatever we have already achieved, and lift up our hearts in gratitude to God, and to those who in times past have labored and sacrificed to give to us these great blessings; and as we recede from the darkness and the gloom of the past, let us rejoice in the faith and hope that we are approaching a bright and more glorious future. And when we shall, in the days to come, engrave the names of those whom we delight to honor upon the tablet of enduring memory, the name of Samuel Finley Breese Morse will stand as one of the highest in the civilized world.

Alderman Breed, of Ward Four, then presented, for the committee appointed to draught resolutions expressive of the sentiments of the city council regarding the great national loss caused by the death of Professor Samuel F. B. Morse, the following, which were ordered to be entered upon the records of both branches of the council.

Council-Chamber, Lynn, Mass.,

April 16, 1872.

Assembled to-night by invitation of the representatives of the nation, in common with her sister cities throughout the land, to tender her tribute of respect to one who, born in Massachusetts, became, in grateful recognition of his services to mankind, by adoption a citizen of the world ; who, fortunate among men, won the admiration of mankind by his success in two distinct professions, adding to the fame of the finished artist the renown of the accomplished scientist ; who, grasping the facts which many others had wrought out, combined them in that wonderful invention which has utilized the lightning which Franklin drew from the clouds, and made it the swift messenger of man, putting that girdle round the world which shall bind in one the nations of the earth; who, passing the ordinary bound of human existence, lived to see every nation share the fruits of his beneficent labors, and to receive from all the recognition and honors so justly his due; and who has left the record of his labors and his life, rounded and completed by every Christian grace, as a precious legacy to his family, his nation, and the world. Therefore the city of Lynn, through her representatives, inscribes upon her official records her profound appreciation of the life-work of Professor Samuel Finley Breese Morse, and especially of those years of toil and privation which resulted in the invention of the magnetic telegraph, whose effect upon the peace and prosperity of the world has conspicuously illustrated the truth that " Peace hath her victories no less renowned than war."

Resolved, That a copy of the above be sent to the family of the deceased, to the press, and to the representative meeting convened at the National Representative Hall at Washington.

For the committee.

B. B. BREED, *Chairman.*

The preamble and resolution were adopted and immediately forwarded to the telegraph office for transmission to Washington. The president then introduced Rev. E. L. Drown, rector of Saint Stephen's Church, who delivered the following address:

Mr. MAYOR AND GENTLEMEN OF THE CITY GOVERNMENT: The first thought which has occupied my mind, in connection with this Memorial meeting, and especially after the admirable preamble and resolution which have just been read, is, that he whom we commemorate to-night was almost a solitary exception to the truth which history has so constantly illustrated, that " one soweth and another reapeth." The late Professor Morse not only sowed the seed, but reaped the abundant harvest. He not only made the great discovery of the electric telegraph, but enjoyed its grandest results of honor and of glory, and the appreciation of his countrymen. I cannot but think of others for a moment whose experience in this respect afforded so great a contrast to his.

I think of one* whose invention has enriched hundreds and thousands, and yet he left his family in poverty and want. In the very city where his widow and orphan child resided, I knew men who were enjoying incomes of from fifty to a hundred thousand dollars annually, derived mainly from his discoveries, and yet the widow was toiling, with her own hands, for her support and the support of her child. I received, not long since, a

---

* The names of these persons were mentioned in the address as delivered. It seems indelicate, however, in consideration of their descendants, to give them here.

letter from London announcing her death, inclosing her photograph; a sad, pale, care-worn face, the expression more pathetic than words, as it told of the ingratitude of men.

I think of another, whose genius has given to some of our American manufactures a world-wide reputation, from whose inventions, also, colossal fortunes have been acquired. The last time I saw him he was an old man, a broken-down man of seventy years, going from door to door with a little basket upon his arm selling lamp-lighters made from wood.

I think of one other, who has long enjoyed a reputation which belonged elsewhere, Robert Fulton, whose name will be forever associated with the application of steam to the navigation of the waters. And yet, from documents I have seen, I am convinced that the honor belongs to an unknown man whom Fulton kept locked up in his house for more than six months while he reaped the benefit of his genius. Who of those present ever heard the name of the real inventor, the humble mechanic, Daniel French?

How widely different from all this was the experience of the late Professor Morse. The mind is almost bewildered by the simple record of the honors that were conferred upon him. I have not had the opportunity to obtain a complete and authentic record of these honors; but, from the limited resources of my own private library, I have gathered the following statement: In 1848, Yale College, his Alma Mater, conferred upon him the degree of LL. D.; and Yale, sir, never confers degrees except *causa honoris*. Soon after he received a decoration of nobility, in diamonds, from the Sultan of Turkey; about the same time a gold medal, inclosed in a massive gold snuff-box, from the King of Prussia; also, a gold medal from the King of Würtemberg, and one from the Emperor of Austria; in 1856, the Cross of the Chevalier of the Legion of Honor, from the Emperor of France; in 1857, from the King of Denmark, the Cross of the Knight of the Dannebrog; and in 1858, from the Queen of

Spain, the Cross of the Knight Commander of Isabella the Catholic. The most distinguished honor conferred upon him abroad was an honorary gratuity bestowed by several European governments at the instance of the late Emperor of France. Ten states, France, Russia, Sweden, Belgium, Holland, Austria, Sardinia, Tuscany, the Holy See, and Turkey, after a deliberation of two days, on the part of their representatives, voted, as a personal reward to Professor Morse, for his useful labors, the sum of 400,000 francs. Banquet after banquet was tendered him in the most distinguished circles of Europe. And after all this, as we all well know, he was privileged to witness, in his own adopted city, the unveiling of the monument which a grateful and appreciative people had erected to his honor.

In the few remaining words I have to offer I propose to confine myself to one single line of thought, leaving to others who are to follow me the more profound considerations inseparable from the greatness of the invention of Professor Morse. I wish to go back to the inception of the telegraph, and call up for a moment our own opinions at that time, and then to recur to his experience in the days when he was struggling to bring out into light and practical use his grand conception.

Who of us can forget the wonder that filled our minds as we first heard of the electric telegraph? I remember, as a boy of fourteen, the amazement with which I would stand and watch the wires and wonder at their mystery. I recall to mind a gentleman of culture, my teacher, and certainly, as I think of him, he was a man, for that time, of learning and intelligence—and I remember one day the gravity he assumed as he said: "I understand something of the principle of the electric telegraph, but I cannot understand how words can be transmitted along the wires." About the time the telegraph came into use I was at boarding-school in one of the small country-towns of New England. The business was almost wholly local, and the town had but little connection with the outside world, yet its public-spirited citizens conceived the idea that a telegraph in the town would be alike a convenience and an honor. The stock was readily taken, the line was built, and an office opened. The gentleman who was first in charge of the office had been from childhood one of our well-known citizens, but from the moment he entered that office and took charge of those mysterious wires he seemed transformed. A new honor surrounded him. We looked upon him almost as a supernatural being. For two days all was quiet in the new office, and the faces of our citizens gave mournful evidence of their disappointment. But on the third day the mysterious tick was heard, which announced a *bona-fide* message. The operator, with breathless interest, received and recorded it. It was honor enough for one day. The office was closed at once, and forth went the operator to tell the great news and to enjoy the congratulations of his fellow-citizens. It so happened that the first message was purely domestic in its character, from an affectionate husband to his devoted wife. But the gentleman in charge of the business could not contain his great secret, and before an hour had passed the domestic arrangements of that happy family had become the public property of all our citizens. I think John Leech most justly represented the prevailing ignorance in one of his sketches in *Punch*. I have not seen the sketch for twenty years, but it is as vivid to my mind as if I had seen it yesterday. Two persons are seated upon the box of a stage-coach; the one with the pale face, the pinched features, the clerical coat, the black gloves, which mark the man of science and of books; the other, the driver, of the Tony Weller stamp, with the capacious stomach, to whom the *summum bonum* of life is roast beef and good English ale. The scholastic gentleman has evidently been explaining the wonders of the new invention, and the interested stage-driver answers him: "And so the 'lectric fluid carries messages from Dover to Calais? What is it like, pray? Anything like beer, for example?"

Let us go back for a moment to the early experience of Professor Morse and trace the beginnings, with him, of all this success, and of these abundant honors of which we have spoken. The late Samuel F. B. Morse was born in 1791, and had this Memorial meeting been deferred ten days it would have occurred upon his birthday, for he was born on the 27th day of April. He graduated at Yale College in 1810, and the following year he went abroad as a young artist, in company with Washington Allston, to enjoy the instruction of the renowned Benjamin West. At this early age he received from the Adelphi Society of Arts of London, at the hands of the Duke of Norfolk, the first of his many gold medals for his first work of sculpture—a dying Hercules. In 1829, he went abroad the second time and remained three years. He sailed for home in 1832. This was before the *Sirius* and the *Great Western* had revolutionized ocean travel and had demonstrated the practicability of steam for voyages of such length. Perhaps it was due to the fact that the *Sully*, on which he sailed, was a sailing-vessel, and thus, by the greater length of time consumed in the passage, allowed ample time for conversation, that on that voyage the idea of the electric telegraph was conceived. Massachusetts—I think it is not generally known—has a larger share in this conception than the simple fact, alluded to in the resolution, that Professor Morse was born here, would give. Among the passengers on the *Sully* was the well-known scholar Dr. Charles S. Jackson. He explained to the travelers the wonders he had witnessed, in Paris, of the electro-magnet, especially the transmission of electricity instantaneously through a great length of wire arranged around the room. The young Morse exclaimed, " Why can't we transmit intelligence in that way?" and in that hour the electric telegraph was born. Before the voyage was finished he had made his drawings complete of the telegraph, as it is now used, with but one exception, to which I shall allude presently. In after years, when his case was in the courts, on the question of the priority of invention, all the passengers on board the *Sully* except one testified to the fact of these drawings. Professor Morse went to work at once. He exhibited in 1835, in New York, a miniature telegraph in successful operation. In 1837, we find him at Washington endeavoring, though unsuccessfully, to obtain an appropriation from Congress. In the winter of 1843, he is again at Washington, pressing his claim for $30,000 to build a telegraph from Baltimore to Washington, a distance of forty miles. Undismayed by all obstacles, in spite of mockeries, he secured the favorable report of the special committee, and his bill passed the House of Representatives. It was delayed in the Senate. On the last day of the session he found one hundred and forty-one bills taking precedence of his own. He waited till after 9 o'clock at night, and went back to his hotel disappointed and discouraged. He examined the state of his finances and found that after paying his hotel bill and his fare to New York his total remaining cash would amount to seventy-five cents. The next morning, as he was going to breakfast, a waiter informed him that a young lady was in the parlor waiting to see him. He went in immediately and met Miss Ellsworth, the daughter of the Commissioner of Patents, who had been a steadfast friend to him while in Washington. "I come," said she, "to congratulate you." "For what?" said Professor Morse. "On the passage of your bill," she replied. "O, no; you must be mistaken," said he. "I remained in the Senate till near 10 o'clock last night, and there was no prospect of its being reached." "Am I the first," said she, joyfully, "to tell you?" "Yes, if it is really so." "Well," said she, "father remained until the adjournment, and heard the bill passed; and I asked him if I might run over and tell you." "Annie," said the Professor, "the first message that is sent from Washington to Baltimore shall be sent from you."

Morse entered at once upon his work. A year passed, and $23,000 were spent without success, for the simple reason that he

had no plan for stretching the wires except through pipes beneath
the surface of the ground. This method cost so much and was
embarrassed by so many difficulties, that the ultimate success of the
whole invention was endangered. At this critical juncture he was
brought in contact with the practical mind and the mechanical skill
of Ezra Cornell. He suggested the present method of hanging the
wires upon posts, and thus the great work was accomplished. Cornell became by this suggestion connected with the telegraph scheme,
and to this fact is due the establishment of the infant, but most
promising, institution known as Cornell University. As soon as
the work was completed Professor Morse hastened to Washington to
redeem his promise to Miss Ellsworth, that she should send the first
message. She sent the noble and fitting words, "What hath God
wrought!" Governor Seymour, afterward our minister to St.
Petersburg, claimed the message for Connecticut, for the reason
that Miss Ellsworth was born in that State. The claim was allowed,
and is to-day as precious as if written with diamonds upon tablets
of gold. That message is deposited in the archives of the Historical
Society at Hartford.

I have thus touched upon the infant beginnings of the great work.
Its grander thoughts, its great achievements, its wonderful uses, will,
doubtless, engage the attention of the speakers who are to follow
me. A word more and I have done.

I said just now that the first medal that Professor Morse ever received was for his sculpture of a dying Hercules. This fact seems
to me prophetic of all his after honor. I know not what thought he
embodied in his work, but we all know the ancient legend: When
the gods and goddesses saw the dying agonies of the giant Hercules, they went to Jupiter and declared that it was not right that one
who had achieved such glorious deeds should suffer thus. And then
(thus the legend runs) Jupiter answered that only his mortal part
would perish, and the spiritual part would be translated to Olympus,

and Hercules should live as a god. And thus, sir, it is only the mortal part of him whom we commemorate to-night that has perished ; the immortal shall live forever. While the thunders roll they shall seem to repeat, while the lightnings glance they shall record, his name. Nay, sir, as to-night I think of those thousands of wires reaching through our crowded cities, through our quiet country places, out through the forests, over the prairies, across the Rocky Mountains, beneath the waters, joining land to land and continent to continent, they seem to me like the strings of some vast Æolian harp, grander than poet's mind ever conceived; and as I think of them to-night, all vibrating to that one great name, it seems as if the hand of God had swept the strings, and I pause to catch the notes of the anthem—Nature's requiem for her noblest son—as it hymns the immortal name of Samuel Finley Breese Morse.

Rev. T. E. Vassar, pastor of the First Baptist Society, was next introduced, and addressed the meeting in his peculiarly effective manner, alluding principally to the private character of the great man who has conferred such a lasting benefit upon the civilized world by his wonderful discovery. His remarks were listened to with deep attention. He was followed by Rev. F. H. Newhall, pastor of the First Methodist Church, Rev. J. B. Davis, pastor of the Free Baptist Church, and Rev. G. Whittaker, pastor of the Boston Street Church, each of whom paid fitting tributes to the worth of the deceased, and spoke of the great debt which the nations of the earth owed him for discovering a system of communication so marvelous. Previous to closing the meeting Alderman McGibbons offered the following resolution, which was adopted :

Resolved, That the thanks of the City Council be, and hereby are, extended to the reverend gentlemen who, by their able and eloquent addresses, have contributed so fully to the interest of this meeting.

The convention was then dissolved.

MEETING AT GOLDSBOROUGH, PA.

At the instance or A. P. Houck, esq., manager of the Western Union Telegraph at Goldsborough, the business community, representing the various professions, trades, and mercantile interests of the place, including Messrs. B. F. Kirkwood and Frank Metzgar of the Northern Central Railway telegraph-line, of Goldsborough, met on Tuesday evening, the 16th April, 1872, at the Western Union Telegraph office, when, on motion, Amos Waidley, esq., was elected president, and B. F. Kirkwood secretary, of the meeting. The object of the meeting having been stated, on motion, the following committee of five was appointed to draught suitable resolutions expressive of the sense of the meeting: A. P. Houck, chairman; Jesse M. Funk, John Kister, George C. Wentz, and Thomas J. O'Neale, who in a short time offered the following resolutions, which were, on motion, unanimously adopted:

Whereas, through the blessing of a kind Providence, it was given to Samuel F. B. Morse, an American citizen, to perfect a practical, and this day a most wonderful invention known as the "Morse system" of telegraphy, by which the whole world is brought into direct and instant communication with itself; and

Whereas, it is our privilege to unite with our fellow-citizens throughout the nation this day, in giving formal expression of the debt of gratitude and respect which we feel we owe to his memory: Therefore,

Resolved, That this community of commerce and of sentiment do hereby show our appreciation for, and recognize in the person and genius of the late Professor Samuel F. B. Morse, through the blessing of God, the originator and inventor of the first, and to this day the best, practical system of telegraphy, known as the "Morse system."

Resolved, That we recognize and acknowledge him as one of the world's greatest benefactors, in that by and through his matchless invention the business of commerce is facilitated; friends living at remote distances apart brought into immediate communication with each other; the press made a mighty power for the development of intelligence and evangelization; nations brought into direct intercourse with each other, and civilization brought with lightning speed to the door of every nation, and thus, as it were, is brought into one family circle, all the nations of the earth.

Resolved, That we deeply sympathize with the bereaved family in the loss of a kind husband.

Resolved, That the foregoing proceedings be published in the York papers.

MEETING AT YORK, PA.

At the request of Mr. George W. Shoch, manager of the Western Union Telegraph at York, Pa., the Hon. Robert J. Fisher, president of the York County Historical Society, in pursuance of an arrangement of the Morse Memorial Association of Washington. to hold a series of meetings throughout the country simultaneously, commemorative of the late Professor Samuel F. B. Morse, called a meeting of citizens at the court-house, on Tuesday evening, April 16, 1872. Accordingly a large number of ladies and gentlemen assembled.

George W. Heiges, esq., through whose exertions principally the meeting was brought about, called attention to the fact that the Hon. Adam J. Glossbrenner had been one of the early friends and colaborers of Professor Morse, and was a trustee, first in conjunction with the late Hon. B. B. French, and then with the Hon. John M. Brodhead, the present Second Comptroller of the Treasury of the United States, of the first telegraph company organized under the Morse patent. He also alluded to the fact that he was actively associated with the Hon. Amos Kendall, the late W. M. Swain, esq., of the *Philadelphia Ledger;* A. S. Abell, esq., of the *Baltimore Sun;* Messrs. R. & R. M. Hoe, the great perfectors of the world-renowned Hoe printing-presses; Joseph Sailer, esq., the present financial editor of the *Ledger,* and other public-spirited gentlemen, in the organization of this company, whose first termini were Washington and Baltimore. and suggested the propriety, therefore, of selecting him as president of the meeting. The suggestion was heartily seconded, and Mr. Glossbrenner, on taking the chair, expressed his gratification on being called upon to preside over a meeting called in honor of the greatest inventor of the present century. David Small, esq., and James Kell, esq., were chosen vice-presidents, and Levi Maish, secretary.

Rev. Mr. Baum, on being called upon by the president, made a most beautiful and impressive prayer.

M. J. Eichelberger, esq., Capt. W. H. Lanius, Prof. S. B. Heiges, Mr. Hiram Young, and Mr. Joseph Root were appointed a committee to prepare appropriate resolutions.

Rev. H. E. Niles was requested to address the meeting, which he did at considerable length. He referred to the fact that he first saw Professor Morse thirty years ago, while on a visit at Washington. He was then struggling to get aid from the Government. He alluded to the trials and difficulties he encountered, and mentioned the names of the Hon. Mr. Ferris and the Hon. James Brooks as warm supporters in Congress of Professor Morse's project. He described the joy occasioned by the news of the passage of the bill appropriating $30,000. [The president here interpolated the remark that it was principally through the labors of the Hon. Amos Kendall and the Hon. Benjamin B. French that that bill was passed.] The speaker stated that Miss Annie Ellsworth, to whom he was related, and who was a favorite of Professor Morse, was permitted to dictate the first message, and that she selected this most appropriate and beautiful Scripture passage: "What hath God wrought!"

He described the extension of the telegraph, and stated that it reached the enormous length of fifty thousand miles. He alluded to the fact that few persons lived to enjoy the benefits of their inventions as Professor Morse did. He lived to see the wonders of his

great work, and had honors heaped upon him by all the powers of
the world.   He was loaded down with medals and badges from
kings and emperors, and received 400,000 francs from the leading
powers of Europe, and saw the unveiling of his own statue.   The
imposing funeral ceremonies were described, and allusions made to
the fact that there are some persons who would rob Morse of his
well-merited honors.   It is true, said the speaker, that Professor
Henry deserves honorable mention in connection with this great
invention.   But Professor Henry himself would not detract from the
reputation and honor of Professor Morse.

He made mention that we ought not to forget that, with all his
honors, he was one of the noble men that were willing to lay them at
the foot of the Savior's cross, and that during the latter part of his
life he was eminently a Christian philosopher.

The speaker concluded his address by narrating an incident, showing how the telegraph has been used, and may be used, for convert-
ing souls and disseminating the gospel.

The committee on resolutions reported the following:

Resolved, That we heartily sympathize in the feelings of veneration and respect for Professor Morse that prompt the people of the
United States to these public manifestations of sorrow at his death.

Resolved, That not one nation only, but the entire civilized world,
owes a lasting debt of gratitude to Professor Morse for the application of electricity to a system of communication as rapid as thought,
and which, pervading the world as the nerves do the human body, in
addition to the vast benefit it has already conferred on the material
interests of mankind, is tending in a large measure to the developing
of common interests, a common language, peace on earth, and good-
will among men as individuals and nations.

Resolved, That a copy of these resolutions be deposited in the
archives of the York County Historical Society, be published in the
newspapers of the borough, and presented to the Morse Memorial
Association at Washington.

On motion of Edward W. Spangler, esq., they were adopted.

G. W. Heiges, esq., in response to a call made upon him, made a short but interesting and eloquent address.

Professor S. B. Heiges was also called upon. He referred to the fact that the Great Electrician had made the necessary preparations for Morse's great invention, and illustrated his idea by highly interesting and suggestive remarks. He expressed his belief that we had not advanced beyond the first letter of the electric alphabet, and predicted great improvements in our system of telegraphing, and other inventions in the same field.

At the request of the president, the Rev. Charles West Thomson pronounced the benediction; after which, on motion of Mr. Charles A. Morris, the meeting adjourned.

A full account of the meeting was immediately after sent by telegraph to Speaker Blaine, president of the meeting held by the Morse Memorial Association at Washington, then in session.

A. J. GLOSSBRENNER,
President.

Levi Maish, *Secretary.*

MEETING AT ROCHESTER, N. Y.

The Memorial meeting in honor of the late Professor Morse took place in Rochester, N. Y., at Corinthian Hall, on Tuesday evening, April 16, 1872. The occasion was considered by many as a merely formal one, and the attendance was not on that account remarkably large. The assemblage was composed of nearly all those men in the community whose good opinion gives influence to the living, and whose regret adds to the fame of the dead.

The meeting was called to order by the Hon. A. Carter Wilder, mayor of Rochester, in the following words:

MAYOR WILDER'S GREETING.

We convene not as citizens of Rochester, or of the Empire State, but as constituent members of this great republic. The nation assembles to-night, and by the aggregated utterances of her more important and thriving cities, voices the nation's estimate of the services to it and to all mankind of him in honor of whose memory she summons this gathering of her children. Europe had, with a frank readiness and heartiness, admitted the largeness of its debt to Professor Morse in his life-time. "The kings of the earth stood up" and lavished unprecedented rewards and honors upon this modest citizen of the republic. His native land has not been forgetful of his services. Respect and honor and emolument have crowned his declining years. Now that she has returned from his grave, she desires again to rehearse his services, and to inscribe his name imperishably in the roll of national benefactors.

It is eminently fitting that our city should be prominent in this commemoration. This was the cradle of the enterprise, which, taking the inestimable gift from the hands of its author, scattered it over the continent, and so nationalized what had previously been but local and, as it were, experimental. Through long years of disappointment and trial, through losses and discouragements and misgivings, was the work steadily prosecuted by our fellow-citizens to that successful issue which only zeal and energy such as theirs could accomplish. We who have been witnesses of the labors and anxieties of these pioneers in the construction of the telegraph can the better appreciate the sorer trials and discouragements of him who invented it. We have thus a measure by which we may gauge both his struggles and his victory. Our action here should testify as well this appreciation as our gratitude to the genius which has bequeathed to us and to the race the richest boon of the century.

The mayor then moved that President M. B. Anderson be chosen chairman of the meeting, and the nomination was carried.

President Anderson on assuming his position, said that before proceeding further it would be well to call upon Divine Providence for assistance and approval in the Memorial services of the night.

He therefore asked the Rev. James L. Robertson to offer up prayer.

At the conclusion of the prayer, President Anderson delivered the following address:

DR. ANDERSON'S ADDRESS.

FELLOW-CITIZENS: We have come together to-night to render our respectful homage to the name and memory of one of the great benefactors of humanity. We join with the sisterhood of American cities in a simultaneous recognition of the genius, labor, and thought which have made the name of Morse known and honored throughout the world. Still more, we would make this an occasion of recording our obligations to those silent thinkers, almost unknown outside of the annals of science, whose achievements made the invention of the telegraph-instrument possible and practicable.

Almost from the time of Franklin the idea of making electricity useful for the transmission of intelligence has floated before the minds of men. Le Sage in 1774, Lomond in 1787, and Reusser in 1794, constructed instruments by which thought was communicated through wires of great length. But the discovery by Volta, in 1800, of the pile which bears his name, gave a new impulse in this direction. In 1819, Professor Oersted made his great discovery of the action of an electric current upon the magnetic needle.

This was soon succeeded by the discovery of electro-magnetism by Arago and Ampère in Paris, and Seebeck in Berlin. The world was then furnished with the three conditions for the construction of the electric telegraph in its present form. The Voltaic battery, the deflection of the magnetic needle by electricity, and the magnetization of soft iron during the passage of an electric current are the three great events in scientific progress upon which the invention of the telegraph depended.

From 1830, when the suggestion of the employment of these discoveries for telegraphic purposes was suggested by Ampère, the minds of men of science in all civilized countries seem simultaneously to have been directed to the means by which these discoveries might be made available for the conveyance of intelligence. In all scientific centers in Europe and America success more or less complete followed these efforts. This is not the place to discuss the vexed question of precedency between Cook and Wheatstone, Steinheil and Morse, in the actual invention of the telegraphic apparatus.

The honor of successful endeavor belongs to them all, but to no one of them does the world owe a greater debt of honor than to our own countryman. His invention has been found so cheap, so simple, so easy of manipulation that it has been more widely adopted than any other. The honors and emoluments which foreign nations have bestowed upon Morse are proof enough of the distinguished place which he holds among the inventors of the telegraph-instrument. It is not necessary to Morse's fame that the reputation of his fellow-inventors should be undervalued. In honoring him we honor them. It would be injustice to his memory did we omit to mention those who at at the same time were laboring at the solution of the problem.

There are three classes of agents which have conspired in giving to man the control of the telegraph. In the first class we should place those students of science who in the pursuit of truth for its own sake, brought to light those laws and forces upon which the whole working of the instruments depends. In the second class we place those indefatigable inventors whose patient thought and persistent experiment perfected the mechanism which made the laws and forces of electricity available to the service of man. In the third class we place those men whose foresight, administrative capacity, and capital organized the telegraph-lines into a system, made them a financial success, and brought them within the reach of the whole brotherhood of man. In each of these classes of workers our countrymen have borne a distinguished part.

The science of electricity was born on our soil, and names worthy to be associated with that of Franklin have never been wanting in the annals of American science. The name of Morse alone is our title to a pre-eminent position in the second class named. In the capacity to organize and administer associated capital our country-men yield the palm to none. What in other lands has been the work of government has among us been accomplished by private enter-prise, and with such success that the highest foreign authorities ad-mit that in our country "the telegraphic system is far more complete and extensive than in the Old World." In this work of perfecting the organization and administration of the telegraph system our own city and our own State have taken a most important part. The names of Hiram Sibley and Cyrus W. Field are enough to establish our claim. Had the Atlantic cable failed, as once seemed likely, we were all ready to grasp the honors and rewards of an overland line to Europe and Asia, which would have been sure of success.

In looking over the history of this great invention we are im-pressed with the unity of scientific labors and practical ends. When Galvani was speculating in his laboratory on the twitching muscles of a dead frog; when Oersted was experimenting with electric cur-rents passing over magnetic needles; when Ampère was watching the effect of electric action upon soft iron, they would have been laughed to scorn had they claimed to be the most practical men of their age. But in fact they were doing more for the material inter-ests of man than all the bankers, merchants, and manufacturers of that day. It is ever thus thoughts go before things. The discovery of forces and laws must precede mechanical inventions. Science must always clear the path for successful art. The speculations of the Glasgow professor, Adam Smith, upon the wealth of nations have wrought vaster and more beneficial results than all the states-men of his age, prolific as it was with great men. The philosophers and lawyers who elaborated by ages of thought the magnificent fabric of the Roman law were thinkers and speculators, but they shaped in their speculations the whole foundations of jurisprudence for the civilized world.

We also see that no great discovery or invention comes by accident. Divine Providence presides over the growth of science and art and civilization. Science had reached such a state at the close of the eighteenth century that a thousand thinkers were hot with action over the facts and laws which were the conditions-precedent of the telegraph. Though the great men whose names we recall to-night had failed in their efforts, the work which they sought to do would have been done. Had neither Morse, nor Wheatstone, nor Steinheil invented the telegraph-instrument, it would inevitably have come to the light in their generation. The doubt and obscurity which hang over the origin of all great discoveries and inventions are not due to the misrepresentation and ambition of men, but to the fact that all great onward movements in science and art are conditioned by what has preceded them, and spring from the aggregate intelligence and common thought of the greatest minds of an age. God's purposes never depend on the genius or power of any one man.

Thus speaking, we do not detract from the honor due to the genius of any one we have named to-night. He must be a very able man who in this age of mental activity makes an appreciable impression on the profession or line of inquiry which he adopts as the channel of his thought. The fact that Morse's name is linked forever with an invention world-wide in its application and immeasurable in its beneficence, is enough for his fame, enough for his immortality.

If material wealth is so dependent on the development of scientific laws and the increase and diffusion of knowledge among men, we see the necessity for an alliance close and intimate between the men of capital and the men of ideas. For if the knowledge of the facts and laws of material science is necessary to the accumulation of capital, a knowledge of the facts and laws of the moral and political sciences is necessary to its preservation. The prevalence of unsound moral, political, and economical ideas among the population of Paris has made that city as unsafe as Mexico for the residence of a capitalist or the investment of his funds. Even now the specter of the International Society casts its grim shadow over the civilized world. Let some moral or economic heresy take possession of a people, and the savings of a generation will evaporate like the feathery snow-flakes beneath an April sun.

Nor can these blessings and safeguards be secured by the mere elements of knowledge, such as may be learned in the common school. Great reservoirs of knowledge must be maintained. Investigators must be supported and rewarded. Knowledge must be increased as well as diffused. It is no accidental coincidence that Galvani and Volta, Oersted, Ampère, and Arago, Wheatstone and Morse were each and all professors, connected with institutions of learning. Have not science and learning some claims upon the colossal fortunes which their votaries have made possible?

If this beautiful city of ours is to hold a true leadership in coming years, something more will be requisite than water, or gardens, or railroads. It must become a center of ideas and culture. May I be pardoned for saying that, in addition to our admirable system of schools, we need endowments for education large enough to bring the means of the highest training gratuitously to every one capable of receiving it; large enough to maintain a body of scientific and scholarly workers who shall enlarge the area of human knowledge; large enough to attract hither, by books, collections, and apparatus, a society of the choicest minds of the country; large enough to furnish a collection of means and appliances for culture that shall make our garden-city the intellectual center of Western New York.

At the close of the chairman's address, W. H. Ross Lewin, esq., proposed the following list of vice-presidents and secretaries, which was adopted:

Vice-Presidents.—Hon. Henry R. Selden, John H. Martindale, E.

Darwin Smith, Roswell Hart, Henry L. Fish, John Williams, Charles
W. Briggs, D. R. Barton, Henry T. Rogers, C. R. Parsons, Samuel
Wilder, C. C. Morse, Newell A. Stone, Charles J. Burke, George
Raines, James H. Kelly, Jarvis Lord, H. D. Scrantom, Samuel L.
Selden, Patrick Barry, John Adams, I. F. Quinby, Freeman Clarke,
Alvah Strong, William Alling, Aaron Erickson, M. F. Reynolds,
F. Smith, N. C. Bradstreet, George D. Lord, F. S. Rew, N. A. Pond,
De Witt C. Ellis, R. K. Gould, A. Stern, Jacob Gerling, Frederick
A. Whittlesey, P. A. Farber, Henry Craig, Jacob Howe, John Stape,
J. H. Gillmore, Alfred Ely, A. A. Hopkins, R. Y. McConnell, John
Gorton, George Connolly, E. H. C. Griffen, M. Heavey, William Croft,
John Van Voorhis, Jesse Shepherd, V. M. Smith, A. Cole Cheney,
E. G. Robinson, John C. Chumasero, George C. Clarkson, Edward
M. Smith, Lewis Selye, John Lutes, Lewis H. Morgan, Herman
Mutschler, George W. Aldridge, D. W. Powers, Charles E. Upton,
William N. Sage, A. S. Mann, George N. Deming, Henry S. Hebard,
William F. Cogswell, George J. Whitney, George H. Thompson, D.
A. Watson, Frederick Delano, P. M. Bromley, Levi A. Ward, Henry
S. Potter, Isaac Butts, Hiram Sibley, C. F. Paine, G. H. Perkins,
George C. Buell, M. Filon, William H. Bowman, William Purcell,
George G. Cooper, John Cowles, Charles F. Pond, C. C. Meyer,
Frederick Stade, Thomas C. Montgomery, V. F. Whitmore, Henry
Hebing, Theodore Bacon, William Aikenhead, C. D. Tracy, S. C.
Hutchins, W. D. Shuart, James O. Howard, William Caring, J. H.
Nellis, John Mauder, Owen F. Fee, Thomas Mitchell, George W.
Rawson, James Brackett, John W. Stebbins, B. F. Blackall.

Secretaries.—Adolph Nolte, E. A. Angevine, Thomas J. Neville,
William S. Fowler, Samuel H. Lowe, J. R. Garretsee, R. Milliman,
Thomas J. Smith, George D. Butler, P. K. Jones, C. S. Benjamin, B.
Frank Enos, Louis W. Brandt, J. A. Hoekstra, George M. Elwood,
G. F. Wilcox, George A. Hulbert, George A. Redman, F. M. M.
Beall, H. P. Mulligan.

DR. ROBINSON'S REMARKS.

The chairman then said that he regretted to announce that Hon. H. R. Selden, who had been expected to address the meeting, was absent; but he would call upon one whom the people of Rochester were ever happy to hear and honor—he would introduce Rev. Dr. Robinson.

Dr. Robinson said that it was the singular good fortune of the distinguished man whose praises were ringing around the globe to-night, to have his merits duly recognized in his life-time. Most great benefactors of mankind were laid in their graves before their discoveries were fully understood or recognized by their fellow-men. Not a few of them had been maligned and treated with contempt. Generations, even centuries, had passed away before the names of many of them had been properly put before the people they had benefited. Not so with Mr. Morse. He had seen his own statue erected on the most conspicuous spot in the nation. Everything had been duly said and done in commemoration of the distinguished dead. There were not wanting, however, those who in his life-time disputed his title to fame; who placed him in contrast with other inventors, denying the same honor to those who put a discovery into practical application as compared to those who have found, often by mere accident, a scientific principle which men have long been eagerly searching for. It was partially through accident that electricity had been discovered. Galvani at a fortunate glance noticed that the skinned legs of a frog jerked when brought in contact with the wire, and concluded that animal-magnetism lurked in them. Volta's discovery came as one of the incidents in the controversy which arose out of Galvani's theories; and the Voltaic pile stimulated Oersted, and his labors turned to practical account the scientific knowledge which had originated in accident. Hence both classes of illustrious men, discoverers and inventors, were worthy of equal honor. Invention required not only ingenuity but accurate calculation. Mathematical calculation was the fundamental principle, the foundation and corner-stone of all sciences. It was to this that the great results before us were due, and to the honor of the great invention the deceased was fully entitled. Whatever might be the claims of the English invent-ors, Morse had preceded them by five years. He had demon-strated in 1837, that thought could be transmitted by wires, and the same year Wheatstone and Steinheil achieved the same results, but five years previously Morse had calculated out, on shipboard, the details of his invention. It was certain, moreover, that the instru-ment of Professor Morse was regarded on all hands as the fittest, sim-plest, and most trustworthy in the transmission of messages. It was no slight merit to have at once invented what had not since been supplanted.

There was one thought which the speaker desired particularly to mention in speaking of the distinguished man in whose honor they were assembled. This was the simplicity of character, singleness of heart and mind, and transparency of soul for which he was remark-able. He was a gentleman in the truest meaning of the term, a Christian in the strictest sense of the word. Whoever met him in conversation must have been struck with his child-like simplicity. It was not cant on his part when he attributed his invention to Divine Providence. It was not cant, but an honest expression of his convic-tion, when he said in his first telegraphic message, "What hath God wrought!" This mode of thought might be attributed to his early education. He was a Puritan of the Puritans—an honest believer in the superintendence of Divine Providence over human affairs. The speaker had met him a few months before, and, allud-ing to his invention at that time, he said it was God's hand that had brought it about. He had not recognized the fact when he had set about his calculation after coming on shipboard at Havre, but he now saw that God's hand directed him. There had been plenty of

time to outlive that feeling. He had, during his life, met with flat-
teries enough to kill it. It was unfortunate that the illustrated papers
had put forward his portrait covered with the decorations of foreign
orders. It was not his disposition to parade these. Such was not
the spirit of the man. He was honest, earnest, single-hearted, de-
vout, pure of faith. Whether as artist and originator of the Academy
of Design, or as the first in this country to use the invention of
Daguerre, he was diligent in the single purpose to be useful to mankind. In the commemoration of this evening these traits should not
remain unnoticed. His desire to benefit the race, not less than his
ingenuity, should be held in remembrance.

There was one characteristic of the great men of the nation which
the speaker wished, in conclusion, to allude to. A large proportion of
them had come forth from among the parsonages of New England.
How much of their strongest traits of character was due to the influence of the old Congregationalist ministers of those States? They
were a sturdy race—men of mind, who had left their mark on the
destiny of America. There was one appropriate closing word to say
in commemoration of the inventor. In remembering how the
nations of the earth had done him honor; how the countries of
Europe had stretched forth their hands, through their rulers,
to greet him; how they were gathered together to-night to pay
respect to the memory of the man who had, as it were, made
the world into a vast whispering-gallery, it would be well to recollect how effective his influence had been in civilizing and Christianiz-
ing nations; how much he had done to arrest war and to check the
feelings that lead to rivalry and hatred among peoples. Let all
acknowledge, in view of such achievement, that there was a nobler
aim than simple mechanical invention.

At this point the following dispatch from Washington was received
and read:

WASHINGTON, D. C., *April* 16, 1872.

M. B. ANDERSON,

    President :

The National Morse Memorial meeting is now in progress in the hall of the House of Representatives, Speaker Blaine, assisted by the Vice-President of the United States, presiding, and the Governors of the several States acting as vice-presidents. The meeting is now ready to receive communications.

A. S. SOLOMONS,
Chairman.

The chairman then introduced Gen. J. H. Martindale.

GENERAL MARTINDALE'S SPEECH.

General Martindale said he certainly had no purpose to employ before them to-night any of that distinguished eloquence which had been referred to. He came with satisfaction to take part in the celebration of a peculiar event, unique, like the character which they commemorated. He supposed that among the men living in this age there was not one for whom could be gathered throughout the land such assemblages as for the distinguished man whom they honored to-night. It was strange that a man who, during all his early and middle life, had illustrated that simplicity of character which they had heard eulogized; a man seemingly in no degree stimulated with that ambition for fame which inspired the masses of men; captivating the young and leading the middle-aged to vigorous action—strange that he should yet, in a silent way, attain distinction which will place him, in the eyes of ages to come, among the foremost men of the century. It is a great satisfaction to know that one can attain eminence in such a way—fame not acquired by mere vulgar ambition over piles of human agony and sorrow. It is a satisfaction to know that one unaffected by this ambition receives the ovation which is offered throughout the country to-night.

What had been said on this occasion, the speaker indorsed. An inventor was not merely a man of genius; he was not always a man of the most incisive scientific investigation; he was not one keenest as a mechanic or chemist, but a man endowed by God to despise and contemn prosperity and power and ambition, with an earnest purpose to consecrate what he learns and thinks to the benefit of man. He is not one wedded to an idea in the abstract, but with purpose to utilize his knowledge. Such a man is enthusiastic, and his enthusiasm makes him happy. Not long ago, the speaker had met a gentleman in social intercourse, on his way to find the north pole, seeking that goal through dangers and privations. He had looked at the discoverer with surprise. What could urge him to incur these hardships? What struck his mind peculiarly was the earnest devotion displayed by Captain Hall—to whom he alluded. That gentleman had said to him that it would be the crowning pleasure of his life to plant his foot on the north pole. How happy men were when actuated by earnest enthusiasm! They never mind obstacles or impediments, but work on steadily to the end. The speaker then called up the picture of Morse thirty years ago, realizing in his imagination, before its time, the consummation that we now enjoyed. What a consolation must the inventor have experienced when seated in his study at a later day to think that his fellow-men, by his means, were conversing as it were with an articulate voice across the seas? However, our admiration now availed the great inventor nothing. His body had been committed to the earth from which it had sprung, and his spirit had flown to the God who gave it. His great example remained to stimulate us. The speaker in conclusion alluded to the ends to be accomplished in the dim future, and the agency of the telegraph in re-establishing the unity of the race. He looked for the time when the association of thought and perfect recognition of the brotherhood of man would come to pass. This power, which was like unto thought itself, would prove most efficient in the consummation of that glorious future.

D. M. Dewey was then introduced, and gave some interesting reminiscences of the introduction of the telegraph into Rochester. He related the call made by Mr. Wells, founder of the American Express, upon himself some thirty years ago, canvassing for the first line from New York to Buffalo. He had procured in Rochester only six subscribers. Hon. Frederick Whittlesey subscribed for two shares, James Chappell for one, and Mr. Dewey himself for another. The names of the other shareholders had slipped from his mind. He eulogized the public spirit of Mr. Whittlesey, and gave a humorous account of the results of his first telegraph-investment.

Calls were made for Dr. Moore, Ex-Mayor Smith, Hon. L. H. Morgan, and Hon. Roswell Hart. The latter gentleman alone responded, giving a few neat excuses for not attempting any formal address on the occasion.

On motion of Mr. Whittlesey the following dispatch was sent in answer to that received from Washington:

To Hon. JAMES G. BLAINE,

 Chairman Telegraph Memorial Meeting, Washington:

The city of Rochester sends greeting to the assemblage at the National Capitol. She claims prominence among the early promoters of Morse's great invention.

M. B. ANDERSON,
Chairman.

The meeting then adjourned.

MEETING AT HARRISBURGH, PA.

The Morse Memorial Meeting in the hall of the House of Representatives at Harrisburgh, Pa., was very well attended. The meeting was called to order by Mr. William B. Wilson. Prayer was offered by Rev. O. H. Miller. Mayor Verbeke opened the meeting by making the following remarks:

We have been called together for the purpose of adding our testimony to the high position one of America's gifted citizens, lately passed away, holds in the hearts of his countrymen.

It would be in vain for me to pronounce a eulogy on the life and character of Professor Morse, when every telegraph-pole throughout the length and breadth of the land stands a monument speaking in thunder tones of his genius.

Universal meetings are being held to-night to pay a passing tribute to his memory, and I am simply here for the purpose of calling this meeting to order and giving my sympathy by my presence.

On motion the following officers were elected:

President: His Excellency John W. Geary.

Vice-Presidents: Hon. Simon Cameron, Hon. John J. Pearson, Hon. W. K. Verbeke, Hon. David Mumma, Hon. Francis Jordan, Hon. D. Fleming, Hon. A. J. Herr, Hon. A. L. Roumfort, Hamilton Alricks, James W. Weir, William Colder, H. McCormick, Dr. George Bailey, John W. Brown, George Bergner, S. O. Thomas, Wein Forney, John G. Ripper, Jones Wister, J. R. Eby, D. W. Seiler, and David McCormick, esqrs.

Secretaries: H. A. Clute, William B. Wilson, H. L. Harris, S. C. Wilson, A. R. Keifer, Ed. Lingle, W. Blair Gilmore, and T. Rockhill Smith.

Upon assuming the chair, Governor Geary spoke as follows:

The past year has been more than usually noted for the departure of many eminent statesmen and other distinguished persons from our midst, and from spheres of usefulness, to that realm of eternal silence from which no traveler returns. These solemn events have not only touched the sensibilities and awakened the sympathies of our people in all parts of the country, but they have given to a long succession of the names of men, illustrious by their services, their talents, and worth, a lasting and honorable place in history.

We have assembled here to-night, fellow-citizens, to pay this last tribute of respect as a memorial to a great man, whose name has been added to the list of the departed, and upon whose mortal remains the portals of the tomb have but recently closed; one whose many virtues and whose inventive genius have caused him to stand out with singular prominence among his countrymen, and whose useful and extraordinary discoveries secured for him the admiration of his fellow-men "to earth's remotest bound."

Samuel Finley Breese Morse, after a long life of eighty-one years, mostly spent in the acquisition of knowledge and in usefulness, has descended to the mansions of the dead. The immortal is separated from the mortal, and the products of his great inventive genius alone remain to the world. Imperishable renown is connected with his memory, and history will assign to his name the measure of its most enduring fame.

Professor Morse was a master in painting and sculpture, and originated the Academy of Design in New York City. He was not only the inventor of the telegraph, but he was indefatigable in perfecting it, and in extending it upon both continents, and upon the islands of the sea, and causing more than one hundred thousand miles of the tell-tale wire to stretch across the lonely plains, to climb the ragged mountains, and to dive beneath rivers, lakes, and oceans, and to proclaim its victories by encircling the globe in advance of time.

It is not my intention to enter upon a detail of his life and accomplishments, for these are topics too familiar to all readers to require a repetition from me. It is enough for me to say, in assuming the position of your presiding officer, that he was substantially rewarded by wealth for his invention; and honors have been showered upon him by academies, colleges, and scientific associations, not only in America but throughout foreign nations, and by almost every sovereign potentate. The utility of his wonderful invention constitutes his best eulogy. He died full of years and full of honors, surrounded with the glory of matured wisdom. "Length of days is in her right hand, and in her left hand riches and honors."

William B. Wilson then addressed the meeting as follows:

As the representative of the telegraphic fraternity of central Pennsylvania, I am compelled to say that we do not consider this an occasion of mourning. A good and pure man, a practical Christian, ripe and full of years, fitted by the benefactions of a life-time to associate with the countless saints that have gone before him, has gone to a better world. Yet while we cannot mourn the transition of a friend and father from this world of care and sorrow to the brighter realms of God above, we feel that this meeting is peculiarly appropriate. We meet to place in history a memorial page bearing testimony of the heart-felt gratitude that thousands of young men and women throughout this land feel toward the benefactor who gave them a habitation and a name, an opportunity to satisfy their ambitions, a means of education, and an intimate intercourse with the world at large. Looking throughout this country, and seeing the honorable positions occupied by those whom the telegraph has reared, who can say that the peaceful, useful family that Samuel Finley Breese Morse has founded does not outshine in true greatness, and will not outlive not only the dynasties of emperors and kings, but the very remembrance of them?

While the fame of an Alexander or a Bonaparte may hereafter be known to the student of musty history, every wave of the electric current will keep alive in the hearts of his children of the telegraph the name and worth of Morse.

The following resolution was then adopted:

Resolved, That the telegraphic fraternity of central Pennsylvania will ever hold in grateful remembrance the memory of Samuel Finley Breese Morse, the able American, who, undaunted by disaster, unchecked by the frowns of patronage and power, nor overcome by

the jealousies of science, perfected and put in successful operation
the system of telegraphic communication, which not only challenges
the world for its simplicity and power, but has been a potent agent
in the rapid advancement of civilization.

W. B. WILSON,
H. A. CLUTE,
Committee.

A. J. Herr, as the representative of the citizens of Harrisburgh,
spoke as follows:

Mr. PRESIDENT AND LADIES AND GENTLEMEN: As we have all
learned, and as we have been told this evening, Professor Morse is
dead. It has been said that the good that men do is oft interred
with their bodies, but how little that is truly good and truly great
has been buried with Professor Morse. He still lives; he lives in all
that perpetuates the remembrance of man upon the earth. He lives
emphatically in his example, his influence, principles, and his labors.
He will continue to exercise a mighty influence upon the people of his
own country, as well as upon all mankind. When such a rare gift as a
truly great mind is vouchsafed by Heaven, it is no weak flame, that
burns brightly for a brief space and then expires and goes out in
darkness. Imagination grows weary in contemplating the perfection
of the invention of Professor Morse. It has infused new energies in
the activity of commerce; it has made one family of all peoples of
the earth, and now Christian civilization places the crown upon his
head, and hails him benefactor of his race. The first message sent
by Professor Morse was, "What hath God wrought!"

I ask the privilege of reading and presenting the following preamble and resolution:

Whereas, in sympathy with the civilized world we deplore the
death of Professor Samuel Finley Breese Morse, which occurred on
the 2d day of April, A. D. 1872, as an event of more than national
importance; that it is not within the power of finite intellect to

measure the beneficial effects which mankind have already reaped from his invention of the electric telegraph, nor to prophesy its influence in extending, expanding, and elevating every field of labor, every branch of science, every condition of art, every department of social and moral life ; that while we lament his departure we yet rejoice that, in the midst of his successes, his honors, and his triumphs, with gracious humility he gave God the glory of his great achievement, saying, on a memorable occasion, " I am sure I may venture before a Christian audience to suggest that the great Author of all good, the Giver of every great gift to the world, intends when such a boon is bestowed that He first and prominently shall be recognized as the author.   It is surely sufficient honor for any man that he be a co-laborer in any secondary capacity to which he may be appointed by such a head in a great benefaction to the world:" Therefore,

Resolved, That the fame, labors, and genius of Professor Morse have entered as permanent properties into the life of our country.

Telegraphic dispatches were received during the meeting from London, Bombay, Poughkeepsie, (the home of the late Professor Morse,) Boston, New York, and other places.

Hon B. F. Meyers was called upon to address the meeting, and spoke as follows:

Mr. CHAIRMAN AND LADIES AND GENTLEMEN : My presence in this meeting to-night is rather accidental.   I came here this morning not expecting to participate in a meeting of this kind.   The invitation to be here this evening came to me this afternoon late; therefore it will hardly be expected of me to deliver an elaborate eulogy upon the life of the distinguished man whose death we are here to-night to mourn.   I can scarcely add anything to the eloquent remarks that have been made by the chairman of this meeting and the chosen spokesman of the citizens of Harrisburgh.   I feel, however, as a member of the press, which has been so greatly benefited by the invention of Professor Morse, that if I kept silence on this occasion I would be doing injustice to that profession.

"What hath God wrought!" You have heard these words quoted here to-night as the first words sent by telegraph. We meet here to repeat to each other the solemn exclamation. God has taken from us a man whose benefaction of the human race is almost beyond estimate. The human machine has ceased its motion, the circuit of life is broken, but the memory of Morse will endure as long as the telegraph-instrument shall click. His soul, as it looks down from that purer sphere to which it has gone, may say, "*Exegi monumentum aere perennius.*" He needs no mausoleum; he needs no memorial stone; he needs no epitaph.

We have come to regard the telegraph as a matter of course. Familiarity breeds contempt. The time was when men were astounded at this great and magnificent invention; now we accept it as a common-place fact.

It is unnecessary for me to recount the incidents of this man's life. He was the son of a clergyman, born in Charlestown, Mass., in 1791; graduated from Yale College, went to Europe to study the art of painting with Benjamin West and Washington Allston, then the foremost artists of America; he was successful in that art, and returned to his native country to found an institution which has since become famous in New York as the Academy of Design. He afterward returned to Europe, where he earned a livelihood by painting portraits at fifteen dollars a head. Truly, the career of this man was a checkered one. The course of his life lay now in sunshine and now in shadow; now in the brightness of success, now in the gloom of disappointments and hope deferred. It was when he was upon his homeward voyage from Europe that the grand idea of the electro-magnetic telegraph was revealed to him. He went to Congress and asked for an appropriation to enable him to construct a telegraph-line from Washington to Baltimore; but Congress did not appreciate the invention he had made, and failed to make the desired appropriation. He went to Europe, but met with disappointment, as well in England as in the capital of the Continent. After six long years of struggle, a struggle against disappointments, neglect, and contumely, he finally returned to his native land to ask again for the appropriation which had been refused. On the last night of the session, when usually, I am sorry to say, much mischief is done, the ordinary rule was reversed, and Congress performed the wise and beneficent act of appropriating the sum of $30,000 to Professor Morse. The trial was made, the experimental telegraph-line was built, and soon continents were linked together and the nations married by this tie of the electric telegraph. And now we can say nothing to add to the fame of Professor Morse; we can say nothing in praise of him that will add anything in the public estimation to what he deserves in the esteem of his fellow-men. He has gone to his long repose—gone to his grave.

> "Such graves as his are pilgrim shrines,
> Shrines to no creed nor code confined;
> The Delphic groves, the Palestines,
> The Meccas of the mind."

Rev. J. W. Stevenson was called upon by the president, and responded as follows:

Mr. PRESIDENT: I feel that this is a very great privilege to be permitted to take any part, however humble, with you and my fellow-citizens to participate in these Memorial proceedings; and to-night as these messages are taken by yonder instrument, it shows that we are in direct connection with hundreds and thousands of American people gathered here and there across this great land.

There comes to me the thought that in years to come many a youth, inspired by the love of science, as he struggles to realize some noble idea for the benefit of the race; as he remembers the career of him around whose memory we gather; the thought that in the face of discouragement, in the midst of difficulties—will say, " O, Professor, the world's not so lonesome, because thou has left the example that labor shall triumph in it." The name lives; the man dies, but the power lives on, and another name is added to American history.

The meeting was closed with prayer by the Rev. J. W. Stevenson.

The following dispatch was sent to Washington:
Hon. JAMES G. BLAINE,

President of the Morse Memorial Meeting, Washington :

A meeting of our people is now in session in the House of representatives; his excellency Hon. J. W. Geary presides, and has delivered an impressive eulogistic address. Speeches have been made by prominent citizens.

WM. B. WILSON,
Secretary.

MEETING AT BALTIMORE, MD.

Agreeably to the call of the Morse Memorial committee at Washington, a large meeting of the admirers of the late Professor Morse was held in Baltimore on Tuesday evening, April 16, 1872, in the Morse Building, on Fayette street, near North street. As an appropriate ornament of the room, a large-sized likeness of the great inventor, dressed in black, was suspended opposite the main entrance. Archibald Wilson, jr., esq., manager of the Western Union Telegraph of Baltimore, had placed one of his best telegraph instruments in a convenient position, and was present with his chief operator, Mr. Charles C. Wolff, to further the wishes of the meeting.

On motion, his honor Joshua Vansant, Mayor of Baltimore, was called to the chair, and the following gentlemen elected officers of the meeting:

Vice Presidents—Hon. Reverdy Johnson, A. S. Abell, William H.

Carpenter, C. C. Fulton, F. Raine, William Schnauffer, E. M. Yerger, John Wills, William R. Cole, J. E. Anderson, C. J. Fox, C. J. M. Gwinn, and Archibald Wilson, jr.

Secretaries—Messrs. Charles G. Kerr and Archibald Wilson, jr.

His honor, Mayor Vansant, upon taking the chair, said:

Fellow-Citizens: Upon the recommendation of the Morse National Memorial and Monumental Association at Washington, this meeting has been convened for the purpose of manifesting, by your presence at least, your admiration of the character of the late Professor Morse, your appreciation of his wonderful and mighty genius, and your deep regret at the irreparable loss which the civilized world has sustained in his death. The committee which waited upon me on yesterday, and requested my presence at this meeting, did not inform me that I would be expected to speak at all, and if they had made such a request of me I should have shrunk from the task, for to the ablest men and the most eloquent tongues must be submitted the charge of pronouncing the eulogy.

His was not the fate which ordinarily waits on genius, for the practical application of his wonderful conception realized his brightest anticipations, and brought him the real appreciation of an indebted world, and he realized while living the full fruition of his every hope.

In the person of Professor Morse, "the insatiate archer" struck a bright mark, indeed; but ere his venerated form lay in the narrow chambers of the pale sleepers, by the practical application of the great conception of his mighty genius, messages of his death, fleet as human thought, scaled mountains, and penetrated the ocean-depths to the remotest bounds of human civilization. We love his memory and admire his genius; let his name be cherished forever among us.

At the conclusion of Mayor Vansant's address, a message from James W. Brown, esq., of New York, president of the Franklin Telegraph Company, tendering the use of the lines of his company, was read.

John T. Crow, esq., offered the following message:
To the MORSE MEMORIAL ASSOCIATION,

at Washington, greeting:

The city of Baltimore, between which and Washington, in 1843, the first electric telegraph was laid by Samuel F. B. Morse, and which transmitted from one to the other the glad tidings as well as the convincing proof of the success of his great invention, unites through the same wonderful agent to-night with the national capital in doing honor to his memory and in celebrating, while illustrating, the triumph of his genius.

The limited circle first quickened by the electric fire has reproduced itself in multiplied and enlarged circles till they have embraced the circumference of the earth. The spark then kindled survived the great inventor's death, and, like the spirit that conceived it, "still lives," keeping pace with that spirit in its immortal circuit, radiating through day and night, and through all seasons and climes, imparting currents of light and beneficence to mankind. Thus hath God wrought.

JOSHUA VANSANT,
Mayor.

On motion, the message was unanimously ordered to be transmitted.

The secretary of the meeting next read a dispatch from A. S. Solomons, esq., at Washington, announcing the organization of the Morse Memorial meeting in the Hall of the House of Representatives.

Messages expressing regret at the death of Professor Morse, from the Telegraphic Staff in Egypt, the Hong-Kong Chamber of Commerce, and the mayors of Saint Louis, Philadelphia, Boston, and Augusta, Me., were then read.

A letter from Colonel Frederick Raine, editor of the German *Correspondent,* of this city, expressive of his regret that indisposition prevented his attendance, was next read.

Hon. Reverdy Johnson offered the following resolutions:

Resolved, That this meeting shares with the world in regretting the loss which mankind has sustained in the death of Professor Morse.

Resolved, That it is some consolation that, although dead, he still lives. His invention, which can neither be fully appreciated nor exaggerated, will forever give him a place in the hearts of his fellow-men.

Resolved, That proud as Massachusetts may be of having given him birth, she will admit that the whole country has a right to claim him; and

Resolved, That Maryland would seem to have some peculiar title in his fame, from the fact that the first practical experiment of his invention was made by wires between Washington and Baltimore, and that the material aid which enabled him to make such experiment was an appropriation by Congress, adopted chiefly at the instance of one of her sons, the late John P. Kennedy, a member of the House of Representatives.

Mr. Johnson addressed the meeting in support of his resolutions, as follows:

Not being advsied that this meeting was to be held, in time to enable me to meditate upon the proper manner of speaking of the great merits of Professor Morse, I feel that I am not now equal to the occasion. The heart, however, speaks in advance of the mind. Every man who is acquainted with the wonderful operations of his invention, and of the blessings it has conferred upon mankind, could not fail, when the tidings of his death reached him, deeply to deplore the event, and to feel that the bereavement is a bereavement to the world. We have had among us many men of exalted genius, talents, and worth, and their memories we hold in grateful veneration. By

such men our revolutionary struggle, which ended in the accomplishment of our freedom, in having made us what we are—one of the
greatest nations of the world, proved successful through their matchless valor and subsequent wisdom in council. The foremost among
those was, as the world as well as ourselves have long since recognized, one of the best, purest, and ablest men for the occasion that
Providence could have selected. Washington, in council and in the
field, not only was never surpassed, but never equaled. It is, however, no disparagement to him to say that the services of Morse have
had a more comprehensive and beneficial operation. Washington
made us a nation, but Morse, by his invention, seems to have imparted nationality to the civilized world. His genius, too, has contributed to make our example better known to the world, and in that
way has contributed more or less to spread the principles of political and
individual liberty throughout Christendom. Men in Europe, at one
time, believed, or pretended to believe, that our political experiment
was but a bubble, which would soon burst. They must now, however, be satisfied that their apprehensions or their hopes have no
foundation. Whatever doubts may have been entertained in Europe,
or with us, as to the permanent success of our form of government;
whatever clouds, from time to time, may have appeared, calculated
to alarm the timid, those who know the deep-seated love of our
countrymen for liberty and union, and their general intelligence and
determination to preserve those blessings, have never shared in
those doubts. This determination, too, and power has been greatly
assisted through the genius of Morse.

By that genius we are literally made one people. We converse
every morning with each other throughout the entire extent of our
wide domain. In a word, we are constantly holding communion
with each other, imparting to each other hope and confidence and
love for our institutions—when they are properly administered—and
causing us to resolve that they shall be so administered.

In the remarks of his honor the Mayor, he said, what unfortunately is a fact, that Morse is dead! But this is only true of him physically. He will never be seen again on earth by any of us, or by any who are to follow us. But we and they will daily and hourly hear his voice. We hear it now in the clicks of the telegraph in this room, and the same voice is being heard to-night, not only by us, but by the whole civilized world. This night he is speaking everywhere. In a spiritual sense, therefore, and in fact in a material sense, Morse still lives!

I knew him personally, though not as intimately as I could have wished. For years, even after his invention, he was comparatively poor, and I feared that his fate might be the fate of most great inventors—to make the fortunes of others, and to enrich the world, but to die in poverty. I have long since, however, been glad to know that this was not his fate. For years he has been as rich as he desired. I have always lamented that our country failed to contribute to this result; other nations making him pecuniary grants, but the nation of his birth, strange to say, never made any. The National government, now that he is dead, are making up as well as they can for this strange omission. The highest officers of every department of the state—executive, legislative, and judicial—are this moment in council in the House of Representatives in Washington, endeavoring to do all that they can in honor of his memory; and this movement has the sanction of every part of the country. Let us of Maryland show that in our estimate of the man and his services, we are not behind any of his countrymen. Sharing with all in the blessings of his invention, we participate with all in sincere and deep regret at his death.

On motion, the resolutions were unanimously adopted; and their transmission directed.

The speech of Ex-President Fillmore, delivered at Buffalo, N. Y., was next read.

A resolution, offered by Mr. James G. Ramsay, recommending the mayor and city council to make an appropriation for a suitable statue of, or monument to, Professor Morse, to be erected in Druid Hill or Patterson Park, was adopted.

A message from the Memorial meeting in Washington was next received, announcing that the Hall of the House of Representatives was densely crowded; that among those present were the President, members of the Cabinet and Supreme Court, and Cyrus W. Field, esq., and mentioning the address, then being delivered, of Hon. Fernando Wood, of New York, who supported, as a member of Congress, Professor Morse's first application to the nation for pecuniary assistance.

On motion, the addresses of Mayor Vansant and Hon. Reverdy Johnson were directed to be transmitted to Washington.

John T. Ford, esq., offered the following resolution:

Resolved, That the thanks of this meeting are given to our esteemed fellow-citizen A. S. Abell, esq., for the use of the room in this building, which he has so appropriately named "The Morse Building," in testimony of his own warm appreciation of, and friendship for, the distinguished inventor while he was still alive.

On motion, the resolution was unanimously adopted.

After the receipt of other telegrams announcing meetings in a number of the principal cities of the Union—

On motion of Hon. Reverdy Johnson, the meeting adjourned.

MEETING AT AUSTIN, TEX.

AUSTIN, TEX., *April* 17, 1872.

Mr. A. S. SOLOMONS,

    Chairman National Telegraph Memorial Association,

        Washington, D. C.:

At a meeting of many of the citizens on yesterday evening, the following resolutions were adopted and a copy of the same are sent to you herewith:

Whereas, the National Telegraph Memorial Monument Association of Washington, D. C., have by circular invited co-operative meetings throughout the country, on this the 16th day of April, 1872, with a meeting to be held at the same time in the Hall of the House of Representatives at Washington, for the purpose of giving a simultaneous expression of grief at the loss of the father of telegraphy: Be it, therefore,

Resolved, That in the death of Samuel F. B. Morse the world has lost one of the lights of science who for so many years has been shedding the light which, by its power, has penetrated the farthest into the darkness of ignorance. His system of telegraphy, unchanged, has grown until it engirdles the globe, bearing messages of good-will and peace to her inhabitants; for to-day, by his system, we learn that the whole world is at peace. We condole with those near and dear to him, for their loss is our loss and their grief our grief.

And be it further resolved, That a copy of these resolutions be transmitted to the above association at Washington, D. C.

JOHN W. GLENN,
Mayor and Chairman.

D. S. RYAN,
    Secretary.

MEETING AT LOUDON, TENN.

In obedience to a call of the mayor of the city of Loudon, Tenn., a number of citizens assembled in the city-hall on Tuesday, April 16, 1872, at 11 o'clock a. m., when Dr. James Mahoney was called to the chair, and S. T. Blair, M. D., appointed secretary.

The object of the meeting was explained by the chairman, as follows:

FELLOW-CITIZENS OF LOUDON: At your request I have called you together to pass such resolutions as your wisdom may suggest in reference to the death of Professor Morse.

I believe it was Cadmus who arranged the alphabet; Archimedes who invented the lever; Euclid who demonstrated the truths of geometry; Galileo who robbed the stars of their mysteries and discovered the perpetual motion of the earth; Cicero and Demosthenes who furnished the models of eloquence; and Watt who discovered the power of steam; but a grander achievement was reserved for Professor Morse in collecting the scattered fragments of scientific experiment and applying them to that wondrous mechanism which has robbed the most terrible of the elements of its mysterious danger and taught the slender current of the wire the alphabet of every living dialect.   But he is no more.

On motion of D. R. Nelson, esq., W. C. Julian, J. S. King, J. J. Harrison, M. D., and F. Beals were appointed a committee on resolutions, and reported the following, which were unanimously adopted:

We, the citizens of Loudon, Loudon County, Tenn., deeply deplore the necessity of assembling to pay a tribute of respect to the late Professor Morse.   We cannot expect to add one scintillation of brightness to his illustrious name, which is already bedecked with as rich jewels as Honor can lavish upon her chosen few.

Resolved, That we condole with Science on the death of one of her most distinguished sons.

Resolved, That we deplore the loss of one who has placed our nation first upon the catalogue of science by uniting the world in electrical converse.

D. R. Nelson, esq., being called upon, spoke as follows:

Gentlemen of the Town of Loudon: If you expect me to speak the praise merited by the late Professor Morse, you anticipate the accomplishment of a task in a few brief moments that a nation will fail to perform in ages to come.   Who can speak the encomiums due to him who is our nation's pride and the world's benefactor? The mind so ponderous with thought would sink beneath its own weight.

From the time the morning stars first sang together to the period when electricity was made to lisp its first intelligible word to man, it was regarded as an' idle sporter with the storm, a destroyer rather than a benefactor.

But a Franklin, one of America's time-honored. sons, entrapped the forked lightning and brought it from the region of the clouds, fettered with the chain of science, while a Morse unchained the cloud-bestriding monster and made it the servant of man.

Sirs, one would but prove his own littleness by an attempt to eulogize him who has ventured so far upon the uncertain path of discovery, and returned to present the human family with a new mode of communication and conversation, which enables men on either side of the globe to exchange ideas as though they were upon the same floor.

Yet he who has done so much for his race mingles with earth no more.   He has gone where mind only exists, having accomplished enough while a companion of matter to give him a name that will live as long as the thunder proclaims the wrath of the storm or the lightning is the agent of its furies.   Time will only add luster and brilliancy to the name he has won among his own countrymen, and magnify his fame throughout the earth.

On motion, it was ordered that a copy of the resolutions be sent by telegraph to the National Telegraph Memorial Monument meeting to be held in the city of Washington.

The minutes of the proceedings were read and approved, after which the meeting adjourned.

JAMES MAHONEY,
Chairman.

S. T. BLAIR, *Secretary*.

MEETING AT OTTUMWA, IOWA.

MAYOR'S OFFICE,
Ottumwa, Iowa, May 3, 1872.

At a regular meeting of the City Council of Ottumwa, Iowa, on the 15th of April, 1872, on motion, it was ordered that Mayor W. L. Orr, Solicitor Eugene Fawcett, and Alderman P. G. Ballingall be appointed a committee to represent this body and take such action as shall be necessary to convey to the meeting to be held at Washington on the 16th instant, in honor of the late Samuel F. B. Morse, our high regard for the memory of that distinguished man, and our appreciation of the wonderful results of his discovery.

In accordance with the instructions of the council, the committee convened at the telegraph-office on Tuesday evening, April 16, and after consultation forwarded the following dispatch to the chairman of the Morse Memorial meeting in session at Washington, D. C.:

OTTUMWA, IOWA,
April 16, 1872—7.45 p. m.

Ottumwa, through her City Council, unites with her sister cities in the testimonial of respect to the memory of Professor Morse.

W. L. ORR,
Mayor.

MEETING AT MOBILE, ALA.

In response to the call of the city authorities of Mobile, Ala., there was an assemblage of citizens to do honor to the memory of Professor Samuel F. B. Morse at the hall of the Franklin Society on the evening of April 16, 1872, to act in concert with all others in various quarters of the Union. As usual with meetings at this hall, a fair proportion of ladies were present.

In the absence from the city of Mayor Parker, the meeting was called to order by President Thomson, of the council, and Mr. H. A. Lockwood was unanimously chosen secretary. Major Thomson, in opening, made a few appropriate remarks, and then introduced Major W. T. Walthall, who, after delivering a prefatory address, read the following resolutions:

Whereas, the recent death of Professor Samuel Finley Breese Morse has called forth the sympathy and regret of the whole civilized world; and

Whereas, it has been determined to give expression to that sympathy and regret by simultaneous action in the principal cities and towns of America: Therefore, it is hereby

Resolved, That we, the citizens of Mobile, cordially unite in the expression of our admiration for the services rendered mankind by the late Professor Morse, especially for his invention of the electro-magnetic telegraph—the most brilliant and at the same time one of the most useful achievements of human genius.

Resolved, That while we can scarcely sorrow for the death of one who had attained a ripe old age, whose work had been so well and so thoroughly done, and who leaves to his family and his country the fragrance of the memory of a well-spent, a beneficent, and an illustrious life, yet we feel that this country and this age have sustained an irreparable loss, the loss of one who has conferred upon them benefits beyond the achievements of the warrior, the statesman, or even, in ordinary cases, of the scholar and the philosopher.

Resolved, That these resolutions be published in the city papers, and that a copy of them be forwarded to the Telegraph Memorial Monument Association at Washington.

Col. A. R. Manning was next introduced by the chairman of the evening, and spoke at length of the great benefits which have resulted to mankind from the inventions of Professor Morse, and of the deep debt of gratitude which the whole civilized world owes to him. At the conclusion of Colonel Manning's remarks, a dispatch was received from the chairman of the National Morse Memorial meeting at the Capitol in Washington, saying that they had convened and were ready to receive communications.

Dr. W. H. Anderson, next introduced by the chairman, said he had come unprepared to make a speech, having been called upon the stand unexpectedly; but as this was an occasion when even the most retired citizen should lift his voice in doing honor to the memory of a great benefactor to every profession and every trade, he could not, though contrary to his rules, refuse the call made upon him. Dr. Anderson thereupon paid a just tribute to the virtues and scientific attainments of the illustrious dead.

He was followed by Mr. K. C. Murray, a member of the telegraphic fraternity, who delivered an address, speaking particularly of the great debt of gratitude due Professor Morse from his "telegraphic children" throughout the world, now orphaned by his removal from his sphere of labor and of usefulness.

On motion of Col. Price Williams, the resolutions previously read, were then unanimously adopted and ordered to be transmitted by telegraph to the central meeting at Washington, and the meeting adjourned.

J. M. THOMSON,
President.

H. A. LOCKWOOD,
 Secretary.

MEETING AT VICKSBURGH, MISS.

In response to a call by his honor Mayor B. A. Lee, and in accordance with a request of the National Telegraph Memorial Monument Association at Washington, a public meeting was held at the city-hall in Vicksburgh, Miss., at 8 o'clock on Tuesday evening, April 16, 1872. His excellency Governor Powers, being one of the vice-presidents of the above association, was called to the chair.

On motion, Messrs. Dedrick and Reinhardt were appointed a committee to draught a preamble and resolutions expressive of the sentiments of the meeting.

While the resolutions were being prepared, Judge Brown was called upon to address the meeting, and in fitting remarks paid a high tribute to the memory of the late Professor Morse.

Senator Warner and Judge Jeffords being both called for, responded in an appropriate and touching manner.

The following preamble and resolutions were adopted:

Whereas, by a general call to all the different municipalities in this country, through the Morse National Memorial Monumental Association, at Washington, it becomes our painful duty to join in a general tribute of respect to the memory of the late Professor Morse, one of America's beloved citizens, and one of the greatest men that this or any other country has ever produced; and

Whereas, the different telegraph-lines of the country have generously thrown their lines open gratuitously for the purposes above set forth: It is hereby

Resolved, That the city of Vicksburgh joins with her sister cities and the whole world in acknowledging the transcendent benefits which Professor Samuel F. B. Morse has conferred upon mankind, and unites in the universal grief which his death has caused to be felt. As his tribute to science has been incalculable, so is our tribute to his memory boundless. His fame will be as imperishable as civilization, upon which he has conferred an immortal benefaction. Our admiration and grief are increased by the fact that, although his labors and his fame belong to mankind, yet America claims his birth, his home, and his resting-place.

Resolved, That the proceedings of this meeting be published in the city papers.

J. REINHARDT,
Secretary.

MEETING AT COLUMBIA, S. C.

On Tuesday evening, April 16, 1872, at the appointed hour, a large assemblage of the citizens of the city of Columbia, S. C., met in the hall of the House of Representatives for the purpose of participating in the memorial services held in honor of the late Professor Samuel F. B. Morse, the inventor of the electric telegraph.

The meeting was held under the joint auspices of the city council, and under the call of the Morse National Memorial Monumental Association at Washington, to all cities of the United States.

On the stand were Governor R. K. Scott, Mayor Alexander, Professors La Borde, Reynolds, and Babbit, of the South Carolina University, besides the speakers designated for the occasion.

The connection of the wires of the Western Union Company had been made, and at the instrument, which was located upon the speaker's stand, direct communication was had with the great meeting at the same time progressing in the Hall of the House of Representatives at the national capital.

On the right of the stand was the United States military brass band of the post, and on the left Thompson's colored brass band, and the floor of the hall was graced by many of the families of the residents of the city, presenting altogether an interesting picture.

The large hall was filled to its utmost capacity, not over one-half the audience being able to obtain seats.

The Mayor, upon taking the chair, said:

LADIES AND GENTLEMEN, AND FELLOW-CITIZENS OF THE CITY OF COLUMBIA: In compliance with a request communicated to me as mayor of the city, which will be read by the clerk of the council, I called the city council together for the purpose of ascertaining their wish concerning the proposal of the National Morse Memorial Committee of Washington to hold a meeting of the citizens of the capital of the State, in conjunction with a National Memorial meeting at Washington, to assemble this evening.

In compliance with the directions of the city council I have convened you, that such proceedings in reference to the brilliant life and regretted death of the inventor of the electric telegraph may be inaugurated as in your judgment the grave occasion demands. Prayer will be offered, when the temporary secretary will proceed to read the communication received from the Memorial committee at Washington, the action of the council thereon, and the programme of their committee of arrangements; after which I will hear and put before you any motions that may be thought appropriate to the subject.

Prayer was then offered by Professor Reynolds, D. D., after which the clerk of the city council, Mr. William J. Etter, read the proceedings of council under which the meeting assembled.

S. L. Hoge, esq., moved that Professor La Borde take the chair as permanent chairman, and in accordance with the motion he was conducted to the chair by Messrs. Hoge, Senn, and Peixotto.

On taking the chair, Professor La Borde thanked the audience for the distinguished honor conferred upon him, and said the occasion was no political question, or any of those matters which divide the community, but what had called them together was to celebrate the genius and achievements of one of the greatest and best of American citizens—a man who never held a public office; never aspired to one; but one who in the paths of science had achieved a renown which has made his name known and revered throughout the civilized world. It is a remarkable fact that the two men who have made the greatest discoveries in the subtle element of electricity were the two whom we honor, perhaps, more than any other Americans. You know to whom I refer—Benjamin Franklin and Professor Morse. The one snatched the lightning from the clouds; the other taught it to be the interpreter of thoughts between man and man in its travel of light around the world. To the lofty genius of Morse, and to the memory of this great inventor, we come to-night to pay our homage. We do it with all the enthusiasm which we should pay to a successful invention of so great importance to all the interests of our civilization.

After music by the military band, James D. Tradewell, esq., was introduced, who prefaced his resolutions with the following remarks:

In the pure life and scientific eminence of the late Professor Samuel F. B. Morse, of the University of New York, the American people rejoiced while he lived; and now that he is dead, desire to pay all honor to his illustrious memory. No man of the present century rose to a sublimer height of civic renown, to a greater extent attracted the admiration of mankind, or became the subject of superior laudations among men of science and genius throughout the civilized world. He filled the earth with his fame, and it will resound throughout all the coming ages. A native of Massachusetts, a graduate of Yale

College in 1810, he adopted the art of painting as his profession, and at once visited Europe, in order to lay the foundation of a successful career on his return to the United States; and returning in 1813, opened his rooms in Boston. His residence in that city was brief, removing to New Hampshire, where he painted portraits for a time with encouragement. Leaving New Hampshire, he located in Charleston, S. C., in which city his success was very marked. Changing his residence, he went to New York, where he resided up to 1828–'29, when he sailed for Europe a second time.

His second sojourn in Europe terminated in the autumn of 1832, when he came home filled with the idea of the great invention of the electric telegraph, the completion of which has made him immortal. As the illustrious electrician and telegraphist, Professor Morse has challenged universal praise, and it is to commemorate in common with his countrymen throughout the United States the greatest art-achievement of the world, that this Memorial meeting of the citizens of the capital of South Carolina is convened to-night.

Resolved, That this assemblage do declare itself to be in full sympathy with the great National Morse Memorial meeting, at this moment in session in the Representatives' Hall in the National Capitol at Washington, convened to commemorate the life, character, and scientific labors of the late Professor Samuel F. B. Morse, of the New York University, and to give expression to the grief of the universal American heart, caused by his recent death.

Resolved, That the fact that this meeting is now in session in this hall, assembled by the invitation of the municipal authorities of the city of Columbia, at the request of the National Morse Memorial committee at Washington, be forthwith announced by telegraph to the National Morse Memorial meeting now being held in that city.

The band of the Eighteenth United States Infantry then gave some excellent music. This concluded, Mr. Richard Cathcart, the secretary of the meeting, read the following telegrams, which he had received while Mr. Tradewell was speaking:

WASHINGTON, April 16, 1872.

MANAGERS WESTERN UNION TELEGRAPH OFFICE:

The National Morse Memorial meeting is now in progress in the Hall of the House of Representatives; Speaker Blaine, assisted by the Vice-President of the United States, presiding, and the governors of the several States acting as vice-presidents. The meeting is now ready to receive communications.

A. S. SOLOMONS,
Chairman.

WASHINGTON, D. C.,
April 16, 1872.

The Hall of the House of Representatives is densely crowded, the Speaker presiding, assisted by Vice-President Colfax. There are present, the President of the United States, the Cabinet officers, judges of the Supreme Court, and the Governors of States, either in person or by proxy. Speaker Blaine has delivered a brief introductory speech. Resolutions appropriate to the occasion have been read. Senator Patterson, of New Hampshire, seconded them in an eloquent speech. Cyrus W. Field was introduced and read the following telegrams:

HONG-KONG, CHINA,
April 16, 1872.

CYRUS W. FIELD, Washington, D. C.:

The Hong-Kong Chamber of Commerce learns with most unfeigned regret the death of Professor Morse, and mourns this great loss to telegraphy and science.

FULLER.

SINGAPORE, INDIA,
April 16, 1872.

To CYRUS W. FIELD,

Washington, D. C.:

The Directors, Officers, and Staff of the Associated Submarine Companies to India unite in deepest sympathies with America for the loss of her great citizen, Professor Morse, whose genius has done so much to extend the electrical science among all classes and all lands of the civilized world.

JOHN W. PARKER.

Associate Justice Willard, of the Supreme Court of the State, followed, and paid a merited tribute to the memory of Professor Morse.

At the close of the speech of Mr. Justice Willard, the following telegrams which had been sent to Washington were read to the meeting:

HALL OF THE HOUSE OF REPRESENTATIVES,

State Capitol of S. C., April 16, 1872.

To Hon. J. G. BLAINE,

Chairman Morse Memorial Meeting,

Washington, D. C.:

The State of South Carolina and the city of Columbia, as represented by the citizens assembled in the Hall of the House of Representatives in this city, tender to their fellow-citizens the expression of their profound sympathy in the world-wide loss sustained in the death of Professor Samuel F. B. Morse. The immense concourse now assembled is moved with the deepest emotion as it recalls the value and extent of the gift which he has bestowed. Patriotism, gratitude, national fame, and personal esteem combine to do him their sincerest honor.

M. LA BORDE,
Chairman.

COUNCIL CHAMBER,

Columbia, S. C., April 16, 1872.

To Hon. JAMES G. BLAINE,

Chairman Morse Memorial Meeting,

Washington, D. C.:

The city Council of Columbia join with the grateful citizens of the civilized world, in expressing its heart-felt commiseration at the incomparable loss to humanity of the great inventor of the magnetic telegraph, Professor Samuel F. B. Morse.

His work is accomplished ; he has been gathered to his fathers, but the great good which he wrought for civilization will live through the countless ages yet to come.

JOHN ALEXANDER,
Mayor.

Attest: WM. J. ETTER,
Clerk of Council.

Attorney-General Chamberlain said that he rose to second the resolutions which had been introduced by Mr. Tradewell.   He spoke of the achievements of science, and the honorable positions among men, as benefactors of the race, which great inventors and discoverers hold.   He said that Professor Morse did not need our praises to make him immortal.   The greatness of his power lies in the greatness of the beneficence of his gift.   He traced a parallel between the fame of those who win glory on the field of battle and those who advance a science, greatly to the praise of the latter. Every being is a personal debtor to this great inventor.   The experience of Morse was practically the same as that of every great discoverer, from the time of Galileo to the present time.

The meeting then, at about midnight, adjourned.

MEETING AT READING, PA.

BOARD OF TRADE ROOMS,
Reading, Pa., April 16, 1872.

A special meeting of the Board of Trade of Reading, Pa., was held Tuesday evening, April 16, 1872, at 8 o'clock—the president, Henry Bushong, esq., in the chair—the object being to join in the National Morse Memorial celebration, being held at this time all over the country, in honor of the distinguished services rendered by Professor Samuel F. B. Morse.

The meeting was called to order by Henry Bushong. esq., president of the Board of Trade.   Mr. C. B. Rhoads acted as secretary.

The president called upon J. G. Hawley, esq., to explain the object of the meeting.   Mr. Hawley arose and spoke substantially as follows:

SPEECH OF J. G. HAWLEY, ESQ.

Mr. PRESIDENT AND GENTLEMEN: We have come together this evening to testify our appreciation of the signal service rendered by the late Professor Morse to the civilized world in the invention and successful working of the American telegraph system.

In 1829, while crossing the Atlantic, the distinguished inventor, whose life has been devoted to the arts and sciences, conceived the idea of the present telegraph system.   For years he studied and struggled, unaided and alone, until in 1843, he impressed the Congress of the United States that there was utility in his plan, and an appropriation was made to aid him in his invention.   From that date to the present time telegraph-wires have been in successful use, and now bind together in bonds of interest and a common humanity the four continents of the globe and all the principal places of the same.   In a few years the telegraph, as a means of communication, will supersede mails, as railways have taken the place of coach-lines.   The practical working of telegraphy is producing a sure and rapid change in civilization and the mode of transacting business between nations and individuals, by uniting the uttermost parts of the earth, and thereby preventing to a great extent the delays and misunderstandings which in the past have caused so much strife and trouble.

Gradually, but surely, diplomacy and diplomats are passing away before the higher civilization of the telegraph, and disputes which in the past have taken years to settle are now satisfactorily adjusted in a few hours.   The telegraph, in practical results, is yet in its infancy, and the good already accomplished through it is the best index of its future usefulness, and now to-night the citizens of the principal cities of the earth are holding converse with each other, and we all know that association and intercourse dissipate ill-will, malice, and the evil passions of men, arouse good-will, and warm the hearts of all mankind into one common brotherhood. These are a few of the many blessings which we have received from the hand and brain of the inventor of the telegraph. Professor Morse lived to see the great good he had rendered to the world, and departed this life mourned by all classes and conditions of men.

In conclusion, I submit the following dispatch, as expressing the feelings and sentiments of the citizens of Reading:

READING, PA., *April* 16, 1872.

A. S. SOLOMONS, Esq.,
Morse Memorial Meeting, Washington:

A meeting of the citizens of Reading is now in progress to join with her sister cities throughout the nation in paying tribute to the memory of the late Professor Samuel F. B. Morse, father of the American telegraph system, and to tender their earnest sympathies to the family of the honored dead.

HENRY BUSHONG,
President.

C. B. RHOADS,
Secretary.

The dispatch was adopted by the meeting, and ordered to be transmitted to Washington.

SPEECH OF JAMES MILLHOLLAND, ESQ.

James Millholland, esq., being called for, said that he was familiar with the progress Professor Morse had made with his telegraph between Washington and Baltimore, the first line he had constructed. He was present in Baltimore at the completion of the line, and saw a game of chess played by telegraph between Washington and Baltimore. Professor Morse met with a great many difficulties at first in the working of his system. He adopted the plan of placing a pipe beneath the surface of the ground, in which the wire was placed. It was found that the insulation of the wire was not perfect, and he was compelled to abandon that plan. He then placed the wires on poles, these to be used only until a better plan for insulation in the ground should be discovered. The poles have been used ever since, though the professor's original idea was that the wire should run under the surface of the ground. Professor Morse invented the instrument for recording the dispatches on paper by indentations.

SPEECH OF HENRY BUSHONG, ESQ.

Henry Bushong, esq., stated that we only fully realize the convenience of the telegraph when we come to use it. If communication by it were cut off we would feel the loss almost as much as we would a stoppage of travel by railway. The telegraph had become a necessity to all the people, and he heartily joined in the tribute which was being paid by the people of the country to the memory of the inventor of the American system of telegraphy.

SPEECH OF FREDERICK LAUER, ESQ.

Frederick Lauer, esq., said that the telegraph is one of the necessities in our country, as well as in the rest of the world. Our experience has taught us that it is a necessity; we cannot do without it. It has benefited me in my business, and so it has every business man. What has it not done in the warfare of the nations? What did it not do during our late civil war? It was of immense advantage to the authorities at Washington. What did it not do in the Old World during the Franco-German war? By it official orders were promptly carried out and troops manœuvered. The telegraph has accomplished almost more than any other invention. It has proved a

great stimulant to business enterprise, and it will prove more and
more so as the spirit of progress marches on.   It is as plain as noon-
day that the telegraph is one of the greatest inventions of modern
times, and useful in the civilization and enlightenment of the world.

SPEECH OF WILLIAM ROSENTHAL, ESQ.

William Rosenthal, esq., was called for, and said that he was here
to-night merely in the capacity of a reporter, and as such would be
pleased to note whatever any other of the citizens might say.   The
object of the meeting was such a proper one—the paying of a tribute
of respect to the father of the system of American telegraphy—that
every citizen of the city ought to be present.   He joined heartily in
the object of the meeting, and he hoped the memory of such a man
as Professor Morse would never be forgotten in the civilized world.
It is impossible to estimate the benefit which has already been
derived from the invention of the American system of telegraphing.
It has done an incredible amount of good to the world.   It is a
wonderful invention.   If we did not know it personally, we could
hardly believe that by a mere touch of the finger of the operator,
sitting at the table there, we are placed in almost instantaneous
communication with the whole world!   We must not think lightly
of the men who in earlier days ridiculed the idea of putting the
distant parts of the world in close communication.   At that time
men of the strongest common sense could hardly be persuaded that
it could become a possibility that by the agency of electricity,
combined with magnetism, dispatches could be flashed from one
end of the continent to the other, much less through the broad
waters of the Atlantic.   In our day we, ourselves, would shake our
heads at the statement of these facts were we not personally cogni-
zant of them.

Mr. Rosenthal next referred to an incident in 1844, when the
idea first burst forth upon the world.   He was present in his native

city, in Germany, when Professor Karmer, a noted mathematician
and philosopher, and who is now connected with the telegraph system of Europe, first operated with a dial, having a printing apparatus
attached. The professor had been a school-mate of his, and he
always recalled with a great deal of pleasure the recollection of that
experiment. The system of telegraphing has been greatly improved
since that time, and he, the speaker, had the greatest respect for such
a man as Professor Morse, who had done so much toward bringing
the whole world in close communication. Telegraphy could never
be overestimated, and it can only be compared in its usefulness to
steam-power.

At this point the following telegram was received from Washington, and read by the secretary, Mr. Rhoads:

WASHINGTON, D. C, *April* 12, 1872.

The National Morse Memorial meeting is now in session in the
Hall of the House of Representatives; Speaker Blaine, presiding,
assisted by the Vice-President, and the Governors of the several
States acting as vice-presidents. The meeting is now ready to receive
communications.

A. S. SOLOMONS,
Chairman.

The telegram adopted by the meeting was sent in reply.

The Board of Trade rooms were connected by telegraph with all
the principal cities in the United States and Canadas, through the
courtesy of Mr. W. H. Runyeon, superintendent of the Western
Union Telegraph offices, who temporarily placed a telegraphic instrument in one of the rooms.

Telegrams were received from Memphis, Tenn., Saint Louis, Mo.,
Boston, Mass., Augusta, Me., Buffalo, N. Y., Hong-Kong, China,
and other places, which were read to the meeting by the secretary,
by order of the president, after which the meeting adjourned.

MEETING AT NEW HAVEN, CONN.

MAYOR'S OFFICE, No. 7 CITY-HALL,
New Haven, Conn., April 12, 1872.

In response to a communication from the National Telegraph Memorial Monument Association at Washington, a meeting of the city government will be held at the chamber of the board of councilmen, in the city-hall, on Tuesday evening, April 16, 1872, at 7½ o'clock, in honor of the late Professor Morse. Instruments will be placed in the room, and telegraphic communication established with the meeting to be held simultaneously in the Hall of the United States House of Representatives at Washington.

The citizens of New Haven are respectfully invited to be present and unite with the members of the city government in this tribute of respect.

HENRY G. LEWIS,
Mayor.

In compliance with the above, there was a meeting held in the common council room, on the night of April 16, 1872. Mr. Fairchild, of the Western Union Telegraph office, had an instrument in the audience-hall, and a circuit was completed embracing Augusta, Me., Saint Paul, Minn., San Francisco, Cal., Chicago, Ill., the Gulf cities, the cities on the Atlantic coast, and the important cities in the interior. The arrangement was such that a dispatch sent to or from any one of these points was received in every place at the same instant. Thus a dispatch from Washington to San Francisco was received South and North at the same instant it was received in San Francisco. The first dispatch received was as follows:

To Presiding Officers of Morse Meetings:

The National Morse Memorial Meeting is now in progress in the Hall of the House of Representatives; Speaker Blaine, assisted by the Vice-President of the United States, presiding; the Governors of the several States acting as vice-presidents. The meeting is now ready to receive communications.

A. S. SOLOMONS,

Chairman.

About 8 o'clock Mayor Lewis was called to the chair. He said: It was not fit that one so eminent as Professor Morse should pass away without some tribute from the people he had benefited. It was eminently fit that New Haven should commemorate Professor Morse, as it was once his home, and the scene of his early education. It was also the burial-place of his father, the great geographer. After these remarks the mayor asked for the nomination of a secretary, and Mr. John S. Fowler was chosen to fill the position.

Dispatches were then read in the order in which they were received. A copy of one received in New York from Hong-Kong was received early in the evening. It was from the Kong-Kong Chamber of Commerce, and addressed to Cyrus W. Field.

A set of resolutions were read by Professor Wayland, and adopted by the meeting.

A speech was then made by Rev. Leonard Bacon, D. D.

New Haven, he said, had many inventors, who had done much for the wealth of the country and the convenience of mankind, and the most conspicuous of them all was the one whose death we commemorate to night. To-night the throbs of the telegraph which we hear so appropriately are heard not only over this country, but the current passes under the ocean, beyond the bounds of civilization— to Turkey, China, Egypt, and the ends of the earth. I cannot but marvel when I sit down to my morning meal that I have before me the history of the world the day before.

The father of Professor Morse lived in the house on Temple street, now occupied by Mr. J. S. Beach, and the house now occupied by

Colin M. Ingersoll, esq., was on the site of his painting-room. Professor Morse was, in connection with his study of painting, much interested in the study of magnetism. He struggled against many obstacles in getting his invention before the public. The first exhibition of his invention was in a room of the University of New York, in 1835, where he sent dispatches there from one end of the room to the other. Then came more difficulty. No capitalist would undertake the enterprise. Congress at first laughed at him. At last, in 1843, Congress made an appropriation of $30,000 to build a line from Baltimore to Washington. For this Congress was censured by many for squandering public money. From that time the science has developed, until now it is a mighty industry, giving employment to thousands. Dr. Bacon referred to some of the more recent advantages derived from telegraphy—the weather-report, the facility of transacting business— and predicted that its advantages are not yet all developed. The last century had been an age of invention, and among the foremost of all inventors stood Professor Samuel F. B. Morse. At this point a dispatch was read from the mayor of Saint Louis, a set of resolutions from Boston, and a dispatch from Augusta, Me.

Professor Niemeyer was then called upon for some remarks. The professor said:

Europe has, until recently, when America asked for a voice among nations, replied, 'What is America? Has she a history?' We have no great military history; we have not the classic art of Greece; we have nothing comparatively in the past. For history, we give them the steamboat, the sewing-machine, and the telegraph. The latter is a bond of peace. It renders possible the immediate explanation and removal of the causes of war. This was Professor Morse's greatest work. He was, however, one of the most highly educated and most genuine artists America had produced. This was shown by his remaining works. There was a struggle in him between art and science, which was determined about 1844.

A letter was here read from Nathaniel Jocelyn, esq., inclosing another written by Professor Morse. Professor Morse spoke of his fondness for drawing and painting, but said his reason taught him to sacrifice his preference to that which was of more importance to the world.

Professor Niemeyer said, further, that Professor Morse was a man of great amiable characteristics, but not to be imposed upon. He, together with Professor Morse, had introduced the daguerreotype into this country, from which arose photography.

Dispatches were here read from Mayor Stokely, of Philadelphia, and extracts from Ex-President Fillmore's speech at the meeting in Buffalo.

Professor Brewer, of the Scientific School, spoke next. He began by saying that Professor Morse was deeply interested in the Scientific School. The electric telegraph as it now exists is the accumulation of the experiments of two or three centuries, but Morse was the great inventor. When Morse offered his instrument thirty-three others were in the market, and others have since appeared, yet Professor Morse's was the instrument used the world over to-day. Many contributions have been made by different men in different countries. England has contributed the self-sustaining batteries. Professor Henry, of Washington, has contributed the means of improving the magnet. The language of the telegraph is to the operator a spoken language, and is to operators, of whatever nation or tongue, a common language, and was thus a link in the brotherhood of nations.

The mayor introduced Mr. J. Murray Fairchild, of the Western Union Telegraph office, who made a brief speech and returned to his instrument.

A dispatch was here read from Washington, saying that the President and Cabinet and Judges of the Supreme Court were present in the House of Representatives, and that the Hall was crowded.

The dispatch further said that it would be impossible to send messages to all the stations on the circuit, as it would require all night to dispatch them. A vote of thanks was then passed by the meeting to the speakers and Mr. Fairchild, and the meeting adjourned.

A copy of the resolutions adopted by the meeting was handed to the operator, with instructions to send them to Washington.

MEETING AT WILMINGTON, DEL.

A meeting was held in the Board of Trade rooms on Tuesday evening, April 16, 1872, to do honor to the memory of Professor Morse. It was called to order by Mayor Valentine, who stated its object in fitting terms. He gave a brief history of the invention of the telegraph, and detailed the labors, the disappointments of Professor Morse, and his eventual success, through the appropriation by Congress of $30,000 in 1843, in the completion of this line. No man ever lived who received more numerous testimonials of merit and appreciation from the different governments of the world. Professor Morse is now dead, and this meeting had assembled to do honor to his memory.

On motion, William D. Dowe was appointed secretary, after which a dispatch from Washington, received a few days ago, was read, asking Mayor Valentine to call the meeting, placing at his disposal the telegraph-wires, and asking his co-operation in furthering the object of the National Memorial Association.

On motion of Dr. Bush, the mayor appointed the following gentlemen to prepare business for the meeting: Dr. L. P. Bush, Dr. H. F. Askew, William Tatnall, John O'Byrne, and Professor Harkness.

A telegraph-dispatch was read, setting forth that the National Memorial Association in Washington was now ready to receive communications.

A dispatch was also read from Cyrus W. Field and from the

meeting in Boston, expressing admiration of the character and services of Professor Morse, and their regret at his decease.

Dispatches were read from Philadelphia, Montreal, Augusta, Me., and various other places.

At the suggestion of Mr. Vincent, which was warmly seconded by Mr. Heald, Rev. Mr. Todd made a brief speech, in which he paid an eloquent tribute to Professor Morse. He remarked that he did not envy any man who could not feel sorrow at the death of all gifted men. The nation at large mourned the loss of Professor Morse; the Church also mourned his decease. Professor Morse was one, like the Apostle Paul, whom great learning had not made mad. He was a humble Christian, as well as a great scientist, and we come together to-night to drop a sprig of evergreen on his tomb.

The committee on business reported, through their chairman, Dr. Bush, as follows :

Whereas, it has pleased the All-wise Disposer of the events of men and nations, in the order of His providence, to bring to a close the earthly existence of one of the greatest citizens of our republic, Professor Samuel F. B. Morse, it seems peculiarly fitting, as is at this moment being done in all parts of our country, to make it a national and public expression of the sentiments of respect to his memory which are entertained by the people : Therefore, it is

Resolved, That in the eminent services of the late Professor Morse, in perfecting and establishing the magnetic telegraph, he has not only distinguished himself and our republic, but has also conferred one of the greatest blessings ever effected by any one in civil life, by the rapid diffusion of intelligence, thus bringing into close proximity the whole brotherhood of mankind, and contributing greatly toward the elevation and civilization of the race, and the establishment of peace and good-will over all the earth.

Resolved, That this meeting not only approve of, but heartily subscribe to, the praiseworthy object of the National Telegraph Memorial Association in their efforts to erect a national monument at Washington to the memory of a man so justly entitled to our respect and veneration.

Resolved, That a committee be appointed to execute a plan for the collection and transmission of the contributions of the people of this city and State to the said Monument Association at Washington.

After the adoption of the resolutions, the mayor was authorized to appoint the committee and announce the same through the newspapers.

On motion, John O'Byrne, esq., addressed the meeting and eulogized Professor Morse, Columbus, Jenner, and other great benefactors, and expressed the hope that their names would be rendered more prominent in history than those of Alexander, Cæsar, and other great conquerors whose deeds were commemorated by a monument of skulls instead of by trophies of learning and contributions to the good of the human race.

Mr. Jenkins made a brief speech, in which he referred to Professor Morse's contribution to the importance of journalism.

Mr. Heald made some remarks, in which he referred to the faith and persistence of Professor Morse in carrying out his ideas, in defiance of the sneers of opponents and the discouragement of friends, until success crowned his efforts. His invention has advanced the age more than a century could have done without it, and he was proud to do honor to his memory.

MEETING AT PHILADELPHIA, PA.

On Tuesday evening, April 16, 1872, quite a large number of persons assembled in the Common-Council chamber to do honor to the memory of the late Professor Morse. The meeting was held simultaneously with others in the largest cities and towns of this country and the Canadas. The hall was connected by telegraph with all the principal cities of the country. The instruments were presided over by Messrs. J. D. Maize and John Wintrup, of the Western Union Telegraph Company.

Shortly after 8 o'clock the meeting was called to order, and his honor the Mayor was invited to preside over its deliberations.

The following officers were then elected :

President—Mayor Stokley.

Vice-Presidents—Henry C. Carey, Hon. Richard Vaux, Hon. Alexander Henry, Hon. Morton McMichael, J. Gillingham Fell, Prof. Charles J. Stillé, Prof. Samuel D. Gross, Coleman Sellers, Rev. J. L. Witherow, J. William Wallace, Hon. Daniel M. Fox, Eli K. Price.

Secretaries—Henry Bentley, of the city lines Western Union Telegraph Company ; S. B. Ramsey, of the Pacific and Atlantic Telegraph Company; William J. Phillips, of the police and fire-alarm Telegraph; Garrett V. Mott, and David H. Bates, of the Western Union Telegraph Company.

Mayor Stokley, upon taking the chair, said he should have preferred that the matter had been placed entirely in the hands of the telegraphers and scientific gentlemen. He would not, he said, make a speech. He then referred briefly to the event which called the meeting together.

The secretary, Mr. Heber C. Robinson, read the call for the meeting.

He then stated that the mayor had authorized him to send the following telegram :

Hon. JAMES G. BLAINE,

> *Chairman Morse Memorial Meeting, Washington, D. C.:*

Philadelphia unites with the rest of our continent in doing homage to the memory of the illustrious deceased, and to-night a large assemblage has come together in the hall hallowed by memories of Franklin, the great discoverer, to pay tribute to the genius of Morse, the great inventor.

WILLIAM S. STOKLEY,

Mayor of Philadelphia.

Mr. Robinson then read the following, among a large number of others which had been received:

NEW YORK, *April* 16, 1872.

CYRUS W. FIELD,

Care Judge Stephen J. Field, Capitol Hill,

Washington, D. C.:

The Hong-Kong Chamber of Commerce learns with most unfeigned regret the death of Professor Morse, and mourns the great loss to telegraphy and science.

FULLER.

MONTREAL, *April* 16, 1872.

A. S. SOLOMONS, Esq.,

Chairman Committee of Arrangements Morse Meeting,

House of Representatives, Washington, D. C.:

Montreal joins the distinguished assemblage now at Washington, in tendering its tribute to the memory of the immortal Morse, whose spirit hovers in our midst, and whose genius discovered the means of uniting, with electric fire, the world in one common brotherhood.

CHARLES J. COURSAL,

Mayor.

WASHINGTON, D. C., *April* 16, 1872.

To the Hon. Mayor STOKLEY,

Philadelphia:

The National Morse Memorial meeting is now in progress in the Hall of the House of Representatives; Speaker Blaine, assisted by the Vice-President of the United States, presiding, and Governors of the several States acting as vice-presidents. The meeting is now ready to receive communications.

A. S. SOLOMONS,

Chairman.

Cyrus W. Field:

The Telegraph Staff in Egypt deplores the loss of the eminent Professor Morse, who has rendered such valuable service to telegraphic extensions all over the world.

GIBBS.

Telegrams addressed to Hon. James G. Blaine, Chairman of the meeting at Washington, were received from the following:

George H. Thatcher, mayor of Albany, N. Y.; Henry C. Robinson, mayor of Hartford; William H. Kent, mayor of Charlestown, Mass.; Joseph Brown, mayor of Saint Louis; Common Council of Milwaukee; mayor of Saint Paul, Minn.; Thomas M. Reed, mayor of Saint John, N. B.; Albert Somerville, mayor of Galveston, Texas; J. J. Endreth, Augusta, Me.; William Gaston, mayor of Boston.

Hon. Benjamin Harris Brewster offered the following resolution:

Resolved, That, in grateful remembrance of the services that he rendered humanity through the power of his genius of invention, which has united by electric currents the peoples of the whole world, it becomes us, the citizens of Philadelphia, to join with the nations of the earth to recognize in an appropriate manner an event of such solemn significance as the removal by death, from his long-time sphere of honor and usefulness, of Professor Samuel F. B. Morse. His fame is of all future time; his works, typified in, "What hath God wrought!" as he said, are for all peoples, but the daily beauty and excellence of his eminent Christianity, his generous culture, abiding gentleness, and broad sympathy are chiefly the remembrance and the loss of his own countrymen, among whom he lived, wrought, suffered, died. As representatives of the city of Philadelphia, wherein Franklin first proclaimed man's power over the lightnings, and brought them from the clouds, bound servants to the earth, it is especially proper that we should unite in expressions of regret and sorrow for Professor Morse, who, at a later day, gave to the lightnings voice, caused them to speak the language of all lands, and to carry hither and thither, as on the wings of the wind, messages of little and great moment. That, while recognizing the mortal death of Professor Morse, we also know that he "still lives," not alone in the infinite peace of the blessed, but in the daily usefulness of the invention he gave to mankind, and in the grateful remembrances of humanity, whom his genius helped forward to a higher plane of enlightenment. With those who were near and dear to him we desire to sympathize, and to offer them such condolence as their great loss demands and our sorrow and regret can convey.

Mr. Brewster then said he had been waited upon by several of the Western Union Telegraph Company's operators to come to the meeting. I sympathize, said he, greatly with the movement. Dr. Franklin, perhaps, next to Washington, was the greatest intellect this country possibly ever produced. He was the father of electric philosophy. He was the founder of the Philadelphia Library and of the Philosophical Society. He was the first to start the paving and lighting of this city. He was a most remarkable man. The resolution, I am glad to see, speaks of this good man. He had a great and a superior mind. I am, perhaps, the only person present who was with Professor Morse when he made his invention a success. I was in Baltimore at the time the political convention nominated Mr. Polk. I went to Washington, also, and while wandering around the Capitol I entered a small room, and saw Mr. Morse with his instruments, who explained the operation, and by his request I sent a message to a friend of mine in Baltimore, State Senator McCully. After this I frequently met Professor Morse, and often enjoyed his society. He was a kind, quiet, and sedate man. This invention of his will do as much and more for this country than the railways. Without telegraph communication the railway system would amount to nothing. Professor Morse was enabled to apply a natural law to a practical result. It is a most happy thing that we can assemble to thank God that Franklin, Fitch, Fulton, and Morse have been among us.

The resolution was then adopted unanimously.

After a number of telegrams had been read by the secretary, Professor R. E. Rogers, of the University of Pennsylvania, was introduced.

Morse, said he, was a benefactor and claims our most solemn admiration. For what do we owe Professor Morse this homage? For the utilization of a great scientific fact. Although I was not acquainted with Professor Morse I feel as if I had been his intimate friend since boyhood. I feel I can say that I, a lover of science, have been a friend and admirer of Professor Morse. My admiration of the telegraph is based on a humanitarian principle. What would the railroad do if it were not for the wire? Let us join, one and all, in this our acclamation of admiration and respect. The theme is one that crowds out words. I once more offer my hearty allegiance to this great movement now going on throughout the entire land—throughout the entire world. All over land and sea the echo comes.

After the reading of a poem by Mr. Beidler, an address was delivered by Mr. David Brooks, inventor of the insulator:

He was, he said, well acquainted with the late Professor Morse; and I remember, said he, when Professor Morse was urging this system of telegraphy. I, too, with others, thought it visionary at the time. The subject was greatly ridiculed, and some wanted a line constructed to the moon. I came to this city to build a telegraph before a pole had ever been erected. After we had erected a line from Lancaster to Harrisburgh, it was six weeks before we could get a message through, and then it started to run of its own accord. Never before was I so much astonished. We had paper then, and did not for years after write by sound. When the telegraph was first built the people did not believe in it, and were afraid of it. For days I was in the Lancaster office and never received a penny. Our copper wire broke so often that we sold it in this city, as we could get no business. Then I went to Lancaster and paid my board-bill. I have traveled considerably in Europe. When I went to England

I was surprised to see but little respect paid to Morse. When I got on the Continent I found he was much better treated. Never has anything been so little improved upon as telegraphy. Professor Morse often regretted this, and often expressed his desire to have it improved upon.

Upon the conclusion of Mr. Brooks's remarks the meeting adjourned.

MEETING AT CHARLESTOWN, MASS.

In the City Council,
Charlestown, Mass., April 16, 1872.

Alderman Souther offered the following resolutions, which were passed.

In view of the decease of Samuel Finley Breese Morse, born in this city April 27, 1791, and who died in the city of New York, on the 2d of April, 1872, the city Council of Charlestown, Mass., expressing, as they believe, the entire sentiment of the people, hereby adopts the following resolutions:

Resolved, That the city council has learned the tidings of the death of the distinguished son of Charlestown with sentiments of profound emotion, and unites with all other communities in the spontaneous tribute of respect for his memory and in appreciation of the world-wide benefits resulting from his living intelligence and genius. While men are justly honored for daring deeds of valor for their country or their race, yet " Peace hath her victories no less than war," and he who has brought all the nations of the earth into immediate communication with each other, thus insuring the time when " Peace on earth " shall reign, surely deserves a place in the catalogue of the world's heroes.

Resolved, That, in view of the benefit to humanity and the world through the invention of the electric telegraph, it is a grateful thought, now, that our deceased son was endowed with courage and energy to persevere through difficulties, doubt, and distrust to a perfect and splendid success; that he was spared to see the results of his labors and privations; that his own eyes beheld his own honor; and that, finally recognized by the governments of the world as a benefactor to his race, his end was peace, and friendship, honor, troops of friends, and all the things that make a green and pleasant age were his.

Resolved, That the city of Charlestown but honors him whose life has honored her, in placing on record this tribute of respect to his memory.

Resolved, That his honor the Mayor be requested to send to the Memorial meeting on the death of Professor Morse, to be held at Washington, April 16, 1872, some appropriate message of sympathy.

THE MAYOR'S MESSAGE.

The following is the message sent by his honor Mayor Kent to the Morse Memorial meeting at Washington, Tuesday:

CHARLESTOWN, MASS., *April* 16, 1872.
To the CHAIRMAN OF THE MORSE MEMORIAL MEETING,

Washington:

The city of Charlestown sends its tribute of honor and respect to the memory of her gifted son.

WM. H. KENT,
Mayor.

MEETING AT SALEM, N. J.

SALEM, N. J., *April* 16, 1872.

At a special meeting of the Board of Trade of the city of Salem the following resolutions were submitted and adopted:

Resolved, 1. That while in great crises of the world's history we would do homage to the great minds called by God to their control; so, in the march of civilization, we recognize the equal claims to the world's gratitude of those who link in indissoluble bonds the sciences to the arts of life.

Resolved, 2. That we behold in Professor Samuel Finley Breese Morse an instance of the beautiful adaptation whereby one mind utilizes for the benefit of mankind the discoveries made by others of the laws of nature; and that while his illustrious predecessor drew fire from heaven, to him it was given to "send the lightnings, that they may go, and say unto them, 'Here we are!'"

Resolved, 3. That among the memorial tablets of distinguished inventors contributed by the nineteenth century to the Temple of Fame, the name of the honored dead shall stand forever renowned.

Resolved, 4. That a copy of these resolutions be forwarded to A. S. Solomons, esq., chairman of the Morse Memorial meeting, held in the city of Washington this evening.

WILLIAM PATTERSON,
President.

T. T. HILLIARD, *Secretary.*

Committee—W. G. Tyler, Robert Guynne, C. H. Sinnickson, J. V. Craven, A. H. Slape.

MEETING AT BUFFALO, N. Y.

The spacious interior of the Central Presbyterian church was completely thronged on Tuesday evening, April 16, 1872, by the people of Buffalo, assembled to honor the greatest inventor of the age, the late Professor Morse. The meeting was indeed a fitting tribute to one "so far advanced in state"—who has passed the portals of the eternal to receive the reward of his labors for the good of the human race.

At an early hour people commenced pouring into the edifice, and before the time of opening the meeting it was filled in every part, a large portion of those present being ladies. The decorations were confined to the pulpit, which was draped with white and black crape. On either side the pulpit were the telegraphic instruments, under the charge of Mr. N. Hucker, of the Western Union Telegraph Company, and Mr. C. L. Goodwin, of the Atlantic and Pacific Telegraph Company. The operators were Mr. Harvey D. Reynolds and Mr. P. W. Brossart. The president of the evening, Hon. Millard Fillmore, and the speakers, occupied the pulpit. The committee of arrangements were on the platform in front of the pulpit. The Liedertafel Singing Society were located in the organ-loft. The tolling of the fire-alarm bell was heard plainly in the church during the exercises.

Shortly after half-past seven, Mayor Brush called the meeting to order, and moved that Hon. Millard Fillmore be chosen to preside, which motion was carried.

The president then read a telegraphic communication, just received from Washington, stating that the National Memorial meeting was then in progress at the House of Representatives, presided over by Speaker Blaine, the Governors of different States acting as vice-presidents.

W. P. Letchworth, esq., then moved that his honor Mayor Brush be chosen vice-president of the meeting. Thomas S. King, esq., moved that William C. Bryant, esq., be secretary, and the representatives of the press present assistant secretaries. These motions were carried unanimously.

J. N. Larned, esq., moved that a committee of five be appointed to draught resolutions. Carried, and the following gentlemen were appointed by the Chair and retired: J. N. Larned, N. Hucker, C. H. Mead, C. L. Goodwin, Robert Jackson.

The meeting was then formally opened by an earnest and eloquent prayer by Rev. Dr. Lord. Hon. Millard Fillmore then delivered the opening address, as follows:

EX-PRESIDENT FILLMORE'S ADDRESS.

FELLOW-CITIZENS: Samuel F. B. Morse, the father of the telegraph, is no more. A great man, the benefactor of his race, at a ripe old age, has passed away and a nation mourns. It is befitting that we should join our lamentations to theirs. He was our friend, for he was the friend of humanity, and we are blessed by his labors.

My acquaintance with the deceased was but slight, yet it was chiefly in connection with the telegraph that laid the foundation of his fortune and his fame, and therefore your committee seemed to think it might possess some interest on this occasion, and at their request I have consented to state it.   I can only speak of one step in that long and weary road which Professor Morse traveled for twelve years from the time he first conceived the idea of his great invention to its triumphant completion in 1844.   None but those who have suffered from the rebuffs of ignorance, the neglect of stupidity, and the cold caution of self-interest, can appreciate the labors and toils, vexations and disappointments, which were endured for twelve long years by Professor Morse.

Some time, I think, in 1838, Professor Morse exhibited in one of the committee-rooms of the Capitol at Washington, what probably would now be deemed a rude model of his telegraph, and among others I went by invitation to see it, but I gave it very little examination, and what he proposed to do seemed so miraculous that I had little faith in it.   Unfortunately, like most inventors, he had not the means to bring his invention to the test and prove to the world that it would perform all he claimed for it, and he asked some aid from Congress to enable him to do so.   The power of the electric current at short distances was known, but the fact was not yet ascertained how far this power could be transmitted, and it was to settle this point that he asked the aid of Congress, but for some reason no aid was given; and the next that I heard was that he was in Europe seeking for aid to introduce his invention there.   But I think he did not succeed, for when I was on my way to the Twenty-seventh Congress, and I think in the autumn of 1842, Professor Morse called on me in New York and requested me to go and see his telegraph-machine, which I did, and saw it operate.   After that he appeared in Washington with it and put it up in one of the committee-rooms, and made another appeal to Congress to grant him $30,000 to enable him to lay an insulated wire from Washington to Baltimore to test the practicability of his invention.   The idea had not then occurred of stretching the wire on poles.

I then gave more attention to the subject than I had done before, and I recollect that he had wire wound on a reel which he said was equal to a circuit of ten miles; that is, five miles out and five miles back; and he showed me how it worked and explained how it would exceed all other telegraphs by transmitting in writing the message, and by recording it there, though no one were there to receive it.

A bill was reported, I think, from the Committee on Commerce, granting the amount asked for, and when it came up for consideration in the House it was attacked by argument and ridicule, and finally passed by a very small majority. Some thought it a foolish expenditure of money upon a chimerical project, and others by way of ridicule proposed to add a sum to test experiments in mesmerism, &c.

I, however, advocated the bill, and though I could not say that the telegraph would do all that its inventor had predicted, nevertheless I thought it was possible and even probable that it might, and if it would I should regard it as a national blessing, and $30,000 was not much for the nation to pay on a contingency of this kind, and the bill passed and became a law on the 3d of March, 1843. I claim no merit for the little assistance I was able to give in this case, as I but performed my duty in the position in which you, my constituents, had placed me.

I trust you will recollect that I have been speaking of events that occurred some thirty years ago, and as I have been compelled to do it without reference to any report of the proceeding, I shall ask your indulgence if I have made any mistake.

Pardon me for adding a few words more. It is always interesting to compare one great man with another in the same condition of life. I think this one of the great charms of Plutarch's Lives. But time will not permit me to furnish any such comparisons as he has made, and I shall content myself with barely naming two or three individuals who have rendered their names immortal by their inventions; and what strikes one as singular is that they have often risen from the lowest ranks of society, and their inventions have no connection with their ordinary occupation or profession.

Arkwright, in England, was an uneducated man, following the humble occupation of a barber until he was thirty years of age; and yet his invention of the spinning-jenny revolutionized the world in the manufacture of cotton goods and made him a millionaire, and royalty itself recognized his merit and conferred upon him the order of knighthood.

Eli Whitney, the inventor of the cotton-gin, was a poor Connecticut boy, seeking employment as a teacher in Georgia, when he discovered the want of a machine to separate the seed from the cotton, and by his invention supplied the want; and, though Georgia defrauded him of his just reward, yet his cotton-gin made " cotton king," and has added immensely to the wealth of the United States and the world. Though he lost his just reward there, yet, thank Heaven, his inventive powers were not exhausted, and his inventions in the manufacture of arms made him also a millionaire.

Robert Fulton, a poor widow's son, of Pennsylvania, commenced life as an artist, by painting miniatures, and yet he made the first successful application of steam to navigation, and his name will be remembered as long as a steamer plows the waters. His invention wrought a revolution in the navigation of the world, and its blessings are felt in the four quarters of the globe.

Like Fulton, Professor Morse was an artist, but he left his easel and brush, and wrought one of the greatest inventions of this or any other age. Franklin called the lightning from the clouds, but Morse caught and tamed it, and subjected it to his will, and of it made a messenger of intelligence which annihilates time and space; it brings all nations so near together that they can, as it were, hear each other speak. It visits every clime and penetrates every obscurity. The great luminary of day can only shine on one-half of the globe at the same time, but the lightning of the telegraph will spread its light by day or by night over the entire globe. In the midst of our grief for the loss of so great and benevolent a man, it is certainly a cause of thankfulness that he was permitted to live so long to enjoy the pecuniary rewards and honor justly due to his great labors. The gratitude and esteem of his fellow-citizens have done for him while living, what have hitherto generally been regarded as posthumous honors. They have erected a statue to his memory in the great commercial city of the Union, while the monument to Washington, in the city which bears his name, is yet unfinished. But no one would abate one jot or tittle from these testimonials of respect. They were justly due, and we cheerfully add our tribute to the memory of the deceased.

At the conclusion of Mr. Fillmore's address, the committee on resolutions entered, and Mr. J. N. Larned read the following

RESOLUTIONS.

We, who are living witnesses, from its beginning, of all that has been wrought upon the earth by the wondrous invention of the electro-magnetic telegraph;

Who have seen the whole civilized world knit into one conscious social body by the great nerve-system of its sentient wires;

Who have seen the impediments of space, the barriers of the sea, and the obstacles of mountain and desert which held the scattering communities of mankind apart, in dumb isolation and strangeness to one another, so fully overcome, within a single generation, that half the cities of the globe are holding conversation together to-night;

Who have seen war averted and peace preserved between powerful and proud nations by the fleet embassy of the telegraph;

Who have seen the circle of human sympathies widen around each individual heart with the stretching of the electric wires, until every calamity carries grief throughout Christendom, and helpful hands reach to each other from the antipodes with one impulse of generous charity;

Who have witnessed in ourselves and in our own age the growth of a broader culture, a more liberal opinion, and a more comprehensive habit of thought, which come from the universal intelligence of human affairs, gathered daily and hourly for the newspaper-press by the mysterious couriers of the telegraph;

Who have seen the advancement of science, the quickening of inventive art, the expanding of commerce, the impetus to civilization that in every way has been given by the flashing currents of the electric telegraph;

We, who have seen from its seed to its harvest, within less than thirty years of our own lives, this marvelous fruitage of one invention, may fitly and well—

Resolved, That the name of Samuel Finley Breese Morse claims its rightful place among the foremost few of those of immortal men who have acted transcendent parts in the civilization of mankind, and the greatness of whose work in the world will be an everlasting growth, which no achievements of future time can ever obscure.

Resolved, That a copy of this expression of the feelings of the people of Buffalo, upon the occasion of the death of Mr. Morse, be sent by the secretary of this meeting to the family of the deceased.

ADDRESS BY THE RIGHT REV. BISHOP COXE.

Right Rev. A. C. Coxe then delivered an address on "the bearing of telegraphy on international interests." He said, it is very well that I am limited as to time and subject—more particularly subject. It is fortunate that I am to speak on a particular point, especially in the presence of the eminent statesman who presides over this meeting, and who knows so much of the trials of Morse in his first attempts. His honor the mayor did me the honor to offer me an opportunity of speaking here to-night, and I felt that I could not do otherwise than say yes, for it was my fortune for some time to be a pupil of Morse, and we lived under the same roof at the time telegraphy first became his controlling idea. All that time he was struggling with a grand idea, which no one about him seemed willing to be inspired with; yet every day he grew more and more interested in it. His perseverance was the grandest thing in his heroic character. But I must not longer indulge in personal recollections, but hasten to the point. It has been said that he claimed to be the author of the first telegraph. There were telegraphs before, but they were most clumsy contrivances, though thought then to be wonderful things. But the word "telegraph" means, to write at a distance, not signal at a distance. And Morse said, "I have taught the electric spark to write at a distance!" With a single spark what facts can be passed around the globe! It is presumptuous to predict what will be the future effect of the telegraph on international interests; but at this very minute there is evidence enough of its wonderful advantages. The whole world is knit and woven together to-night. If the telegraph had been invented in former ages, what marvelous things would have resulted! I am quite convinced that many events considered the darkest in history, could never have been accomplished.

Visiting Professor Morse not many years ago, I was delighted with the simple old man. "Yes, here they are in a box, and you shall see them," said he, referring to his countless orders and decorations. And then he showed them to me. He was a knight of many orders; he had received honors from every kingdom, and presents from several kings. It was his darling thought that the telegraph should be held so sacred a gift of God that it should always be respected in time of war. This was a glorious thought. It was the glory of Morse to be a soldier of the Prince of Peace. He trusted in Him alone. Thank God for that, while a nation's tears are being showered upon his grave. And now he has gone to wear much brighter decorations than those of earth; to shine as the stars forever; to gain the reward of those who have served well their fellow-men, and to receive the plaudit of his Maker.

At the conclusion of the bishop's address, the Liedertafel sang a chorus entitled "Rose-bud in the forest," and the following address on "The relation of telegraphy to Christian civilization" was then delivered by Rev. D. H. Muller.

ADDRESS OF REV. D. H. MULLER.

Mr. PRESIDENT: To appear before this audience, to hear the eloquent recitals dropping from your lips, and to represent on this platform a city whence flew the first telegraph-message, are honors duly appreciated. Memorial words need to be spoken to sympathetic ears. We are mourners this evening to the extent of our knowledge and love. To deepen in our memory the name of a great inventor, and to increase our knowledge of his work, we are assembled. The beautiful tribute of the right reverend speaker fitly falls upon the brow of Morse, while the shortness of an arm drops my praise at his feet. The relation of telegraphy to Christian civilization is a subject so comprehensive as only to detain us at its threshold. Civilization is intelligence developed; barbarism is intelligence neglected. Christian civilization is divine and human action combine to secure complete conformity of a people to the divinely appointed laws in society, for which God has fitted man. Its ideal is the perfect condition of human society. He who concedes that this state is preferable to barbarism, welcomes the agencies that promote it. The electric telegraph is a child and servant of Christian civilization. It springs from the fruitful soil whence come the poetry, history, science, and philosophy that move the world. Like all ascendant forces in modern civilization, it is the offspring of an occidental mind—the novel contribution of the western race to the world. Types of civilization that grow obsolete in their relations to the future are swallowed by oblivion.

God, who directs civilization, lives in His plans for the future. He turns the great wheels always in one way, that we may see and catch the secret, find how they move, and throw about them the belts of inventive and creative thought. No invention more fully serves this element of progress than telegraphy. Its instincts are prophetic; its vision fixed on coming generations. No soil binds it, no geographical lines limit it. Its elasticity meets the expansive disposition of civilization. Increased facility of intercommunication gives added power for impression. Great was the discovery of printing; greater the discovery of paper, by which the rags of the beggar are turned into the oracles of light. Wonderful is the natural precursor of this invention, the agent that gathers space in its arms, and brings Pekin as near as New England was to Buffalo aforetime. But more wonderful is the lightning racing with Time around the world, leaving him twenty-three hours and fifty-nine minutes behind, and making the Brother of the Sun my neighbor, into whose ear I can pour truth and love. Penetrating daily life, its necessity to advancement makes each soul a debtor. It fashions and perpetuates civil liberty, and, by promoting justice, and intelligence, contributes to national peace.

By it the administration of law is rendered more certain, furnishing an antidote to ignorance, treachery, violence, and following crime with feet shod with wool. Its magical utterances superintend commerce. Diplomacy balances itself on its wings. Its hands are raised as the peace-maker; its voice ruffles the dignity of legislation, and makes senatorial wisdom nervous with its shocks. Joy and sorrow flow and reflow in the empire of friendship through the agency that makes the globe a magnet in the fellowship of worlds. It bows its head at the altar, and sends from the sanctuary its benedictions to the unwise. As men measure the almost infinite distance of the stars by an arc of a few seconds, so its present development faintly shadows the possibilities of the future. Men may weary of steam, and float along other currents, but electric speech they will never outgrow. It will scale heights that seem to imagination summitless; it will send out its line to the whole earth, and drop words to the ends of the world; it will as a rightful king gather precious treasures, and lay them at the feet of that higher King. This hour tells us no power is held in eternal bondage. This audience emphasizes the truth that usefulness is the greatest glory. It is nobler to be a Mott than a Carnot; greater to be a Morse than a Napoleon. Upon the harp of a thousand strings, stretched over hill and valley, in deepest seas and over widest continents, an invisible hand strikes; its music, mingling with Heavenly melodies, murmurs over the grave of Morse the thanks of all generations.

An address was then delivered by William Dorsheimer, esq., on "The connection of telegraphy with literature and art." He spoke as follows:

MR. DORSHEIMER'S ADDRESS.

LADIES AND GENTLEMEN: There is a natural association between the name of Morse and the subject which has been assigned to me. He was an artist, and at a time when literature and the arts were struggling here with an uncongenial soil and climate. Copley, West, and Allston had taken their easels to London; Irving and Cooper were finding in Europe a support they did not find at home. The stern sectarians of New England had contributed a few huge tomes to theological literature, but Franklin and Jefferson were still the only famous men in American literature—the one for the homely skill with which he popularized a philosophy most noticeable for its shrewdness, the other for the insight he had into the forces which yet control our politics. In a country like this it could hardly have been otherwise. Who would leave the work that lay before him, the work which was to yield money and place, and give his hours to idle books or a barren canvas?

No questions were then pressed by the elders upon the young more earnestly than these: Will you give up the quick returns of commerce, public station, the fresh laurels to be gathered at the bar, the honors of politics, and choose in their stead the obscurity of unknown endeavor, penury, and neglect? Will you leave the real and seek a mere ideal? Will you turn away from the present, its hands full of precious gifts, and seek your rewards in the homage of generations whose applause can never reach your living ears; whose laurels can never rest upon your living head? In a practical age, among a practical people, of what use are letters and the arts? These questions Morse answered with an emphasis which made his answer understood. The prizes which practical men value most were won by him, and in a profusion never before known in our country.

His training as an artist was necessary to his great work—"the swelling prologue to the imperial theme." Who but a dreamer could have thought that a messenger would be found who should neither be seen nor heard, and be swift as calculation? Who but a tender lover of nature would have thought that the mystic force which never reveals itself to the human eye except when nature takes on her most awful aspect, could be brought down and persuaded to carry the daily thoughts of men? Who but one accustomed to do his work, not for the profit it would bring him, but for the truth and beauty of it, would have dared to breast the jeering obloquy with which wisdom always assails whatever it does not understand? No, it was not an accident that the inventor of the telegraph was found among the little band of American artists! He is their gift to the world.

There is another relation between this man and my theme. Literature and the arts are the telegraph by which the centuries have always held their intercourse. Were there time enough I might trace the unbroken line which stretches from the heights where Hebrew prophecy was first proclaimed, to the cottage where Tennyson pours forth the music of his delicious song. Surely it was not an accident that the telegraph was found by one whose purpose in life it was to carry forward the endless wires over which all human knowledge and every human hope have come.

We do not suppose that books will be sent by cable from one country to another. That is not the service the telegraph is to do.

Its work is a greater one.   It will make nations ready to receive the thoughts of other nations.   Seas and continents still divide us, but time and distance place no barriers before our thoughts.   To-day, for all races of men, "one morn is in the mighty heavens."

The telegraph will bring the thinker before his audience.   It is hard to conceive that the cold neglect which through all the past has chilled the impulses of genius can long continue under the full sun-light of our day.   No Galileo need fear the dungeon now, nor Cranmer dread the stake.   Not now need Erasmus shrink into his lonely cell, nor Sidney mount the scaffold.   Never again shall a Milton, amidst poverty and obloquy, gaze upon the majestic vision which "he saw with that inner sight which blindness does not dim," describing it to those who heard not.

No. A man may find his hearers now; if not at home, then elsewhere.   The true word bravely spoken to-day, though it fall upon the deaf, goes forth over those wires and finds a sympathetic heart—finds an answer somewhere.

Art and literature, they are the thought of man; the telegraph, it is the messenger of human thought.   The press, the school, the platform, the stump, these are the forces now at work to awaken, to train, express, and perpetuate the thought of man.   An American artist gave to the world the most active and subtle of these agents. May we not hope that the debt will be soon repaid, and that the great agents of intelligence will yet arouse the dormant genius of America, and lead forth from among our people great masters of literature and of art?

The following address was then delivered on "The influence of telegraphy on commerce," by George S. Hazard, esq. :

ADDRESS OF MR. HAZARD.

The influence of telegraphy on commerce has been from its inception of such vast and increasing interest, that in the brief remarks I propose to make it will be only possible to touch in a general way some of its important results to the commerce of the world. Thirty years have scarcely elapsed since the first memorable message flashed over the wires, and now telegraph lines extend to almost every civilized nation upon the face of the globe, stretching over mountains and across valleys, seeking the beds of rivers and the depths of oceans. "Their line is gone out through all the earth and their words to the end of the world."

For a moment permit me to call your attention to the extensive net-work of this vast marvel of the age, through which vibrates unceasingly the burden of human thought and intelligence. Europe possesses 450,000 miles of wire; America, 180,000 miles; India, 14,000 miles; Australia, 10,000 miles. There are in addition 30,000 miles of submarine cable in successful operation beneath the Atlantic, German Ocean, the Baltic, Mediterranean, Red, Arabian, and China Seas, the Persian Gulf, Strait of Gibraltar, Gulf of Mexico, and the St. Lawrence; and the extensions now average 100,000 miles *per annum*. No other human invention has ever reached such vast proportions and developed such mighty results. So thoroughly has the telegraph system commended itself to the exigencies of commerce that the merchant no longer hesitates to regard the daily and almost hourly use of the foreign and domestic lines as an absolute necessity.

Transactions involving immense amounts are constantly being conducted by these metallic messengers with a fidelity, correctness, and dispatch which are astonishing to the uninitiated. So completely has the telegraph changed the old methods of business, by equalizing values and diffusing intelligence, that men of capital no longer possess the power of controlling the markets, and the merchant of moderate means is often the peer of the millionaire. The correspondence which formerly was finished at the office now pursues the merchant, in the form of the inevitable telegram, to the social fireside, suggesting thoughts and cares which he would gladly lay aside for the quiet enjoyment of his home; but the business must be considered, and an order given on his correspondent at Chicago, San Francisco, or perhaps through the ocean to London or Liverpool, or perchance his vessel may be waiting orders at Cairo, Constantinople, Bombay, or Shanghai, and to some of these messages he may receive replies dated an hour or two before the time he sent them off, for the telegraph is no laggard, but an industrious friend, and a constant admonition to its patrons to think quickly, execute promptly, and, if possible, be a little ahead of time.

Commerce is king, and the electric telegraph is the brightest jewel in this monarch's crown. These two forces, commerce and the telegraph, are inseparable, going hand in hand in their mission of civilization and religion to every kindred, name, and tongue under heaven, teaching the whole family of nations the great problem of human rights, making mankind more congenial, more homogeneous, more forgiving.

Manifold as are the uses of the telegraph, none are more beneficial to commerce than its recent adaptation in reporting meteorological observations, enabling the corps of observers to forecast the weather, often with surprising accuracy,—warning the mariner to beware of the approaching storm, or, notwithstanding threatening skies, that no danger may be anticipated, and that he may safely proceed on his voyage. Although the system is new and was inaugurated under many difficulties, it may no longer be considered an experiment, as it is rapidly commending itself to the approval of the country.

Thus the mysterious and silent wire, traversing more than seven hundred thousand miles of land and sea, bearing messages of peace, good-will, and prosperity to all peoples, has become the medium of international intercourse through which the channels of trade may be controlled and a world-wide fraternity promoted.

"I'll put a girdle round the earth in forty minutes," said the mischievous Puck. Shakespeare probably did not intend to make a prophet of the little sprite, but he made him unconsciously utter a thought which found a response in the nineteenth century, and was warmed into life by that truly great and good man whose memory we have met together to cherish and embalm in our "heart of hearts," as one who, under Divine Providence, was permitted to develop to the practical use of man that inestimable gift—the electric telegraph. Then let the name of Samuel Finley Breese Morse, as a benefactor of his race, go down to future ages of civilization "till the earth shall be filled with the knowledge of the glory of the Lord as the waters cover the sea."

The closing address was then made by George J. Bryan. esq., on "The effect of telegraphy on journalism." It was as follows:

ADDRESS OF MR. BRYAN.

"But mightiest of the mighty means
On which the arm of progress leans,
Man's noblest mission to advance,
His woes assuage, his weal enhance,
His rights enforce, his wrongs redress—
Mightiest of mighty is the Press."

Truly has the poet sung, "The pen is mightier than the sword." There is "a power behind the throne" greater than the throne itself. Journalism—the free press—is the corner-stone of human liberty. Charles X and Louis Philippe lost their crowns by vainly endeavoring to crush it out. The two great English-speaking nations of the world have been taught by their untrammeled journals that " it is preferable to die freemen rather than to live slaves." To the "Art preservative of arts," to the press, the world is mainly indebted to-day for whatever of constitutional liberty it enjoys. I love to hear the rumbling of the steam-power-press better than the roar of artillery. It is silently attacking and vanquishing the Malakoffs of vice and Sedans of evil, and its parallels and approaches cannot be resisted.

I like the click of type in the composing-stick better than the click of the hammer of the musket in the hands of the soldier. It bears a leaden messenger of deadlier power, of sublimer force, and of surer aim, which will hit its mark though a thousand years away.

How telegraphing has revolutionized journalism! How by its magic wand the mighty events that mark our day and generation pass into magnificent procession before us! Its condensed eloquence, its epigrammatic sentences, surpass all attempts at oratory. How, for instance, we were thrilled as we were told that Chicago—the city of the continent that most truly reflects the genius, the wonderful progress, of the American people—was burning. How its appeal for aid to our famishing brothers worked a response as princely as it was electric. While the proudest monuments of human genius in the devoted city were still burning, the same wires flashed back the munificence of our large-hearted people. Our whole population rose, as it were, *en masse*, illustrating "that a touch of nature makes the whole world kin."

Some of the grandest events of modern times have been chronicled by this stupendous agency: the union of the Atlantic and Pacific Oceans by the completion of the Pacific Railway; the series of mighty battles before Richmond; its fall; Sherman's march to the sea, and Sheridan's ride to Winchester, twenty miles away. How the boldest held his breath for a time as the wires flashed to an astounded people the news of the assassination of Abraham Lincoln, whose unselfish patriotism and heroic devotion to human freedom endeared his name, like another Washington.

But the other day, lightning-presses, reproducing the cable intelligence, kept us advised of the profound sensation felt throughout the British Empire as the heir-apparent to the throne lay at the point of death. The deep sympathy felt for the prince and his noble mother illustrated that we have not yet forgotten those ties of a common language, of a common origin, laws, and literature, and like grand achievements in civilization, which should insure between the two nations a continuance of our present peaceful and mutually beneficial relations.

O, how the public journal photographs by its telegraphic and other news the sum-total of human existence! It reflects as in a mirror the ambitions, the struggles, the agonies, the joys, the sorrows of our race; it paints, as in the recent case of the French Emperor at Sedan, the uncertainty of all earthly power and grandeur; it pictures to us, as it did in the colossal struggle between France and Germany, the sanguinary horrors of cruel war. From the golden lands of California to the Atlantic, from far-off India, yea, to the uttermost isle of the sea, the magic wires bring to our live journals messages full of weal and woe, of deep import to all interests and all classes. But for journalism, telegraphy would be comparatively useless. Our presses scatter its treasures broadcast throughout the land, and they make newspapers an actual necessity. The press and telegraph combined may safely be pronounced, next to Christianity, the most powerful agencies in the world in promoting the civilization, the happiness, and the intellectual advancement of the human race.

Magic wires are stretching themselves in all directions over the earth, and when their mystic meshes shall at length have been perfected our globe itself will be endowed with a sensitiveness which will render it impossible to touch it on any one point and the touch not be felt from one end of the world to the other. And this work is but just commenced; it is but the beginning of the dawn of the world's great jubilee. It promises a day of more refinement, more intellectual brightness, more moral elevation, and consequently more human felicity than the world has ever seen since its creation.

At the conclusion of this address the resolutions previously read were adopted unanimously, after which the Liedertafel sang, very finely, "The Knight's Lament."

The following poem, written by Miss Mary A. Ripley, was then read by R. T. Spencer, esq.

"WHAT HATH GOD WROUGHT!"

[The first message sent over the line from Washington to Baltimore, in 1844, was dictated by Miss Ellsworth, and consisted simply of the words, "What hath God wrought."]

"What hath God wrought!"   Behold the mystic path,
Whereon the thought of man may travel forth,
As on a highway cast up by His hand
Who founded the firm earth.   Through forests dim,
O'er rock-based mountain, through the dark defile,
Winding along the river's verdant bank,
Or, breast to breast with chariots of fire,
The trembling chords stretch on.   The timid bird,
Resting its weary wing, dreams not its perch
Is tremulous with the tale shall move the world,
And make the throbbing heart of nations beat
With a yet stronger life—still hamlets wake
From drowsy slumbers, shake off slothful ways,
And join the world's great march to nobler goals
And more exalted heights.

"What hath God wrought!"
Beneath the flowing currents of the sea—
Far down in the mysterious depths, where foot
Of man may never tread, where human eye
May never pierce—there go these lines of thought,
These marriage-ties, that join the continents
And bind together alien lands in one,
With common joys and hopes and sympathies,
Whose perfect blending shall bring in the dawn
Of the millennial day.

"What hath God wrought!"
In all the ages, whether darkness laid
His raven wing upon the rolling sphere,
Or whether tides of light o'erflowed its coasts,
God wrought His will by some anointed soul
Whose clearer sight looked out beyond the mists
That shroud the narrow gaze; who dared to lift
His prophet-voice, and teach the laggard Time
A truer wisdom and a grander life.
With ceaseless travail moves the old world up

Among the shining spheres; but all her wail
Is changed and glorified into a hymn
So full of triumph that the angels wait
To hear its jubilant strains.   And so the toil,
And tears, and blood of these appointed ones
Bear onward through the errors that oppose—
Bear upward, through the hate that would drive back—
The helpless world that lies upon their heart.

So he, whose name is on our lips to-day,
Hath fought his fight and won his golden crown.
Poor words of ours fail in the utterance
Of his great patience, yearning to achieve
A good for man which grows and rounds with years—
Whose influence threads the labyrinths of life
And floods the nations, blending with its power,
In one grand melody, the peasant's cry,
The monarch's shouting, and the woman's wail.

"What hath God wrought!"   No need to lift on high
The storied shaft to blazon deathless deeds.
The globe all woven o'er with restless wire,
Bearing swift messages through air and sea,
Clasping with del'cate threads the old and new,
Forcing the wrinkled world to rouse itself
And stir with fresher blood—this shall repeat
The well-learned story to the future age.
Our praises faint, drowned in the gathering surge,
That, borne above the tumult of our day,
Lifts up itself to meet the Heavenly grace
And mingle with its glory.

              Rest thee, then,
Crowned with the honors thou hast nobly won;
Rest, victor spirit, for the battle's done.

TELEGRAPH DISPATCHES.

The following telegram to the meeting was received over the wires of the Atlantic and Pacific Telegraph Company.

COUNCIL CHAMBER, DETROIT,

April 16, 1872.

The following resolutions have just been adopted:

Resolved, That this Council, as the representatives of the people of the city of Detroit, unite with their fellow-citizens throughout the United States to-night in the expression of the highest appreciation of the services and genius of the late Professor Samuel F. B. Morse, in the invention and application to public purposes and benefits of the system of electro-magnetic telegraphy, which in the twenty-eight years since 1844, has united cities, States, countries, reducing months to minutes, resulting in the gain of time alone in communication with each other an enormous addition to the usefulness and practical application of the abilities of mankind.

Resolved, That this Council sympathize with the feelings that have invited this simultaneous manifestation of respect for the memory of this gifted man, and cheerfully participate in it as a just and well-earned tribute, due not only from this country and people, but from all nations of the civilized world.

Resolved, That the city clerk be instructed to transmit a copy of these resolutions of respect and sympathy per telegraph, forthwith, to A. S. Solomons, esq., Chairman of the committee of arrangements of the National Telegraph Memorial Monumental Association, for the meeting now in simultaneous session with our own in the city of Washington, D. C.

F. RUHELE.
PHILO PARSONS.
FRANCIS ADAMS.

Attest:

 CHARLES M. BERGMAN,

   City Clerk.

Telegrams were also received from Toledo, Cleveland, Chicago, and elsewhere, but not in time to be read before the meeting.

The doxology was then sung by the Liedertafel and audience; the benediction pronounced by Rev. Dr. Shelton, and the meeting adjourned.